The Hunters

The Hunters

A novel

John Bolger

Story

Story Press

An imprint of Resolute House

Story Press, an imprint of Resolute House.

THE HUNTERS. Copyright © 2011 by John M. Bolger. All rights reserved. Printed version printed in the United States of America. Ebook version created in the United States of America. No part of this book may be used, reproduced or transmitted in any form or by any manner whatsoever without written permission except in the case of brief quotations embodied in critical articles and reviews. For information please contact Resolute House publishers by visiting www.resolutehouse.com and clicking on the link regarding permissions.

Story Press/Resolute House paperback and ebook versions published 2012. The Library of Congress has catalogued the paperbook edition as follows:

Bolger, John M.
  The Hunters.

  ISBN 978-0615708911
  ISBN 0615708919
    1. Title

Cover artwork and design by Drew Maxwell.
Additional cover design by Story Press.
Book design by Story Press.

Special thanks and gratitude to Pam Houston for her tremendous help with the construction and editing of this novel.

Thanks as well to my other heroes, mentors and friends who helped me with many aspects of this novel, the related book of short stories, and their various drafts: Ron Carlson, Jim Gannon, John Bergstrom, Sheila Roberts, Ellen Hunnicutt, Liam Callanan, Justin Winslow, Tom Bontly, Nick Flynn, and my father.

For Kerry

He who regards himself in this light will be afraid of himself . . .

For after all what is man in nature?

~ Blaise Pascal

The Hunters

Fall

Waves. Large swells.

Their crashes interrupt the wind.

She stands on the beach, refusing to look at him, looking out at the cold water.

The waves blast the shore with surprising force, each seeming more ferocious than the last. Above them, winter threatens: dark skies filled with wind and swirling mist. And with each crest, the waves' fury momentarily surpasses the roar of the low wind as it rushes across the dunes, sending the cold sand everywhere.

What did he do? he asks her against the wind.

She won't look at him, won't cry, holding her arms straight, cocking her wrists at an awkward angle, and bending back her fingers, first one hand and then the other.

What did he do? his voice swallowed by the storm.

She pulls back her fingers, staring at the waves.

1

Paul Kruk gropes in the cold darkness and finds the heavy canvas flap of the mess tent. The rough cloth is so dark that he can't tell it apart from the other dark, cold shapes around him that might be branches, shrubs, hanging animals or nothing at all. He pulls back the wing.

Inside, the gas heater sputters and hisses. The heat, sound and even the dim red light it emits are a little overwhelming after marching silently through the dark woods to his truck, after waiting patiently in the cold all day. He sits down at a picnic table in the red half-light of the heater, pulls off his hat and gloves, and waits.

His numb skin feels raw and his jaw aches as he begins to thaw out. A pot of chili is simmering on the stove beside him. He feels tired and rubs his eyes in the warm tent, listening to the heater and the bubbling sauce.

The smell of propane dominates the mess tent, but Paul can sense the suggestion of wet earth lingering beneath it: dirt and clay; moss on rocks; brown leaves and rainwater; worms.

The sudden flare of a match makes Paul jump up in spite of himself. Brien Grace is in the far corner of the tent, smiling at Paul's surprise and placing the flame inside the gas lantern. Paul curses with relief and watches as Brien lights both sacks of the lantern, blows them out and then turns the gas all the way up. The large tent slowly becomes visible as the yellow incandescent globes begin to shine.

"What were you doing in the dark anyway?" Paul asks, but Brien merely shrugs.

Paul stands and pours a cup of coffee.

Brien has his back to him. And says nothing.

"Somethin' wrong?" Paul asks.

"No," Brien says and digs through the shadows on the

far side of the tent.

Paul lifts the lid off the blackened pot on the stove and takes a long sniff of the chili he made yesterday morning. He finds a bowl and a spoon.

"You kill one?" Paul asks, carefully pouring his chili. He tears off a piece of French bread and adds, "I didn't see anything hanging outside. Too fucking dark."

Brien doesn't say anything, but is busy digging through the cooler on the other side of the mess tent; the ice bangs loudly against the sides. Paul sits down and takes a long sip of the coffee. He feels its heat on his numb lips and tongue, and it warms his sore throat when he swallows. He sets the coffee on the table beside him, eats the chili. Feels better.

Paul watches Brien, who is still ignoring him, scraping through the ice and food in the cooler. He and Brien have been best friends since before Paul's father died. They went to grade school and high school together. Brien went on to college and graduate school, and he has nearly finished his psychology doctorate; Paul joined the army, then returned to town and ran his father's restaurant, Kruk's Diner. Seventeen years ago when Paul married Susie McCormick, his high school sweetheart, Brien was his best man.

"I heard Drew got one today," Paul says between mouthfuls. He tears into the bread with his teeth. Drew Fisher and his brothers always take the site two hundred yards east of Brien and Paul's campground; it's a tradition, as is driving into town for the night when someone from either group gets a buck.

Paul chews, saying, "So maybe we'll get to celebrate tonight."

Brien is still silent as if he knows. But he couldn't know, Paul thinks. He couldn't possibly know—because it's only an idea. Still, Brien's silence unnerves Paul.

Paul looks down at his bowl and says, "See the girls

dance."

Paul stops and frowns.

"It's only the first day though."

"Hey Paul," Brien says, turning around.

Paul looks up.

"Here," Brien says, tossing something.

Instinctively, Paul uses both hands to catch it, cradling it gently toward the side of the tent and the ground, letting it sink into the shadows beneath the table momentarily. Raising it, he feels its weight, its strength, and knows as he lifts it into the yellow light of the lantern.

Paul looks at the heart wrapped in plastic and smiles.

"Buck?" he asks.

Brien shakes his head and says, "Doe. A big one. About an hour before sunset. She's outside."

"Nice job, Professor," Paul says.

The headlights of Paul's truck lit the cold dirt road on Saturday morning—the first morning—and beside him Tom Grace wanted to shine the deer with his high powered light.

"Not in the morning," Brien said from the back.

"Why not?"

"Just because," Brien said. "First day, you know?"

They were silent for a time, rocking from side to side with the truck as they took ruts and pot holes. The digital clock read: 4:28. Paul was sleepy and took a sip from his mug—the coffee was warm but tasted like plastic. And in his left hand, the wheel twisted violently over and again.

"It's right here," Brien said.

"Where?" Paul asked. The forest flashed on either side in an unbroken chain of lifeless branches and trunks.

"Yeah," Tom said, pointing, "There's the path."

Paul pulled his truck to a stop and turned off the engine, and they got out, went around to the back and quietly lowered the gate. Brien and his brother carefully pulled out their guns and gear. On the side of the road, they unzipped the thick leather gun cases, freed their twin Remington rifles, and propped them against tree trunks.

When they spoke, it was just above a whisper, and the wind passed between them more loudly, rustling the leaves on either side of the barren, frozen road and carrying their scents into the forest on the opposite side.

"When'd you put up the tree stands?" Paul asked.

"Two days ago," Brien said, adding, "But we scouted the woods a couple weeks back."

"Where you gonna hunt, Paul?" Tom asked.

"I got a blind up here," he said, pointing vaguely to the dark road ahead. "I saw it last year, checked it out last night, before poker."

"I hear Craig and Drew and those guys are planning a drive," Tom said.

Paul turned to him and said, "Oh yeah? Maybe I'll join them."

"Good luck, Paul," Brien whispered.

"You too," Paul returned, getting in the truck, gently pulling the door shut, starting it. Paul waved to Tom standing by the road, his rifle in one hand and his gear in another, and then to Brien, who was already moving up the embankment, toward the hardwoods.

A few miles later, he turned onto an iced-over dirt road that followed the banks of the winding Pine River for six miles through the forest of pine, oak and birch trees.

Six miles out of the way.

He found the overgrown access road he'd wanted— one that Drew's group wouldn't use because it was on the far side of the ravine, through which the Noname River flowed.

It was cold, and the sky was a dark blue. His flashlight helped him find the way for the first hundred yards; then he had to keep it off and feel his way to the ridge. He was quiet, but there were leaves, the crunching leaves. Still, he was glad it hadn't snowed.

Snow, of course, was better for silence. Better for tracking. But, for his purposes, the snow would ruin everything. No tracks, no tracking.

He knew where to make the blind, knew there was an old dugout in the right spot; he found it and slowly began to camouflage himself.

Yet, it wouldn't be today anyway. Maybe Sunday. Probably Monday.

If at all.

In his blind, he knelt to move a log, adjusting it one last time. Everything was gray and imperceptible. He pulled out warm bullets, one at a time, from his shirt pocket, and loaded the internal magazine, slotting each of the five golden hulled and amber-tipped .30-06 Springfield rounds into the cold rifle, and he chambered a round by quietly drawing the bolt up and back, then with two fingers and his thumb slowly pushing the bolt forward and down again. He made sure the safety was on. He wrapped his blanket around him and waited: watching as daylight came to the land, as things gained definition, grew into shapes discernible from each other, waiting: as the trees became pine or oak or birch, as the ridge took on a pitch, and then as the pencil lines below became the scrub trees on the valley floor through which the frozen river wound its haphazard course; and he watched and smiled when he could see the other ridge.

Where the other blind would be.

Straight across, perhaps a bit down. But it was still too early, and the shadows still hid it, and he waited; and then checked his watch and now it was time, four minutes to sunrise, and—right on cue—a salute of shots echoed through the forest. Some were very distant, miles and miles away, others only a mile or so. Sometimes they came in a series of quick successions, five or so, sometimes just one loud burst, or two.

The first day of hunting season had finally begun.

The orange line of light began to cut across the tree tops on the ridge opposite. He took out his binoculars, leaned against the wall of his dugout and scanned the opposite bank. He found what he was looking for.

The blind was well constructed. It was, in fact, quite a bit below him, and was to his left, further down valley than he remembered, which was much better. Perfect. Paul could only make out the orange cap of the man sitting in the other blind, but Paul knew it was him as he watched the blaze orange hat through his binoculars.

It had taken Paul two hours to pack on Friday afternoon. He'd gotten out his gray-green duffel bag and then an orange hat and placed a black face mask right next to it. He'd considered them, losing all sense of time, and then coming back with a quick breath.

The woods were three hours away—he could be there by sunset if he hurried.

It was the most natural thing in the world. He was just going hunting. Just like every other time.

He finally decided to halve all his gear. In one pile he put the orange hat, a blaze orange hunting vest, an orange rain poncho, a bright pink hunting tag that he would pin to his back, his hunting license with its hunter's choice option, heavy Sorrel boots and waterproof pants. After rummaging through some boxes, he added a Buck knife, binoculars and a compass. Then he remembered four pairs of wool socks and added two pair of long underwear, a couple flannel shirts and a thick gray wool sweater.

The other pile had a waterproof outfit, the face mask, a license plate, a roll of duct tape, and a pair of jungle boots. He put these items into a trash bag and then he'd put it into his duffel bag, packing the first pile around it.

In the kitchen, he removed a container full of chili sauce from the refrigerator. He'd made it at the restaurant that morning. He packed it in his truck next to the propane gas he'd promised for Brien's heater.

He went into the basement and opened his hunting closet. Paul lifted the .30-06 Winchester his father had bought a mere month before the surgery that killed him. Paul unzipped the carrying case and felt the polished gun stock and the high-powered 50 mm scope—

His wife startled him.

"You're home early," he said.

"Bill let me off work so I could say goodbye to you," Susie said.

"And how is the Doc?" Bill Percy had cleaned Paul's teeth since he was a boy. They'd become friends through Susie, even though they were a generation apart, and were in a Wednesday night Sheepshead group together.

"He's fine. He told me to tell you to stay warm and not drink."

"That's a bad bet," Paul smiled.

"And be careful," she added. She was suddenly serious, worried, like she was every year when he left.

Paul zipped up the gun and asked, "Wanna help me pack?"

She asked lightly, "Are you almost ready to kill Bambi?"

"He's no Bambi."

"Well, Bambi's dad then," she said.

"I probably won't even see a doe," Paul said.

He watched the orange hat with his binoculars again just before nine. Silent, unmoving.

He's patient, Paul mused.

The drive was scheduled for eleven. It was a stupid time to drive. Dawn was the best time. Drew Fisher and his brothers were not terrible hunters and had been coming up here as long as Paul and Brien.

But a late morning drive? They just want to meet up and have lunch.

Five guys scattered on the ridge—excluding himself, of course—and three guys driving the ravine. A stupid group. Paul had overheard the plan from Drew's younger brother last night before poker. He also told Paul in detail where everyone in the group would be placed.

He put down the binoculars and waited.

Just after ten, he fumbled for his binoculars. It took his eyes a moment to adjust to their frantic swaying. Then he found him.

Paul watched as the man in the other blind stood, stretched. Yawned.

Not all that patient, after all. Young.

Paul focused the glasses. It was the same face he'd seen in his sister's year book, the same face that had surprised him when he arrived on Friday night, the same face he'd played cards with the night before.

It was him. It was Craig.

Paul smiled.

Craig stamped his feet a bit, rubbed his arms and shoulders, and sat back down.

Not yet, Paul told himself. Later.

Paul had seen him almost immediately on the first night. Craig was supposed to be in the other group, at Drew and his brothers' site. Paul's headlights had shone on the Fishers' tents briefly before he turned into the site he and Brien share, parking beside Brien's black GMC truck and Bert's white Ford truck.

Brien and Tom had already put up the mess tent and the sleeping tent. They helped him unload his gear and sleeping bag.

"Got up here as soon as I could—snuck out of work at two," Paul said.

"Don't you run the place yet?" Tom asked.

"Run it? Sort of. But you guys know who really runs it," Paul said. Brien smiled; Paul had managed the restaurant ever since he graduated from high school, but his mother was still in charge of things, even after a heart attack, and still made her famous Two Rivers soup.

In the sleeping tent, there were five cots. Two men sat on folding chairs beside the heater playing cards. That's when Paul realized who it was.

"You know everybody here?" Brien asked him.

"Not yet," Paul said. The two men stood up.

"This is Bert Vance, my future business partner."

Bert smiled and added, "If we both finish our dissertations on time."

They shook hands. Bert had a full dark beard and blue eyes and was tall, about six and a half feet.

"And this is Craig Bunder. Tom's friend," Brien said.

It was him. Paul disguised his shock. Craig had blond hair, a big square jaw, dark eyes, and large muscular hands like Paul's. He looked young, maybe eighteen.

Paul knew he was twenty-eight years old.

"Hey," Craig said.

"Hi," Paul said, shaking hands, forcing a smile.

Later, while he and Brien ate a sandwich in the mess tent, Paul asked, "Wasn't it supposed to be just four of us? Not that I mind. Plenty of room in the tent and all."

Brien answered, "Yeah, Craig was supposed to stay with Drew. But there's eight of them, and they only got enough room for six in their tent. One guy's sleeping in his pickup."

"He'll be cold," Paul said, smiling. They took beer from the case and drank.

"Anybody planning to go into town tonight?"

"No. We'll get a poker game going."

Paul stared at Craig. Paul had a full house: Jacks over Sevens. Craig was bluffing. Paul knew it.

Brien had folded at the outset, and Bert and Tom had folded after drawing cards.

Craig considered his hand. After a moment, he called Paul's bet, tossing in three red chips, "See your fifteen. Raise you fifty."

Craig counted out the five blues and moved them toward the pile. He leaned back and started smacking his tin of chew with his forefinger.

"Three blues is the limit. Thirty bucks," Brien said over his glass of Beam and Coke. Craig dropped three blue chips in and held the other two over the pile, watching Paul. Then he leaned back in his camp chair, so that his head was almost touching the side of the sleeping tent, his hands half-stretching, half-dangling back beside the cots that they had stacked on their sides.

"It's my deal," Tom said. "So I call the ceiling, and I say fifty."

"You didn't call a new limit when you dealt," Brien said, looking at him, "So the old cap stands."

"But I'm the dealer."

"It doesn't matter," Brien said. "If you change the rules, you gotta tell us before we ante."

"It's alright guys," Paul said evenly, leaning back against his chair, "Let him raise. He's bluffing."

Craig didn't meet his gaze: "It'll cost you fifty then."

He tossed the two blue chips into the pile.

"Oh, come on, Craig," Brien griped, yet Paul had already counted and pushed a stack of five blues into the pot.

He smiled and said to Bert, "If I lose, it'll just be less money to tip the girls with after you get the first buck."

Bert laughed and took a swig of his beer.

"What d'you got?" Paul asked.

"You show first," Craig said.

"You were called," Brien told Craig.

But Paul laid down his cards, saying, "Full boat."

"Wow, that's pretty," said Brien. "All natural, too. You didn't need any of those damn wilds."

Tom rolled his eyes at Brien. "Look—call the game the way you want it when it's your deal. Until then, shut the fuck up."

"Beats me," Craig said, putting his cards face-down in the pile of discards.

Tom said, "Aren't you gonna show us?"

"I don't have to. Paul won."

"Aw," Tom moaned, suddenly indignant, "Come off it! You were called."

"No, he's right," Paul said. "He doesn't have to tell us if he doesn't want to."

"Paul's right," Brien muttered.

Later, Paul overheard Tom whisper to Craig, "So come on, what'd you have?"

Paul watched as Craig's mouth formed two words:

Flush. Hearts.

Paul considered this for a moment. Then decided Craig was a liar.

In the mess tent, Paul finishes eating the chili. Brien goes outside to get the others for the tradition.

Paul takes the doe's heart out of the plastic and puts it in the warm water that Brien poured and heated. Paul massages the heart, pumping it with his meaty hands, forcing the blood out, the clean water in. He lifts it from the water and squeezes it, lets blood and water drip from it. He dips it in again and repeats this gesture several times, after which he places the heart into a bowl of clean water.

The water is cold and fresh from the old spring up the road that was nearly iced over. Paul filtered it on his way into camp; he had to knock down a few icicles to get at the pipe that some missionaries had put in decades ago, but the trickle of water was still fairly strong, and the woods were quiet and he was glad to be up north as the water filled the collapsible jugs he'd brought up. Just the sound of the water and nothing else. The sound of the water among the icicles and rocks, the sound pleasing, a gentle cadence in the woods. Now the sound of the lantern burning and the sound of the heater blazing. The sound of the water dripping into the bowl. He cleans the heart, watching the tiny swirls of blood, like little feathers that curl in the wind. The water and blood dripping into the bowl. The water and the spring are a part of a tradition, a ritual, a part of the fabric of—

Craig pulls aside the flap of the entrance.

"Hey," Craig says, bowing as he enters the old army tent.

With one squeeze, Paul pumps whatever blood is left from the heart.

"Hey," he says, keeping his gaze on the heart. He picks the heart out of the water and dips it in again. Cleaning it.

"I heard Brien got one," Craig says. Paul doesn't understand how Craig can bluff like this.

"That's right," Paul says. "A big doe. Look at the size of her heart."

Paul raises the dripping heart from the bowl and holds it in the dirty light of the lantern. Craig's eyes widen a bit. It is maroon.

"Wow," Craig says. "Mother fuckin' big doe."

"That's right."

They filter into the mess tent one by one, grabbing coffee or beer or whiskey. Drew Fisher comes by and pats

Paul on the back as Paul is busy with the heart. Drew had seen a huge buck near the ravine, but he hadn't gotten a clear shot. Paul'd thought Drew already got a buck that day, but the story Bert told him was wrong: not a buck, a doe; not big, a yearling; and it wasn't Drew, it was Drew's brother Mike Fisher who had gotten the doe.

Drew and Paul laugh, shoot the shit a little. He and Paul played football together in high school—Drew was quarterback and safety, and Paul was fullback and on the offensive and defensive line. Drew's a lawyer now. Got his own practice in Appleton. Paul's still running his father's restaurant for his mother in Two Rivers and wants to buy out his mother, but he and Susie can't afford it yet.

Paul slices the heart into several thin strips. He marinates them with a brush, dipping it into a butter and garlic sauce, smoothing it across each piece, and places them on a small grill. Both he and Drew purposely avoided the topic of their most obvious bond, and Paul's thinking now about Drew's twin brother who drowned in the Wolf River and what a tragedy that was. How Adam's death precipitated all of this—everything that is happening or might happen.

Craig and Bert are talking about the girls, about the bar. Craig can't wait.

Bert says, "I got a wife, so I don't know if I'll go."

"So do I," Drew says. "So do Paul and Brien."

"Oh, you gotta go, Bert," Tom exclaims. "It's a tradition!"

Paul watches Craig.

Craig can't wait to see them strip. To dance. Naked.

"But we won't go tonight, anyway," Brien says and sips his coffee.

Drew nods.

"Why not?" Craig asks.

"Because nobody got a buck," Brien says. "We only go if somebody bags a buck. It's tradition."

"And if nobody gets a buck," Tom shouts, "We just stay here and pull our dicks while Paul strips!"

Everyone laughs.

They eat the heart with pieces of French bread. It's good.

"Tastes like a steak sandwich," Tom says.

"Tastes like chicken," Craig says.

They laugh. Paul pretends to join in the laughter, watching Craig.

Drunk. Like he was that night.

They all go out and look at her. She hangs in the darkness. Brien and Bert and Tom shine their flashlights over her body. They are silent as they look at her, hung on a series of coarse ropes. She is erect, her hindquarters dangling several feet above the ground. Her innards have been torn out. The incision runs vertically just below her chest and continues to her stomach, her abdomen. It looks damp with blood where the fur meets the hole. She is massive.

"Probably 175 dressed out," Brien says, as if hearing Paul's thoughts. "Would have gone 200 on the hoof."

Paul looks at her face. Her tongue hangs out the side of her narrow mouth. Her forelegs are tied behind her head, and the hooves stick up behind her ears in what might almost seem a comical gesture, except the eyes are open, staring, like she's in pain.

"Tomorrow, a buck," Tom says, raising his beer. They drink.

"You comin' with us tomorrow, Craig?" Tom asks, adding, "We've got a couple good tree stands."

Paul looks at him casually, naturally.

"Nah," Craig says. "I'm gonna stay put until I get one."

"How long do you have up here?" Bert deadpans.

Craig smiles, but ignores the joke: "Drew said he'd

give me a ride back Monday night if I don't get a buck tomorrow. If I do, I'll catch a ride back with Tom."

"Are the Fishers planning another drive?" Paul asks.

"No, most of them decided to hunt Willow Creek. But I figure the ravine's gotta pan out for me."

"It's a good spot," Brien says. "Me and Paul used to hunt it all the time. Remember you got your first buck in that ravine?"

Paul nods.

"You gonna get a buck, Paul?" Bert asks.

"Hopefully I'll see one," Paul says quietly. "I don't have a doe tag. Plus I only got two days up here. Gotta be back home day after tomorrow, on Monday afternoon."

"Why?" Tom asks.

"My wife," Paul says.

Bert smiles and nods.

Later that night, Craig and Tom go to see the girls anyway. Brien lights a tiny fire, just enough to keep the bears away from the camp. Brien uses thin tinder and kindling from hardwoods that is dried out and dead on the trees and doesn't use any leaves, cones or old logs, so there's little smoke. Out of habit, Paul is careful to always stay upwind from whatever smoke there is. On the last night, they'll make a larger, celebratory fire, and those who have gotten a deer will stand or sit beside it.

Paul, Brien, Drew and Bert play Hearts in the tent. When Drew's brother Mike shows up, they switch over to Sheepshead. Drew and Mike leave around ten-thirty.

They gather the playing cards and chips and put them away, and clean up the beer bottles and soda cans. They throw the paper plates in the fire—the sudden flare illuminating the tops of the pine trees of the camp—and seal the food scraps and other garbage in plastic bags and hang them from a tree. They fold up the card table and the camping chairs, and store them in the various trucks. Then they bring out the stacked cots, unfold them and lay their sleeping bags on top of them.

Paul is cold and tired as he crawls into his sleeping bag.

"Early day tomorrow," Brien says, from two cots down.

"You're going out, too?" Paul asks.

"Yeah, I told Tom I'd hunt with him again—hopefully double his odds.   If I hit a buck, he'll come over and slap his tag on it."

"Shouting distance?" Paul asks.

Brien smiles, "Not exactly, Paul. But close enough."

"Dangerous game you're playing," Paul says, smiling.

"Yeah," Brien says.   "The DNR won't catch me, though. I'm too smart."

Paul's sleeping bag is warm, surrounding him, protecting him. Listening to the other two sleep, Paul thinks, but it won't be tomorrow, or even tomorrow night. It'll be Monday if I'm lucky.

There is the sound of the wind and the cold outside, and the sound of the gas heater hissing and the sides of the tent shaking in the wind. There is a low wind that gusts against the sleeping tent and the whole encampment, and there is a high wind that is nearly constant among the tops of the trees and sounds like the rush of a river.

One of the ropes that holds up the doe creaks every so often in the low wind, but the heater sputters and hisses, and it's warm inside.

And then he can no longer feel the sleeping bag around him. His wife stands silently inside the warm tent in the darkness, the buck he shot as a boy lies in the crackling leaves, his sister walks on the beach of the Great Lake. The waves rolling in slow huge swells over the heart in the cold water where feathers stir the wind. The huge doe hanging outside and an Indian chief singing and torches and pine trees creaking in a slight breeze and the scent of pine trees in sunlight. His father's voice.

And somewhere in all that he wakes up to find himself back in the tent and Tom stumbling over something, laughing and saying, "Shhh," and Craig crunching some potato chips loudly, and Bert snoring, and Brien rolling over and muttering, "Any chance I can talk you fuckers into shutting the fuck up?"

Tom laughing and Craig laughing, undressing, crawling onto the cot beside Paul's.

In the silent darkness, Paul listens to his drunken snores. It's just a notion, nothing more. It'll be Monday, if at all. Because it's a notion. A nothing.

The sky is overcast. In the blind, Paul takes out his canteen and drinks. The water is very cold and tastes metallic. He waits in the darkness.

Above, snow looks likely.

Snow. What bad luck.

Dawn does not so much arrive as the world takes on a dreary pitch and remains that way. But eventually he can see the nameless river, a thin tributary of the Pine River, which in turn runs north to the Menominee River—the border of Wisconsin and the Upper Peninsula.

And later he can even see the dark, opposite side of the ravine.

Sometimes he watches the other blind with his binoculars. Morning thoughts are slow, sober, steady, as he thinks it over and decides the plan is firm. He knows now that he can lie if he has to—he lied right to Bert's face. Twice.

And more thoughts: Paul never got used to seeing them after the gutting; remembering: he and Brien came up here more than twenty years ago—the year he turned seventeen, the fall after Dad died, leaving the restaurant behind—and Paul killed his first buck and walked up to it and stared and eventually Brien came over from his blind and saw him standing over it and pointed to the tiny hole, saying, "Right behind the shoulder. Nice shot Paul," and Paul slumped down beside the buck and cried and cried.

He couldn't stop crying, didn't know why.

That was long ago.

Still, he'd never gotten used to seeing them afterwards.

And he thinks of Drew's brother Adam who drowned in the Wolf. How it's all just now and now and now, and then the now ends and becomes the past, and we end too and become the past, and the past flows through the now, causing new problems in its wake.

But the dead have no problems, except for one.

Snow begins to fall. Snow might ruin this opportunity. But here it is, falling through the woods in huge flakes. And opposite him, across the milky surface of the frozen Noname, in the other blind, the orange hat is hidden. Curled up for sleep. Paul checks his watch. It's ten o'clock.

Suddenly Paul sees it, melting out of the hardwoods, and then back into them, moving slowly, silently, below him, among the trees of the valley floor, visible for a moment, then camouflaged once more. Paul picks up his binoculars and looks for the rack. Eight points, at least.

Binoculars down, silently, he has the Winchester in his hands and sights the buck. With a fluid motion, he raises his gun to the other blind.

Craig has seen the buck, is sitting up, lifting his gun; he's using a shotgun with slugs, so he has to wait until the deer comes into the limited range—100 yards. Craig's orange outfit is like a neon target; even his face is fully visible now between the cross-hairs. The buck is coming closer—if Craig gets the buck, he'll leave.

It'll ruin everything.

Paul knows he has to take a shot, but he's not ready. He moves his rifle back and sights the buck, which is raising its head, listening, scenting.

Paul aims two feet ahead of it, then three feet, and flicks off the safety with his right thumb. He takes a breath and holds it; he re-aims and gently squeezes the trigger. A loud blast and a jerk of the gun—a punch to his right shoulder—and the buck is off, bolting back into the trees. The shot destroys a part of a stump just in front of the buck. Paul shrinks back into his blind, lying against the dirt.

He peers up and slowly brings his binoculars up to his eyes with one hand. His binoculars between logs, Paul finds the opposite blind. The shotgun is still frantically trying to follow the buck. The loud blast that rips through the heart of an immature oak is only a futile gesture—the buck is long gone.

Paul lies flat again, listening. People heard the two shots; someone nearby might have even realized they came from different makes, but it's unlikely: just two shots in the crowded woods on the day after opening day.

Discouraged, the orange hat sinks back into its own blind.

He lies there, thinking: Craig stays until Monday night.

On the stage, the Asian woman is dancing slowly, dressed in a yellow bikini. Tom slaps Paul on the back; they smile.

"Glad I got the buck?" Tom asks. "Keep the tradition going?"

"Skinny little fucker," Paul tells him, referring to the buck's six points.

"Me or the buck?" Tom asks with a laugh.

"Both I guess."

"Where's your buck, Paul?"

Paul smiles, saying, "You just put your tag on that buck. Your brother did the shooting."

"Maybe," Tom says with a wink. "Maybe not. You'll never know."

"I guess not."

The bar is filled with men in heavy wool sweaters, men in flannel shirts, men in long underwear tops and jeans. Their heavy coats are slung across their bar stools and chair backs or hung on antlers of mounted trophies.

Smoke fills the air; usually that would be bad: Paul would have to change clothes, wash his hair and beard with the freezing cold water in the morning—the deer can smell the smoke, and it scares them away. But this trip Paul wants to scare the deer away from the ravine.

Four other dancers move throughout the bar. The men cheer, laugh, whistle.

On stage, the Asian woman gestures as if to take off her top, then stops, laughing at the men. The men holler, clap and hold out dollar bills until she picks a man, takes his money, and dances in front of him. She removes her top slowly, seductively. She has small breasts.

Beside him, Brien has his arms folded as he watches the show.

Paul leans over, "What do you think?"

Brien looks at him, "I think they're earning their keep."

Paul nods. Brien adds, "I think it's going to be an early morning, Paul."

"We get to sleep-in tomorrow. Til seven."

Brien shrugs. Brien used to be as wild as Tom. Even more so. Now, he has three kids. Each one made him more quiet, reserved and sober. More like Paul has always been.

Brien packs a dip in his lower lip, looks at Paul and says, "If Megan asks, this never happened."

Paul nods.

One of the strippers comes around to Paul. She has short brown hair, almost a butch cut and is wearing a leather outfit. She has a nice body and a thin, boney face. She makes a slow, catlike move toward him, then loses her composure, the act, and backs up laughing. She walks over and gives him a hug: "You look like you had a crappy day—no deer in the woods?"

Paul laughs and reaches into the front pocket of his jeans to pull out a dollar. She suddenly comes close to him, her hands smoothing his flannel shirt from his shoulders to his chest, and puts her mouth beside his ear as if she's going to whisper something to him, but she just makes a low, moaning sound. He can feel her breath on his ear and neck, and her cheek and then lips brushing his beard. Paul pulls out a bill and hands it to her.

She backs up and laughs again. She calls out to the crowd around her, "This one's too nice to be a hunter."

She works her way over to another hunter, puts her arms around him and begins a new game. Paul turns around.

Behind them, Craig has paid for a lap dance. A tall, blond woman smiles at Craig as she lithely straddles him. She massages his shoulders, then rubs her naked breasts in his face. She rocks against him slowly, gaining momentum, her hair whipping him in the face. Then she stands, kicks up a leg over her head, grabs it by the ankle, and holds it. Somehow she slowly turns in a half-circle, bringing the outstretched leg over his head. Craig leans in and sniffs her like an excited dog.

Everyone around bursts into laughter and applause, and Paul feels the explosion of sound and it wells within him as she completes her turn and crouches against Craig's lap, her breasts on his knees. He rubs her back and buttocks, and she humps against him, and then reaches back, grabbing his hand, placing it into her hair, and driving wildly, her face contorted as if Craig is pulling her hair, reining her like an animal.

Then amid the applause, she stands, kisses Craig on the forehead and moves to the next group of tables.

On the ride home, the wheel twists in Paul's hand again and again as the truck clambers over ruts in the dirt road. It's begun to snow again—the small flakes fly through the headlights at the truck like stars falling from the darkness. They're a bit hypnotic, and Paul has to avoid looking at the flakes, has to stay focused on the road.

Craig and Tom are crammed into the jump seat in the back. They're drunk and talking about the whores. That's what Craig calls the dancers, while Tom calls them the talent. But maybe they are whores. Paul is too tired to think about the distinction between strippers and whores.

The road goes on and on through the pale woods. Snow lines the unplowed road: in some places, piled several inches high. And the woods go on and on in a barren, unbroken repetition. Craig slurs his words just a bit.

"It shoulda been me with the buck."

"Bullshit," Tom tells him.

"This morning I saw one. A big buck. Twelve points, at least."

Tom answers: "So why isn't it hanging on the line?"

"I think somebody else is hunting the ravine. It was weird, like somebody missed him right before I fired. But probably it was just an echo from somebody a mile away but he heard it too and it spooked him."

"It's crowded as fuck up here," Tom says.

Paul watches the road.

The clouds cover the stars, and outside the band of the headlights, there's absolute darkness. He did it on a night like this.

Brien is asleep, his head bobbing against the window

of the passenger side. Craig and Tom are finally silent too. Paul realizes that the noise of his truck is also like the headlights, a bubble of sound in an otherwise silent world.

Empty woods. There's no one here.

There's nothing to stop anyone from anything.

Paul checks the rearview mirror: asleep like kids in the backseat. The pale woods go on and on and on, and the deserted road carves right through its emptiness.

On the windy beach beneath a black sky and the roar of the storm, his sister picked up a piece of meat wrapped in plastic, covered with sand. No—Paul saw now that it was a stone striated like a muscle with red, pink and gray colors. Kristen tossed it up in the wild air and caught it.

She threw it at the fierce waves. It disappeared immediately with a tiny splash that was inaudible above the raging storm.

Paul Kruk, his sister said to the splash of water.

When Paul had started high school, Kristen was seven years old. They'd spent a good chunk of those days away from the heat of the restaurant, sneaking along the rusted rails of an abandoned railroad track to a long, winding ravine, and then down to this same stretch of Lake Michigan. She'd told him then that the sound of his name was like the kerplunk sound a rock makes when it hits the water. And now she threw another stone in the water, ignoring his questions.

Paul Kruk, she said again to the water in a child-like way.

Why didn't you go to the police? he asked her, yelling above the storm.

She bent and found another one. The October wind picked up and swept a bit of sand into her face. She threw the stone into the water and looked at him, her head cocked slightly to one side.

Paul Kruk, she said, wiping at one eye with her sleeve.

Paul was surprised that her face was remarkably unmarred. The bruises were only on her legs, arms and stomach as if he'd known not to mark her face.

Oh, sister. My baby sister.

His silence and tears seemed to offend her: she chucked another stone and repeated angrily, Paul Kruk.

She bent to find another stone.

Is it because you don't want to go to court? Paul whispered. We can get a good lawyer who'll keep your name out of the papers. Maybe Drew over in Appleton—

Paul Kruk, she whispered as another stone hit the water.

What do you want then? Paul asked.

She stared at the indifferent waves. A smirk passed over her face. Finally she answered his question.

I want him dead, she said. Then laughed at Paul and herself and the sand, waves and sky.

A hand shakes him: "It's seven, Paul. Good morning."

Brien. Paul sits up and looks around in the dim light of the sleeping tent. Tom is stretching in his sleeping bag. Brien is pulling a pair of jeans over his long underwear.

"Where's everybody else?" Paul asks, reclining a moment longer.

"Bert went out with Drew, so did Craig," Brien mutters.

"Oh," Paul yawns.

"There's some hot coffee in the thermos over there on the card table."

"Can I help you take down the tents?"

"Just this one. Bert already packed up the mess tent for me."

"Okay."

At nine, Paul closes the gate of his truck and watches as Brien ties the last knot on the ropes that bind the deer to the roof of his truck—Tom's buck lying beside Brien's doe.

"Too bad you didn't go out today," Tom says. "I bet you'd've gotten one too."

"Yeah," Paul agrees. "Hey, Brien?"

"Yeah?"

"I'll follow you to Iron. Gotta stop for gas there."

"So do I," Brien says.

"Cool."

The sky is threatening rain. Rain will spoil his chance. Paul screws on the gas cap and flips the gas tank panel shut. He walks inside, trying to wipe the smell of the gasoline from his hands with a paper towel as he goes inside. It's not enough, and he washes them in the bathroom.

At the register, the woman behind the counter looks at him. The clock above her reads 9:37.

"Forty-five, thirty-three," she says.

"Put it on my card," Paul says. She takes the card. He gets his receipt, makes sure that it has the time and date printed on it, and shoves it in his pocket.

"I don't know how you do it," she says.

"What?" Paul asks quickly.

"Hunting," she says, nodding at his orange vest. "I just don't get it. Ten years up here and I still think it's barbaric."

"Do you eat meat?" he asks simply. At her slack expression, he walks out.

Outside, Brien shakes Paul's hand and says, "See you in a couple weeks."

"Yeah, let's get together," Paul says. "Play some cards."

"Sounds good."

"Later Kruk!" Tom calls from the truck. Paul waves.

Paul washes his window, waving as the truck pulls away from the gas station; the Graces head south, toward home.

When he's sure they're gone, he gets into his truck and starts it. He pulls out his radar detector: he'll make up most of the time on the paved roads. He heads north, toward the forest.

The orange hat will rise from its blind. A deer will pause beside the frozen river at the very bottom of the ravine, looking for open water. As Paul lies flat against the belly of his blind, he will raise his rifle, watching.

When he reaches the right spot on the dirt road, Paul pulls over to the shoulder. He opens the garbage bag. He moves his seat all the way back and quickly changes into the cold clothes from the bag: a black waterproof coat and matching pants, the black facemask, and a pair of black leather jungle boots. He slips the orange poncho over all this and pulls up the hood. He peels a strip of duct tape, steps outside and affixes the fake license plate over the real one.

He hauls the Winchester out of the truck bed, frees it from the leather case, locks the doors and heads into the woods.

When Paul finally stopped crying, Brien told him what to do: you circle the anus first and pull it out and tie it in a knot so you don't get shit all over the venison. And then start at the belly and work your way up to the chest—be careful not to pop the bladder or the stomach—and then scoop out the innards and reach up and pull out the lungs, rip out all the shit inside the thorax, and leave it all for the raccoons. Tie him up and drag him back to your truck.

Save the heart. We'll eat that later.

His first buck.

When he can no longer see the road, he lies down and

pulls off the poncho, leaving it bunched up at the base of a pine tree. He takes a long breath, glances at the silent woods surrounding him, and continues through the short pine trees.

A sudden crimson mist, the orange hat will sink back into the blind—the shot gun falling, bouncing on the logs. The body will be stretched awkwardly, legs sprawled and visible. Paul will watch the right leg quiver for a full five seconds; then that too will cease as the world becomes absolutely silent once more. Paul will slip back into the trees where his orange poncho awaits him.

He crawls slowly up the embankment, the ground wet and cold beneath the waterproof jacket and pants. His breath is coming too quickly. He can feel his face is sweating beneath the ski mask.

He pauses before continuing, waiting for his body to resume a slower pace.

Using his elbows, his knees, he pulls himself up the slope. He lies flat a full minute. He slowly pulls his binoculars to his face, and raising his head ever so slightly, looks down at the broad expanse of the ravine. It is snowing.

He waits, contemplating whether it should be a head shot or a chest shot.

He uses the binoculars to study the tops of the trees. There is no wind. The big snowflakes are falling straight down into the ravine.

Then he slowly returns his view to where he can see part of the orange hat and part of Craig's face.

Head, he decides.

One shot only, make it count.

He waits.

His sister stood on the beach. She wouldn't look at

him.   She threw the stone at the indifferent waves and laughed.

The orange hat suddenly moves into view, and Paul sets his binoculars to the side.

The Winchester rifle in his hands, Paul has Craig through the cross-hairs.

Craig has seen a deer, is sitting upright, must be trying to tell if it's a buck.

Amateur. You'll only scare it away.

Paul uses the forefinger and thumb of his right hand to zoom in a bit with the scope and takes a slow, steady breath. He exhales and holds his breath. Craig puts his shotgun to his right shoulder, exposing his left side, his rib cage.

Paul brings Craig's image closer, aiming between his left ear and temple.

One shot only. The head.

Paul flicks off the safety.   Between the cross-hairs, Craig has tilted his head and has closed his left eye. Craig is gripping and re-gripping the stock of his shotgun. His hands must be sweating as he tries to get a bead on the animal.

Not removing his left hand from the rifle stock, Paul twists the dial on the back of the scope, zooming in. The orange cap comes closer; it sways slightly with each breath Craig takes.

Paul zooms in one final time before floating his right hand back into position, his index finger on the trigger.

She is dressed in contradictions: a plaid skirt like those Catholic school girls wear, but the black t-shirt and the tall, pointed black leather boots tell the rest of the story. She almost runs into the pub, fresh and flushed from the late September air. Laughing with her friends. She's been dancing next door, and now she's in the bar. His bar.

He hasn't seen her since Drew's wedding. He watches her walk toward the bar as he lines up a shot. Their eyes meet. He feels it instantly, knows it immediately. The chemical connection, the electricity, all that bullshit.

She looks away as if playing coy, but he knows. She and her friends sit at the far side of the bar. He takes his shot and makes it, and then lines up the eight ball and finishes off the table. Then he steps to the bar where his leather jacket is slung over a wooden stool and takes a sip of his beer. While Tom racks the pool balls, he leans against his pool cue and takes a moment to take her in: bright red lipstick, dyed hair falling in lazy tangles, tight t-shirt accentuating her breasts, shapely white legs stretching down into those black boots.

She is gorgeous, and as she glances up one more time at him, he decides to go over and talk to her.

2

Craig is embarrassed and pissed off. His face is hot. The walls of the sleeping tent feel confining and close—the entire hunting camp seems twisted and bizarre suddenly.

This isn't the way it's supposed to be.

Kristen's brother is pumping his hand with his huge mitt of a hand. Craig has big hands too from the war, but Paul was in the first war and he has all that time in lifting and hauling and cutting in the kitchen of his restaurant. If it came to a fight, it would be a tough one. Craig thinks he might be able to take him, but it would be close.

He doesn't want any bullshit. He just wants to take the Cure. Tom brought him up here for the old traditional Cure.

Kristen's brother. Fuck.

A woman walked toward their table balancing a tray peppered with shots of Jameson. The Jameson Girl was how she introduced herself—as if this stop in Appleton, Wisconsin were part of some big national tour arranged by marketing executives, and she its star. Tom paid for two shots, and even though Craig knew he'd have a hangover tomorrow, he held out his hand for the shot. The Jameson Girl smiled as she picked out a shot from the tray and handed him one of them.

Tom was shaking his head dramatically behind her, mouthing the words, "No, no, no," to Craig. But Craig ignored him.

"Thanks a lot," Craig muttered, but purposely ran his words together: "Thanksslut."

Tom shook his head in exasperation at Craig, and when the Jameson Girl turned toward Tom, he smiled at her and managed, "Yes, thank you—don't be a stranger, we'll be right here!"

The woman smiled at him and moved on.

"You're a moron," he told Craig as the opening strains of Purple Haze filled the bar.

"What? She was a slut," Craig deadpanned.

Craig held the golden colored liquid up to the yellow lights of O'Danny's pub as Tom frowned at him from across the table. Together, they gulped back the shot. Tom slammed the glass on the table and grabbed his beer to chase it immediately. Craig gently placed the glass on its wooden surface, and while he tasted the whiskey and felt it in his throat, he looked around the bar at the patrons.

That's when she walked right in to his pub. He recognized her immediately—she was from Two Rivers, and he was from Manitowoc. At Drew's wedding, he'd driven her in Adam's Porsche from St. Mary's to the Elk Country Club. And here they both were in Appleton. Tom saw his look and laughed.

Craig watched as she looked at him again, and it was her look—the way she lingered over his face with a look that was genuine before going back to her conversation with her friends with false excitement. That look was what got him.

"Hey," Craig feels himself saying to Paul.

"Hi," Paul says, and it's almost shy the way he says it. Craig goes back to his drink, while Paul turns away awkwardly and leaves the sleeping tent.

He's supposed to take the Cure —just like his dad and grandfather did when they got back from Vietnam and World War Two—and now it's all fucked. He was supposed to stay with Drew. He knew Paul and Brien were friends, but he didn't know that Paul would be up here.

And fuck it man, this is supposed to be his time. His time and Tom's time up here. Their cure. And Brien's time too, even though Brien was just a hobbit. Craig's supposed to take the Cure and be done with it. He served the country in a time of war. He deserves to get the fucking cure. Paul had been called up on Reserves, but didn't go to Iraq or Afghanistan.

Fuck it. Fuck it all.

The Cure, what a laugh. What fucking cure? It's like, thanks Tom and Drew for ruining the weekend, thanks for putting me in the same group with my ex-girlfriend's brother.

The first night they were together, he watched her for a while from across the bar, and then decided to just go up and talk to her. And that's all it took. He and Kristen talked the rest of the night. They talked about music. She liked a lot of the same bands, and that was cool.

The rest got a little fuzzy. They were both drunk. She played pool with him, of that much he was certain. He had a joint, and they smoked it at some point in the little gravel alley that runs between O'Danny's and the Tea Tree Shop.

But the first time they kissed—he wouldn't remember if it was in his car or in the alley. What he'd remember is that the first night they kissed, they had sex. He would remember that much. She took him back to her apartment. They messed around for a while. Then she went and found some condoms in a drawer, and they used them on the couch in the living room and on the rug. He'd remember her facial expressions, sometimes serious, sometimes smiling, and her moans, and three distinct positions, her body moving in the half-light coming through the curtains from the street lamp outside her apartment window, and he remembers that she called out once, Yes, fuck me.

Then she came. Or faked it.

Craig has a pair of aces with a king kicker. He draws two, but no help. Paul scares everyone out. But Paul has shit, or is slow playing something good. Fuck it.

Craig raises, and Brien launches into yet another scolding session about the rules, while Tom has another panic attack in response. Craig watches Paul's expression as he holds the chips over the pot, suddenly realizing that he's made a mistake, that Paul really has it. Craig decides he has to ride it out and just hope that Paul doesn't raise over the top.

Paul baits him, saying, "It's alright guys. Let him raise. He's bluffing."

Craig lets go of the chips, saying, "It'll cost you fifty then."

Tom and Brien continue to bicker, while Paul jokes with Bert, and Craig feels the blood rush to his face. This is all wrong.

"What d'you got?" Paul challenges.

"You show first," Craig feels himself saying.

"You were called," Brien tells him.

Before Craig can respond, Paul lays down his cards, saying, "Full boat."

Then they want Craig to show his cards, and he won't. He can't stand pickup games like this with people who argue over the most basic rules, but he feels bad about that, and about losing, and breaking the rules, and the look he saw in Paul's eyes, and the whole thing now, and he just wants the weekend to be over and done.

Greeny was drawing dead. All of them knew it or suspected it.

Pair of kings in the flop. Craig was just baiting him.

Better get out now Greeny, Teron warned him.

Above them, a fighter screeched into view and they all watched as it roared against the last glow of sunset in the west and into the distance, the rumble lasting well after the fighter was gone. They were playing Texas Hold 'Em and smoking a joint. The card table was the scorched hood of a Humvee that had been propped up at its corners on stacks of rocks, cinderblocks and bricks that looked thousands of years old and had weird designs carved into them.

It was a Tuesday, and earlier that day, Hawker or Brando had killed a sniper. They'd been on patrol and had all heard the shot whiz by their heads, and they'd later joked that if he'd gotten the sergeant who was on point, the shot would have taken all of them out like a line of dominos. The sergeant had given them the evening off because the fire team had saved his life and tomorrow Lieutenant Batman was going to cowboy up into the old city.

They were celebrating on the back of the hill behind the ammo dump of the makeshift base, dozens of supposedly loyal Iraqi security forces covering the perimeter. Teron had just named Private Danials, bestowing the handle Greeny on him, both because he was new to the Suck and because he'd somehow managed to buy a bag of Kabak. Craig had been partial to the nickname Jack Daniels and was still a little sour that Teron had named him.

Teron spoke up, Man been in the Sand only two weeks and he gets yeh.

Teron held up the joint and admired it.

Yeh in the Sand man, Teron muttered taking a hit off the joint and passing it on to Hawker.

Dark haired Hawker looked down his severe, twisted nose at it strangely, pretending he was downright scared of it, and then passed it to Brando.

Sandman, sandman, Brando said softly and started cracking up.

Gotta admire Greeny, Greeny got balls, Teron was saying. He was happy, and his speech had become a fake kind of talking, black talk that Craig knew he normally wouldn't use. In front of the lieutenant or the sergeant, he sounded pretty much white.

Dude, keep it down, Craig said, You want to wake up

the sergeant?

Sandman, sandman, Brando whispered, exhaling smoke and laughing, Sandman got the sergeant.

I thought yeh was coke, Hawker said.

No man, Teron said, Yay is cocacola but yeh is jus' delicious yeh.

Yeh and yeh?

Yay and yeh, Teron corrected.

Yeh and yeh, Hawker said, There's no difference.

This ain't yay, Teron said, taking back the joint, This a gorgeously beautiful blunt of African black tar Kaff Kaff rolled by my new friend Greeny here. Of the stuff of quality that would make King Haile Selassie himself proud.

Then he became Bob Marley and said, And here I and I marooned in Babylon.

Teron slapped Greeny on the leg, who pushed more chips into the pile, scarcely looking up.

Cough cough, Brando said and started cracking up again, lolling his head from side to side, whispering, Cough cough, cough cough, to the stars.

Craig turned over his pair of kings that matched the pair on the flop. He took a hit and watched Greeny's face drop as he realized he'd lost. Craig exhaled as he leaned forward and swept the pile of chips toward him.

Greeny turned over his hole cards that made a king-high straight on the river and threw his hand into the pile of discards in disgust.

Brando sang at the night sky, In a little hilltop village, they gambled for my clothes.

Don't take it so bad there Greeny, Hawker said, Private Blunder here always wins.

Greeny recovered and took a long pull off of his canteen.

Hey Teron, Greeny said.

Yah mon, Teron said.

What's your nickname? Greeny asked.

Terror, Hawker said before the beatific smile melted from Teron's face.

Craig smiled as he looked over his new friend. Craig had to admit it: Greeny had made a friend of Teron and himself and Brando and Hawker. They would definitely have to stop pretending like he didn't exist.

They go outside to look at the doe hanging on the line, but mostly just to get outside of the tents. It's cold and pitch dark, and they all are shining their flashlights everywhere. Brien is starting to build a fire, and Tom helps him.

Craig stares into the fire and is thinking about Greeny now, thinking about the card game they played a few weeks before the day he almost died. But back then, he was thinking about the woman he dated before Kristen and thinking that if he lived, he'd go back to the States and see what she was up to.

Craig considered the woman he dated before Kristen a real whore. Brittney. She'd just had a kid when they first met.

She was a former cheerleader, and now she was a secretary at an accounting firm. And Craig met her standing in line at the Jam Jar, a bar that just opened in Appleton, and Craig laughed at the way she wanted to talk to him non-stop, and before he knew exactly what was going on, they'd spent more than an hour talking and then walking around Appleton, and the way she looked at him made him think that she wanted him—and the warmth of her voice, the sound of her laughter and the teasing lilt in her voice—and his pulse raced, his throat felt tight, his saliva tasted electric. But he wasn't sure if she was just fucking with him—she kept waving that huge diamond ring on her finger in front of his face, but the ring too was just another big turn on for him, and then when she mentioned the Karma Sutra, he knew he was in.

And so, when they approached her car, she touched his arm, and then they were kissing, and she was leaning back against the car and grabbing him, pulling at him, more physical than any woman he'd ever been with, so he brought her back to his apartment, and they spent the day trying out the various positions, and even pretending like they were inventing a few new ones. It had been a while, and a while was an understatement—at least a year.

It wasn't until she met with him a few more times that he found out that she had a baby, and a few times after that that the baby was only eight months old. And he told himself that it didn't matter, that it was just sex, and that she and her husband were already on the way to a divorce, so what could it matter? But somehow it did matter, and it did make him a little sick over the whole thing, but he wanted her anyway.

Her husband was Indian. Craig's father would have said he was a brown Indian rather than a red Indian. Craig tried to not let the existence of the husband bother him, but the existence of the baby bothered him more.

Eventually, Brittney didn't want to hire sitters for the baby, so he'd come over to her house. They had sex while the baby lay on the rug, sleeping just a few feet away. At some point she'd come, and at some point she'd mention that she loved him, and at some point she'd have to nurse the baby. While she was nursing the baby, he'd tell her that he had something to do: an old friend in town, a job interview, a meeting—whatever, it didn't matter—she'd understand and nod without a word, and he'd slip out of the house and walk through the woods behind the house that ran for about a quarter mile until he reached an old park on the other side where his car waited for him. And the whole time he was thinking how stupid he was, that he would probably get killed if her husband ever found out, that he could have come home early from his business trip, and then he'd be dead.

Later that night, Craig and Tom wind up at the bar, and the old guys stay at the hunting camp. Tom wants to go bowling, so they drive an extra half-hour on the back roads to Wabeno. Craig sparks up a one-hitter to pass the time. The trees are flying by in the darkness.

"Did I ever tell you about Brittney?"

"The cheerleader milf?" Tom says, laughing.

Craig laughs out the smoke from his lungs and passes the one-hitter to Tom, who waves it off, nodding to the tree-lined road ahead. Craig shrugs and sparks one up.

It wasn't the Indian husband that caused Craig and Brittney to break-up.

It was love. She fell in love with him.

They were lying on the carpet of her home. She mentioned leaving her husband.

Craig leaned up on one elbow and looked her right in the eye.

"That isn't a good idea," he said.

"Why not?"

"You can leave him, but not for me, okay?"

"What do you mean?"

"We're just here to have fun, right?"

"I thought we were falling in love," she said to him with tears in her eyes.

He took her hand: "I'm sorry. This is great, but you have to know that, that I'm not in this for the long haul."

She started crying.

"I'm just here for fun," he said. "I thought you knew that. I thought you wanted it that way."

"What's wrong with me?" she said.

"Nothing, but I'm only twenty-two. And you're--"

"Old?"

"No, of course not," Craig said softly. All of this was

way too melodramatic for him; he was ending it now before it got too bizarre. "But I'm just having fun right now. I don't want any commitments."

Then he added as serious as he could, "Of any kind."

She was silent for a long while. When she spoke, it was cold and just above a whisper, and it scared him to the point that he did as she directed as quickly and efficiently as possible:

"Get. Out."

A few months later, he met up with Kristen at O'Danny's, and she too had another man.

The next night, Brien has gotten a buck, and everyone heads in to town.

The jump seat of Paul's truck is a bit cramped for Tom and Craig. The bar is forty minutes away.

"Look at what he's done with these young guys. It's amazing. It puts Favre in the top five right?" Brien says.

Everyone agrees. They list the top five. Paul says: Johnny Unitas, Brett Favre, Joe Montana, Roger Staubach, and Bart Star. Craig's list is: Brett Favre, Joe Montana, Tom Brady, Peyton Manning and Dan Marino. Brien's list includes Joe Montana and Steve Young, and Tom says, "Dude, Favre has almost as many touchdown passes as Young and Montana combined. Plus, the talent Young had around him was better."

Brien asks if anyone remembers a better quarterback transition than Montana and Young, and nobody does. Tom jokes, "How about Rex Grossman and Kyle Orton?" to a couple chortles.

"Who did they replace?" Craig asks, trying to remember the Bear's first string quarterback from the start of the season.

"Sid Luckman," Tom says, and everybody laughs.

The conversation turns. Tom starts talking about melting glaciers, ice ages and a warm up in Greenland that was part of a natural cycle. He's defending Bert's position from an earlier conversation, playing devil's advocate.

"I'm just saying. How do we know? The earth probably froze completely solid at one point, even at the equator, and probably spent a couple million years boiling over. So how do we know what's causing it. How do we know what caused the warm up in Greenland?"

Brien isn't buying it and is annoyed: "Perhaps it's because we've deforested the entire planet in the last four centuries, replaced it with grids: air conditioned houses, dustbowl farms and sprawling cities that generate their own weather patterns. You look at ancient history: farming in Greenland. How about what's happening now?"

"There's definitely something going on," Tom says. "I'm just saying it might not be man-made."

Craig is remembering a series of photos they showed his unit during BCT of the field of oil wells that were burning and the plumes of smoke rising into the air.

"Yeah, it must be all those volcanoes," Craig says, and Brien laughs.

"Seriously, Tom," Brien says.

"Sorry, man, just shooting the shit," Tom says, and he goes back to staring out the window at the trees that line the frozen road.

They are silent for a time, until Tom adds, "Fucking hobbit."

And they all burst out laughing, except Paul.

"I prefer the term, 'Ring Bearer,'" Brien deadpans.

More laughter.

"What's a hobbit?" Paul asks as he handles the ruts in the iced over gravel road.

Tom's explained this to Paul once already. He does so again. As a psychologist during the war, Brien was a non-combat officer.

"Paul was in the first gulf war," Brien tells Tom.

"Yeah but he was on reserves in Germany for the

second one."

"But he's not asking about me being confined to the base."

"Then what's he asking?"

"He's asking about Tolkien."

"Oh," Tom says.

"Didn't you see the movies?" Craig asks. Paul shakes his head.

Tom explains: "A hobbit is a three foot tall character. A dwarf in a fantasy book. That can't fight."

"We're not dwarves," Brien says indignantly. "We prefer the term 'little person.' And we can fight. We're just too valuable to be allowed to leave the Shire."

They all laugh. Paul nods and gives a weak smile.

Craig is still smiling: Brien for all his education is a hawk like the rest of them, and he's tall, not as tall as his friend Bert, but taller than Paul or Tom or himself. And the idea of being in Iraq and being forced to stay on the base like a sitting duck except on rare occasions is just insane. It'd be like waiting for Lebanon all the time.

The forest trees line the darkness just beyond the edge of the snow-covered road.

Craig is thinking about being on the water at the Grace family cabin. In their forested bay on Lake Grace. Surrounded by evergreens, huge red and white pines, and oaks and birch trees, their leaves already yellow, orange and red, autumn in the air. He lay on a long, inflated raft and smoked his last joint. When it burned his fingers, he flicked it at the glassy surface and let his hands dangle over the sides in the cool water and felt a sense of serenity come over him. He would fight and die for his country. It was a simple decision, and this would be his last moment of peace before he too joined the earth with its lakes and forests as dust and ash.

And the next morning, he went to his parent's home in Manitowoc, and then he began to pack, and two days later he was signing in for BCT at Fort Jackson, and ten weeks later he was in Baghdad, thinking he'd probably die there, ready to die there.

But he didn't die. He made it back.

Craig wonders if Paul's Basic was nine weeks too. He wonders if Paul knows that he was in love with Kristen.

The second time he and Kristen were together they just made out and talked. And that was cool.

The third night they were together they had sex, drunk, in the alley behind the bar.

Another night she ended up puking all night while he held back her hair.

The next night they were back to being strangers. She sat at the bar, and he played pool, just as when they'd met. She was talking with a friend.

Cigarette smoke thicked the air, and he lit one up and took a drag. He wanted to talk to her, but he wasn't sure. The music was pulsing through the place. Jane's Addiction.

He lined up a shot and caught her purposely turning her head to look away from him. He took the shot and made it. He chalked the cue. He realized that she was looking at him, pretending she wasn't.

He finished off the table on a four ball run. Tom cursed and dug in his pocket for quarters for the next rack. Craig smiled at him and found his drink. They played another game. Radiohead filled the bar. Creep, followed by Paranoid Android. He kept noticing her pretending to be looking somewhere else whenever he looked on that side of the bar.

He went up to see her at the bar, smiling at her as he approached. She pretended to look away.

"Hey," he said.

"Hey," she said back, and she looked at him, then down at her lap.

"You okay?" he asked.

"Look, I fucked up," she told him.

"What?" he said, surprised. "What do you mean?"

"See, I'm dating a friend of yours," she said, not looking up.

He realized that she was drunk.

"Yeah," he said softly and walked away.

It was his shot, and he went on a little three ball run, but when he stood up from the table, Tom had an odd expression on his face. Craig noticed that Tom was subtly pointing to his right, pointing behind Craig.

Craig turned around; Kristen was just behind him.

"That's it?" she said. "'Yeah'?"

He smiled.

"I didn't realize you were dating someone," he told her.

"I wasn't," she said immediately. At his look, she added, "I was—it's complicated. I am."

He couldn't stop himself from saying, "I realize that's your decision."

"What do you mean my decision?" she said. "It's a fact."

"Look, I thought it was over between you and Adam. Otherwise, I didn't think you'd go cheating on him."

Her eyes narrowed immediately.

"Fuck you," she said quietly. She turned without a word and melted into the crowd.

They drink whiskey again tonight. Another night celebrating their return. Hendrix is blaring from the speakers. All Along the Watchtower.

Tom orders whiskey from the start. They have been talking about the World War veterans. They've been talking about the way some of them took the Cure, but never came back.

"I saw dead people, lots of them, but it didn't register,

you know, because I didn't kill them," he's saying above the noise of the bar. "You know?"

Craig nods.

"I remember one," Craig says.

"What?" Tom asks above the music.

"Did I ever tell you about the day I almost died?" Craig asks.

"Tell me again," Tom says, and so he does.

When Craig has finished telling the story about the day he almost died, Tom slaps him on the back once, and goes to buy more shots.

Craig finds himself swaying among the strippers and hunters, thinking about the window in the stone wall.

Tom hands him another whiskey. Craig nods and downs the shot, thinking about the window, thinking about the person in the window in the stone alcove in the ancient city.

He can't remember the age or gender. A dark jacket over a white tunic.

That's it.

After Adam disappeared, Craig didn't talk to Kristen. Craig went up and then down the river, looking for him. He'd just vanished, right in front of all of them.

But when they found Adam, Craig was at her apartment in Appleton. Kristen sank into him and began weeping, and the weeping did not stop. Tom came over and gave her a hug too. Craig didn't want to make it awkward for her. He just wanted to help. He slid out of her grasp, as she turned and sobbed into Tom's shoulder.

The wind is icy as Craig steps from the heat of Drew's Suburban. Drew turns off the engine, steps out, and shuts the door. It's as if the cold and silence of the frozen world engulfs them both—the darkness is broken only by the intermittent vapors of their breaths, ragged in the moving air.

"The wind better die down, or the deer will never go near the ravine," Drew whispers. "Too many scents."

Drew pulls open the back, where Craig's shotgun is.

"Remember," Drew says, "Brown is down."

If anyone in the group gets a doe, Drew will put his doe tag on it.

"That stripper went down," Craig says grabbing his gun and unzipping it from the cold leather sheath. "Last night."

Drew's smile appears more like a grimace in the frozen twilight before the dawn. Craig sets his gun case inside the Suburban and gets his backpack.

Drew pulls his Ruger .44 Carbine out of its black gun case.

"You ever see this? It was my brother's."

Craig nods, thinking about how Adam drowned right in front of all of them.

Drew is looking at the rifle.

"He was a great guy," Craig says.

Drew nods.

"You okay, man?" Craig asks.

Drew nods and zips up the case hurriedly.

"I better get to my blind," Drew says with a weak smile.

"Lunch?"

"You bet," Drew tells him as he closes up the glass window of the back of the Suburban. "I'll start the drive a bit earlier today. Then we'll meet up. Say noon?"

"Noon," Craig says.

Drew laughs and wipes at his eye as he heads to the driver's side door.

About a year after Adam's funeral, Craig and Kristen started hooking up again. She was back from her internship in New York and had finished her master's degree at Lawrence.

She'd stopped dyeing her hair, and it was as if their time together was new too. As if she might be able to put Adam's death behind her, her alleged betrayal behind her. She was on a celibacy kick, and that really bothered him. Still, he tried not to let it. They spent whole days and nights together. She was thinking about a doctorate at the University of Chicago, but also thinking about staying for him or having him move with her.

It might be love, she'd finally admitted. And then one morning, things got weird, and she stopped speaking to him.

Craig stumbles in the darkness to his blind. His head is pounding. He waits for the dawn. He can't see a damn thing in these woods. It's not like being on the water, like when Adam died. He could see everything that day: the shudder when the red kayak got lodged in the center of the river, Adam's expression as the kayak jarred, slanting suddenly downward, Kristen's look as she called out to him.

He notices that his shoe lace of his right Danner boot has come off. He hasn't tied the shoe laces of any of his boots since Iraq. A trick one of the sergeants taught him: just tie a knot in the laces at the right place and then all you have to do is quickly wrap them around the tines. Saved him plenty of time when the sergeants ordered a line up. He fixes the shoelace now, wrapping it around the little metal tines, and feeling the stiffness in his right heel. It's different than pain: it's as if the bottom of his foot isn't even there. He was lucky.

The Humvee he was in was the third of the six in the convoy. The old city loomed in front of them. There was dust everywhere, and the hot winds were kicking more of it up. They were all sweating, and Billy kept wiping his forehead with a rag.

Man, it's gotta be a hundred and fourteen today, Billy said.

Summertime Iraq, Teron muttered, Hell of a place to pick to have a war.

Someone had thrown logs and telephone poles across the road, and he watched as Greeny and Hawker and some of the others pulled them to the side of the road.

Over the radio, he could hear Brando singing, I held the scabbard as the soldier drew his sword, I rolled the dice as they—

And the sergeant said, Cut the chatter Private Merrill. This ain't American Idol.

Sir, yes sir, Brando said and for once he was quiet.

He digs his bottle of ibuprofen out of his backpack, and as quietly as he can, pulls out two pills with his forefinger. The pills are more for his head than his foot. He chugs some water and then lies down. He sleeps for a time.

When he wakes, he feels better. It is after dawn. The sky overhead is clouded over, and snow has begun to fall.

He pulls out his wooden hitter box and crushes the cigarette-like pipe into the bottom of the dugout side. There's just a little grayish green of the northern lights at the tip. Just enough to chase away the boredom. Spice it up a bit. He hits it and holds the smoke. He exhales it slowly, intermixing inhaling and exhaling, feeling the smoke stay in the very bottom of his lungs.

He takes a long drink from his canteen, and then quiet pulls out his tin and packs a dip.

He thinks about the weekend. Paul has been acting so strangely.

Maybe he thinks the break-up is Craig's fault, or he's pissed because she ended up getting engaged. Or maybe there's something worse going on. Maybe he knocked her up; maybe she had to go to the abortion clinic next to the Charter Fishing building. She couldn't have had a kid. He would have seen her probably, would have heard about it anyway. If they don't want to tell him, there isn't anything he can do about it.

Maybe Paul wants to hurt him. Perhaps Brien or Drew are in on it too.

If they want to hurt him, there isn't anything he can do about that either. Let them, he thinks. It's a relief, thinking this way. There isn't anything to do. Craig is actually happy as he considers the thought. He looks up into the lazy snow that drifts through the bleak tree branches. It's better to let your life happen, watch it like some kind of a movie.

The last time he saw her was in the fall of last year; she was sitting on the curb in front of a bar, hugging her knees to her chest. He waved at her. She looked at him and then stared at the ground before her, brown hair falling into her face. She didn't push it away from her eyes. He sat down next to her. The remnant patches of the grainy snow were melting in the sun, but the dusty curb was dry.

"Hey Kristen—been a while," he said.

She didn't look at him. She was staring at her knees.

"Listen," he said. "You want to grab a beer or something?"

She looked up at him; Craig was taken aback by the look of abject hate filling her eyes. His legs felt week, behind the knees and in his calves suddenly. He shouldn't be here talking to her. It made him sick to his stomach.

"I'm busy," she whispered.

He stood and took a step away, and then looked at her again.

"Well, maybe later?" he offered, feeling as if he was losing himself in that look.

She said, "I won't be around."

"What does that mean?" he asked, but she just shook her head and looked down the street. He shifted his weight and followed her gaze a moment at the street lined by dirty clumps of the still-melting snow.

It was empty.

He tried again: "I'm leaving. For Bahgdad probably."

She made a shrug-like gesture and a noise that might have been a laugh.

"Well, sorry to bother you," he whispered, frowning and suddenly angry. He bit down on the inside of his frowning lower lip and regained his cool. He walked on.

"See you around," he said over his shoulder.

She didn't say anything in return.

Two weeks later he was heading to BCT, and ten weeks after that he was overseas.

He lies in the blind, thinking about basic combat training. What a cluster fuck.

He was among non-whites on a constant basis for really the first time in his life.

Before he entered BCT, Craig's father had told him to watch his back, and he meant while in country, not overseas.

You didn't want to talk with Craig's father, really about anything, because he always brought race into it. It didn't matter what the subject was. Ask him about sports, and out of nowhere, he'd say those guys can hit and run, but they haven't designed one yet who can coach a team or play QB. He didn't even watch the Bears-Colts game. Ask him about politics—he'd say he was a lifelong Democrat, until the party got taken over. But let them have it, he'd say: Whenever the Blacks get a hold of something, it's all used up anyway. Blacks this. Mexicans that. Jews own everything. He had a poem of the racial slurs for the various ethnicities that was thirty words long that he made Craig memorize as a four-year-old boy. Craig's father's distrust of race, of all other races beside what he thought his was, was a part of nearly everything he did or said.

But Craig had found out in Basic that that's not the way it is. Race was always there, in part because his black counterparts like Teron always brought it up. White cap'ain goin' make me scrub da latrine 'gain, Teron would say, putting on a fake accent for show.

But you end up relying on those guys, and although race is always always there, you end up joking about it or feeling bad about it, and making fun of yourself, and you end up relying on those guys and they rely on you, and then suddenly race really isn't there, if only for a time.

He watches the sky in the blind, a blanket pulled around him, watching the little flakes of snow fall through the branches of the forest ravine, thinking now of the day he almost died, in the third Humvee in a convoy of six.

Four distinct blasts obliterated the first Humvee. And he was the first one out of his, jumping out before it had fully stopped.

There was quiet as the blast echoed through the canyon of the buildings, and the quiet was a moment, a moment of realization and inability, the realization that Greeny was probably dead, and the others, Brando and Hawker and the Lieutenant, were all in that one too, and the inability, the heaviness of his weapon, the fact that he couldn't see a target in the glare of the sun and that his back felt weak, exposed like a target, and the moment seemed to last, seemed to stretch out, and then the rip of the M-60 from the second Humvee in the convoy, directly in front of his own, tore the silence, and returned time to normal. Someone was shooting at him, and it was like hornets spinning past his head, and he saw the shadow in a window, just fifty yards or so away. He clicked off the safety of his M16-A4, and then he and Teron were weapons free, and beyond the noise of his machinegun, there was a stone wall that had an alcove-like window, and the wall was turning to dust as they fired at the muzzle flash from the window, and he clearly saw the figure inside the window in the stone wall wore a dark leather jacket over a white tunic, who fired at them still with a Kalashnikov, even as the stone frame around the window kicked up dust, and then the figure was suddenly gone and the back wall beyond the window was turning to dust.

Someone shouted fireinthehole, and he sprinted to the far side of the Humvee and crouched down, the metal hot and an acidic petroleum scent in the air; he cradled his rifle and plugged his ears out of habit from BCT.   Then the blast.

He stood—someone was shooting at them with a hand gun, a little popping noise in comparison to the blast, and then he heard the sound of the sniper fire, little whizzing rifle shots, and then he heard the ripping blasts of an AK-47. On top of the Humvee, the M-60 was unmanned. He crawled up there and realized that Billy lay in the bottom of the Humvee.   It looked like he was trying to strangle himself: both hands pressed against his neck, his fingers and hands wet with blood.   Trying to stop his life from flowing out of him; it wasn't working.

Craig was about to help him when he stopped—he saw its intensity before he heard it: the flame-up in a window near the top of an apartment building. An AT-4—a fire blazing toward him. He turned, now hearing the initial flushing sound followed by the rocket's roar. He leapt out, but he never landed—a hot blast on his heel and the world turned sideways.

There is a deer approaching in the woods just to the northeast of his blind. Craig hears it before he sees it, picks up his shotgun, and quietly sits up.

He woke to a roar and the brief high-pitched screech of

tires as a fighter touched down. Overhead the sky was black, and the stars were invisible beyond the stark, overwhelming lights. He tried to move, and when he couldn't, he panicked.

He realized he was strapped to a gurney on a runway. His mouth was dry, and he could taste the dust and grit. He could sense the drugs and saline in his body. Nearby, a huge Lockheed Starlifter had started up, and its engines obliterated all other sound.

A sergeant leaned over and tried to yell above the noise of the aircraft: We had to immobilize you as a precaution. You're lucky—the rocket cremated the Humvee. The explosion threw you into a stone wall twenty yards to the east. Your neck appears to be okay. And you'll keep the foot. We're shipping you to Germany. So lie still.

The deer is a doe. Brown is down, Craig thinks as he lifts his shotgun.

The deer approaches the kill zone.

He feels his breath coming too quickly, just like back in the old city. Only this time he can see everything so clearly: the twitch of the doe's left ear, twice it twitches, the graceful steps it takes as it walks, then trots, then walks again, uncertain of itself, along the sloping path that lines the pitched ravine, and the deer's eyes, scanning for danger.

He leans forward, shifting his breathing as he shifts his weight.

His heart is racing.

He moves his finger toward the safety

It was a river that killed Adam.

A river the color of coffee being poured out, filling up a mug.

Running full with fresh rainfall.

Below a waterfall, white and rushing.

They had just paddled five stretches of the Wolf River, and were at their portage point before the river became too dangerous, when Adam Fisher got stuck in a hole. Someone found him three days later, nearly fifty miles downstream, bloated and scarcely recognizable, his legs broken and still pinned inside the crushed kayak.

He was an expert and had spent the past decade on the toughest rivers of Alaska, Colorado and Utah.

Some of the others, including his fiancée and his twin brother Drew, had already taken out, and were carrying the red and blue and black kayaks to the gravel road, where they had left a car with a trailer on the back. There were nine total in their group.

Earlier, he'd been playing in the water, practicing hand rolls and enders with his buddies. He was like a ballet dancer, graceful and smooth. The Wolf was running high that day—the spring melt had filled the river above its banks—and so it was off the charts. The Wolf ran through some tough stretches, and they'd decided to take out before the Menominee Reservation.

He was enjoying himself, smiling, laughing. Rolling beneath a waterfall he'd just launched off. They'd found a hole, and some of the guys—Adam, Drew, Tom Grace and Craig Bunder—were trying enders, but only Adam was really launching out of it. They all took out, but Adam headed fifty yards upstream and worked on some Duffek turns out of an eddy below the waterfall. Then his fiancée came back from the truck with her camera.

She took his picture, and she sat down on a flat rock, near the water's edge, pulling off her drysuit, toweling off her hair, warming herself in the sun.

Adam leaned back, looking up at the blue sky, and drifted lazily back toward the hole, and that's when he got stuck. The tip of the kayak lurched forward and down at an oblique angle, and suddenly he was jarred forward and felt the breath leave him. Then he slapped the water with the paddle—a weak angled smack—but nothing came of it, he was still frozen there, angled up, with the mouth of the kayak turned slightly toward the waterfall.

He gave an awkward laugh and pushed at the water, a determined frown on his face. He must have known that the kayak was caught on something, but he didn't know that the tip of the kayak was wedged between a limb of a submerged oak tree and a boulder beneath the water. His legs were numb from being cold all day, so he didn't realize that water was coming through the skirt, that the kayak was filling with water, with the weight of the river.

"You need the rope Adam?" someone called.

His fiancée waited on the shore, watching in silence.

Adam shook his head, pushing again at the water.

"I think," he began, trying to move the mass of water with his paddle. "I think I got it."

He pushed at the water again, and suddenly the boat shifted again, turning him nearly parallel with the river. His head underwater for a few moments, then free of it momentarily—he hit the water with a flat, useless smack, and then popped the skirt and tried to wiggle free of the kayak. He looked awkward now, like a bird caught in a net or a dog trying to climb from the water into a boat.

His fiancée stood and took a step toward the river.

"Adam?" she called.

"Get the throw rope!" someone called.

"I think," he began again. He must have realized at this point that something was terribly wrong, certainly he would have felt the leaden water weighing down the kayak and pinning him to it.

Tom Grace ran up with the rope bag in his hand. Adam's twin dove in the water and began to swim to the hole.

Craig threw his boat in the water, pushed off with one leg and began paddling toward his friend.

"I think this is," Adam called once before being pulled under.

3

Drew Fisher carefully takes a step forward into a layer of frozen leaves. He tries not to make a sound, but does anyway. The purpose of the drive is to make a bit of noise, flush the deer up valley, where the others wait in their blinds. Still, he doesn't want to scare them from a mile away.

And he doesn't want to make so much noise that the others think he's their target.

He scans both sides of the ravine for hunters. The world around him is gray, and snow is silently drifting through it. All it would take would be somebody not paying attention, not looking for blaze orange, just firing.

He continues on through the valley floor. The scrub trees offer little resistance.

He reaches the Noname River. Back when he was trying to be a painter against his father's wishes, he would have taken a picture of the creek, in order to use it as a template to make a painting of its surface.

It's beautiful: stark black contrasted with sections of white, like polished marble whorls.

His brother Adam used to pronounce its name as *noh-nam-ey*, as a joke, as if the Indians had named it, rather than by the paradoxical name their great grandfather had given it sixty years ago on a hiking trip, to appease his grandchildren, the Grace and Fisher cousins, who needed a name for everything. This river is the border between the land his family owns, the broad acreage that remains of his great grandfather's vast estate, and the public land that borders it.

The stream is only about five feet across here, so he decides to jump it. He checks the safety on his Ruger again. Assured, he runs and leaps over, expecting to slip backward on the snow. However, he lands safely on the other side, takes a couple quick steps forward, and continues his quiet march through the woods.

On the beach, Lake Michigan was a perfect blue. The sun was brilliant, and Drew lowered his sunglasses and sunk down in the beach chair with a rum runner. He loved Door County.

Overhead, the private jets were completing a long slow arc before being brought in for their descent to the private air strip to the south. Cessnas and Hawkers and Learjets. Even the occasional Gulfstream. Like toy planes on a carousel.

Their two boys were playing in the grayish-white sand, building clumps that might be castles or train stations, depending on the game they were playing.

He took a sip of his drink and closed his eyes. The lapping sound of the waves was relaxing.

Beside him, he could hear that Sharon was covering herself in lotion again. She wasn't speaking to him today.

He could also hear that Kristen was hovering nearby. He looked at her from behind his glasses. She looked beautiful in a backless black suit. She kept stealing looks his way. His brother Adam was swimming in the water, jumping through the waves.

When Sharon had her back to him, Drew waited until Kristen looked at him again; he held her gaze, then nodded to her with a slight smile. She nodded back, ever so slightly.

Drew leaned back in his chair, took a sip from his drink and closed his eyes.

A deer bolts toward him, a stampede of legs running over the ice and snow and bounding beautifully over the shrub trees. Drew's heart pounds, and he fumbles for a moment with the strap of his Ruger rifle. He knows he has time to put his rifle to his shoulder and click off the safety before it is on him.

He is wrong. Feeling the slowness of his movements, he pulls the gun strap down from his left shoulder, over his wrist and raises the rifle up again to his right shoulder—but the deer sails past him. He turns and aims, but the safety's on anyway. The deer is gone.

He turns back to the east, hearing brush crash. Four more bound toward him exactly like the first—beautiful, graceful as they leap toward him, oblivious to his presence upwind of them, following their mother or big sister through the small woods of the valley. He flicks off the safety and aims at the closest one that sprints toward him. The gun gives him a gentle punch in the shoulder—an insignificant pain, followed by the adrenaline and the desire keep the gun down, level, as the deer bounds past him, and then fires: one-two-three-four shots in a rapid sequence, until it loses a step and falters: its right leg kicking straight out, sliding out on the snow, and it falls.

The other deer scatter and are gone.

Drew looks around to see if there are other hunters in the area. He doesn't see any blaze orange, nor any blinds on the walls of the valley.

He puts on his safety as he approaches. He leans the gun carefully against the crook of a small birch tree. He bends down and looks at her.

The deer is looking up at him. Drew realizes he's landed two shots. Only two shots, but two nonetheless, as his father would have said.

He's hit the thing's shoulder. There's another bloody tear in its abdomen. Nothing that's going to take it out quickly and painlessly. He's surprised it went down in the first place.

He pulls out his Buck knife from its sheath. He wipes its fixed blade on his jeans out of habit, and then kneels and takes her face below the jaw line with his left hand.

The deer tries to lift its head. Its back legs kick out once and again. It's just stunned, and Drew knows this is dangerous. He pushes down with his left hand, feeling its rapid pulse and hot breath, and with a quick downward thrust, he stabs through where he envisions the jugular vein is, down through the coarse, tough throat, out the other side to the other jugular and into the cold snow until he feels the blade stopped by the ground below. He knows from the spray and pump of blood that he got at least one of the jugulars. He stands, holding the wet blade and watching as the blood mists and pumps from its neck.

Nothing else is necessary, his dad would have said. Leave it for a while. Let it go peacefully. Nice and quick. Good job. Better than blasting its brains out into the snow.

The mist ends, and the pumps quickly become weaker, and weaker, and then cease altogether.

He kneels beside the deer and watches its eye. He thinks for a moment he can see the iris and pupil changing as its life fades and vanishes, but then it looks precisely the same to him, and he isn't sure if it's gone or not. He puts a hand on the body. He can't feel a pulse, and the rib cage is still. He opens his pack and fishes out his gutting gloves and his twine.

Outside, the wind chimes were now illuminated by the lights of the pool deck. They hung in the night air like luminescent jellyfish, their long legs dangling and draping across the dark sea. Drew silently stepped into that sea of night and plunged into the thick humidity of August.

He walked down the path amid the overwhelming sound of the crickets and other night insects to his father's boat. There will be certain songs that will remind him of his brother. Certain images, certain places. The old, beautiful boat is foremost among them. The Hinkley that his father said they had saved. As a family. And it was true that their father had bought the ruined thing out of receivership at a sheriff's sale down in Florida, thrashed by two hurricanes and worn from years of seawater and the misuse of its former owners, but it was the brothers who had salvaged it.

After they'd cleaned it from stem to stern, he and Adam had stripped, varnished and coated this big old wood boat one October. The other brothers were all at college. He and Adam worked shirtless, their torsos, forearms and hands splattered with iodine-colored speckles of the lacquer, and coated with the rich brown dust of the wood, like mahogany, like the color of Adam's guitar. It took a full week to repaint and stain the exterior. Once the exterior was finished, they'd repaired the interior. They'd had to hire a friend to overhaul the old engine, and once that was complete, they'd put on a new coat on both the exterior and interior, and then it was ready.

The boat hung in the sling of the lift, like the leg of an injured man. He ran his hand along the hull. In the morning, he and Adam were going to take it over to Washington Island, through the Strait, which would take a bit of careful navigation.

He climbed into it and downed the last of his vodka tonic. He set the glass on the empty captain's chair and felt his way into the dark cabin and to the cot inside.

He imaged how the boat might fall; how he might die, right here, right now.

We're all in this together, he said to the night. There was darkness and bright light and then a voice. A lovely voice.

Kristen was standing at the door of the cabin, amid the sounds of the chirping insects throughout Door.

So where's your brother? She'd asked, her voice enough to wake him from the brief moment of sleep. She was beautiful.

He sat up and shrugged his shoulders as she stepped into the old boat. She slipped her hands over his shoulders.

She bent and looked at him a moment meaningfully, before positioning herself on his lap, her hair falling around his face like a waterfall.

Drew had known where his brother was that night. And so had she.

His brother Adam was at the Beach Club, drinking with and probably fucking one of the waitresses for old time's sake.

His hands are cold, so he rubs them together and blows vigorously on them before putting on the gutting gloves. He's going to have a nice big cup of coffee and head home after this, he decides.

He rolls the deer over and makes an entry incision just below the diaphragm, keeping the blade pointed upwards, and cuts through the hide and skin first, and then the abdominal wall. He uses the blade to peel back the skin and abdominal wall on either side. He switches positions and uses his other hand to guide the knife, working his knife to its abdomen, where he cuts around the carcass's udder, forming an island around the udder, which he then pulls out and squeezes. There's no milk, so he throws it into the frozen leaves beside him. He slices down to the pelvis and stops just above the vagina.

He cuts around the vagina and anus, making a circle with a deep incision. He grabs the spool of twine. The knife cuts through the twine as if it isn't there. He then pulls the vagina and anus out and ties them off with the twine.

He then pushes and pulls them back and up to where the udder was. He ties off the bladder, which is about half-full, and he begins to pull it out. He reaches in with the knife and cuts it free, but as he removes it, he realizes that it's leaking, maybe the bullet passed through the bladder, or maybe he accidentally put a tear in it, so he throws it to the side, and then rolls the carcass onto its side, and pushes it hard so that the legs bend at their joints until it is nearly resting upright on its stomach to try to drain the urine from the deer and prevent the meat from being spoiled. Its head slumps to the left and its legs to the right as he holds the body upright.

He lets it fall back onto its side. The innards have spilled out and are hanging out of the body. The stomach's been ruptured too, or at least one of its four chambers is leaking. There's blood, urine and stomach juices everywhere as he reaches in and cuts the remaining organs away.

He sets down his knife by his backpack and pulls the carcass by the forelegs away from the entrails. He rolls it onto its back and uses the twine to tie off the esophagus. He cuts out the diaphragm, then feels inside the chest and reaches up to check the remainder of the esophagus. It's wet and slippery inside the deer's body. He decides to cut the chest cavity open all the way so that he won't cut off a finger. He's not going to mount it anyway. He cuts up and through the tough section of the breast bone, and after he's cut it open and dried his hands with a towel, he cuts out the rest of the windpipe.

He rolls it onto its stomach again and lets it drain. He stands and swings his head around his shoulders in the quiet woods, stretching out his aching shoulders, neck and back. His gloves are covered in blood. He waits; his father would have told him to wait ten minutes. He doesn't want to look at his watch, though, because he doesn't want to get it covered in blood and piss. After what seems like five minutes, he rolls the deer back over, and begins to pack it full of snow, trying to find the freshest snow. The remnant heat from the carcass will melt the snow, and clean it out.

On the boat, the drone of the motor on the water was steady and slow. Drew looked at his brother Adam lying in the back.

They were both hung over. Drew leaned against the steering wheel, while Adam lay on the couch beneath the American flag, pretending to sleep.

The only way to tell them apart was that Adam had his shirt off and wore different sunglasses.

The water of the Strait of Door off Washington was filled with whitecaps. Big clouds grew to the west. Adam sat up and studied it. Lightning flickered in the clouds, and a nearly constant thunder grumbled in the distance, filling the silence. They both knew it was dangerous, that they should turn back now.

This would be better in a sailboat, Adam said, You know?

Where were you last night? Drew asked him.

Adam shrugged.

Then he asked, How's Sharon treating you these days?

Drew laughed.

I'll take the drive home, Adam said, and he went to the cabin below to sleep it off.

Drew continued toward the island alone as the storm clouds grew. It loomed to the north, large and solemn, seemingly primeval, wild with forests above the angry water, like something out of a dream.

He flips the deer over again and lets it drain out. While it's draining, he pulls a plastic bag and a towel out of his backpack. He ties the fore and hind legs together for the drag out, and packs the abdomen full of snow again. He picks out the heart and liver from the entrails and cleans them up before storing them in the bag. He decides that he needs to warm up, so he blows on his hands and then presses them together under the towel.

Dr. Finkel's waiting room was small. Drew felt cramped sitting there.

Sharon said that this was for their own good. She held

their first-born child in her arms. The baby started crying, and Sharon cursed under her breath and handed the baby over to Drew. The baby squirmed in his arms and smelled like urine. Finally the doctor let them into his office.

"Dr. Finkel, Mr. Fisher, who's on first?" Drew said, holding a hand out and smiling. Dr. Finkel gave him a weak, almost imperceptible smile. He had a limp handshake.

The office, too, was quite small, and Drew couldn't feel at ease in it.

The session began slowly as Sharon listed her grievances. Drew bet himself five hundred that the psychiatrist would change her prescription at the end of the session. He wished Adam were here so he could bet him. He supposed that Adam was though. He imagined Adam in the corner of the room, smiling at Drew's plight, shaking his head.

Then Sharon said, "And Drew spent all this money on law school, but he isn't sure if he wants to still be a lawyer, or how he'll make his living."

"I like painting," Drew said for Adam's benefit, deadpanning, "I've sold a couple paintings."

The psychiatrist looked at him. In the corner, the pretend Adam was laughing.

"Maybe I'll make a living as a painter," Drew said, but only to mess with Sharon.

"It won't be as a painter," Dr. Finkel told him flatly.

Drew began to tune out after that as pretend-Adam became indignant: The good doctor here has never even seen one painting of a deer that you've done. Not a single one. They look almost identical to the photographs.

Drew started laughing at that, and at the non sequitur, both Sharon and the doctor looked at him sharply.

Drew starts the drag out. He's barely gone a half mile when he realizes that he is dizzy. He stops a moment, and leans against a tree. He needs to get out of the ravine. He walks over to a part of the ravine wall and starts to climb up, but it's too steep. He slips on the wet leaves beneath the snow and nearly falls. He stops again, feeling dizzy and nauseous.

Adam leaned against the boat as Drew looked over the hull for imperfections. The sun was blindingly bright that morning, and the air was heavy and still. The bottom of the boat was still drying from the expedition up to Washington Island the day before.

I'm going to ask her to marry me, Adam said.

Who? Drew asked.

Kristen, his brother said with an incredulous look on his face.

Without hesitation, Drew walked over and gave Adam a hug around his neck.

Drew follows the Noname River, dragging the doe behind him.

Then he approaches the spot where Craig's blind is. Craig will help him drag it out. He sets the doe down on a flat plain near the river and walks up to the blind.

"Craig," he says in a half-whisper. Then says it again. This is dangerous. He's going to get himself shot. He approaches from the side, and peers upward, calling again in a louder voice. But the blind looks empty.

Where is he?

Drew steps forward again. He looks up toward the blind. He knows that Mike, his cousin Jack, and Craig are supposed to be somewhere on this ridge, and that this one should be Craig's blind. Maybe he left.

"Hey," he calls, "Anybody in there?"

Silence is best usually, but no deer will be coming into this valley now that it's coated with blood. He walks to the side of the blind.

"Hey, anybody here?" He walks toward the logs and rocks that make up the blind.

There's someone inside: he can see a set of boots, pointing in different directions. Large flakes of snow cover them. He steps up and over a fallen tree that camouflages the western edge of the blind. There's a shotgun in the snow at an odd angle with its barrel beneath the snow and the butt of the gun a bit above parallel, resting on a snow-covered rock. There's someone sleeping on their side inside the blind.

Drew recognizes the black jacket beneath the blaze orange vest. He's about to yell to get up, get up you lazy sack of shit, when he sees the blood.

Craig is on his right side with his mouth open in a pool of blood.

"Craig!" Drew shouts as he runs in. Craig's left ear is bloody, and Drew turns him over by his shoulder. Part of the right side of his head is missing. Drew instinctively drops Craig's shoulder, and the stiff body falls back where it lay; Drew braces himself on the logs that line the blind. His left hand draws itself through something sticky—blood, bits of flesh.

Drew wheels around, stumbles a few steps, and vomits at the snow-covered stump of a rotted-out elm. He heaves three times. His eyes are full of tears, which he wipes away with his right hand along with the excess spit on the side of his mouth. He wipes his hands on the snow and leaves on the ground. Then he straightens. He can't see; he's crying.

He wipes at his eyes again, opens his backpack, and rummages through it until he finds his cellular phone. He calls 911. He's roaming, and there's a weak signal. The line is filled with static and a series of odd high-pitched tones. Then an operator announces the service carrier, which he doesn't recognize. When the line is picked up, there's a loud crackle that hurts his ear.

"Sheriff," a voice announces through the static on the

line.

Drew wipes the tears from his eyes as he talks.

"There's been an accident, someone in my hunting group has been shot, has been killed," he said.

"Are you sure he's dead?" the voice asks.

"Yes."

"Where was he shot?"

"In the head, behind one ear, and out the other side, toward his temple."

"Did you check his vitals? Is he breathing, does he have a pulse?"

Drew stops. "What?"

"Sir, you need to perform CPR if he's not dead."

Drew considers Craig's body a moment, then says quickly, "I can see his brains. On the logs of his blind."

"Sir, we just need to figure out whether to direct you in CPR and to call in a chopper. Can you do that?"

Drew walks over. There is an orange hunter's hat soaked through with blood lying beside Craig's head. Drew tentatively reaches out and touches the left side of Craig's neck.

The body is cold. What remains of his face has gone pallid.

"There's no pulse. He's, he's frozen," Drew says, trying to stay composed, but he feels himself losing it again. "Look, he's dead okay? Oh, fuck, he's dead."

"And no breathing signs?"

"No, didn't you hear me—he's dead," Drew says, and seeing the crimson on the logs, his stomach turns again.

"And he was shot in the head?"

"Yes, half of his head is gone," Drew feels his voice crack as he spins around toward the valley. The valley continues to spin, even though he knows he is still now. He vomits again briefly, holding the phone away from him, and then he straightens and puts the phone back to his ear.

"Calm down sir," the voice says. "I'm coming myself

with my deputy and an ambulance. I'm gonna put my assistant deputy on the phone and you can talk us to your location. One more thing, who shot him?"

"I don't know."

"Did you shoot him. Accidentally, sir?"

"What? No. I don't know. No."

"We're on our way, sir, just tell us where to go."

Drew tells the assistant deputy how to take the roads, and the proper unmarked forest trails, to their location.

While the assistant deputy is narrating the directions back to him over the dispatch, Drew hears something.

There's a buzzing. He carefully steps into the blind near the body.

Drew realizes that the sound is coming from Craig's backpack, splattered with a spray of bright blood. His own phone still on his ear, Drew moves closer to the backpack, bending down so as not to touch the walls or anything else in the blind. By the time he unzips it, searches the pocket, and finds the phone, it is silent. He pulls out the cold machine and scrolls through the received calls; he sees that Tom Grace has called.

He pushes the button on Craig's cellular to call Tom back. He immediately ends the call. He thinks a moment, wiping the tears from his eyes with his sleeve, and then calls Brien Grace.

Hypothesis: The realm of experience created through psychoanalysis allows us to grasp along what imaginary lines the human organism, in the most intimate recesses of its being, manifests its capture in a symbolic dimension.

4

Brien Grace sits in Manitou on a wooden bench in the darkness of the mess tent. This is his favorite time of the hunt—thawing out after a successful day.

His flashlight illuminates the side of the bowl of chili he's eating and the surface of the chili, which looks vaguely like the surface of an alien planet. The propane heater beneath the wooden table gives off an aura of red light and casts a weak shadow of the boards of the table and bench on the far side of the tent, and it looks like nothing, or perhaps like a gallows, which makes him smile slightly and grimly, because he knows there is a shadow being cast outside the tent behind him from the bright light of the lantern, and he knows that it looks like a woman hanging from a noose. It's the shadow of a deer. His deer hanging outside. His doe.

He takes a bite of chili and notices the blood on one of his fingerless wool gloves. He gutted her without wearing them, so there must be blood on his pants or jacket or flannel shirt, which means that if he wants to hunt with Tom tomorrow, he will need to wear his fatigues, or the deer will smell him a mile away.

It's all so primitive, the hunt, and now, as with each trip, he rationalizes his presence—the necessity of thinning the herd; the lack of a wolf population to function as predator; the necessity as omnivores of engaging with our prey; the tradition that his father taught him; the comradery, camaraderie, brotherhood of the weekend—yet he's lying when he doesn't just admit that he loves it, every bit of the hunt. Except the gutting.

Back when he was pre-med in college and going to be a medical doctor, he approached it with a clinical accuracy like the carcasses were his cadavers. Now, he's more careful, even says a Chippewa-Ojibway-Anishinabe prayer or poem that his wife Megan taught him before he cuts them open: please great spirit please bless the creature that I have just killed and that my family and I will eat, and bless all creatures and beings that sustain us, amen.

Today, as he knelt over the doe, he thought about the prayer, and even as he slid the knife under the skin and ran it up to the diaphragm, he thought about the process and its strangeness. Yet all that stopped after the blood rushed up from beneath the skin.

He stands, goes over to the flap and leaves the tent. The pale darkness of twilight remains in the west as he makes his way to the hanging water jug on the other side of camp. He stuffs his gloves in his coat pocket and washes his hands once more beneath the frigid water from the hanging plastic ten gallon jug. As he grabs the spout, he can hear newly formed chunks of ice bumping against the sides, like tectonic plates pushing up from beneath the earth's mantle, and stirring within the soft jug as the cold water rushes to his hands. He quickly shuts off the spigot and turns back to the camp, wiping his hands on his shirt, then blowing on them to warm them up.

Manitou is completely still. The place was named by his father, although it was his great-grandfather who first began using it. Brien, Tom, Paul and the Fisher boys have been coming up here since they were kids. Though Brien thinks of it with a sanctity reserved only for the most important people and ideas in his life, Manitou is merely a few groups of pine trees, bunched here and there, with a gravel logging road nearby and a mud track to pull up their pickups, cars and SUVs, and a couple fields, almost regularly spaced apart, for the tents. He's been here when it's summer, and you really can't even tell there's a campsite here at all because there's too much undergrowth.

His deer hanging in the blazing light of the propane lantern is an eerie sight, the abdomen carved right out like that. And his hiking boots rest beneath her as Van Gogh's shoes. As when Heidegger analyzed the peasant's shoes. He can hear Kristen's voice now, chastising him for his foolishness: Heidegger, for God's sake.

There is blood on his slippers. No. He looks at his hunting slippers, made of a tan split-leather and lined with comfortable white fleece. He got the tops of them wet when he washed his hands, and the water in the half-light looks like blood.

He decides he should call her, and then decides against it. He studies his doe for a time; then crosses Manitou to the hissing lantern, which he shuts off. The darkness and silence are immediate.

In the darkness, the only thing he can see is the silhouette of the deer above the cold fire pit. Earlier Brien had noticed that there were ashes in the fire pit from a long forgotten fire. The rope creaks in the darkness, as when they hung Dietrich Bonhoeffer, or Roger Casement, Roger MacEasmainn, hanged by a comma.

The one has nothing to do with the other, she'd say here, and he would smile against her skin, smile his smile telling her that she was wrong. Outside, through the window of the hostel, Dublin would be just waking up, and they had finally left it all behind. For each other.

I find any link offensive, she would add. A horn would sound as the city woke from its European dreams. Two backpacks would lean against a cracked wall beneath an antique-framed window. Perhaps not Dublin, perhaps London. Or Prague, Paris, Amsterdam, Berlin, Krakow or any other number of cities instead, where the weight of history would surround them as much as any blanket.

He would lean up in the bed on one elbow, tracing a finger across the curve of her breast, to her ribs and down to her hip bone, and he would say, just to see her angry blush, Or when they hanged Connolly or Pearse.

She would say, But they didn't hang Connolly or

Pearse. They were shot.

He would stare at her, running a hand along her body, and mention the peasant shoes again.

We have the Musée d'Orsay for one day, she'd say.

So Paris then.

He would kiss her body, and while his lips moved over her soft, pale skin, she would murmur, What's with the imperial executions? Are you killing yourself for me?

She would allow herself to be kissed and would whisper, I can be whatever you want.

This is not how it happened, but Brien imagines it this way as he goes back to the mess tent of Manitou, bringing the unlit lantern with him.

Why are you thinking about her again? Aren't you ashamed?

The heavy, coarse fabric of the tent wing is scarcely discernible from the other cold autumnal shades that may signify something. He feels his way inside the dark tent, back to the light of his flashlight that lies on the wooden table, illuminating his bowl of chili. Tom will be back soon and so will Paul and the others. He sits down. He finishes off his chili, and then goes back out to the water jug to wash the bowl. He rinses out the bowl in the cold water and washes his hands again and goes back into the mess tent.

He turns off the flashlight and sits in the darkness. He will not call her.

He won't.

In the darkness, he thinks about her, but he will not call. He considers his predicament, and he thinks he might weep for a moment, but will not let himself cry.

.

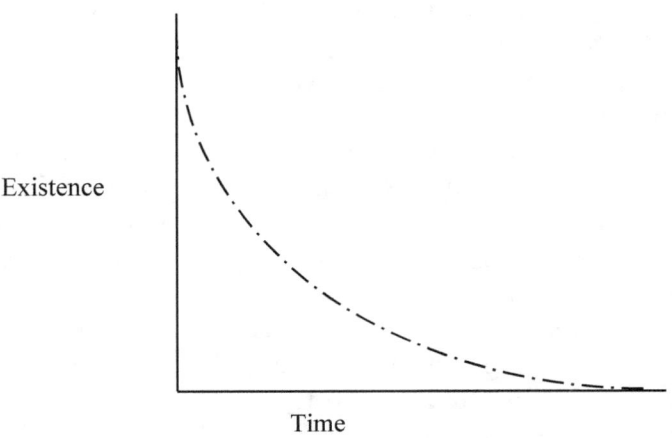

Time

Where Existence is defined as the subjective life of an individual.

Brien arrived at the camp at ten in the morning. He was tired from his escape from Chicago five hours earlier. He'd picked up Tom in Milwaukee, where he'd been staying over at a friend's place, stopped by Two Rivers to get their gear and see his family, and made great time on the way up to Manitou.

And he couldn't stop thinking about Kristen as he and his younger brother began to set up camp in precisely the same manner that their father had originally fashioned decades ago, but without their father's presence, as they'd done for half a decade now. Tom and Brien set up the camp without speaking, but Brien couldn't stop thinking about last night.

Their rendezvous had not gone well, just as it had become strange the first time five years prior, and after the wine glasses and coffee cups had been placed in the sink, and she'd gone back into the living room of her Lincoln Park apartment and turned off her ipod—the song by Feist suddenly interrupted on a beautiful wavering note, the words of which Brien heard as "my world"—an awkward silence had fallen between them, she in the entrance of the kitchen and he looking at her and at the Chicago night sky in the window behind her; then Kristen had walked over and stood before him for a moment, and only a moment, looking at him, and then as he had been considering saying something or even doing something, moving toward her, touching her arm, anything, she'd grabbed him by both wrists and said, "Thanks for staying tonight. I'll be okay tomorrow, I know it."

Before he could respond, she'd leaned up on her tip toes, kissed him on the cheek and said, "Please, no matter what, don't tell Paul. He'll just worry."

"Okay," Brien had said.

She'd turned abruptly and walked toward her bedroom, saying, "You sure you're okay on the couch? There's a nice hotel on Michigan Ave," which hadn't made sense, given what had transpired earlier. He'd made a joke about the poverty of graduate school, and she'd pointed to the blankets and pillow on the couch and said sleep well and closed the door to her bedroom, and Brien had felt relieved.

After she'd told him goodnight, he'd spent a good portion of the night on her balcony of her apartment as sporadic bursts of light snow blew past the little lights to the east beyond the big park and into the vast dark emptiness of Lake Michigan. The first snow of the season, little flakes signaling the beginning of something more, and here he was, a married man at her apartment in Chicago— his colleague, his friend, his best friend's sister, and thinking about the absurdity of his situation: she lay in her bedroom, possibly asleep, and he stood on her balcony, and his wife was asleep at their home in Two Rivers with their three children, and he could not let it go no matter how he tried that this was not what he wanted, and eventually he moved silently back inside, quietly sliding the balcony door closed behind him, and then sat on the couch again, and he listened to see if he could hear her moving in the other room, and when he decided that he couldn't, he then decided that might not mean she was asleep: it might mean she was staring at the ceiling, awake; that perhaps she too couldn't sleep, but that that didn't mean she wanted him in her room, or her bed—to quietly knock on the door until she answered and to slip beneath the covers with her.

Eventually he had forced himself to be still, to not-think about the situation and to just accept it. He lay down on the couch and watched as the dim lights on the ceiling shifted and moved—lights cast by the traffic on Clark Street and maybe even the traffic on Lake Drive on the other side of the park, altering the ceiling, even at this great height, so that the white ceiling seemed to waver like the concrete at the bottom of a disturbed pool on a sunny day, and he thought about the headlights of all those cars and all those cabs, signifying all those people, each one an individual, unique in thought and capability, with a destination that night all their own and completely different than his. And eventually the lights became the echoes of lost wraiths wandering the old park, searching endlessly for the vanished City Cemetery, and after an indeterminate period of darkness and a roaring of white noise like a distant jet, he was lying in the woods of the hunting camp, the multicolored fallen leaves scattered all around him: he was on his back with his hands comfortably interlaced behind his head, amid the boxes and crates of his hunting gear, because for some reason he hadn't set up the tents; he was staring up into the sky, watching the snow glide gently through the bare branches of the oak trees overhead, and the top of the pine trees beyond his feet toward the Fisher's site were already covered with stark white snow. To his right and in the distance, his father had been strung up on the hunting line and was calling to him kindly.

Brien remembered that eerie dream then as he unrolled

the mess tent in Manitou to the south of the hunting camp below a set of white pines, while Tom began kicking with the heel of his boot the big, rolled up, tied sleeping tent into position on the north side of the encampment, near the shrub trees and spruces.

Their father now dead these five long years.

As he pulled each of the lower corners of the old army tent into position and staked them, Brien thought about the way Kristen had said to him the night before, "If you leave, I swear I think I'd jump off that balcony," and how it was a non sequitur because they'd just attended the conference together, and he'd come up to her apartment to show her his dissertation and said three times that he was going to make a reservation for the hotel as the conference was over now, but he'd let her comment go and pulled his dissertation out of the laptop bag—his dissertation that was meant to be more than the culmination of his successful clinical psychology research at Lawrence and during his clinical residency overseas in Iraq, but also the synthesis with his failed work as a graduate student of philosophy, prior to abandoning that doctorate after completing his course work, when he was all-but-dissertation. He thought about how she'd let out a sharp laugh when she saw the introductory quote of his dissertation from *De la Psychose paranoiaque dans les rapports avec la personnalité*, and how she'd quipped, "Yes, Brien, you might as well completely piss them off before they start reading your work," and he thought of how she'd let out a sigh, almost a moan, and muttered something that sounded affirmative and might have been the word "Well," and how she then read aloud the quote in flawless French and then translated it into English.

As Brien struggled to push the tent up and open, he thought of how her voice had sounded as she read certain passages aloud, and how her polished, black nails had looked against the white pages as she turned each page. He crawled inside the tent, and then pushed each pole into its proper hole, and raised the ceiling, thinking about the way she'd scanned each page and then stopped when she found something with which she disagreed and had written a comment in the margin. When she got to the chapter about suicide, she'd skipped it—the entire chapter—and Brien had realized that she was quite possibly ill.

Outside the tent, he pulled each of the six guy lines taught and staked them into the dirt and remembered how good her coffee tasted as he sipped it, and how everything was ordered just so in her apartment, everything was white and black, and new and quite clean, just the way he'd envisioned on the drive down, just the way he'd hoped—the couch was black and leather, and the rug was white and wool, and the table was an opaque, faux-marble square piece of glass that rested on black iron runners.

Brien and Tom pulled the old and very heavy oak picnic table from underneath a canvas tarp beneath a squat spruce tree on the far side—the western edge—of Manitou, just to the north of where they'd put the deer line, where the table spent the majority of the off-season—at least when Paul or Drew weren't using it while up north for a fly fishing or camping weekend in the summer—and while they moved the old, bulky table across Manitou, past the black-sooted fire pit, and into the darkness of the even older, bulkier mess tent, Brien almost told Tom about his strange dream about their father. And about how he'd woken without an alarm at just before five ante meridiem, and gathered his dissertation silently from her glass table and slid it into the front section of his black laptop bag, and had even held his breath as he'd walked quietly over to the front door, which he'd silently opened, and about how it had not been until he'd stood in the empty hall and had slipped on his loafers over his bare feet and his leather coat over his t-shirt, and had walked quickly to the elevator, that he'd allowed himself to breathe normally again.

Brien sat down at the table, which as a tree had once stood in the very center of Manitou beside the fire pit many years ago before Brien and the others were born. After the tree had been split open by lightning one summer night, their father (with the help of his cousins Jim Grace, Johnny Noclezney and Drew Fisher's father) had cut and shaped some of its wood into thick boards, which they sanded and stained with dozens of coats of lacquer, and then hammered together into this table. The rest of the tree had been ceremonially burnt over several seasons, until there was no more wood from the oak tree, but for this table.

He thought of, and almost told Tom, how he'd driven home to Two Rivers from Chicago, wracked with guilt, even though—for the second time—nothing had happened.

I have a wife and kids, he'd thought the whole way home, and he'd spent the week in Chicago at a conference with a young, beautiful woman, and now was going to go hunting. I have a wife and kids.

He'd arrived in Appleton, where his wife Megan was waiting with his family.

Megan greeted Brien at the door. Shannon in one arm, and Sean and Connor running out from behind her to give him a hug.

His kids wrapped their little arms around him, and Megan joined in the hug.

She looked gorgeous. He was more relieved than ever, but he knew this was only the beginning.

So he is the first of the hunters to get a deer. A big doe. His father would have told him to be proud, but never gloat. His mother would say that he should prevent the venison from spoiling. His father who marched with Father Groppi. His mother who taught birding and conservation.

He opens his notebook in the dim light of the heater and lights a match. He reads the first of the three quotations he has copied into the pages of the notebook. He turns the page and reads the fourth quotation regarding the interplay of the three terms, but it only makes it worse.

He shakes out the match and places the burnt stick on the table.

In the darkness of the mess tent, he hears a truck driving on the gravel road that borders the hunting camp. It's either Paul or Bert. Bert had miraculously shown up just as Brien and Tom had hauled the deer to the road. Bert gave them a ride back to camp, before heading into town for beer with Tom.

The truck pulls into Manitou, the headlights casting weird, wandering shadows of the saplings onto the side of the mess tent. Brien doesn't know which one it will be: it will be either Bert and Tom, who will have beer and whiskey for the poker game, or Paul, who will be wondering where the hell they were when he went to pick them up.

Brien thinks about turning on the light, but stays in the darkness. He hears one door slam.

Paul.

Brien crouches to the side of the tent and waits.

Paul shuffles in. He sits down with a heavy sigh. Brien can scarcely contain a chortle. Brien waits a bit, listening to Paul breathe: Paul has his hand on his brow, the weight of his head in his hand, and his mouth is moving like he's praying.

Brien silently feels for the matches and opens them, knowing that Paul can hear him. He manages to pull out a single match and places it silently in the darkness against the strike zone. He strikes the match.

Paul jumps and swears.

Brien laughs at Paul's face—he looks as if he's just had a bucket of ice water poured over him.

"What were you doing in the dark anyway?" Paul asks.

Brien shrugs and thinks about how he was thinking

about her, yet again.

Steam rises from a mug as Paul pours coffee. Brien decides to pull another trick on Paul and bends into the shadows to fish in the ice chest for the doe's heart. His hand surfs among the beer and the ice and food for the heart.

Paul starts talking, asking him about the hunt, while Brien searches for the heart, but he can't find it. He's like the Tin Man.

Brien feels the heart, grasps it.

Brien calls, "Here," tossing the heart to Paul.

Brien laughs as Paul's baseball talent comes through, and Paul catches it and smiles at him.

"Nice job, Professor," Paul says.

Brien smiles. Paul's sister used to call him professor back when she was in his class at Lawrence, but now she's moved on, and she's virtually a professor in her own right.

And the smartest person he's ever met.

It wasn't without some preconceived plan, the rigor of which will, I hope, become apparent as it is revealed in its entirety, that last time I brought your attention to a case whose particular significance resides in its showing in miniature the reciprocal interplay of those three grand terms we have already had occasion to make much of—the imaginary, the symbolic, and the real.

Brien's tree stand overlooks a small clearing: a meadow, a grove of haphazard saplings and beyond that the hardwoods, where Tom sleeps in his tree stand. Brien waits, staring at the multicolored leaves on the ground below, occasionally sighting the far trees.

The problem has a solution, and the solution is simple. Admit that you are a fool. Go home to your wife and kids, to your true love.

A slight breeze carries a bit of winter's chill.

The zero sum game. But this is not a game—this is how to live. The process matters. The old philosophies are correct. Father was correct. Honor and duty and truth and love.

The binoculars have fogged again.

But Kristen: her mind is not right. She is in danger. And if she does something to harm herself?

The emptiness of a dead woods in winter.

And even if not, what then? What happens when you choose to live by a code that no one else follows?

It's the same either way. Plato and Nixon.

You can live by a code, but it may not matter to the end result. Pitch that perfect game just like Harvey Haddix. Excel in every respect.

He carefully, silently, lifts the blaze orange poncho, reaches into the breast pocket of his waterproof shell, and pulls out a cloth that his wife bought him. He cleans the binocular lenses.

Father had been abandoned by the Fishers and the Graces. Forced out of two businesses he should have inherited.

His father had said to turn the other cheek. That only we can undo ourselves.

Fishers, Graces, he'd said: The old injuries must end. That the fighting must cease. Christian brotherhood, he'd said. But for all his magnanimity, virtue, and caring, he became like Job, without the divine reprieve.

He sets the binoculars on the blanket, folds the cloth, and puts it in the pocket of his waterproof coat.

But the world will do what the world does best.

Shiva. The destroyer.

That boy outside the temple in Baghdad, missing a leg and an eye. Begging to the American soldiers, and to their psychologist, for alms, for water, for anything; the soldiers later joked that you should shrink heads here, and you later wept, for you could not help those who live in Baghdad.

The divides were too great.

The wind blows gently through the woods, and Brien pulls the blanket around him more tightly and listens to the wind as it sounds across the entrance of the hood of his coat.

In the hostel in Paris, the obvious question Kristen would ask him would be this: why is it that you now want to destroy that which you love best for something that clearly is not love?

He would look at her, unable to admit to her that he does not love her.

She would continue, lovely and yet practical as always: Or if it is love, it's only your love for what you can't have.

Prompted, his answer to her would be: I don't know. Maybe because I'm afraid that it all doesn't mean anything.

That's not a good enough answer, she would say before picking up her backpack and leaving him in that empty, silent hostel.

It is cold, and Brien adjusts his gloves, pulls his wool hat down more tightly, just above his eyebrows.

A dark and empty pit after the silence. Not even the echo remains.

Oh father show me the way. I cannot, I do not believe.

I do not believe as you believed: *For the leader; according to "The Deer of the Dawn." A psalm of David.* Your creed was an ancient song whose music has been long forgotten. And you clung to it.

But that creed might be wrong.

You would never admit to yourself what Grandpa always said: that the old virtues are often quoted by those who do not possess them, and that only the names of people and places, the names of towns and events retain meaning.

His grandfather who waded ashore among the bodies in North Africa during Torch, who survived the rout at the Kasserine Pass; young American men floating in the waves or lying in the dirt on another continent, their bodies contorted, their eyes open. His grandfather, who said you can't see what you're shooting at in war, they'd say fire at that hill, and so he'd fire at the hill with everybody else and soon the hill was smoking in dust, and then they'd yell cease fire, and they'd all stop shooting, and later they'd inspect the ruins of the hill and find dead men up there, dead men in various uniforms: German or Italian or French.

And what Brien saw in battle.

Rudra. Hara. Bhairava. Mahākāla.

The boy missing an arm. The heat of Baghdad. The soldiers who went out and never returned to the base. The bodies lying on the side of the road.

Shanti.

A psalm of David. And the echo of the words by a peaceful man hung on a tree as the bulls of Bashan surround him.

Something has moved out of the hardwoods. There is something moving through the shrub trees toward the frozen meadow. Brien silently sets down the binoculars and pulls his rifle up from the dusty floor of the stand.

And he forgets the thoughts he will remember later; thoughts that he will forget once again when he receives the call from Craig; the internal discord he will have with himself on the way back, the buck and doe tied atop the cover, as he drives south, his brother beside him in the passenger seat, his notebook in his backpack in the back of his truck on the way home.

How his father had said to forget the old injuries, but embrace the old virtues.

How he met Kristen in Chicago for their first rendezvous, when she told him about how she ran.

He sees the buck at that moment and has his rifle up. He sights the antlers: eight points. Flicks off the safety. Waits for the shot. Aims for the proper place, just behind the muscle that controls the foreleg. Holds his breath, sights again, and slowly applies the pressure to the trigger with his index finger.

Five years ago, on his way out to Chicago to meet her the first time, a line of thunderstorms had dominated the northern half of Illinois and the southern half of Wisconsin.

It should have been a twenty minute flight, but his plane had already been delayed coming into Appleton, and then they'd been delayed again on the tarmac in the cramped little thing, watching the weather worsening and listening to the rain pound the metal roof. It'd been night by the time they got moving.

The thunderstorms and winds were so bad that they had to peel to the east over the Lake, bouncing and swaying over the black waters. They were forced to head down into Indiana, dipping through northwestern Kentucky, and even then, huge black clouds greeted their little plane, intermittent brilliant flashes illuminating them—visible for a moment like purple towers before they were plunged into darkness once more.

A nervous, gay flight attendant handed out cups of water to everyone, as if he was making an apology for the ordeal the travelers had all endured, or hoping to do one last good deed before perishing.

And suddenly they plummeted, and the cup of water Brien was drinking went flying into the air, and when it fell back from the ceiling of the plane, when the plane had righted itself and he no longer felt helpless, the water soaked him and an elderly woman beside him, and they both laughed nervously. And he thought he would probably die that night and never see Megan or his kids again.

But eventually they touched down despite the heavy rain, and Kristen was at O'Hare waiting for him.

She greeted him with a full hug and a kiss on the lips.

It was the profoundness of their desire for the other

combined with the impossibility of the situation that made things awkward between them. He believed that if they would put it into words it would have been something along the lines that they wanted each other, and had for some time now.

As she pulled him to her, he noticed the way the delicate muscles on either side of her neck stretched into her jaw, and decided he wanted her, right down to her calves, her ankles, the soles of her feet.

But here he was, married with three kids, placing her into the role of the temptress. He had been her counselor; he had been her professor.

"Is this a conflict of interest?" Brien joked. They were announcing and repeating passengers' names over the loudspeakers, asking them to please report to white courtesy telephones.

Kristen allowed him to hold her for a time, her body young and beautiful.

"Clearly it's exploitation," she told him.

"Why am I here? With you, I mean."

"I don't know. I think—I think it's good to see you, you know?"

"Yes, you too."

She stepped back, and they walked from where she'd met him at security. He couldn't let it go.

"There are ethical concerns," he joked meaningfully; he nodded at her. "My student and my patient."

She leveled her gaze at him; she'd had enough of this: "Brien, you're married. And my brother's best friend."

"Well that makes things much easier doesn't it!"

"Yes, it does," she said with a slight smile.

"It really is good to see you, and I mean that as a friend and for all the right reasons," he told her. "We could just talk, as friends."

"I would like to talk. I need to talk."

"Okay. My conference doesn't start for a few hours."

.

Tom is rallying the crew to go out to the strip club.

Brien looks up at his deer, both of them hung on the line. The doe he shot, hanging beside the buck he shot. At least Tom had to gut the buck.

He has one thought, which was if his father was still alive, Brien would have joked to his father that Pascal was wrong, that we love the hunt more than the kill because the gutting sucks, and his father might have grunted or even smiled.

He pulls out his flashlight, turns it on, and looks at a different section of his notebook. It reads:

If I take death into my life, acknowledge it, and face it squarely, I will free myself from the anxiety of death and the pettiness of life—and only then will I be free to become myself.

He turns off the light and lets the darkness engulf him.

The coffee shop was in O'Hare, and it was remarkably deserted. She didn't waste any time: "There was an announcement, that it was safe, and we should go back to work. That there was no emergency. And we started back up the stairs. I was on the 30th floor when it hit. I didn't feel it. I can't believe it now, given the images I've seen and the stories I've heard, but I—"

She cupped her tea in both hands. Brien took a sip of his coffee and set it back on the table. After she steadied herself, she resumed, but her voice lost some of its confidence as she continued.

"But there in the stairwell, I didn't feel it. And this big guy, very fat, came out, and he shouts, 'Run for your lives!' in this high-pitched voice.

"Imagine that—run for your life. I started laughing at him. He was angry and terrified, and said, 'A second plane just hit this tower.' And I did feel it then, vibrations running through the building, and suddenly I became very very scared—a second plane? I couldn't believe another plane had hit, and I didn't understand—I figured that the first was just a private plane off-course, like the one Kennedy died in. A second plane? Or were they missiles?

"And then I ran, and I kept running. I didn't wait to see them fall. I was forty blocks away when they finally came down. I was in a cab. I found a cab, it felt like the last cab in Lower Manhattan, five blocks away, and the driver was Muslim, and he whisked me away from there like some angel.

"All those people. All those firefighters. I just kept thinking about all those innocent people and firefighters.

"And I thought about that man who said run for your lives. There's a good chance he didn't make it out. I ran down those stairs. I ran, literally, for my life."

She stared at him for emphasis and added, "For my life. You ever run like that?"

"No," Brien answered quietly. "Not really. Not like this."

"There's a point where you think about giving up, even knowing it might mean the end of you, the very end of you, where you try to convince yourself that the danger isn't even real, where you tell yourself that it's in your head and you could quit if you wanted, and maybe it'd be alright because you can't catch your breath and your holding your high heels in your hand, and the cement is hurting your stocking feet with each step and your knees when you fall. But for some reason you go on, and a guy like that—he was all red-faced and out of breath even before I saw him, and the look on his face—he was in shock and exhausted by the time he'd reached the stairs, maybe he'd done the same thing that I did—walked down, then heard the all clear and walked all the way back up, and got to his floor when the second plane hit."

Her blue eyes had welled with tears. She paused and composed herself.

"He didn't make it out I don't think," she concluded softly. She took a sip of her tea. Brien steadied his emotions and made no comment.

She recovered and went on, "I mean of course I hope he made it out, and I never did see any memorial to him, but I just have this feeling."

She took another sip of her tea and then said: "And I laughed at him."

"You can't—" Brien began.

"I know," she said, stopping him.

He wanted to reach out and take her hand, but thought it might be misconstrued.

She continued: "Anyway, there were others in the stairwell. Police officers telling us to keep moving. Firefighters heading up. A couple guys in suits. Maybe they were FBI, I don't know. They went up, while we ran down."

Brien pours himself a cup of coffee. He sits down in the darkness and listens to the others get ready to go to the strip show.

After Adam died, Kristen went to New York.

And she's the face that launched a thousand ships. After what happened to her, they all enlisted: Tom, Craig, even himself.

He sets the cup of coffee on the table his father made and puts his head in his hands in the darkness of Manitou.

He wanted to tell her that forgiveness seems nearly impossible, but with effort and calmness, that it too is possible. Instead, he let her slip away from that first long meeting with some books of his that he lent her.

He volunteered and shipped out three months later.

The truth is that he didn't even remotely have the

power to heal the people he tried to treat over there: men and women, boys and girls, soldiers, people: blank stares; shaking; becoming afraid, or cruel. Those that wouldn't leave the base, or wouldn't come back to it. And the two that had been blasted by the IED in the Humvee: a young woman who looked right through him; a young man who was unable to form new memories. In both cases, the neurologist couldn't figure out what had happened to the frontal cortex, said they must be malingering.

The truth is that at his lowest times he felt he was another instrument of discipline and fear that they used against the soldiers to toughen them up.

Brien and Tom stop at Iron Mountain for gas. They say goodbye to Paul and are a half hour south, when Tom remembers the trash. Back at Manitou.

They decide to go back for it.

Manitou is silent and empty: snow drifting through the trees; two large dusty gray squares, marking the ground where their tents were staked, in stark contrast to the dark, wet ground all around.

The three black trash bags covered with a light dusting of snow rest in the leaf-strewn mud beside the sunken tracks from their trucks. They load the trash into the back of the truck and head to the dump.

It's about an hour drive, and Tom quickly falls asleep. Brien is alone with his thoughts: he keeps thinking that this may be his last deer hunt. He needs to become more responsible.

They turn off the wet, paved forest road onto a frozen gravel road leading to the dump, and Brien guns the truck down this wide, ice-covered path, lined by snow and ice a couple feet high, pushed back and crushed time and again by the blades of large plows. Brien accelerates toward the valley, which is filled by five huge snow-covered mounds. Seeing something he doesn't like, Brien steps on the brake, well short of the first frozen trash mound, and the truck skids to a stop.

"What the—" Tom begins to protest, then sees it too and is silent.

A black shadow moves through the waste. Brien feels his heartbeat accelerate a bit, the old primal instincts.

A bear is digging through the garbage dump. A cub.

Brien holds up a hand to Tom, slides out of the truck silently and moves slowly to the back. He opens the Lakeland cover of the GMC, slides the three bags of garbage to the back and lifts them out. He closes the cover slowly and carefully. He silently moves toward the heaps of debris, toward the cub. There are bottles in the bags, and they make frozen chipping sounds in this silent place.

Icicles fang the far wall of the ravine. A grimacing monster in a nightmare.

The bear cub stands, haltingly, at Brien's approach. The snow falls silently between them.

Brien takes a few more steps forward, then hears it: a crunching sound to his right.

Brien freezes in mid-step.

Above the low hum of his truck's engine, the crunching sounds continue. He looks slowly to his right. A big black bear is just forty yards away, on the side hill initially obscured from his view by a short red pine.

It sits in a pile of garbage, chewing its way through a torn, half-eaten pizza box. Its fur is slick with slime or mud. Its muzzle is covered with paper and other debris.

The big mother bear. He can hear her breathing.

Brien cannot move for a moment.

The big bear is looking at him as she smacks her mouth loudly on the box. She makes a noise like a sigh, followed by a loud grunt.

The bear cub makes a slight noise, which it in turn

follows by a sort of screech. It takes a tentative step toward Brien, then another. Then the mother bear rolls to the side to get a better look at her cub, then swings her head with a loud grunt and a sort of grin toward Brien. She has big yellow teeth.

That is the moment that Brien swings the bags with both hands backward and then forward, letting go of them almost gingerly. He is walking backward even while they are in the air. They land with a crash that disturbs the stillness. The cub begins to run toward the closest one, and Brien moves to the door of the truck. Brien opens the door, gets in, closes and locks it in four precise, careful and quick movements. He throws the truck in reverse.

The cub leaps up into the air like a cat pouncing on its prey and lands on the nearest bag, and Tom bursts out laughing. Brien looks out the back as the trees flash by on either side.

"Holy shit," is all Tom can say at first. "Holy shit holy shit holy shit holy shit."

Brien is still looking out the back, backing up. He glances back at the dump briefly and sees the cub shredding the garbage bag while the big mother bear saunters over, turning her head a bit in their direction and tilting it upwards too, obviously grunting, as if scolding them or muttering about them to the sky. Tom starts to laugh again, and when they're finally at the end of the iced-over road, Brien slams on the brakes and spins the truck onto the forest road, joining in Tom's laughter.

"Fuck man, that was hilarious," Tom says. "I gotta call Craig and tell him."

Brien throws the truck into drive and floors it. Tom is dialing. Brien's heart is pounding, and he forces himself to relax.

"And me without my bear license," Brien says in faux sadness. He turns off the forest road onto the paved road, heading south for home. The sun suddenly breaks through the clouds and lights up the snow that is falling everywhere and the wet road begins to shimmer.

A moment later, they approach a forest road where Brien has to tap the brakes: a Ram truck has pulled to an abortive halt, mid-way onto the road before them. Brien maneuvers quickly to the left, around the truck, with his heart still pounding.

Tom points, as he listens to his cellular phone, saying, "That looks like Paul's truck."

Brien looks at the driver, who is squinting against the sunlight, apparently blinded by it, and who has a thick beard. Brien sees something odd. Something that doesn't make sense. Something he doesn't tell Tom.

Brien's cellular phone begins to ring. He pulls it out of his shirt pocket. He glances at the caller id.

Craig is calling him.

What are you doing? Why are you doing this again?
For love.
Have you lost your mind? Love?
Love.
No, death.
Not death.
Death.   Cut away all evidence of your real feelings and just live within the shell that remains. Hollow shell in an empty world. Cold, sterile, lifeless. Not love, not hope, just death. Not even a penny in the world, and even if you had money, what would it matter?

He is your love. Money is irrelevant.

No he is not your love. Your love has died. Drown. Nothing remains.

Something remains.

All that remains is the hunt.   Sex, the weapon of choice.

Yet one thing does remain, yes that is the yes, yet yes remains yes yes.

Yes.

5

Your story has ended.

It begins on a riverbank in summer. Everything in the world was perfect.

It ends on a beach in the fall, when you set his fate. Winter fast approaching the great lake, your brother ready to do what was necessary.

Don't think about it.

The desolate forest in late fall. The empty woods as the snow falls.

Keep moving.

Kristen walks through the woods of Two Rivers. Her mother's home is not far from here, but she can't go there yet. She can't face her. There is snow falling through the trees, and the drifts are a foot or so deep in places.

Her story is already over: it began on a riverbank.

The riverbank where you watched him die. A young man drowning. Only twenty-eight years old.

You were four years younger than he. Engaged. You often asked yourself what that word meant. You fought it for a time, fought the implications, someone's property, all that, then decided it meant love. He said soul mate. A musician and a sap. At the time, you teased him, soul mate. Bullshit. He would show up with flowers and songs he'd written, good songs, but still you teased him. Why? Certainly because it was sappy, and you are not that, but also to keep power, a bit of distance, control.

And now? Gone, gone.

Nearly a decade later, and the man you used to replace him is dead. Killed.

Used by you to replace Adam. Used him, plain and simple.

And then what he did to you. His revenge.

Had to be stopped. Had to be.

Killed. Found by your fiancé's brother.

She stops. She is having trouble breathing. She puts a hand to a tree.

Listens.

Stands, listening to nothing. To silence.

The woods are so quiet. Is there a hunter out today? She's dressed in dark clothing, it's dangerous. This is a private stretch of land, the owner an old man, but you never know. It's always possible this time of year. She scans the dark forest, the snow slowly falling among the pine and birch trees.

She will see her mother, go to her home, have tea with her. Her boots will get a bit muddy first, her clothes will carry the telltale signs of having hiked through the woods. Wishes she had a dog to walk, an excuse to walk to her mother's home. She hasn't seen her. Parked her car near the diner. Decided to get some exercise. That's all.

She continues, stepping carefully over a rotted out log. Her story is over.

It ends when you tell Paul. The hunter. When you were young, you hunted together. Paul taught you. He was always an amazing shot. His time in the Army only made him better. His nickname overseas in the Gulf War was Oswald because he was such a good shot—bunch of sick fucks, nicknaming her brother after an assassin, or would-be assassin, depending on who you talk to.

What has he done?

You cannot admit the truth of it even to yourself.

Up ahead, mother is home, the lights of her home are on. You will go there, you'll be safe there. No, you will never be safe again. Never. What he did to you. His revenge for, or hated of, what? Your power? Freedom? Intellect? What was it that he hated about you?

Had to be stopped. He will never hurt her again.

She stops again and listens. What are you listening

for? There's no one here.

She stares as the snow. It's sizzling. No, or is it?

The snow sounds odd to her as if it is making a sound as it lands. Like sizzling or crinkling. She decides it's just her imagination and looks around again. Just the woods.

She steps forward cautiously, moving toward the house through the forest. It's funny, you lived here even before daddy died. You were so young, barely knew him. You were a child when he went. Gone.

And no money, your mother would balance the books, still does. And you would try to help her. There's no money in restaurants she'd say. No money. She'd make the books balance though. The food was always good. The place clean. She is organized, efficient. Like Paul.

She's also a fair cook. Your father, they say, was better.

Paul, everyone says, is almost as good as dad.

And you? You wanted to get out from the time you were six.

And you almost escaped. You left, got out. High school was a joke for you, but you took it seriously, and studied hard. Got a near perfect score. Got a full ride out East. And everywhere else. But then Adam kept coming around with that bullshit talk, it wasn't bullshit, with that talk about being soul mates, and you fell for it, you fell in love, it really was love in fact that time, and you came a lot back then, it was more than the sex though, it was love. You decide to stay near town, go to a good school, maybe it was a better school, who knows, aren't they all about the same?

But Boston. Say it with a sigh ages and ages hence. The paths in a yellow woods. You stayed here to be close to Adam.

And now what are you doing: seducing Brien. Are you insane? But maybe it was always Brien, ever since you were a kid, you fell in love with Brien when he was hanging around the house, always so kind and tall and good looking.

And smart, he could talk to you. He can talk to you.

No. He's married. Three kids. It wasn't Brien. It was Adam. You chose Adam because he was talented. Not for his wealth. But maybe Brien, maybe it always was.

Brien is too noble to fall with you. If he were unmarried, or perhaps childless, jesus you're cynical, when did you become that way? It was when Adam died.

She has reached the verge of the clearing where the woods end and her mother's yard begins. She looks at the house, trying to see if there is any movement from within. There are lights on upstairs and in the kitchen and the family room. Mother's home. That's good. She will see you. Hiking. You must be calm. She can't know you know. She doesn't know about you and Craig anyway. Just a friend of Paul's friend.

Craig. Why did you choose Craig? Initially it was because of Adam. His infidelity if you want to call it that. But it wasn't cheating really, you always pushed Adam away. Wanted to be independent. Sex was a weapon. No it was liberation. Now that's bullshit. You don't even remember anymore. Sex was sex. You had only been with Adam, but you didn't want to be hurt. That's it, isn't it? I didn't want to be hurt by this man who said he loved me, said he was my soul mate, said all this romantic bullshit, when he didn't have to do that. Let's just enjoy each other. Let's keep it light and just be with each other, experience each other. He was a football player, you should have known better. He couldn't play soccer for shit, it was fun to get him on your field and school him. And then in the sunlight, lying on the grass of the soccer field afterwards, he had the light in his eyes, making them so amazingly blue. It was love, you agreed with him. And then he started messing around with others. And you knew it. You could tell. So revenge: you flirted with Drew that night in the boat. When you were drunk. Did you kiss him? It's possible. Jesus, Drew, why Drew? To get even. Isn't that always your why? Andrew so different from Adam. So guarded, calculating, hurt always. How could identical twin brothers be so different?

Kristen sees her mother now, moving from the family room of her ranch home to the kitchen. Her mother. She will witness that Kristen has gone for a long hike and make her some tea and tell her the news. So that you will not be fooled later, so that you will already know, will have excuses as to why you are not attending the funeral. You will not have to act that you haven't heard the news. Oh God you will not have to act. You cannot act well your feelings always bleed out no matter how you try to put a lid on the boiling pot the steam comes screaming out and last week with Brien in your apartment there is a perfect example. And with Drew you were seduced into that boat by your hurt and also the money, the Fisher money. You were drunk and hurt and seduced by it all. The money they casually wasted. You had never seen people spend so much on so little. Never seen so much money period. Child of a soldier turned businessman in a small town. All we ever had was the restaurant and there were times, pretty much every lunch and most weeknights, when we were eating what Dad couldn't sell that night or the night before.

Her mother is in the kitchen, doing the dishes at the sink. She can see the steam rising from the sink. Her mother's movements as she washes up from cooking for herself, probably yesterday's dinner. The sun is setting somewhere behind the clouds, and the darkness is coming on rapidly. She is cold now, the heat of her walk through the woods gone, the sweat on her shoulder blades and lower back becoming cold, and still she waits.

You made that mistake with Drew, that was bad, but it was harmless, you didn't even kiss him, did you? Woke up in the morning, still drunk, lying beside Adam. But that mistake with Craig, the first time, before you were engaged to Adam. Almost ten years ago. Craig was so rugged, so powerful. Like Adam, but less caring, less talented. Regardless, you confessed that to Adam, and if there's an afterlife, except there isn't, then Adam now knows about betraying their time together, being with Craig after he died too, and about Craig's death. You are a careless girl, you hurt them. No, you are strong, and they hurt you, they did this. Adam lied and cheated on you. Don't do that to his memory. Adam asked for your forgiveness, and you forgave him. And he forgave you for being with Craig. You were both young. But you kept making mistakes didn't you and then Craig, after Adam was dead, that mistake too. God is everywhere, Adam told you. God is nowhere, you told him, but you were laughing, and you told him you didn't know, you were afraid of crushing his belief, what would it do to this beautiful man? Adam, I'm sorry. He can't hear you: Adam in the ground these eight long years.

Craig will be in the ground soon too, they are probably transporting his body south right now. You should feel sorry for Craig.

But you don't.

You used Craig. You used him again after Adam died. And what did you do then? After you were done using him again? After he had fallen in love with you, became obsessed with you? You left him. Went to work for a company. Why did you go to New York? What were you thinking? Six years of studying Thompson Woolley, Weisstein, Calkins, Gilligan, Mitchell, Evansgardner, Chesler, Raugust Howell, Hollingworth, and all the men too, and you go and do what, what exactly: you go to New York to work for a corporation, a multinational conglomerate. One of the biggest companies on the planet. Six figures felt good though. Money for the first time. Friends. Nights out. Couldn't relate to anyone, though.

Not anyone, but a lot of them. Outside the office it was worse. In the restaurants and bars. A lot of people couldn't even speak human. But mostly it was your fault: you were too used to studying, too used to being introverted, and you had the line up between work and self. At work: work was work, and there was no destruction of that perfect line between work and life. People would come in and tell you their plans to move up the company ladder, or how to network better, and many would confide many things, even dark things. But outside: you couldn't relate. Walk into the Village and sit alone. Central Park: alone. Restaurants in Manhattan: alone. Biggest city in the world, and you're alone. Except in certain quarters: a few outdoor types, hikers and rock climbers, people who liked to get out of the City, and some waiters, bartenders, people that liked to talk about art. And Mary. You and your friend Mary, getting out for weekends.

And then, it all vanished: the building shaking. Smoke. Running.

A piece of an arm on the concrete sidewalk outside.

A shoe, a woman's shoe, broken in half.

Don't think about it. Don't think.

Your friend, Mary. Still missing. Gone. Forever.

Don't you think about it.

And then you went running home like a little girl, and back into Craig's arms. But you were celibate, chaste now. Chaste? That term hardly applies. You were dating, but not dating. You were friends. You were watching the events of the world, it felt like the beginning of the Third World War, the end of the world, and you needed to be away and protected. And then what he did to you. He had to be stopped.

Don't think.

Inside the lighted house, her mother has finished washing the dishes. Kristen sees her walk into the living room, sees the blue lights of the television come on.

How could Adam and Drew have been so different? Twins and yet miles apart. Drew lacked a moral compass. If she kissed him. She can't believe she allowed herself to be so weak as to kiss him. God. Why would she ever have done that?

She begins to walk up to the house. She has to stop thinking. She has to be strong. Her mother will see her clothes and make her tea. Her mother will tell her the news. She will act in shock before her mother, and her mother will be oblivious.

Be strong. The investigations have already started. There's little time.

What has Paul done? You can't even admit it, can't even think it to yourself, it's all on Paul. You little saint you.

She knocks on the back door. Refreshing walk through the woods, the good daughter, coming to see her mother. Opens the door and walks in, calling for her mother.

He will handle everything. She won't need to talk to him. He will know what to do. A fish from the sea upstream, like instinct, second nature.

The first thing he will need to do is to destroy the rifle.

Heat. Even without the fire in the furnace, the place was white hot. He was sweating by the time the old man was ready to go.

"Don't look into it directly," the old man had told him. "Even with the welding helmet."

"Okay."

The furnace was roaring as he opened it, and he used the heavy iron tongs to place the long cylindrical object inside. If the old man was surprised by the object, he couldn't tell behind the tempered, black safety shield. The rusted tongs wouldn't budge, and then the old man nodded and made a ripping gesture to him, and so he pulled them apart, letting it go. The metal made a loud clanging noise as it fell inside the furnace with the other scrap metal.

He watched as the oven heated up, thinking about everything and nothing. Thinking about words. His new words. It was the same as when he was in the army. He had a new vocabulary now: ferrous scrap processors; induction furnace and electronic arc furnace; magnetic separation.

A thin orange line of melted steel emerged. And that was that. The old man tapped him on the shoulder and gave him a thumbs-up.

Back in the old man's office, they were both sweating as they took off the shields and peeled off the coveralls. He hung up the coveralls in the locker on the far side of the office, and the old man did the same. He placed the shield on the old man's desk.

"Two grand," was all the old man said.

The old man had told him it would be one thousand

before he'd seen what the scrap was, but he had brought four just in case. He went to his truck and counted the money, his stomach sick and his palms sweating, even in the cold night air. The old man followed him, standing in the doorway of the plant, his breath like smoke in the air.

The old man didn't look at him after he handed over the money. Just backed off a step, looking out at the dark road.

6

Sheriff's department.

Hey Jimmy. It's me.

Investigator O'Reilly, to what do I owe the pleasure?

You know, Sheriff. I'm just calling to shoot the shit.

Well good. How's things?

Fine, you?

Just getting ready to do a little Christmas shopping. Wife's fine.

That's nice.

Kids are growin' up too fast.

Sure. I know all about that one.

The dog—

First time in a while that I haven't had to talk through your deputy Matt.

Yeah, he's out getting ready. A big storm is on its way.

It hit Madison about ten minutes ago. Snowin' pretty good here already.

Looks pretty bad. I saw on the weather report—clouds all the way to mainland China, and the jet stream's just gonna funnel it all to us.

Pretty bad.

And just in time for the darkest evening of the year. That's a little Frost for yah.

Lots of frost I'll bet.

You bet.

You thought about what I said?

Yeah, Rick. I thought about it.

You thought about it?

Yeah. I did.

You think a lot about it?

Plenty. Rick, it kept me up at night, the wheel's

turning, grinding up all those years of rust with your well-oiled theory.

Come on Sheriff. Don't fool with me.

I seriously did think about it, Rick.

And?

And I thought about it. That's all I got.

You think I'm wrong.

Yeah, I gotta be honest here, Rick, I think you're barking up the wrong tree.

I'm gonna need to bring in the ATF on this one, I can see that already. I'd rather you help me out here because I hate dealing with the feds. Keep it local, you know?

Look, I didn't say I wouldn't look into it.

So you'll look into it?

I'll go and see him.

You're not taking this seriously.

I said I'll go and see him.

I want to be there.

So we'll both go.

I can be there today. In four hours.

Not now.

When?

I'll tell you when.

When?

When it's when, that's when.

Stop fooling with me, Sheriff. Say when.

Next week.

Monday.

Sure. We'll have breakfast with him.

You're not taking this seriously.

What? We'll have breakfast, when we go to see him.

Breakfast.

Yeah, at his diner. Where he cooks, everyday, like he's done the last ten years, with his mother.

Jimmy.

Like his father did for thirty years before that.

Jimmy.

I like it better when you call me Sheriff.

Sheriff. Look. You know the guy.

Yeah, I know the guy.

You're an officer of the law.

Look, I'm conducting my investigation. You can conduct yours, but I'm conducting mine, and that's that. I've said too much to you already.

You just want to give him a head's up—an early Christmas present.

Hell, it ain't even winter yet.

It's sure felt like it for some time.

That's true I suppose.

So Monday then.

Second Monday after New Years.

Wait—what? You said—

Got some shopping to do. Bye now.

Sheriff—

Bye now, Rick. You come find me after the holidays are over, once it's winter.

Winter

Snow falling in large flakes under a gray sky. The lighted headlights of the funeral procession creep through town, winding through Two Rivers toward the Lake on its way to Manitowoc. The fumes from the exhaust are visible in the air, like breath, like factory smoke.

He watches it pass from the window of the shop. Feeling nothing.

The snow stops, and he counts seventeen cars and that is when he sees Tom Grace's car, and then Brien driving his truck with Megan in the passenger seat. Somewhere in the twenties, he loses count and starts over.

He watches the lighted headlights and the fumes of the cars and trucks as they crawl through town, and the snow begins to fall again.

He watches and counts thirty-nine more cars and trucks in the falling snow, telling himself he is feeling exactly nothing.

7

It has snowed for four straight days. The old expression goes: big snow, little snow; little snow, big snow. But there has been no stopping the snow, though the snow has changed: dark snow falling from black clouds at noon and little snowflakes sliding down quickly at night; ice pellets pelting the drive and big snowflakes meandering everywhere; fine ice crystals raining down and thunder filling the clouded dome; bright blinding snow falling in the hazy sunlight and blowing snow in gusts of wind; sleet.

From his desk, Paul watches the snow fall outside his window. He's heard the Eskimo have twenty different words for snow, and now he knows why.

Today, big flakes are falling straight down rapidly, as if there's so much snow above them, weighing them down, that there's no room in the air to dawdle and float down gradually, as Paul has observed that big-flaked snow will most often do.

The storm has covered the gray and icy December snow with a fresh full layer a foot thick.

The snow has coated the bark of the naked elms and oaks and cedars and aspens that stand, irregularly spaced, in Paul's front lawn. Sitting in his office, which would have been the nursery back when he and Susie were still planning on kids, Paul watches the snow falling. Forecasts have indicated that another full foot of snow may fall here in Two Rivers. He wishes it would fall through the day and night for weeks and cover the entire world.

Today is Monday, his day off, and he just got a call from his mother at the restaurant. He's going to have visitors soon.

He puts on his fleece, a waterproof shell, and a hat and gloves. He pulls on his Sorrels and laces them. Cooper, his black lab, is running around him in circles, tail wagging. Paul goes into the garage and starts the snow blower. He hits the electric garage door opener, and before the door is even halfway up, Cooper bounds out into a world of white.

Paul cuts a path into the driveway. The tracks from Susie's car are long gone. The forecast called for more than two feet of new snow, and by Paul's estimation, when it is over there will be a lot more. There's so much snow falling he can't see. He shuts down the blower and gets his ski goggles from inside the garage. He fits them on over his hat and pulls the hood over his head and the drawstrings tight. Cooper runs in, covered with snow. It's ridiculous to snow blow when it's still coming down so hard, but he's going to have visitors. It takes him a half-hour. He works the entire driveway and feels better.

He decides to shovel the walk to work off some steam. He turns off the blower and stores it in the garage near his work bench. He takes the first shovelful carefully and turns it over to the side; he does this two more times, and then gingerly prods at the lowest layer, testing for ice beneath the snow. There is none.

He takes several large shovelfuls quickly, throwing the snow into the air, some of which blows back onto the walk beside him. He begins to work faster.

The snow is heavy, but his back is strong and he is determined.

He is sweating and tired by the time he finishes. He feels even better, and he stamps off his boots in the garage and goes inside. He won't let himself have a drink. Not now. It's still morning.

He towels off Cooper and pulls the pebble-like ice crystals from between the pads in his paws. He goes upstairs, and showers and dresses. Then he finds himself in his office again, sitting behind his desk, looking out his second story window at the snow.

He stares out the window for what seems a long time because it is a long time. He realizes that more than an hour has passed, and he's hungry, but he doesn't move.

Last night, the Packers beat Holmgren and the Seahawks in the divisional round of the playoffs. He knows that normally he would feel a great pride and satisfaction in their win. But he doesn't.

His mother had said that two men were looking for him. She told him who they were and that they each ordered a plate of chicken and dumplings, and black coffee. But then as she was standing there pouring the coffee, they changed their orders to omelets, and the one she didn't know also ordered a glass of orange juice, while the one she knew ordered a side of potatoes and a side of venison sausage.

He stares at the snow coming down, thinking and not thinking for a long time.

Then he sees them coming up the driveway. A squad car and a truck. The emergency lights of the squad car are not on. That one is Jimmy Baker. The Sheriff.

Jimmy played on the O-line in high school, and they'd been rivals then for a girl, and things had gotten ugly at a couple parties sophomore year, and after one party, there was a fight in the dark night, wrestling in the soft, dry snow beside a station wagon, but no punches were thrown, and he and Paul are friendly now.

Paul makes his way down to the kitchen and opens the refrigerator. He pulls out and opens a jar of pickles that he pickled at the restaurant. He snakes one out with a forefinger and thumb from among the meandering vines in the Mason jar and takes a big bite.

The doorbell rings, and so that is how they will find him: crunching on a big mouthful of a homemade pickle.

He and Susie were in a big fight. There were no insults. That wasn't how their fights went. Just a sullen silence between them that sprouted up unexpectedly and grew around them, filling their home. The silence had lasted almost two months now, and last night without warning she'd broken a plate in the sink.

The silence, he knew, was his fault and was driving her mad. He also knew that the silence would eventually pull them apart.

This morning before she left for work, she rolled against him and then put both hands into his beard and clenched her hands just enough so that it hurt him.

She stared into his eyes. She didn't say anything. She didn't have to.

Then she stood and stripped off her clothes and went into the shower. When she returned in her dental hygienist uniform, he was pretending that he'd fallen back asleep.

She slammed the door to the garage on her way out.

Cooper is at the door, tail wagging. Paul shoos him to the side and opens the door. Outside, there's Jimmy, standing with snow in his black curly hair, wearing a big sheriff's coat. Another guy stands just behind him, in a black overcoat and wearing a cowboy hat, with a grave look on his worn face.

"Hey Jimmy," Paul says, not smiling, concerned. "What's what?"

"Mind if we come in out of the snow, Paul?"

The snow has already partially filled the valley of the walk with a new u-shaped layer a few inches thick.

"Something wrong?" Paul says; he looks at the man that he knows is a detective. "Who's this?"

"Nothing's wrong. This is Investigator Rick O'Reilly—he works for an insurance company, kind of like a detective. We better just come on in and tell it to you like it is."

"Sure thing," Paul says.

He stands to the side and clenches his gut as if to make

himself smaller, and they walk into the mudroom. Cooper greets the men, sniffing them, tail wagging rapidly.

"Go on now, Cooper," Paul says, and the black lab goes and lies down on his checkered blanket.

Paul nods the Mason jar at them.

"Pickle?"

They both smile and shake their heads. Paul finishes off the pickle and fishes out another one.

"Look," O'Reilly says. "There's no easy way to say this, so I'm just going to say it, okay?"

Paul nods.

Before O'Reilly can continue, Jimmy chimes in: "First, we just want you to understand that you're not a suspect."

"In what?" he says, the acidity of this new pickle suddenly a bit overwhelming.

"The Bunder kid's death."

"Craig? You mean you think it was a murder?"

"Nobody said that," O'Reilly snaps.

Jimmy's talking to Paul as if he were a child: "The detective works for the insurance agency. They want to see if it was an accident. They want to see what caused it."

"Oh, I get it," Paul says. "You guys don't pay out if he killed himself."

"It wasn't a suicide," O'Reilly says. "The insurance company hires me to investigate whether there's an adequate reason to support the theory of an accidental shooting. And you're right: our company only releases the assets for accidental death and dismemberment."

"I get it. Who do you work for?"

"The N.R.A. Endorsed Insurance Program."

Paul is quick to pull out his wallet. He has his N.R.A. card and his insurance card in one of the sleeves. He shows the detective.

"You guys got me too. It's ten grand right?"

"That one is," O'Reilly tells him.

Jimmy adds, "Craig'd taken out a couple accident plans, so he had a lot more in play than that."

"Who'd he designate?"

"I really can't say," O'Reilly tells him.

They still haven't taken off their coats or gloves.

Paul nods. He shoves his wallet back into his back pocket.

"So what do you want with me?"

"See, I hate to ask you this, Second Amendment and all," O'Reilly says, and suddenly becomes formal, "but we're here to ask you to surrender your rifle."

Paul's mother was the first one who noticed the change in him—the sourness, the solemnity. Paul had always been reserved, but now he'd become nearly mute.

She'd asked him about it, in the kitchen of the restaurant as Paul was cutting up fish for the fish chowder, but he'd merely shrugged.

"They're testing all the rifles from the woods that weekend," Jimmy is quick to add. "That's why we gotta take your rifle. They want to test everybody's gun that they know was up there."

"Not everybody's, just the one's that match the round," O'Reilly says.

"Okay," Paul says and pops the last piece of the second pickle into his mouth.

"Mr. Bunder was in your group," O'Reilly states, adding it again as a question: "In your hunting party?"

Paul nods between crunches. He swallows the last of the pickle.

"You own a Winchester rifle?" O'Reilly asks.

"Yes," Paul says.

"Thirty ought six?" he asks.

"You know it," Paul tells him with pride.

"You left the woods on the day that Mr. Bunder was

shot?"

"What day was that again?"

"Monday afternoon," Jimmy tells him. "You weren't in the woods that day?"

"No, I left with the Grace brothers on Monday morning." Paul says, adding carefully, "So, is there a criminal investigation in all this?"

"Yeah, but it's pretty limited," Jimmy tells him. "There's also this here insurance investigation."

"What's the criminal investigation entail?" Paul says before he can stop himself.

"There's a theory out there that somebody shot him accidentally," Jimmy says, showing with a wry smile what he thinks of this hypothesis, "and probably realized it and didn't report it because they were scared or for whatever reason. It's still manslaughter though."

"So, did you have to get a paper from Judge Crandon to come down here or something, Jimmy?" Paul says with a smile.

Jimmy's good-natured look vanishes. "Oh no, but I could Paul, you know that. Are you saying I need to get a warrant?"

"No, no," Paul says, serious too now. "Come on down to the basement and I'll open up my hunting chest for you."

Brien Grace stopped by the diner two days ago at closing time. He didn't say anything—just ordered a Miller and a bowl of chicken noodle soup. He ate while Paul mopped the floors and cleaned up the place.

When he'd finished eating, he put some money on the table for his tab, which he knew Paul would not give him, and then stared at Paul, until Paul was forced to stop what he was doing and come back to earth. Paul leaned on the handle of his mop and looked at Brien.

"What's going on Paul?" Brien asked. "What's up?"

Paul considered this and smiled.

"Nothing," Paul said.

"Everything okay?"

"Yeah, Brien," Paul said.

Brien looked at him. They'd been best friends for more than thirty years. Brien's wife Megan is Susie's good friend.

Paul gave a slight smile and waved a hand, mumbling, "Just some financial stuff, you know. Makes Susie nervous. Which makes my life a pain in the ass."

But Brien wasn't buying it. This was the same person who had held in his laughter when Paul's mother had presented Paul with his father's Winchester rifle on his eighteenth birthday, when Paul had been hunting with an identical rifle for the past three years, and Brien had laughed later when they were alone because Brien knew that Paul had been sneaking the rifle from out of his parents' attic without his mother's permission over the past three years. But Paul knew different and knew better.

Paul went to the refrigerator, pulled out two more beers and gave one of them to Brien. He opened the beer and took a long pull.

"You know," he began, taking another gulp of beer as Brien watched him intently, "ever since my dad died, I've had to make the money and the tough choices for Mom and Kristen. I've felt like I've had to be patriarch of the family."

He took a pull off his beer and laughed. This was the same speech his father gave him a few months before he died on an operating table.

"But we're a dying breed, we Krukowski's," Paul said. "No kids for Susie and me. So, really, it's just about keeping this restaurant going. That's it."

Paul took a sip of his beer and set it on the table. He folded his arms over his chest before continuing.

"You know I'm the sort of person who'd do anything for my family. Hell, even my friends that are brothers like you," Paul said, and the emotions hit him because it was the truth, and he saw it so clearly now, but he pushed on, into the partial truth.

"And it's the kids, Brien," Paul said, real tears suddenly coming to his eyes. "It's the kids that make a marriage and family complete. It's family that we'd do anything for right? Lay down in traffic for them if necessary, right?"

Brien took a sip of his beer and nodded.

"We don't have that, you know, Susie and me, and it's just different than I thought it'd be."

Brien bought it. Paul returned to silence and listened in guised awe to the psychologist—his best friend and surrogate brother—counsel him about his supposed problems.

Paul leads them into the basement. He gestures to the combination lock.

"I keep it locked up, just in case, you know with all these teenagers breaking in and stealing guns over in Appleton and down in Milwaukee."

Jimmy nods.

"Good thinking," O'Reilly says.

"It's the Chicago gangs," Jimmy says.

Paul begins to enter the lock combination, but he straightens half-way through and looks at them, "You're sure about this Jimmy?"

Jimmy nods solemnly. O'Reilly just wants to get on with it.

Paul dials in the last number of the combination and pulls the lock open. He takes off the heavy lock, opens the door wide and pulls the string for the overhead light bulb hanging inside. He steps aside, and O'Reilly and Jimmy look inside at the three shotguns and the Winchester rifle that line the wooden gun rack set into the wall. There's a shelf with a sheathed 9 mm handgun and a dozen or so boxes of various ammunition.

"They're all registered, Officer," Paul says to Jimmy with a smile.

Jimmy chuckles.

O'Reilly pulls out the Winchester, checks for a magazine and opens the chamber.

"It's empty," Paul assures him with an uneasy laugh.

"Gotta make sure, though," O'Reilly says.

"There's the case," Paul says, pointing.

"Thanks," O'Reilly says, pulling it from the hook where it hangs. He sheathes the rifle and zips it shut.

"You need the ammo?" Paul asks.

"No," O'Reilly says, "We won't make you pay for the rounds. We'll just test the rifling pattern."

Jimmy states again: "They're testing all the rifles of this make of the hunters in the woods that weekend."

Paul considers this for a moment.

"I don't get it. If you think he was shot by a Winchester rifle, won't that show up?"

"There are gun-specific marks on the bullet, like fingerprints," Jimmy says.

"Right. The locks and grooves?" Paul offers.

"Land and grooves," O'Reilly states dourly.

"They're just gonna check the rifling pattern," Jimmy says.

Paul nods and locks the hunting closet.

A month ago, Paul was in the kitchen of his restaurant, pounding out butterflied chicken breasts on the butcher block table that he was going to wrap around smoked ham, provolone and Swiss cheese to serve as a cordon bleu special that evening.

His sister, Kristen, barged into the kitchen. She stood there looking at him. She had this crazy look on her face. It was a look of mischief and knowing and horror.

She didn't say anything, just stared at him. He was too

scared to say anything.

Then one corner of her lips turned into a slight smile, and she walked out.

The snow has begun to fall more sporadically now, drifting and meandering a bit, but big flakes of snow are still falling, and every so often the wind pulls chunks of white from the trees or his roof, making the snow seem to swirl up and around instead of down.

Jimmy and O'Reilly left five minutes ago, telling Paul that they would call him once he'd been cleared, which Jimmy assured him would be in no time. The sheriff gave Paul his pen and had him sign a form for his authorization to allow them to test his rifle. The pen is sitting on his desk as Paul watches the snow.

He waits an hour, watching ESPN, and then goes upstairs to his office. He pulls open a drawer and finds a key. He uses the key to open a locked drawer in his desk. He takes out an oblong object wrapped in towels and goes to the garage, whistling for Cooper to follow.

This is what Brien told him: We see the tip of the iceberg, but there's ninety percent underneath. We think we know things, think we know people, but we don't.

It is about an eighty mile drive from Two Rivers to Milwaukee. It takes him more than an hour and a half in the storm to reach the park overlooking the bay in the city's northern suburbs. He considered heading all the way down to Chicago, but the weather changed his mind.

The snow is coming quickly again, but this time it's falling much faster and in tight flakes, almost like rain. He gets out of his truck. He opens the truck door and lets Cooper out into the blasting wind and billowing snow. He puts the bundle, wrapped in towels, into his coat, which he zips up.

Somewhere above the thick clouds, the sun is setting, but it feels like night as he makes his way down to Lake Michigan from the rampart-like stone terrace of the park on the concrete switchbacks of the icy bluff. He stops momentarily to watch the countless waves rush inland and smash against the ice. The roar is steady, but as he nears the shore, it becomes more singular and he can hear individual waves rushing through the drift ice and often cresting. He reaches the bottom.

The waves are ferocious against the mounds of fast ice. Paul stands on a support made of huge concrete blocks, leading east about a hundred yards out to the huge mounds of ice, where the collisions of the waves catapult water a dozen feet into the air. Below this concrete dock, the flat, snow-covered shore also seems to stretch out to the mounds—but Paul knows that only the first twenty yards is beach, and the rest is snow-covered fast ice, under which there may be water, even riptides.

At the water's edge, where the waves pound, the ice mounds are spaced about five yards apart and reach a height of ten feet, like small pyramids or the crenellations of a fortress. And further out, big dark chunks of pack ice roll with the surf, and smaller pieces of drift ice, like thousands of large ice cubes, fill the water.

Normally, in the spring, summer or fall, Cooper would be dashing back and forth on shore, barking at the waves and biting at the water in the air. But here, the dog instinctively knows that this ice is dangerous.

And more danger: black ice covers the surface of the concrete dock, several inches thick. It is transparent in places, and filled with milky white swirls in other sections. His father would have called this glare ice, a term left over from his days in the navy, training up in the frozen-over bays of Greenland, somehow preparing for action in the Mekong Delta.

Paul walks slowly, taking small step after step on the

smooth, thick glare ice until he is ten feet from the edge.

Every ten seconds or so another wave pounds the hills of ice, and water fills the air before soaking the new, frozen shoreline.

He pulls the bundle out of his coat, and frees it from the towels. It is a gunstock. He examines the crisscrossed markings. It's a thing of beauty really.

A wave smashes into the ice directly before him, sending a shower of frigid water onto the ice-covered dock upon which he stands. If he were to fall in, it would be difficult, perhaps impossible to climb out, and he would surely be hurt by the drift and pack ice and crushed against the mounds of fast ice.

There is only this wooden stock that is left of his father's rifle. He wants to keep it as he stares at the surging waves that crash against the frozen shoreline. He runs his thumb across the pattern carved into the stock and feels the craftsmanship of the markings with his thumb as he stares at the exploding water.

Further out, the drift ice rolls with the large waves. The drift ice does not approach the shore of fast ice. By the time the waves begin to crest, the drift ice slips backward into the shallow behind the surge, while the large chunks of pack ice tumble in the surf, often smashing against the mounds of ice.

All of this will vanish in less than a month, or whenever we get a hard rain or a couple of full days above freezing.

He can't make up his mind.

He turns away from the surging waves, looking up at the trees that line the cliff.

When his father bought his rifle for himself at a gun show, he also bought a twin rifle for his son, and these rifles were not registered. Paul had felt an overwhelming sense of pride, excitement and responsibility as they drove home with the guns. His father did not tell his mother he'd bought the second rifle for their son, but only that he'd bought a rifle for himself because he just wanted to take the boy hunting and he didn't want a lot of questions.

Paul used the rifle his father secretly gave him to kill his first buck a few months after his father died, and Brien thought this first rifle was Paul's father's rifle. The second rifle, his father's real rifle, was presented to Paul as a birthday present from his mother when he turned eighteen and she believed he could handle it. Paul had hidden his father's rifle in the attic and taken out his real rifle and registered it and put it up on his wall on display until he married Susie a year later, when she told him that he'd have to lock that gun up if he wanted to have kids.

After his sister told him about the rape, he'd gone up and gotten the other rifle, which he had always assumed he would eventually give to his son when he and Susie had kids. He'd brought both rifles up north to the hunting camp, his rifle and his father's. The rifling marks on the bullet they'd taken out of a log in Craig's blind matched this second rifle, the stock of which he now holds.

Paul examines the bluff, then the landscape that surrounds him. He came here this past summer on a day when it'd been nearly a hundred degrees and quite humid. Cooper had spent the day fetching tennis balls from the lake while Paul considered his plan, contemplating whether he could actually do it.

He'd also stood on this very concrete dock with Cooper, who'd patiently watched the shadows of the dock. There are huge catfish and trout that like to lie in the shadows of the concrete blocks in the summer here. He stood there sweating, while Cooper sat next to him, drying off and blinking in the blinding light, looking into the shadows. And together, they saw the fish—three or four huge brown trout, their fins scarcely moving, bobbing slightly with the rise and fall of the waves.

As he left, he saw three boys, all dressed alike, their hooded sweatshirts up, their baggy jeans low on their hips, walking down the switchbacks. He saw them, and he knew they were up to no-good.

Probably going for a quick smoke or to split a joint. Then he saw they had sticks and knew what they were up to. Three boys fishing with sticks.

He watched from the ramparts above the switchbacks as the three boys stabbed at the fish in the shadows. He remembered feeling sick, the way he did when boys he knew as a child used to hunt with sticks and grill forks for spawning salmon in the ravines that line Lake Michigan and would line them up, six or seven in a row, on the muddy banks of the river.

He felt sick as they pulled something out of the water, but he didn't know why.

And now he is cold.

And now he has thoughts of being as cold as cold.

Such extremes here on this inland coast. Here in the suburbs, and also in the barren farm country just to the north that stretches across the mid-section of the state, and up in the forests, the lakes and hunting lands that begin north of the farmland. People die of hypothermia every winter here, or are frozen to death when their car breaks down on a back road in the Northwoods. And in the summer they die of heat exhaustion, or sun stroke, or are found dead in their apartments or cars. The wind chill gets it below negative twenty, the humidity above one hundred ten. And somewhere between negative twenty and one hundred ten, you're supposed to survive.

Cooper is beside him, whining. The dog's typically patient look is gone; Cooper looks at Paul with his ears cocked. He just can't figure this one.

Paul turns away, and immediately Cooper walks the glare ice and then sprints for the shore. Cold and heat, light and dark, water and air and ice and fire. These things are not opposites. Even animals, the hunter and the prey.

He turns back to the water.

The waves explode like fireworks off the ice. This inland sea doesn't think beyond itself, it just is.

His arm rises almost automatically, and he carefully moves his feet apart for balance. He hefts the stock up into the air. It hangs there a moment, a thing of beauty against a terrible sky—then vanishes over a mound of ice and is gone into the roaring water.

Cooper looks at the water and then at Paul with a sheepish look; he doesn't want to fetch it.

"It's okay, boy," Paul tells him.

On the way back up the bluff on the concrete switchbacks, the snow changes to ice pellets. The wind picks up and begins to blow harder. The ice pellets are like hail, small and less perfectly formed, but they still hurt when he looks slightly up from the frozen-over snow beneath his boots. But he does look up, and his face is stung by dozens of pellets. The ice pellets are being launched up horizontally, more than horizontally—it's amazing, the pellets seem to be launching from the huge waves of the Great Lake and blown by the wind up the face of the cliff. He wonders what the Eskimo would call this. The wind sounds like the engine of a jet plane, and he decides it's time to get out of the storm.

He puts Cooper on a blanket in passenger seat of his Ram truck and heads toward Two Rivers. Cooper curls for sleep, soaked and cold.

On the long road back, he has to drive slowly through the gusting blizzard. He sees few other cars. It's as if he is the only one left out in the storm. The snow falls in an endless, hypnotizing procession, and he finds himself talking to himself, even though he tells himself to stop. He wishes he could find a hockey or basketball game on, but there's nothing. As he nears Manitowoc, the black ice has taken its toll: he counts seven cars in the snow-filled median or in the ditch to the side of the interstate on a twenty mile stretch. There's even a semi-truck that's plowed its way into the rolling hills of snow that fill the ditch beside the freeway. All of them have been marked with bright orange, square tags.

He decides to avoid the downtowns of Manitowoc and Two Rivers, and to come into Two Rivers well north of town; he stays on the freeway and gets off I-43 at Denmark. The sign for the sale of the Kafka Real Estate Company is partially buried by a snow bank. He skirts Denmark on R, crossing Rosecrans Road, and heads toward Cooperstown, but north of Cooperstown, he thinks better of it again and heads north again on P rather than BB. The snow seems even thicker, if that is possible, as he gets on KB and crosses the Neshoto River. In the mesmerizing snow, he works his way back on Sleepy Hollow Road, 163 and then G, until he gets to 42, which he takes south.

He passes Sandy Bay Road, and then turns onto Nuclear Road. He drives past the nuclear reactor. It looks like a gigantic prison.

Then Paul's heart jumps for a moment. Up ahead, a squad car's emergency lights fill the darkness, and flares have been set up. He realizes there's a tanker overturned on the shoulder of the road. The black ice must have gotten him.

A sheriff in the snow is waving him forward.

It's Jimmy. Paul decides he has to wave to him as he drives past. Jimmy waves back.

Just two ordinary citizens going about their business in the shadow of the nukes, Paul thinks as he drives home.

and then he is in the air, his whole being in the air, suspended, weightless over the log of the blind, and then he is leaping from a swing at his grandmother's farm outside Manitowoc, as the chains of the swing jangle and then snap free, and lands effortlessly, painlessly on the thick lawn beneath the glowing stars where he begins to run up toward the lighted house that glows brilliantly, and he runs toward the house, but it is receding before him somehow, and it is at that moment that he realizes that it is all receding before him, slipping soundlessly away like a wave, and its opposite, a dark, swirling presence, looms behind him now, like a rolling thunderhead, and he stares at it for a time as it morphs and swirls, ever shifting, and then he goes back to the swing, which is now as it should be—a proper rope swing tied to a huge branch of an ancient oak tree—near the fallout shelter his grandfather built before his father's birth, to wait out the storm and take shelter if necessary, and he swings for a time, sneaking glances at the darkening sky, but the clouds are gone now, and he is alone on the creaking swing on the lawn beneath the stars.

8

Tom has never seen so large a funeral. The mass is held in an old Episcopalian church with high white walls. Simple and plain: no statutes or stained glass or candles. One large brown cross on the wall behind a large white marble altar.

The mourners have filled it beyond its capacity. Many standing in the aisles, at the back, in the wings and even on the second floor with the church choir. When they can no longer fit inside, they walk down to the basement, where apparently there are speakers.

There are readings: Craig's sister reads from Psalms; his cousin reads from Ecclesiastes. There is a homily, of which Tom will remember only a part.

The procession has risen, and Tom stands too. He feels weak as he walks to the front of the church. Tom, Brien, Drew and Mike Fisher, and two of Craig's cousins are pallbearers.

The coffin slides on rollers down the aisle and out the church door. Bob, the funeral director, is young and professional. He coaches them to the hearse. At the curb, he steps away to open the back door, leaving them on the sidewalk as large flakes of snow begin to land on the perfectly smooth surface of the brown coffin. Tom watches as each snowflake slowly loses its crystalline form and becomes a drop of water.

Bob returns, places his hands on the head of the casket and leans in confidentially. Now lift with your knees, not with your back, and walk it up to the door, he tells them, With your knees.

The coffin is heavy. Very heavy. All of them strain a bit under its weight.

Craig's mother is weeping uncontrollably. His father's

face is blank.

They slide it on the runners up and inside. They step away, and Tom's vision blurs. Bob walks to the back door of the hearse and flips up a few locks, securing the casket in place. Tom feels himself double over slightly and let out a sob before he can stop himself. He holds a cloth over his eyes.

Bob announces, Please turn on your lights and follow us for the burial service.

Brien and Megan take Tom in their arms, and he is no longer crying. They are crying, but he is not.

And then he is again.

They had reached the tertiary road above the ravine and the Noname River at just before noon. The gravel road immediately became a dirt path with ruts and tire tracks frozen into its surface.

Brown sheriff squad cars and an ambulance marked the place above where the accident had occurred.

A deputy sheriff told them that they'd removed the body. That the EMTs had him in the ambulance and that they'd need a statement from them.

Tom couldn't believe it. He wanted to see. He slammed his door and walked right past the deputy. When the officer called out, he ran and tried to get to the ambulance.

Brien caught him and held him back.

Tom takes in the crowd again.

The only person who isn't there is Kristen. And that surprises him. Then he realizes that Paul isn't there either. He would have expected to see Paul too, but especially Kristen.

The honor guard lines up. They are old men with rifles.

"Company. Attention," one of them announces.

They do their best to follow his commands.

"At arms," he orders. "Ready."

The seven veterans point the rifles into the air.

"Fire." Tom flinches at the blasts in spite of himself. They fire two more times.

Craig's family is sobbing as the priest says the final prayers. It's terrible.

Tom leaves with Brien and Megan. He can't bear to stay here another moment.

On the way home from the Noname River, the snow had started to fall more heavily. The sun was beginning to set behind the clouds, and the dreary countryside began to slip into a dust-like dusk.

Brien said something to Tom, "It's all just a matter of chance. And we think we're so smart, but really, it's just chance that makes up our lives."

He meant it to be helpful. Tom was weeping. He couldn't stop.

Brien wept too. And then he started trying to help, telling Tom to let it out, to talk to him.

But Tom couldn't talk about it, because his thoughts didn't make any sense: Tom had told only Craig about the girl he saw lying in the ditch in Samarra after al-Askari, and now the knowledge of that story has died with Craig. How we die when we die, but our world dies too—the things we think and see and hear and touch and believe and hope and know—all of that dies with us, and so the death of an individual is the death of an entire world.

They go to a small Irish pub in Manitowoc. It reminds Tom of the pub his great grandfather used to own as a hobby up on the island town of Grace.

Brien orders three Bloody Marys while Megan finds a table and politely encourages Tom to follow her. He's dazed, and they are being kind to him.

Brien comes back with the drinks, and then goes back up to the bar and gets the beer chasers, which are half and half's.

The Bloody Marys are good and spicy, but Tom can't stop thinking as he takes a sip, and then he finds himself crying again.

Tom finds himself thinking about insignificance.

The nothingness. Of everything.

Megan has a hand on his shoulder. She's talking to him. He is thinking about the insignificance of things.

All is vanity. Irrelevant. It all adds up to zero. Zilch.

Like his studies. Like the war. Like his writing.

He'll have to put it aside now. It just doesn't matter.

Nothing does.

Back when they played poker on the hunting trip, Bert had asked Tom about his writing. Tom had shrugged it off, until Brien chimed in that Tom was a good writer, and just being modest. Craig insisted that he tell them about the play he was writing, and Tom eventually relented, and he told them about the play, which was a sort of morality play, and he watched their faces as he tried to explain it: two families vying for the truth; the one representing a sort of Christian teleologic faith that leads to a compromised version of it, and the other a kind of fallen ideal of a circular Celtic spiritualism and Greek stoic logic.

He watched their faces, and he realized he'd gone too far, and that his tone had a sort of self-importance as he talked—the sort of thing that Brien and his father used to do, the sort of talk in which he and Kristen always hid—but then he decided it didn't matter and so he continued: But the truth is illogical, and existential, and illusory, because objective truth may not even exist, and so it escapes both families' attempts at claiming it.

It was silent in the tent once he finished. Bert stroked his full beard once and nodded briefly as he began to deal the cards. Brien's eyes were full of hope and understanding. Paul was oblivious, mixing a drink on the far side of the tent.

Craig deadpanned: How'd you like to have to follow that?

And they all laughed.

The bar is essentially empty.

Tom sits on a chair at a tall table, sipping his Bloody Mary.

There is a game on the NFL network. It's a Thursday, but the Packers are playing the Cowboys tonight. The announcer is talking about Brett Favre and Tony Romo.

Comparing, contrasting.

"Irrelevant," Tom finds himself muttering.

"What's that Tom?" Megan asks sympathetically.

"Nothing," he says. "It's just that it's all so meaningless."

"Don't be like that," Megan says.

"It's true," Brien announces. "It seems meaningless when we're grieving. And that's okay."

They are silent for a time.

Then Brien adds, "Usually it seems meaningless to me, even when I'm happy."

And Tom lets out a brief, spontaneous laugh, but Megan gives them both a worried look.

On the way to the bowling alley, in the dark woods, Craig asked if Tom remembered his girlfriend Brittney.

You going to call her up? Tom asked him.

Maybe, Craig said, hitting his one-hitter and croaking with the smoke still in his lungs, Maybe I'll ask her if she's ever heard of a donkey punch.

Tom knew Craig was trying to be funny, but he wasn't in the mood.

Jesus, Tom said, That trailer looks so lame.

I know, Craig exhaled, serious too now, One messed up commercial. That director. He's a real misogynist.

Tom glanced at Craig for a hint of sarcasm, but found none. He thought about that as he pulled onto the dark, deserted street running through the small town of Wabeno.

The neon beer signs in the bar blazed against the cold darkness. Craig took one last hit and blew the smoke out the window as Tom pulled the truck into one of the straight lined spots in front. Craig packed a dip, and they went in.

The bowling alley was empty, even though the bar on the other side was full. They bowled for a time, and then a group opened up a lane next to them.

A woman from that group was flirting with Tom. She was quite sweet, and far too good looking to be single in the Northwoods. Craig smiled at Tom when she left to talk with a friend at the bar.

What's wrong with that one? he asked Tom.

Nothing, Tom said, She's just not the one I'm looking for.

Who are you looking for? Craig asked, A man?

Tom laughed and waited for the pins to set.

Seriously, who are you looking for? Craig asked.

No one you know, Tom lied.

The sheriff stands and thanks Tom for coming in. Tom shakes his hand, nods solemnly and sits down. Sheriff Baker is friends with Tom's brother from high school.

"I just want you to know that you're not a suspect," Sheriff Baker says.

"So you think it was a murder?" Tom asks quickly.

"No," the sheriff says. "I don't. But I just need to tie up a few loose ends."

Tom nods.

"So you got anything you want to tell me, Tom?"

"About Craig?"

"About anything."

Tom shifts in his chair.

"Craig was," he begins. "Craig was a good person. Overall. He could be an idiot. And wild. But he was a good person."

"Did he have any enemies?"

"Enemies? No. He had lots of friends."

The sheriff nods.

"He served the country," Tom says, and that is all he can manage.

The sheriff nods and waits for him to regain his composure.

Then the sheriff asks: "How did he know everyone that was up there?"

Craig and Tom were sitting on the couch with Kristen, and she was laughing.

Craig had made her laugh—it was the first time she'd laughed since before Adam had disappeared.

Then the phone rang, and Kristen answered it. She listened for a second before she began to break down. He and Craig were both hugging her. Then she was in his arms, and they were both sobbing.

The weekend after the funeral, Brien calls up and insists that Tom come over to Drew's house.

It's been a week, he says.

When he gets there, Drew, Brien and Drew's brother Mike Fisher are ready to play baseball. Mike has on his uniform from when he used to play in the Minors. Mike nearly made it to the Bigs—he was pure finesse, had four distinct beautiful pitches, but he could never throw a fast ball above 85 miles per hour.

They walk over the baseball field, which is three blocks away.

Tom tries not to think about the times he played little league and high school baseball with Craig. Together, they won seven first-place trophies.

On Lake Grace, Craig was happy. He'd made up his mind.

I'm going to volunteer, he said.

Tom nodded and explained, Officer Training ends in a month for me.

So maybe you'll be my commanding officer, Craig offers.

Possibly, Tom said.

That would suck, Craig deadpanned.

You have no idea. You have any idea how to peel a potato or clean a latrine?

Craig said, You have any idea how many C O's get killed by friendly fire?

They both laughed.

What about Kristen? Tom asked. I thought you were going to Chicago for her.

It's all over between us, Craig told him.

That night, Tom is sitting in the dark, still soaking wet from the baseball game with the Fishers, when the doorbell rings.

He turns on the outside light.

She is standing in the cold on the front porch of his duplex. She is shivering, her breath visible. He opens the door.

"What are you—" he begins, but she just walks right in.

"So, this is your place?" she says looking around. He realizes she's been drinking. She pulls off her hat and scarf, and her long brown hair looks lovely in the half-light. She has on a skirt and a blouse. She could be dressed for a meeting or maybe even a funeral.

"Yeah," he says, and he begins to add, "Where were you—"

And then she is in his arms, just as when Adam died, but this time she is suddenly kissing him, and the kiss is one of desperation and desire, and although it is what Tom has always wanted, her kiss is even more than he had hoped.

Black cruel river slowly slides past. Bubbles, insects, twigs in the darkness.

Drew sits on the riverbank. He is exhausted and sobbing.

His brother is gone. Mirror image. Forever gone.

He has finally stopped looking. The police and paramedics and park rangers and tribal law enforcement are talking about it, theorizing in whispers. The parking lot is filled beyond capacity with emergency trucks. The sun has set, and the darkness is coming rapidly.

He sits under a blanket, exhausted and cold.

Is his brother gone? No. He can't be.

Kristen runs by him, frantic, barking orders, yelling at the cops, Tom, anyone.

Has the river taken him into the darkness below the surface of its shadows?

A search and rescue team finally arrives with a boat and scuba divers, and she turns her fury on them.

Is he gone? Only the river knows.

Craig shows up a few hours later. He is soaking wet. He searched the rapids below for Adam, and somehow he survived them.

Drew watches as Craig skirts the crowd to avoid Kristen, his face worn and tired.

He begins to cry when he sees Drew.

Drew grabs him around the neck with one arm, and they cry together.

9

Drew steps up to the plate. He taps his boots dramatically with the bat, and then adjusts his cap for affect.

He takes a practice swing with the bat once, and again. He squares his shoulders and cocks his elbows.

Tom is pitching. Drew had suggested that Mike pitch, but Brien and Tom laughed at the idea. Mike, the baby of the family, used to play with Brien and Tom back in Two Rivers when he was just a kid. He was a phenom even back then; threw the Grace brothers out dozens of times.

Tom leans forward, pretending to look at the catcher, shakes off a couple imaginary signals, and stands upright for the pitch. He winds up and throws.

The pitch is coming, and Drew swings—the snowball explodes like fireworks, and Mike and Tom and Brien are laughing. Drew sprints to first base as Brien drops to the ground over at the short stop position to scoop-up a new snowball from the ground in front of him.

Drew reaches first base as he sees the snowball out of the periphery of his vision—Mike extending for the catch and missing it.

"Oh fuck," Mike says, and runs to where the snowball landed in the foot of powder that covers the ground—to pick it out or make another one.

"Safe!" Drew shouts as he runs toward second.

Tom runs to cover second; Drew sees Tom blocking the plate, glove extended expectantly for the throw from first, and Drew closes his eyes and dives head-first into the snow at Tom's feet. The cold of the dry snow is a shock, and then he collides with one of Tom's legs, and the weight of his cousin falls on top of him.

Drew pulls himself up and scrapes the cold snow from

his face. Tom lies in the powder beside him, holding one arm in the air, the baseball glove clutching a mass of snow, which may or may not be the snowball.

"You're out!" Brien screams, throwing his right arm down in an exaggerated gesture like an umpire.

Drew immediately jumps to his feet and starts kicking snow at Brien, covering his big Sorrel boots. Brien crossly folds his arms, looking the part.

"That's bullshit, I was safe!" Drew shouts. "There wasn't even a tag!"

Brien stands toe to toe with him as the two start barking at each other.

Then Brien makes a wild gesture, throwing him out of the game, and pretends to write in an imaginary pocket notebook while Drew tries to get at him and Mike holds him back.

After the baseball game, Brien pulls him aside when Tom is out of earshot.

He is serious now and whispers, "Thanks Drew. I think it helped him."

Drew nods, looking to make sure Tom couldn't hear. "We need to get him out more—I know how this goes. He needs to get out. Especially after just getting back from overseas."

"I agree."

"I'm serious Brien. Right now. Let's get him up north. Up to Grace. You can stay at your place, and Mike and I can stay at ours."

"When?"

"Tonight."

Brien laughs: "Not now."

"Soon."

"Okay."

Jimmy over in Two Rivers has asked him to come in

and talk about Craig's death. Drew drives from Appleton down to Manitowoc to stop in and see his father's modification to the factory before heading up to Two Rivers.

The sheriff's office has been renovated recently, and the whole place still smells of new construction.

Jimmy is a good guy. Drew and Jimmy used to play football back in high school, before his father moved the family to follow their company headquarters' move to Appleton.

"So you knew Craig?" Jimmy asks him.

"Sure," Drew says. "We were friends."

"Before we go any further," the sheriff says quickly. "I just want you to know that you're not a suspect in all this."

Drew nods.

"You know how it is. We were on that case together when you were a DA."

"A volunteer ADA," Drew corrects. "Just fifty or so misdemeanors that I've prosecuted."

"Anyway," Jimmy says. "You got any thoughts?"

"Seriously? You're really doing a criminal investigation?"

Jimmy shrugs, "Not really. He was from Two Rivers, so the family has asked me to do a little work on the case."

"Geez, I mean I think it was an accident," Drew says. "I freaked out when I found him. I mean of course I did, but I freaked out because I'd just killed a deer, a half mile or so upstream, and I thought: what if one of those rounds I fired? You know? And they took my rifle when they arrived to test it."

"Yeah," Jimmy says.

"That's about it. It's a pretty sad story."

"Depressing," Jimmy says.

The next day at the office, the day is getting away

from him.

The phone suddenly rings, interrupting his work.

"Drew Fisher," he announces into the speakerphone.

"Hey there, heard you stopped by the factory yesterday."

His father's authoritative voice always shocks him from whatever he's doing.

"Yeah, had to come over to Two Rivers to see the sheriff."

His father sounds as if he is clearing his throat.

"You sign up for those pro bono cases I told you about?"

"I did the volunteer prosecutor work already," Drew answers.

"What about the defense side?"

"What about it?" Drew says flatly.

"Look, you don't have to, but trust me, it'll be good for you, no matter how it works out. It's good networking, for starters."

"Why am I doing this?" he asks. "Shouldn't I be helping you with the business?"

"Not yet," his father tells him. "Give it time."

His father spent years grooming Adam for the job, and now that he's gone, he can't choose between Mike and Drew.

"I've given it time, and now you want me to volunteer in criminal work. What does that have to do with running a business?"

"We've been given so much; it doesn't hurt to give back, Drew."

There is a pause.

"Sorry, Dad," Drew says. "It's just been tough. A tough time."

"I know. First Adam, and now this. That's why you need a break. Shake things up a bit. Anyway, we're slow around here, so I don't have much to send you, at least for the next couple of months anyway. Except collections, and you'll look better filing those if the judges know you're helping out with those deadbeats on the criminal side of things. Play both sides, show them you're objective. Okay?"

"Okay."

"Atta boy. And why don't you and Sharon come over for dinner tomorrow night."

"I'll make sure she can."

"You guys have plans?"

"She has book club I think."

"Yuck."

"They don't really read the books, Dad. They just drink wine and gossip."

"Like I said: 'yuck.'"

Drew laughs.

"One more thing," his father says. "Remember: if you get Judge Crandon, watch out. He's the devil."

Judge Crandon looks down at him from the bench over a pair of reading glasses. He does not have on his black robes. He seems more human that way.

"So you're not appointed by the Public Defender's Office."

"No your Honor," Drew says.

"That's fine, just so we know. And you don't want any compensation from them, even though, technically, you know you'd receive it?"

"That's right your Honor."

"Okay, well, George, take him to see the one that's claiming he has no money, the one that wants to represent himself. See if you can reason with him counselor," Judge Crandon says.

"Thank you your Honor," Drew says.

Drew turns toward the bailiff, who is whispering into an old phone at a desk near the wooden bar that separates the court from the gallery of wooden seats.

"George," the judge patiently says.

The bailiff slams down the phone immediately and gets his keys ready.

The judge continues: "I don't want a kangaroo court in here, counselor, and he may have some legitimate arguments—I'm not going to make them for you—but I don't want the court of appeals looking at a transcript of a maniac, got it? So see what you can do, and you'll have my thanks."

Drew nods and collects his brief case and his heavy wool overcoat. He follows George to the side of the courtroom.

"Oh and counselor," the judge says. "You'll need this."

Judge Crandon hands him a thin document, which Drew knows is the Complaint.

"He's already been served with the Information," the Judge states.

Drew nods.

The bailiff stands and points toward a side door. On the other side, they come to a door with a thick Plexiglas window. The bailiff presses a button on the wall, and they wait for clearance from the security on the other side. Finally, the bolt of the locking mechanism inside electronically snaps open with a boom.

Drew has to wait while they bring his client out and secure him in the holding cell. He reviews the file again, bored.

Drew's potential client is white. And his head is shaved clean. That isn't a good sign—a skinhead or trying to beat the drug tests.

He doesn't look impoverished, though it's tough to tell because he is in an orange jumpsuit. But well groomed.

About Drew's age, maybe a bit older.

Drew offers his hand for an introduction, but the potential client is shackled: handcuffs around his wrists that are bound to the floor. He raises his hands to waist level and gives a slight shrug and smile. Suddenly the room seems starker to Drew. The lights are florescent and coat the room in an odd, annoying hue. There's nothing in the room other than concrete and metal that is bolted down.

"You the attorney?" the potential client says with a sneer.

"Yes. Drew Fisher, nice to meet you."

He is suddenly formal: "Friedrich, if you will. How do you do?"

Drew pauses: "I think I'm in the wrong cell."

Friedrich stares at him.

Drew points to the complaint, "This one says 'Oscar.'"

"Yes, quite, formerly," the potential client says, adding with a sneer, "That was my old name."

"So you're Oscar?"

There's an awkward pause as the prisoner looks at the wall and mutters for a moment. Then he looks back at Drew and his eyes narrow: "Just call me Friedrich, got it Matlock?"

"No problem."

Friedrich adds, "Look, man, I can't pay you, but they say I don't qualify for the public defender."

Drew realizes that Friedrich is ashamed that he does not have money.

"If you want, I can represent you pro bono," Drew offers.

Friedrich's eyes light up, and he suddenly sounds vaguely British, "Yes, that would be a capital idea."

"Okay," Drew says. He sets down his briefcase near the entrance of the holding cell, folds his overcoat in half, and sits on a metal stool bolted into the floor beside the metal table that separates him from his client. He sets the complaint between them.

"Let's start with the charge," he tells his client.

Friedrich nods.

"One count of intoxicated driving," Drew says.

"That's bullshit," he says.

"One count of driving with a detectable amount of a prohibited chemical substance in your blood."

"There was a huge storm, I couldn't help skiddin' out."

"One count of reckless driving."

"The cop's a total dick," Friedrich mutters.

"Be that as it may," Drew begins, flipping to page two of the complaint and adding, "they're also charging you with—"

He stops and scans pages two through five of the complaint. It's unusual.

He looks at Friedrich and announces, "Seventeen counts of possession of or manufacturing a narcotic, keeping a drug house, possession with intent, et cetera."

Friedrich grins widely, eyebrows raised: "Now that part's true."

The commissioner enters the small side courtroom, and Drew stands up.

"Please be seated," he says. He is the commissioner for Judge Crandon and the other Manitowoc Circuit Court judges. The gatekeeper for the system.

The clerk calls the case, and the stenographer begins typing.

"Appearances," the commissioner says. The assistance district attorney announces for the record that he is representing the state.

"Andrew Fisher appears on behalf of Mr. DeMareni, who is in custody, but not in court," Drew states. "Your honor, this is a probable cause hearing, which is an evidentiary proceeding. Therefore, my client's presence is required pursuant to Wisconsin Statute section 971.04, sub 1, sub d."

The commissioner nods and looks over at the bailiff: "George, where is he?"

"He's locked up, Commissioner," George says from his desk at the side, "Got in a fight, so we had to separate him."

"Well," the commissioner says, "Get him in here. We'll be in recess until he is produced."

George huffs off to get the defendant with a clacking of keys and handcuffs.

Drew reviews his notes in the quiet courtroom: the commissioner, the assistant district attorney, the clerk and himself all reading in silence. Whenever any of them turn a page, a ghostly sound echoes through the vast, unchambered room.

Minutes later, George brings Friedrich in. He wears an orange jumpsuit and looks very haggard: unshaven, worn and nervous. When the bailiff has shackled the defendant to the floor and placed him in a chair, the commissioner nods at the assistant district attorney.

The assistant district attorney says, "Commissioner. This is a simple case. The sheriff, Sheriff Baker, was out during a snow emergency. He saw an overturned truck. The trucker was passed out. He'd taken pills. A chemical component in the pills was a homemade barbiturate. We discovered that he's been manufacturing pills and other drugs. A lot of them. That's it. Therefore the state asks that you bind him over for trial."

"Your Honor," Drew begins, "there was a huge storm that night. There were as many as eleven accidents reported that night."

"I don't care," the commissioner says.

"Excuse me, your Honor?"

"The accident is the least of his worries."

"Furthermore, the drugs are homeopathic in nature."

"Counselor," the commissioner says ominously, "You don't really want to go there, do you?"

Drew pauses a moment, then continues: "Your Honor, when the sheriff went into that cab, he was acting as a community caretaker. But the subsequent search of the cab was unlawful. His subsequent confession, the arrest, all of it, it's all fruit of the poisonous tree."

"Objection," the district attorney announces.

"Grounds?" the commissioner asks.

"Commissioner, the state objects on multiple grounds, not the least of which is procedural. This is a preliminary hearing as the commissioner is well aware. The state's burden is probable cause. That's it. Slightly more than an arrest warrant. If the defendant wants to make some sort of constitutional challenge to the search, then he has to file a motion in limine or the like. After he's bound over."

The commissioner nods and looks at Drew, "I agree. You may have arguably meritorious grounds to bring a motion based on a fruit of the poisonous tree, but that's for the judge to decide. For the purpose of this preliminary hearing, I'm going to find that the state has met its burden of probable cause that the defendant has committed a felony within this jurisdiction, and we are going to bind you over for trial."

The commissioner makes a note on a piece of paper, then continues, "As to bail?"

"The state would ask for fifty thousand dollars, commissioner."

"Your honor, my client is indigent. I am here on a pro bono basis as part of my firm's attempt to help out persons in such difficult circumstances. As a result of the accident of which I spoke earlier, my client lost his job. He has no other means of support, and he has substantial student loans and other loans hanging over his head. Therefore, I feel that a signature bond of one thousand dollars is ample to secure his appearance in court."

"Your honor, the state is certain that this defendant has more means than we have been shown. Furthermore, the fact that he is in the transportation industry, is in other states for many days of the week, and—"

"I just got done saying he's been fired," Drew interrupts.

The commissioner holds up a hand.

"I'm going to set bail at fifty thousand dollars. Clerk give them a new date."

The clerk has already slotted the date; the result was predetermined before oral argument.

"March 30 before Judge Crandon," she quickly announces without looking up.

"Thank you commissioner," the assistant district attorney says, closing the file.

"Thank you, your Honor," Drew says, entering the date into his PDA.

"So we lost?" Friedrich wants to know.

Drew is speaking to him on a telephone. Friedrich is unchained, sitting on the other side of a partition of glass.

"It's just the beginning," Drew says.

"And you'll file that, that thing," his client asks.

"Motion? Yeah I'll file a motion to dismiss based on an improper search of your vehicle, and an improper search of your residence," he says.

"One other thing," Friedrich says.

"What's that," Drew says.

"They said they're revoking me."

"In your other case?"

Friedrich nods.

"You'll have to take that up with your probation and parole agent."

"Can you represent me at the resentencing hearing?"

"Sure thing."

"They're moving me up north. Up to Winter."

"Okay."

"It's going to be another great fucking Christmas," Friedrich says with a sour look on his face.

Sharon is angry at him again. She doesn't want him going up to the cabin in Grace with the guys. Thinks maybe they could go up to their house in Door County or to their condo in Elkhart with the kids.

Drew tries to explain it to her, but she just won't listen.

They are about halfway to the island town of Grace when Drew pulls his Suburban onto a side road and to a stop.

"A toast," he announces. They all look at him—this isn't like him, he knows. He pulls out a large thermos. He pulls out five plastic mugs and pours into each one.

"What is it?" Tom asks, sniffing.

"You'll like it," Drew says of his hot cider mixed with whiskey.

"Hair of the dog," Paul mutters, taking a long pull. It's practically the first thing he's said since he arrived in Appleton from Two Rivers.

"To brothers," Drew says. And they touch mugs and drink.

When he's finished taking a long pull, Drew puts a cap on his mug, places it on the floor of the Suburban, and cranks the gearshift into drive.

The wheels spin in the snow.

"Ah shit," Drew says, and floors it once. The wheels just make a sliding, grating sound against the snow. He tries to rock it, by pressing the pedal half-way to the floor intermittently. It doesn't help.

"Let's push it," Paul says.

"You could probably push it all by yourself, Paul," Tom tells him.

Brien, Tom, Mike and Paul all get out and take

positions in back or on the side in the deep snow. They stand in the snow, and push, rocking it, until Drew feels traction and pulls the Suburban out of the snow on the shoulder of the road and back onto the plowed road.

Through the window, Drew gives the four of them a thumbs-up and a smile.

Tom gives him the finger back, and all of them start cracking up.

They reach Bent's Camp at just before noon. The clouds momentarily part—just long enough for Drew to need his sunglasses when he takes off his helmet.

They took their sleds over the ice of the huge lake and opened them up, kicking up snow dust everywhere. The trip was getting a little monotonous for Drew. He wanted a bit more of a thrill.

But Bent's Camp is special, and Drew feels it as he steps inside. Like the Burnt Bridge Bar, Voss's, Dairymen's or some of the other gems up here in the Northwoods. It's made of wood. Like the Grace and Fisher cabins, but even more so. There's birch on the ceiling. White panels of birch. Surrounded by a darkly stained polished oak. Beautiful really. Thick oak beams that rise from the floor to ceiling in support, and pine, signature logs, running laterally throughout, even on the interior walls.

They go up to the bar, but Brien and Tom won't drink. They have covered two hundred miles this morning, and plan on another hundred or more after lunch.

They order some Bloodies and beer backs, and Paul orders a shot of whiskey as a side.

Tom tells Drew that this is the sort of time that Craig would have loved.

"So, let's do something he would want to do," Drew returns.

"At the Dam Bar, I bet they're running the water.

Let's go there."

"Sure," Drew agrees. "Right after lunch. The soup here is almost as good as at Kruk's Diner."

Paul gives a wince-like smile and belts back the whiskey.

At the Dam Bar, they are taking their sleds across the open water.

They pull their sleds from the road onto the ice before the little bar. Outside, near the dam, Drew can see open water—a section fifty feet wide and more than two hundred feet long. Two riders race their sleds over the width section of the open water. A couple dozen people in coveralls, parkas or snowmobile suits stand beside a row of fifty or so sleds, watching the riders race across the water.

They laugh and go into the little bar. Order some beers.

On the screen, Brad Paisley and his band are playing a country rock song.

"Kruk, you look just like the drummer," Tom jokes.

They all laugh.

"You look like a skinny version of the singer," Paul tells him, and Tom punches him in the arm.

On the television in the corner, ESPN is replaying a couple plays in slow motion of the Giants victory over the Packers in the NFC Championship game last week. They keep showing Favre's last throw for an interception in overtime. They'll head home tomorrow and get home in time to watch the Giants play the Pats in the Super Bowl. It was supposed to be Brett's game though, and they all know it.

Drew takes a swig of his beer and pulls Brien aside.

"Listen," Drew says. "I have a client. I need to have a psychological evaluation performed on him. But he's a defendant, so I'd like it to be someone independent, someone I know, that way I can keep it confidential if I need to. Can you do that?"

"Sure thing, Drew," Brien says. "Happy to help."

"Great," Drew says. He turns, raising his beer and asking the group, "Now who wants to cross that water?"

The crowd is waiting. Mike, Tom and Brien have just crossed. Paul guns his engine and shoots across the ice for the water to cross at the width-wise section.

The water here is a dark metallic color, in sharp contrast to the ice that lines it.

"There's no way," Drew mutters to his helmet as the big man takes his sled wide open toward the hole in the ice. Paul hits the open water and his sled gives off a huge plume, a white rooster's tail in the middle of winter. He crosses quickly and makes it to the other side.

Brien, Mike and Tom are waving to Drew.

Drew kicks his boots into the stirrups. He gives them a thumbs-up.

Drew starts toward the water, then swerves to the right. He can almost hear their moans as he veers away, followed by their guffaws as they realize what he's going to do next.

He guns it to the west, past the sleds that line the shore, toward the main section of the lake. Then he slows and spins the snowmobile around. He revs the engine. Once. Twice.

He can hear his breath in the helmet and see them jumping and waving, cheering him on, on the southern side of the open water. The long section, lengthwise, of open water lies before him.

He's done open wheel racing for years, started when he was a teen with Adam and Mike. This is nothing.

He revs it again and knows he will make it.

Then everything is shaking and roaring as he guns the sled and releases the clutch.

He is aiming right at it, right at the open water. He is

going 90 when he hits it.

Nothing changes except rather than the smooth sound of the ice, he hears the rushing sound of the open water. He is nearly across, with only about fifty feet left to go, when he sees a small object floating in the water, to his right, a piece of ice or debris floating there, and before he can stop himself, he veers to the left, and the whole sled shifts to the side, and he's losing it, and he panics, thinking he might fall into the crust of the ice, decapitate himself, cut off a leg, an arm, and then dark, smooth water comes right up at him with a hard, overwhelming, frigid splash.

The assistant district attorney grabbed him as he made his way out of the facility. They were surrounded by glass on all sides, between the glass doors to the facility and those leading outside.

"You really know how to pick a winner," he said.

Drew said nothing in return—he was so very tired of the attorney bravado, and although he's conservative, or perhaps because he is so very conservative, such bravado from district attorneys was more than annoying; it was offensive and fairly unsettling.

The assistant district attorney looked young, mid-twenties, and wore an ugly faux-smirk as he passed over a document. Drew took it.

A rap sheet. Seven pages long, and although Friedrich appeared to have beaten most of the charges many times, Drew got the picture immediately.

"I believe there's also a copy of an interstate compact agreement with North Carolina and one with Texas in the file," the ADA said. "Jurisdiction on two imposed and stayed sentences in each jurisdiction. You want a copy of that too?"

Drew nodded.

"We won't be pleading this one for less than a series of consecutive sentences with a total bifurcated of forty years. Twenty-five in and fifteen on ES," the ADA told him.

"What about ten of initial confinement and twenty-five on extended supervision?"

"Not a chance," he said smugly. "He's got like thirty charges here alone."

"I'll take the offer to my client," Drew said.

The ADA left, and Drew sat in the cold of the unheated entrance on a nearby bench, reviewing the rap sheet. It wasn't good.

Just then his cellular phone began to ring. He looked at the caller I D.

He answered it quickly, whispering, "Hey I didn't expect to hear from you so soon."

"I need to see you," the woman on the other end said.

"Oh, baby, I can't, I'm sorry, I gotta work," he said.

"What are you doing after work?"

"You know, kids, the usual," he said.

"Your wife going to be there too?"

He didn't say anything in return, just stared at the floor between his feet and ran a hand slowly through his hair.

"Look, Drew, I'll make it worth your while," she said.

He looked around the empty entrance room.

"Then I'll see you tonight," he said, adding, "Ten o'clock."

"Where?" she asked.

"The usual place," he said.

He is drowning in the darkness. In the freezing cold.

It is like his nightmares.

A hand seizes him and pulls him upright out of the water. Steadies him.

It is Paul. He has jumped in and lifted Drew up from the water with one hand. Drew finds his footing on the shallow bottom of the lake and stands—the water is up to his chest. He pulls off his helmet and gasps for air. His nose and the back of his throat are burning. He pitches the helmet on to the ice, where it clatters away from them. He coughs and chokes and then gets his wind back. He wipes the water from his eyes.

He turns to Paul to thank him, but before he can, Paul points downward and dives. Drew dives too and feels the nose of the sled as Paul is heaving it off the bottom of the lake. Drew gets out of the way, gains his footing on the bottom and offers a bit of assistance to Paul. They come up again, freezing cold, but now the water seems warm, at least compared to the air. Drew gasps for breath as he holds the nose of the sled out of the water with both hands by one of the skis. He is dizzy, and the water is blurry.

Paul quickly squares his shoulders, grunts a moment, and with Drew's assistance, pushes the sled up and out of the water, onto the ice, where Tom, Mike and Brien haul it the rest of the way.

"Thanks," Drew says.

"Refreshing!" Paul exclaims with a wide grin.

"Let's go back to the bar guys and hit the dryers," Brien says.

Drew climbs out onto the ice, while Paul hauls himself up on the other side.

Drew has never been so cold in all his life.

"My brain is frozen!" he yells. His ears are plugged with water.

"What brain?" Tom asks.

Brien works on his dissertation:

A human being is a being in time.

The being in time consists of perception, as separate from objective reality, and is situated in the present moment, perceiving beyond the present moment.

Its perceptions beyond the present moment are of the past and the future.

Therefore, the "present" for a being in time consists of the past and the future.

10

It is nearly Christmas Eve.

Brien makes his way through his darkened house by the light pollution of his and his neighbor's holiday decorations. He and Megan have just returned from a Christmas party and paid the sitter.

He looks out at the deserted street. It's cloudy tonight, but the clouds break for a moment and allow the moonlight to shine through.

He is as lonely as the moon.

Upstairs, earlier, the lights were on. The high-pitched whine of their nearly broken hair dryer down the hall sounded as lonesome as a train whistle or a harmonica in an old folk song.

His wife was getting ready for a party.

Their kids were with a sitter up in their son Sean's room.

Brien stood on the hardwood floor of the landing in his coat and tie. He needed to bring in the dog.

It's freezing out there.

He flipped on the light switch of the landing.

He was staring at the floor, at himself, staring back up at him: part of his face was on the ground, beside his leather boots, on the wooden floor boards, below his stocking feet: a puddle; snow melt from his boots on the hardwood floor; and in it, his thin, clear reflection.

Brien called the sheriff as he'd requested. Brien sat in his office and told Jimmy what he remembered. There wasn't a lot to tell really. He held his cellular phone to his ear and watched the snow fall. It had been such a strange time.

"Anything else Brien?" Jimmy asked him.

"No that's it," Brien said, leaning back in his office chair. The notes for his upcoming lecture after the Christmas break were displayed on the laptop computer on his desk. "It was just a normal hunting weekend, until Drew found Craig. By the time we got there, the sheriff's cars were everywhere."

"Thanks for calling me back."

"Anytime, Jimmy," Brien said.

"Call me if you think of anything else," Jimmy said.

You need to call Kristen, Brien had told Tom. They had been on their way home from the hunt. Before they'd remembered the trash. Before they'd seen the bear. Before Drew had called Brien on Craig's phone.

Why? Tom had asked.

Because I'm not going to, he'd said simply.

The forest had flashed by on either side of the truck, and the forest road had been wet with the beginning of the snowfall.

But why do I need to? Tom had asked.

Because she needs someone right now, Brien had told him.

They'd been silent for a time.

Then Brien had added, And it can't be me.

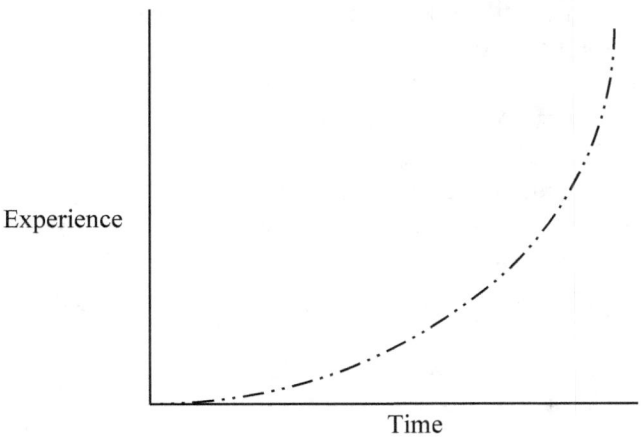

Experience

Time

Where Experience is defined as objective reality as encountered by the subjective individual.

Winter lasts forever.

Brien's routine is the same each day.

He gets up early and shovels the snow, each grating of the shovel against the hardened snow and concrete underneath like the cough of an old smoker. Then he goes to the gym and works out alone. He drinks a pint of water at the gym. He arrives at home in time to help his children get their breakfasts and makes a pot of coffee.

Upstairs, in his office, his dissertation is waiting, looming like a monster.

He works on it all day, except for a break for lunch. The only variance to this is when he has to grade papers, and then he is solely focused on that for the whole day and his dissertation gnaws at his stomach.

He makes dinner: something simple for the kids, such as pizza or hamburgers or mac and cheese; something more complex for Megan and himself, such as shrimp with fettuccini or a Greek salad or steaks.

He reads his children a few bedtime stories and helps them to say their prayers.

He shovels the snow and takes his dog for a walk on the frozen sidewalks and roads of the little town of Appleton, a bag of freezing shit usually tied to the leash. He gets in bed, and Megan is already asleep.

But tonight as he stared at the ghostly reflection of himself in the puddle at the bottom of the stairs, he knew that everything was about to change. That this might be their last Christmas party together.

He had kept his promise to himself. He did not call Kristen.

She didn't call him either until after Thanksgiving.

Brien was getting ready for his lecture in his office. It was one of the last classes of his final semester teaching as a non-professor. After this, he'd start a private practice with Bert and moonlight as an adjunct somewhere. Maybe here at Lawrence.

He was looking over a page of his notes on his laptop, an exhibit that he would project onto a screen in the classroom.

TIME AND MEMORY: What makes up the "present" moment for the being in time?

PAST	PRESENT	FUTURE
Retention (Perception K)		Protention (Perception I)
------------------------------	X	------------------------------
Recollection (Memory)		Projection (Foresight)

Definitions:

Where X stands for the being situated in the present moment, perceiving the present actuality.

Where Retention (Perception K) is the ability to perceive present actuality, prior to its becoming the past actuality.

Where Recollection (Memory) is the purposeful or unintentional ability to recall past actuality.

Where Protention (Perception I) is the ability to perceive present actuality and understand its import on future actuality.

Where Projection (Foresight) is the purposeful or unintentional ability to envision future actuality.

Where Perception is a form of intelligence in terms of a being's capacity for data storage.

Where K and I stand for Knowledge and Insight.

Where Memory and Foresight are meant in terms of a being's capacity for data retrieval.

Where Actuality is defined as objective truth, or that truth beyond the perceiver's subjective perspective.

Brien's cellular phone rang, and he shut his laptop and answered it.

"Hey," she said sadly. It was Kristen.

"How are you?" Brien said immediately.

"I'm in a bad place."

"Yeah?"

"Yeah."

"What's up?"

"Guilt," she said after a pause. He could tell she was upset, might be crying.

"Why? What's wrong?"

"I did something, Brien. Some things. Really bad."

He moved on his chair. "I see."

"Worse than you can probably imagine."

"Remember," he said, laughing. "I was in the army. So, I can imagine a lot."

He could hear her breathing on the other end.

"Seriously, what's up?" he asked.

"Let's not talk in specifics," she said.

There was a pause.

"Okay," Brien began. "Why do you feel guilty?"

"Because I don't feel guilt. Because I don't feel bad about it."

"No?"

"No, because I know I'd do it again."

"The bad thing?"

"Yes," Kristen said. "A thousand times. A thousand times a thousand times, if necessary."

"So you feel guilty for doing something that you'd do again if you had another opportunity?"

"Yes," she said, and it was the helpless way she said it that broke his heart.

"Then don't feel bad," he said simply.

There was another long pause. He was trying to figure it out, and in a vain sort of way, he hoped it involved him, even though he knew that it didn't.

"Kristen," he began after a time, "you felt bad for surviving on September 11th. Guilty for running. For being lucky, and for not stopping and giving up when you were hurt and exhausted."

Another pause.

"You'd do that again?" he asked.

"Yes, of course, that's different," she whispered.

"You know, Nietzsche wrote—on three or four separate occasions—about the ancient Egyptian and Greek concept of the Eternal Return. That whatever happens in this life will happen in the next one, and the one after that, for all eternity. Like reincarnation without any form of karma that alters our state of being. I was never able to figure out why he wrote about such an odd theistic construct, which was clearly the dogma of ancient pharaohs and kings."

He paused, but she said nothing. Usually she'd chime in here with something wry, or a comment about a museum she'd been to recently—something witty—but she was off her game today.

He continued: "But I think he was trying to emphasize the importance of human choice. If something happens once, then it's just as significant as if it happened an infinite amount of times. Each act, each gesture, takes on an almost overwhelming significance for the very reason that it only happens once."

"I'm feeling sick," she said.

Brien was in the kitchen, adjusting his tie in the reflection from the microwave when Megan walked down stairs. She looked great.

"Wow," he said.

She laughed, "Thanks."

She walked into the living room and checked on the kids and the sitter.

"You can call our cellular phone, or the restaurant

where the party is with any questions, but basically, if it's something serious, you know how to dial 9-1-1, right?"

Joan was in high school, and she nodded and gave them a brief view of her braces.

Megan wrote down some instructions. She looked so pretty as she thoughtfully tapped her pen against the counter in between each instruction, pausing and thinking about each of their children.

Brien allowed himself to hope that the party would not be as bad as he'd envisioned.

He didn't know what to say to her anymore. There was silence on the line for a long while, and he felt himself falling into that silence.

He added, "You know, Kristen, instant karma isn't only religious dogma. Or a catchy tune by John Lennon."

She didn't laugh at the joke, and he continued: "It's a real psychological construct. Human beings have a need to be judged. Not later, but here and now. Not in the afterlife. Not by a court. But by themselves. And instant karma is a psychological response to that need. There's evidence that people accidentally make their worlds worse due to their guilt."

"I was afraid you'd say that," she said.

"Kristen," he said to her. "What's happening? What's going on?"

"Life," she said, with an audible sob. "Life is happening."

On the way to the party, Megan sat in the passenger seat, looked at her reflection in the visor mirror and put on lipstick.

Life is happening? he asked her.
Yes, she said.
That's a good thing, he said.

No it isn't, she said.

Yes, Kristen, life is always always a good thing. You know that.

She was silent for a long time.

Meet me, she finally said.

What?

Meet me halfway. I can come up from Chicago today.

He didn't need to ask what she was asking.

Where?

In Milwaukee.

He thought about it for a moment before he decided that she needed to talk to him, and that was all. He was going to help her, and that was okay.

Okay, he said.

The restaurant was an old wooden building on the west side of Appleton. It was full of dark wood and lit candles. Other than that, everything was green and red, or gold and silver. Christmas décor hung everywhere, even from the giant antlers of a great moose on the far wall, and the waitresses were handing out champagne. There was mistletoe of course, and as they passed under it, Brien pointed up. Megan smiled at him, a controlled tight smile, and allowed him to kiss her cheek.

"P D A," she said. "Come on, Brien."

The first person they saw at the party was Susie Krukowski. She was dressed up for her, which meant she'd put on a black skirt, a green Christmas sweater, heels and a bit of makeup.

Megan gave her a big hug that seemed sympathetic and whispered something conspiratorially in her ear. Susie turned to Brien immediately, hugged him and gave him a brief kiss on the cheek.

"Where's Paul?" he asked.

"He had to work," she said with a pout on her lips.

Megan's face was stone for a moment, then she said,

"Are you coming on Friday night?"

"You betcha," Susie said. It was their girls' night out.

They went off into the party together arm in arm. Brien found the bar and ordered an IPA for himself and a chardonnay for Megan.

The café she'd picked out was a small greasy spoon located on the first floor of an old hotel that had been converted into an apartment building.

He was early, and she wasn't there when he arrived. He went into the café and took a seat at the counter. He ordered coffee. He pulled out his laptop and saw that he had a few hours left on the battery. He worked on his dissertation for a time before he realized she was more than an hour late.

He was about to order without her, figuring she'd changed her mind, when she called him: I'm outside the restaurant, I want to drive somewhere else, come out.

He saved his dissertation on the laptop.

He packed up his things and walked out of the café onto the city street.

He approached the corner. She wasn't there. She called again.

I'm behind you, she said.

He spun around. An empty Milwaukee street, but for the cars parked against the embankment of snow on the side of the plowed street.

Not there, turn left.

He turned left. The empty, snow-filled crosswalk was just before him.

Turn just a little right.

He looked.

Brien, I'm waving at you, she said.

He saw her, waving at him from her Saab. I see you, he told her, laughing, and hung up the cellular phone.

She was smoking. As he was beginning to cross the

street, she pulled the car up and around in a wide half-circle. He stopped and hopped back onto the curb. She pulled next to him. He opened the passenger door, and was about to sit down, when she started screaming.

Brien turns in time to see Drew kiss Megan briefly on the lips.

Susie is standing nearby. Drew turns and kisses her on the cheek.

The bartender produces the beer and wine.

"Cash bar tonight?" Brien asks.

The bartender nods and announces, "Seven fifty."

Brien pays for the drinks. He waits for his change, watching Megan.

Drew is laughing with Megan, an arm around her waist. Megan tilts her head back and laughs at the ceiling. Susie is making a mock frown, then she joins in. Megan points over at Brien, and Drew waves. Brien waves back.

"A spider! A spider! A spider!" Kristen screamed.

Brien backed up and looked inside. She looked terrible: her eyes had deep bags under them, and she looked as if she'd been crying. Brien looked at the passenger seat of her car.

"Kill it! No, wait, don't kill it," she ordered: "Sweep it out. Pick it out."

Brien was trying to determine if there was in fact a spider or if she was just hallucinating.

"I don't see a spider," he told her calmly, deciding that the hints he'd seen of delirium had now made themselves manifest. The question was why.

"Please," she said. "I don't want to get bit by it."

"I don't," he began, readjusting himself to look closer. "I don't see anything."

She shrugged, suddenly placated.

"It must have crawled out," she said.

As he climbed into the passenger seat, she lit another cigarette from the one that was already lit and flicked the first one out the window.

He was sitting in the car, feeling a bit cramped, with his laptop case on his lap. The car smelled like damp clothes and smoke.

"How rude of me," she said, laughing, "You must think I'm losing it."

"No— " he began.

"How are you, Brien?" she said with a smile, and she put both of her arms around him, squeezing his neck tightly, but taking care not to get the cigarette too close to him.

"Fine, thanks," he said. "I was a little worried when I got your call."

"That's—" she began. Then stopped. She was on the verge of tears.

"That's why you're such a good friend to me," she said. "And I mean that, Brien."

"Thank you," he said. She had the heat blasting in the car. Wet cigarettes.

"I want to talk to you, but let's not right here, okay?"

"Okay," he said.

Drew walked over. Brien put the chardonnay back on the bar and shook his hand.

"Thanks for putting together the snowmobile expedition," Brien said.

"Not a problem," Drew said. "It was fun."

"You get that water out of your ears yet?" Brien joked.

Drew laughed and grabbed a handful of peanuts off the bar.

"You see that client of mine yet?"

"They scheduled me for after New Years. Said they had to do intake or something."

"That'll give you plenty of time. I just need a report

before March," Drew said. He ordered a drink and said, "How's Tom doing, Brien?"

"He's alright I think," Brien said. "Shocked, like all of us, but he seems to be doing better."

Drew nodded.

"These things take time," he said.

Kristen put the car in gear and maneuvered her way through the plowed downtown streets. Brien pulled his seatbelt down, but it got stuck half-way as she tapped the brake. She drove through the downtown high rises and office complexes, smoking fervently and talking rapidly about nothing that made much sense the whole way.

"By the way, Brien," she said quickly, "I've been thinking about your dissertation. Did you know that your theory in your dissertation that the human being is a being in time consisting of the past and the future contains three assumptions?"

"I can think of one," Brien replied.

"First," she stated, "is that an objective reality even exists."

Brien smiled at her.

"Second," she continued, "is that subjective reality is a part of objective reality. And, paradoxically, the third is that subjective reality is also separate from objective reality."

She took a corner too sharply. Brien pulled on the seatbelt. It caught again, and he couldn't get it buckled. Finally he relaxed, loosened the belt slightly, and then slowly and smoothly pulled the belt over and into position.

Suddenly Kristen turned south on Water Street, and Brien was thrown into the seatbelt. She drove south until the buildings changed from modern glass and steel to cream city brick.

She pulled in front of an old building in the Third Ward.

"I saw this, this morning," she said, stopping before one of the buildings on Buffalo Street, adding, "Alright, I'll tell you the truth, I cased it out a couple months back and I have a deposit on it now."

Brien looked at it. It was a nice old building.

"Come on," she said, getting out.

They were hustling in the cold to the big old door of the building, when suddenly she exclaimed, "What an airhead! How stupid can I get?"

She walked back, digging through her purse. She had on a black skirt, black leather boots, and a warm looking winter coat. She had beautiful legs.

She plugged the meter and skipped back to him, whereupon she thrust her arm through the crook of his elbow, and leaned against him. He could feel her breast against his arm as they went inside the building.

The entrance hall had a tall ceiling and was filled with old brick arches.

"They're selling off lofts and renting office space," she said. She had a look in her eyes now: confident, controlled, charged.

He nodded as they got on an elevator. He wanted to know where they were going.

"We could move in here, Brien," she laughed. "Start all over."

She pressed a button for the fifth floor. And the elevator began to climb slowly.

He was about to ask where she was taking him when she put a finger to his lips.

She rubbed a hand across his cheek.

"You haven't shaved," she whispered. "I like that."

She was standing just a bit too close to him. He smiled down at her and said, "Thanks."

She wasn't well, he reminded himself. He forced himself to look at the numbers on the elevator. She had placed her head on his chest. There were not two ways of interpreting the gesture.

"Oh, will you look at that," she said, pointing her hand at an old emergency sign which read: Push Here To Turn On.

"How convenient," she murmured.

Brien smiled and read the rest of the sign: If the red light is flashing, help is on the way. He was going to say something, but the elevator door opened, and she skipped away from him out of the elevator and into the ugly, unfinished loft of the abandoned fifth floor.

"What do you think?" she asked spinning around with her arms outstretched, fingers extended. She looked gorgeous. And dangerous.

"Of this?" Brien asked.

"I'm thinking of opening a practice here. My own practice," she said. "As a sole practitioner."

"It's great," Brien said, smiling at her. He looked around at the spacious loft and added, "It is a pretty big place for a sole practice."

"I'll live here too," she said happily. "Look, here."

She pointed to a piece of red tape on the dusty floor that began in the center of the southern wall, ran to the center of the room, turned at a right angle and ran twenty feet, and then turned again to continue running to the northern wall.

"It's divided. Equally in half," she announced seriously.

"This half," she said, jumping to the eastern side of the red line, "will be for work."

Brien nodded. He could see yellow and green lines of tape, probably denoting a conference room, a reception room, and at least two offices, all of which were complete with rectangles symbolizing desks, a conference table, inn tables and the like.

"And this half," she said, jumping to the western side. "Will be for life."

Again, she or someone else had used tape to symbolize the walls of the various rooms and the furniture within: couches and coffee tables; a big shower and a huge bed.

"Wow," Brien said, impressed. This was not what he'd expected.

"Thanks," she said. She took his hand and held it for a long time. Too long.

When he looked around the room wearing an expression of hope for her benefit, she dropped his hand and turned toward one of the large glass windows.

"One side for work and the other for life," he said happily.

And then the sudden, frightening non sequitur, like the ones in Chicago, the suicide threats. She spun back toward him and asked, "How do we live, Brien?"

"I'm sorry?"

"How are we supposed to keep going?"

Brien paused for a long time.

"You mean how do we keep going to work each day as a psychologist? Or just as a human being? Or how do we keep from killing ourselves?"

She laughed and said: "I should have preferenced this with a 'my client thinks that life isn't worth living' remark, but I didn't and I'm not going to."

She looked at him and continued, "Because it's what I think. It just keeps going on, and it's all so bad. I just don't see the point half the time."

"What about progress?" he offered.

"That's almost funny," she said. She suddenly turned from him and walked to a dusty window that looked out on the frozen city.

She was looking out, and he realized that she was crying. He walked over. She was clearly having a breakdown of some sort, but he couldn't figure out why. It wasn't because she wanted him, he knew that now. He took her by her shoulders, trying to comfort her.

"Tell me what's wrong, Kristen," he said.

"I don't know why I'm here," she said. "With you."

"Third time's a charm?" he asked.

She grabbed him and pulled him close to her.

It was a hug, but it was lasting too long. Her hands were moving on his back, her cheek brushing across his chin, rising toward his mouth.

"Wait," Brien managed. "Kristen, wait."

She let go and stepped back.

"I think," he began. "I think we're just—"

She read the look on his face and cut him off.

"I'm sorry," she said immediately.

When he began to apologize, she held up a hand, adding, "No, I'm so sorry."

She backed away, and then hurried to the exit for the stairs and out of the loft.

Brien looked around. It would make a lovely office, and a lovely apartment, someday.

The party is over. Brien is feeling good, but the party is over. Megan leans in to give Drew a hug goodbye. He presses his hand between her shoulder blades, against her skin, on the open portion of her dress.

"Just go ahead and kiss her," Brien finds himself saying.

They both look at him.

"Seriously, take her home," he says. "Or get a room at the Copper Leaf."

Drew backs off a step. Megan manages a fake laugh. Brien turns to where Susie is talking to a couple on the other side of the room.

"Susie," Brien calls. Susie turns.

"Come on over here, we're swingers tonight girl!" he calls.

Susie stares at him, then she smiles, gives him a big wink, and blows him a kiss. Brien turns back to the others.

Megan has stopped laughing now, and Drew has left.

When Brien went outside, Kristen was gone. He walked up Water Street until, eventually, he managed to hail a cab for the rest of the way. He found his truck.

Once inside, he started it and waited for it to warm up before heading home.

He pulled out his cellular phone and called Paul.

He sets the alarm of his home and walks upstairs by the light of the moon and the Christmas decorations inside the house. The light in their bedroom is still on.

He brushes his teeth, takes a piss and walks into their bedroom.

Brien looks at Megan, who is still awake. She is reading a magazine, ignoring him. They had fought in the truck on the way home. It was a stupid fight.

Brien looked at his home beyond the headlights of his truck.

It's a nice little home. It's enough.

He had played the fool for too long.

It's time to grow up. I do not need what I haven't got.

There was a snowman that he built with his sons melting in the front yard.

After his father had died, when Brien was at his lowest, he had made a prayer, a simple prayer for help, and Megan that summer, that very summer, had walked right back into his life.

In the window upstairs, he saw that the lights of the hallway to his sons' rooms were still on, though he knew the kids were asleep.

He parked the car in the garage and walked into the house.

Lead me beside the calm water. Restore and guide me on these paths.

I will not fall. I will not fail.

He entered the house, and Megan shot him a look and immediately hung up her cellular phone.

"Who was that?" he asked.

"No one," she said strangely.

"So, have you come up for another round?" Megan asks simply, not looking up from her magazine.

"You don't even know what we're fighting about," he says.

She simply smiles. She's not fighting with him, he realizes. He's fighting with her. Or with himself.

"How about what you said in the truck?" she asks.

"I don't know why I said that," he admits, feeling foolish.

"You don't," she says as if it were a statement rather than a question.

"No," he says. "And I'm sorry. And I don't know why I said that to Drew. I didn't mean to. Or to Susie."

She stares at him. She smiles and motions for him to join her.

He slips off his clothes and into bed. The sheets are cold, but her body is warm and he kisses her. They lie like that for a time, holding each other and kissing tenderly. Then he remembers that the lights are on and the blinds to the room are up. He stops kissing her and gets up. He pulls the string to close the blind.

Across the span of dark shrub trees and lawn, the lights of his neighbor's house are on, and he sees his neighbors—dressed in flannel pajamas, both of them hunched over in the window. They appear to be trying to fix a window; they look up at him. He realizes he is stark naked as the blind finally comes down.

He goes back to the bed and lies down on his side beside Megan.

"I think I just gave the neighbors a show," he says.

She smiles as she sits upright, pulls off her nightgown and pushes him onto his back. She gets on top of him, whispering, "At least it was a good show."

The problem is that you cannot admit the truths even to yourself.

Adam is dead. Craig is dead. But you are alive.

Why did Craig do it? And why did you set his fate?

And now Paul? What have you done to your brother?

The central problem is one of admission. There is a wisdom to the Eastern and Western religions that demanded confession.

The central problem of truth. And of violence.

Truth is truth. It does not know itself, it just is.

Violence is violence. It is blind. Unknowing.

Begetting only itself.

11

The freeway is full of cars in the cold dark. Red, angry lights all the way into Chicago. A sluggish progression back to Lincoln Park on the Kennedy.

Kristen's Saab is automatic and is switching constantly between second and third gear, straining back and forth as she uses the brake and gas.

She has the radio on. Switching stations. She is trying to drown her thoughts with music, news, talk shows. She can't stop thinking about Brien. What has she done? What has she become? A married man. Her brother's best friend. In some ways, her own best friend. Their meeting. God. He'll know. He'll figure it all out. Knows she's falling apart already. Senses something's wrong with Paul, too. Their meeting, it's all ruined now.

Up ahead the traffic has stopped. She slows and stops too.

Waiting in the glare of the brake lights.

What had Brien said when they met up at O'Hare? Every meeting is a miracle. Even accidental meetings are miracles.

Nice sentiment. The problem is that there are no miracles. Events occur. We assign meaning to events. We designate the good events as miraculous.

Adam alive. You met him, fell in love with him. What is that? A miracle? No because then Adam drowns. If meeting him were miraculous, then what of his death?

There are no miracles. Miracles: tell that to six million. Placed in ovens and burnt alive. Thrown in pits, mowed down by machine guns. Led to the showers and gassed.

Every meeting, Brien said in O'Hare.

And you, you said, God is either absent or not listening.

God hears, Brien said, Hears it all. How can she not hear her own cry?

Traffic begins to move again, slowly.

Ahead of her, there is an accident, a half dozen emergency vehicles crowd the side of the road, lights blazing in the winter dark.

That thought of Brien's, that would have been wondrous advice, if not for knowing that it was Megan's influence on him. Brien, once an atheist, or at least an agnostic. Not a believer. In this way, you and Brien were the same. You and Megan opposites. Although Megan was always such a good person, such a kind person, and you respect her. You do. Too bad she's married to the man that you could have loved. You could still love him. No.

What about Tom?

Poor Tom. Poor kind talented Tom. Means so well. Funny. But so wounded by the world. Just being in it has wounded him.

And now you have as well. It had to be done. But did you have to be with him? It was him or Brien, they were the only ones left you could possibly ever love. And you chose him.

The traffic pulls to a stop. She exits at Addison, deciding to take Lincoln Ave to Webster or Armitage.

You could leave. You could just simply leave.

Would Tom follow you? You could leave in such a way that he would be alright, that he would give up.

And Brien? Would he follow you—you'd like that, wouldn't you?

Beneath the red light of the freeway exit, she pulls to a stop. A worn man with a sign stares at her as she waits to pull onto Addison.

Would Brien? Possibly. If you sent him a letter. A

letter from the other side of the world. But you wouldn't send him that letter. Would you? You wouldn't do that. You won't even leave, you'll stay on and on.

Damaged. Can't even see the word for your occupation, therapist, without breaking it into two component words: the rapist. Damaged beyond recognition, beyond recall.

The light turns green. The homeless man is yelling something, but she can't tell if he's begging for money, cursing her, or warning her. Are her headlights turned on? Yes. Turn signal? Yes.

If you leave, what about mother?

Paul will care for her.

Paul.

Paul would understand. He never made you stay at the restaurant, always said you were meant for something else, but let you work whenever you needed money.

And Susie. Susie has always been so kind to Paul, so good to him.

But Susie is not who she appears to be either.

No one is.

She picks up her cellular phone and calls the sheriff again.

When she called this time, it was different. After he answered, she hung on the line for almost five seconds before hanging up.

He hung up and stared at the tracer id on the phone. It was the eighth time she'd called this week. Usually she just hung up as soon as he picked up.

She called back an hour later. He answered and listened to her breathe.

Sheriff's department, he announced again finally, and not unkindly.

I'm sorry, she finally said. I have the wrong number.

That's okay, have a good day now, he told her, listening to her hang up.

A prank phone call, he thought, placing the phone in its cradle.

Now why would a sweet girl like Kristen go and do a thing like that?

12

Jimmy doesn't want to deal with this right now. This snow is screwing up his entire week. Five wrecks in as many hours.

The station is flooded with calls for help, and he's going to have to get involved now, too. Sixteen years in the Department, and he's still just a glorified tow truck operator.

Jimmy goes into the garage. The smell of the oil and gas of the place still gives him butterflies. These are his cars. His rigs. There are six Fords inside with souped-up engines, each of which, when the roads are clear, can get up above one-thirty without any strain at all.

Matt has just finished attaching chains to the tires of their respective rigs. He's washing his hands in the sink on the side of the garage.

"Still glad you went to college for this?" he asks Jimmy.

Jimmy smiles. Matt always likes to bust his chops for going to school at U.W. Green Bay when he didn't need to to become a cop.

"Just remember that that degree's why I'm your boss," Jimmy tells him.

"You were an English major, right?" Matt needles him.

"With a concentration in criminal justice," Jimmy says with a mock-defensive tone in his voice.

Matt smiles at him as he hits the garage door button. The wind and snow immediately fill the entrance, and Jimmy has to zip up his coat.

"Careful out there, pops," Matt yells as he climbs into his squad car. Matt is still smiling at him as he heads out into the storm.

Jimmy frowns at him dramatically and mouths the word "rookie" for his benefit before he climbs into his own rig.

Jimmy was escorted to Tributary Seven by a deputy from the Forest County Sheriff. It was snowing, covering the twisted naked branches of the oak, maple and birch trees and the tops of the pines and firs with a layer of snow. They slowed their cars as the road conditions worsened: as the road changed from paved to gravel. The snow drifted through the trees, and the sky grew darker.

As they turned their respective squad cars onto the path that took them deep into the forest, Jimmy began to talk to himself as the trees passed by: "Whose woods these are, I think I know, his house is in the village though. He will not mind me stopping here to watch his woods fill up with snow."

He continued through the darkening woods as his squad car took the ruts in the road: "My little horse must think it queer to stop without a farmhouse near. Between the woods and frozen lake, the darkest evening of the year."

A deer walked to the edge of the woods in front of them, trotted across the path, and then cantered away on the northern side. Even now, the woods are full of life, even as winter sets in.

"He gives his harness bells a shake to ask if there is some mistake. The only other sound's the sweep of downy woods and dusty flake."

Several more deer crossed the road behind their vehicles. Jimmy watched them in his rearview mirror. The woods go on and on and on. Their squad cars climbed the frozen ruts of the path. Jimmy whispered aloud: "The woods are lovely dark and deep, but I have promises to keep. And miles to go before I sleep."

They pulled their cars to a stop at the overlook point, which looked like a bomb had hit it; it had been driven over by so many squad cars and ambulances.

"And miles to go before I sleep," Jimmy muttered as he zipped up his jacket and headed out into the cold.

They both had on winter hiking boots and tromped through the snow of the woods toward the ravine. They stepped over a drooping yellow police line that had been strung rather uselessly through the forest trees.

The deputy had been the first on the scene and described the condition of the body they found, and what the witness, Drew Fisher, had told him. He'd photocopied pictures of the scene, and gave them to Jimmy almost hesitantly, as if he were breaking a law.

"Great," Jimmy said.

The deputy nodded. He lingered a moment, unsure if he was still needed.

Jimmy sucked in a big breath of air and exhaled.

"Smell that?" Jimmy asked.

The deputy cautiously sniffed at the air, as if it contained cholera.

When he shook his head, Jimmy exclaimed, "Football weather! Week seventeen and the Outback Bowl. I got twenty on the both the Pack and Badgers."

The deputy laughed.

Jimmy thanked the deputy and said he was going to hang around for a bit. The deputy climbed carefully up the ravine and was gone.

The snow had only lightly covered the ground, and he could see frozen footprints in the mud and dirt of the ravine beneath it.

Their report said that the Grace boys had called it the No Name River.

As he scanned the tiny stream below, he found himself muttering the introductory lines of the other poem he memorized in college, though he doesn't remember much of what it means, "S'io credesse mia risposta fosse a persona, questa fiamma staria senza scosse."

He squatted down and read the report carefully. The bullet came from the southeast. He looked at the diagram, and where they estimated the shooter was, sitting below the blind, shooting upwards at the blind from Tributary Seven. That miraculously the bullet missed the trees and continued upward into the blind.

It doesn't make sense that way.

He looked at the log, wiping away the snow with a gloved hand. Beneath the snow, someone's drawn on it with a sharpie, noting precisely where the bullet was recovered.

He sat down in the blind, shrinking down just a bit to match the Bunder kid's height. He drew up a pretend shotgun and aimed. This was where he would have been sitting. He looked at the report. What they couldn't figure out was why there were no tracks where they had approximated that the shooter was. In a quarter mile radius, they did not find a single track that was not attributed to their own investigative search.

He said aloud as he looked down the broad valley, "Giammai di questo fondo non torno."

But the skull altered the trajectory of the bullet. That's what they missed. Like the way water alters a ray of sunlight: the way a stick or a fishing pole in water appears to angle upwards, toward the surface.

They had missed it.

He walked down the valley, found a place where the ice on Tributary Seven was thick enough to hold his weight, and crossed to the other side. The shrub trees were sparse here, and he made good time. He found a winding narrow deer path that ran up and up.

When he neared the top of the southern ravine side, he eyed the opposite wall.

He pulled out his binoculars, whispering, "Odo vero."

He saw that the blind where the victim died was partially obscured by an outcropping of stone and trees.

He moved to his left and up, climbing the pitched face of the ravine carefully, testing the earth beneath the snow with his hands and his boots before committing his full weight to each step. He glassed the opposite side: as before, Craig's blind was partially obscured.

He moved upward, and then suddenly he was on top of it. The killer's blind was part of a natural depression in the side wall, the infantile beginning of a side-ravine from the spring melt, and was so well camouflaged beneath a set of pines and an outcropping of birch that he would not have discovered it had he not been searching, had he not almost stumbled on it.

He stayed outside of it, intentionally. He scanned the opposite blind with his binoculars. He had a perfect view. A perfect shot.

He decided to film this. Look for a shell casing. Anything.

But he already knew there wouldn't be anything.

"Odo vero," he whispered as he got out his video camera and prepared to document the lack of evidence he'd unearth.

Then he had an idea. He filmed the blind, filmed what he envisioned would be the line of the shot. He paused the camera and looked carefully at the snow-covered ground. Where would the shooter need to step? The walls were steep, so he chose the flat ground. Where the ground would be flat enough for water to pool, for the mud to become soft. He used a glove gently to push away the snow. And again. And a third time. Until he hit the earth beneath the snow. And then, as he pushed the rest away: there they were.

The first was a single footprint made of snow, of the snow that must have been falling when the shooter left the blind. The snow that was crushed by the boot as it left the blind in the falling snow: the remainder; a raised fossil of snow. The rest of the snow was not compacted and so had been swept away, but this one footprint of snow remained.

The second was the indentation. The soft mud, earth made so from the prior mist or rain or snowmelt, and in it, the second print, frozen into the ground. The shooter took several more steps, being careful, but in his haste, the ground gave away, just a bit, and then froze as the temperature dropped. The tread frozen in the mud.

He took several photos and some video of both of them, whispering all the while:

"Odo vero."

Kruk's Diner has only six people in it, and one of them is Rick.

"Hey, Rick, you made it."

"You're late," Rick says, glaring at him.

"Yes, I know. Sorry. Couldn't be helped."

Jimmy takes off his winter coat, shakes it once quickly to get the snow off, and slings it over the back of the chair. He nods at one of the tables, where two older women are picking at their breakfasts, before sitting down.

"He's not here," Rick whispers through clenched teeth.

"It's early. Have some coffee," Jimmy tells him.

Paul's mother comes by. She's worried.

"Goodmorning Jimmy," she says. She's a big woman, and very sweet.

"Good morning. I'm starving," he says, picking up the menu.

"You're looking for Paul?" she asks.

"Oh, yeah, nothing special, just gotta ask him a favor, you know," he says.

"Sure," she says, but clearly she doesn't.

"Is he here?" Jimmy asks.

"No, it's his day off," she tells them.

"Now how could I have forgotten that?" Jimmy announces, banging a hand on the table.

Rick raises his eyebrows. He can't believe this.

"So," Jimmy says and looks at the menu. "I'll have a coffee."

"Me too," Rick finally mutters, acquiescing.

"You want sugar or cream?" she asks.

"Black for me please," Jimmy says.

She fixes her eyes on Rick.

"No thanks, just the coffee," he tells her.

"And a quick meal," Jimmy announces, setting down the menu. "Rick, this is the place. This is the place I was telling you about. Remember?"

Rick just stares at him.

Jimmy continues, smiling: "Rick, this is where they have the dumplings. The chicken and dumplings. For breakfast."

Rick's mouth actually opens just a bit.

Jimmy is chuckling now, "They're so good they eat them for breakfast. For breakfast Rick! And the potatoes, these café-style potatoes, sliced just perfect and the special seasoning. Wow! And the venison sausage."

Paul's mom is smiling fiercely.

Rick manages to say, "Right."

"So, anyway, Mrs. Krukowski," Jimmy says, turning slightly to look up at her again, "we'll just start with the coffees, and then bring out an order of the chicken and dumplings for each of us whenever you get a chance."

She nods and hurries off to get their coffee.

"What are you doing?" Rick asks.

"What?"

"Ordering chicken and dumplings," Rick whispers angrily.

"I know it sounds odd for breakfast, but trust me, it's absolutely fantastic," Jimmy says emphatically.

"You stalling for him or something?" Rick asks, incredulous and irritated.

"What? No," Jimmy says, gesturing around the room. "Look, Rick, he's not here, but we might as well eat."

"What if he," Rick begins, and then leans in and whispers even softer, "What if he runs?"

Jimmy sits back in his chair, the jovial look gone.

"Then you have your man, and your investigation as to whether to pay out those proceeds would pretty much be over."

"And yours?" Rick asks.

Jimmy's patience with him is growing thin. This is his investigation.

"You let me burn that bridge if we ever come to it."

"Fine," Rick finally relents, but quickly adds: "But I'm sure as shit not eating chicken and dumplings for breakfast."

"That's fine Rick," Jimmy says, happy again, "I like their omelets better anyway."

It was a long way back from the Northwoods. Back to Two Rivers.

He needed to make one more appointment, so he called ahead. It's always best to call ahead.

Jimmy listened to the scanner, listened to the chatter from the other jurisdictions. Eventually, he turned on the radio, and thought about the case, and then a song came on and he sang along with it: *where the silver leaf of maple, sparkled in the morning dew; I braided twigs of willow, made a string of buckeye beads. But flesh and blood needs flesh and blood, and you're the one I need. Flesh and blood needs flesh and blood, and you're the one I need.*

Paul is nervous. He's playing it off okay, but he's nervous, and Jimmy can tell. And Rick O'Reilly can tell too, which is why he almost gleefully leaves with the rifle.

Jimmy stands there a moment, in the laundry room of Paul's home, the black lab looking up at him from his bed in the corner, the snow falling into the house in big light flakes from outside. Jimmy notices a pair of Sorrel boots resting beside the dog, and they look to be the right size, but of course they're the wrong make.

"How are things, Paul?" Jimmy asks, looking at Paul directly.

"Sure, Jimmy, you know they're fine," Paul says back.

Jimmy nods and says, "You give Susie my best now."

Paul nods too, saying, "Say hello to Amy and the kids."

Jimmy entered the morgue. A visit here was always pointless, but a criminologist had told him in college that it was an important part of law enforcement, so he always went anyway. He nodded to the woman at the entrance, and she passed him a clipboard beneath the glass plane that separated her little office from the rest of the world.

Jimmy filled it out quickly and passed it back, and he walked to the door, which buzzed and emitted a loud electric click. Jimmy opened the heavy door and walked inside the small entrance. Everything here was made of metal and concrete. He pushed a button for the elevator and waited for it to arrive. He was bored.

The big metallic door slowly opened with a low, tired sweep. He entered the long galley of the elevator, designed to transport dead bodies into the shelving units below, and hit the button for the basement with a single knuckle of his forefinger.

While the elevator slowly began to descend, he announced to the chrome walls, "Let us go then, you and I, while the evening is spread against the sky like a patient etherized upon a table."

The elevator reached the bottom with a slight shudder, and the door slid open. As he walked to the row of refrigerated shelves, he paged through the report from the Forest County Sheriff's Department, noting the entrance and exit of the bullet, noting that the coroner had determined that death was instantaneous. Almost merciful.

As he read the report, he whispered, "Half-deserted streets. Muttering retreats. One-night cheap hotels."

The bullet was recovered from the scene. Lodged in a log on the west side of the blind. A diagram illustrated how the round most likely ricocheted upwards slightly, went through one smaller log, before being stopped by a bigger one.

It was a .30-06 caliber round.

"Sawdust restaurants. Oyster shells."

The coroner had concluded, as Jimmy had, that the investigating officers had placed the shooter too low. That he could not have been on the valley floor.

"Streets winding like an argument."

And that the shooter had to be firing from a higher position.

"Insidious intent."

Furthermore, the position, angle and distance of Mr. Andrew Fisher when he shot his doe, not to mention the make and caliber of his rifle, led both the coroner and Forest County Sheriff to rule him out as a possible suspect.

There were three rows of three shelves.

He paused before the shelf that contained the body.

"Do not ask—"

The coroner arrived, breathless, from a different door.

"Sorry, Jimmy," he breathed, running a hand over his balding head, "to keep you waiting."

"I've only just arrived, Nick," Jimmy said smiling, adding jovially, "Let us go and make our visit."

Nick stepped up quickly, heaved up the handle and pulled out the cold, metal shelf.

Craig Bunder, pale, naked and dead, lay on it.

Jimmy drives through the bleary snow-filled night. There was a prank call that someone was going to destroy the nuclear reactor. He drives by it, and it looks like a great fortress in the dark. The red lights wink at him between the gusts of the crazed storm. He continues through the bleak night, thinking about the rifle. If the testing pattern shows that Paul is the killer. But it won't. There's no question that it won't.

The snow has grown more intense, and Jimmy can hardly see.

Suddenly something looms out of the darkness like a giant whale. Jimmy turns hard to the left, pumps the brakes, and even so, skids for more than thirty feet, watching the road with the realization there's a truck, without any running lights on, taking up the southbound lane of traffic. Jimmy comes to rest easily against a snow bank. He backs up gingerly so as not to spin his tires. He turns on his emergency flashers and his search light, which he shines over the hull of the darkened rig.

The truck has turned over and is lying on the driver's side.

Jimmy backs his squad car up even farther and affixes the headlights and search light on the cab of the truck. There's somebody in there. He gets out and approaches it cautiously, sniffing in the air carefully as he does: it's a tanker; it could explode, but he doesn't see any fire or smell any gas.

The guy inside is hurt. He can see that—the trucker is crumpled around the steering wheel and the driver's side of the windscreen. He runs back to the squad car and calls on the radio for an ambulance. He gets flares out and marks the rear of the overturned tanker, placing them well away from the rig with three flares spaced about a hundred feet apart.

Another squad car pulls up. It's Matt; his emergency flashers are off. Jimmy makes a whirling signal with his right hand that tells him to get his flashers on. The blue and red lights fill up this night of snow and darkness.

Jimmy finishes setting the flares and runs up to the front of the truck. Inside, illuminated by the lights of his squad car, the trucker is unconscious. Matt steps out of his squad car and stares at the trucker.

"How the hell are we supposed—" Matt begins, but Jimmy has already wedged the tip of his boot into the front grate by the driver's side headlight. He grasps onto the grill of the truck and pulls himself up. He works his way carefully to the top, pulling himself up and onto the passenger side. He crawls to the passenger door and stands unsteadily in the wind and swirling snow; he looks down into the cab, but the lights of his squad car are blocked by the steering wheel. He turns on his flashlight and shines it through the passenger window. He peers in: a splintered driver's side window and blood.

He bends down and taps on the window with his flashlight. The trucker doesn't move. He opens the passenger door carefully, pulling it slowly up and toward him.

"Hey, you okay in there?" Jimmy calls. "Sir, can you hear me?"

No response. He lowers himself through the open door and into the cab of the truck, so that his belly and upper body are leaning on the doorframe, just as Matt climbs on top of the overturned cab. Jimmy kicks around wildly for a moment in the cab with his boots; he steps momentarily against the gear shift—it suddenly slides out of gear and his boot slips off the shifter, and he almost falls. He swears and pulls himself up; he finds footing with his left foot on the headrest of the passenger seat. Matt holds the door open for him with one arm and steadies him with the other. Jimmy lowers his right leg to the driver's side seat and allows his body to slide all the way into the cab, using his hands on the sides of the door frame to hold on and steady himself.

He lowers himself further, then turns and looks at the guy. The trucker is wedged between the steering column and the driver's side door, his bald head covered in blood.

Jimmy squats carefully and reaches two fingers down to the trucker's neck. He feels for a pulse, but there is none. He quickly moves lower and feels again for a pulse. He's got one, but it's faint. He realizes that he recognizes the trucker, but he can't place where he's seen him before. Jimmy catches the scent of gasoline, and his stomach suddenly feels sick.

"How is he?" Matt calls from atop, where he holds open the passenger door.

"He's gone into shock," Jimmy tells him.

"The ambulance is here," Matt calls.

The wounds to his head look serious. There could be neck trauma, but he can smell gasoline, and there are three flares out there. Before he can stop himself, he lifts the trucker up and begins to haul him upright. He stands him up and lifts him toward Matt, who is lying down on the passenger side of the overturned tanker and holding out his right arm expectantly for the trucker. Matt and Jimmy pull-push him through the passenger side door.

Matt hauls him up the rest of the way and then lowers him down to the EMTs that are waiting for him with a stretcher.

Jimmy turns back to the wreck: there's an open prescription bottle of pills lying against the shattered driver's side window of the cab. He picks them up and looks at them. There's no prescription label on the bottle. Jimmy slips them into his pocket. It could be medicine for the trucker.

He clambers his way up and out of the truck.

Back in the snow and darkness, the snow intermittently red and blue, he sees a vehicle approaching and uses his flashlight to direct it around the wreck. It's a pickup truck. He can tell from the silhouette inside that the driver is waving, thanking him.

Jimmy waves back at the dark figure inside the pickup.

Spring

It was Sunday.
She left early, to attend mass, Palm Sunday mass.
When she arrived home, he was still in bed. Asleep.
She left again for the church auction, and he got up and headed out to work.
When he returned, she was already upstairs. In bed.
He turned on ESPN and opened a beer.
That was Sunday.

13

Paul closes up Kruk's Diner. He locks the back door. He walks to the front, pulls the chain to turn off the neon "Open" sign, and locks the front door. He turns off the ovens, the burners for the stoves and the fryer. Empties the small refrigerator and puts the uncooked beef patties, chicken breasts, and left-over soup into the back of the walk-in refrigerator where it's coldest, and then adds the lettuce, tomatoes and other vegetables on the metal shelves near the door, and the loafs of white and wheat bread, rolls of French bread, and bags of sesame buns.

He wipes off the tables and puts up the chairs. He washes the smudges from the windows and doors; sponges down the counters; mops up the floors; closes the register—counts the cash and change, and adds the credit receipts.

He grabs his keys, his jacket. He turns off the lights, locks up the office, and leaves through the backdoor. He steps out into the evening and makes sure the door has locked behind him.

Outside it's an early spring twilight, and the post-sunset colors are spread out to the west in a beautiful combination of purple and pink against the heavens. The snow melted yesterday, and although it's chilly, it feels like a spring night. It's been a long winter, and Paul is glad it's over.

He starts his truck. The parking lot and streets are wet, and the colors of the sky reflect upon them, making the world seem a sort of globe of colors in which he and his truck are suspended. He makes his way through the small town of Two Rivers, his hometown. A person watching him would observe that he wears his seat belt, stops fully at every stop sign, and uses his turn signal when he changes lanes on the two lane highway.

He drives home.

The radio is not on. He realizes that is odd, so he turns it on, and spends the next five minutes of his commute changing from station to station. Each station, each program, is more annoying than the last. He finally shuts it off again and continues his drive in silence.

He takes County Road O through the farms and then the woods. By that time, it's dark: the woods having cut off whatever light still lingers in the west.

You can do this, he tells himself. You can.

At home, the house is dark. He feels a moment's panic that Susie's actually done it, actually left, but then he remembers that she has Bunko tonight and is out with the girls. With Sharon Fisher, Megan Grace, and the others.

Their dog, Cooper, greets him at the garage door, starving for attention and needing to go out. He lets Cooper out back, and the big black lab sprints for the woods that border their backyard.

"Cooper!" he calls once from the doorway, his voice loud in the stillness of the spring evening. The air, the very sky, feels big tonight.

He steps into the wet, brown lawn and lifts the tarp that covers his snowmobile. He produces a six-pack of beer, the bottles rattling and sounding loud in the big air of the big sky as he walks back inside. He pauses at the doorway.

Above him, the stars are out and alive. He can see Orion to the south, just above the woods. He envisions Orion as an archer, inverted and partially facing the east, firing an arrow into the earth.

Then he turns on the floods, and the stars disappear.

He closes the door to the backyard, hoping Cooper won't mess with the raccoon he's lately been treeing and then barking at madly. He carries the beer to the couch.

He opens a beer and turns on the television. He hides the six-pack behind the far side of the couch, beneath some newspaper in case she comes home early.

The Blackhawks-Red Wings game is in between periods, so he changes channels to the local news. There's a serial killer on the loose in the middle part of the state of Wisconsin. A college boy from Milwaukee, a Greenpeace advocate, went to the killer's house, asking for a donation. The man apparently invited the boy into his house. A week later, the police found the house abandoned, the boy's remains scattered in a fallow field behind the man's house. They also found a little cemetery with dogs, cats, even a horse. And people—

Paul changes the station. The hockey game is on again. The Red Wings are up one to nothing.

He told himself he wouldn't drink. But just this one beer.

He watches the game. The Red Wings score another goal. After the face off, play is stopped because there's an octopus on the ice. He changes stations. The Favre retirement speech is being aired again. The talking heads on ESPN are saying what a hero he is. What a true champion. Paul watches and then turns it back to the Blackhawks game.

It went well. He tries not to think about it, but he can't stop.

It went smoother than planned. He tries not to think about it.

He walks to the door and looks out at the empty dark backyard to where the woods begin. He knows he should call the dog, but instead he finishes the beer and watches the dark woods opposite the flood lights of his home.

There's somebody standing in the woods, looking at him.

The third period starts. The Red Wings score again.

Who's outside? Could be a neighbor. Could be a cop or that psychokiller.

Maybe nobody's out there after all.

Out the living room window, he doesn't see anyone. Just the dark, silent woods. He needs to bring Cooper in soon but decides to let him play a bit.

He opens another beer and then another and another. He goes into the cabinet and pours a bit of whiskey in a glass and downs it. He tries not to think about it.

At first, he didn't know if he could do it, didn't know if he had it in him. He figured he could hunt him, but he wasn't completely sure if he could plan it well enough and patiently wait for him like a deer. Or stalk him like a bear. He'd hunted wolf and bear and wild boar. So he figured he could. But he wasn't sure. Because there's always an element of chance in the hunt.

It was much easier than he thought. Scanning the kill zone with the binoculars, watching for any signs of movement. Looking up valley for any witnesses; calmly studying the valley for a full minute. Carefully backtracking from the blind. Crawling backwards beneath the trees and down the hill, and then slipping into the orange poncho, standing, moving silently to the road, into the truck. Pulling out from the glove compartment: a pair of costume glasses, a fake beard and a different orange hunter's hat.

Starting the loud truck in the silent woods.

Smoothly moving away from the valley and the Noname River. Easier than planned.

Except for the drive out: passing the tall man walking down the road, struggling with a tiny buck, the ropes slung over his shoulder, the man with the beard, the man with the blue eyes, the man who briefly looked up and then pulled the deer to the side of the road, the man who straightened, a hand in the air to wave, but also as if to ask for help, the man who looked up and saw, had to have seen, Paul as he passed.

They made eye contact, even through the costume—the fake beard, the fake glasses—even as Paul forced himself to look away and step on the gas. The man who probably recognized the truck, even though the license plate had been switched.

The game is over. The Red Wings beat up the Blackhawks again.

He takes a couple more pulls off the whiskey bottle and opens the last of the six-pack, then decides it's time to clean up.

He takes a long piss in the bathroom. A pair of pale palm leaves from the mass Susie attended three days ago have been tucked behind one corner of the wooden frame of a picture of the two of them and Cooper. The priest had spoken of giving oneself to the smiters, not hiding one's face in shame, of God taking the form of a servant, and the plot to steal this servant during a festival. At least that's what Susie told him the next day, when she was trying to reach him. He could feel her reaching out to him, but he couldn't do it, just couldn't take her hand in return.

Paul walks to the back door. Somebody's standing in the woods, watching him.

He looks out at the dark woods for a long time, waiting. He doesn't know what he's waiting for. For the man to move?

He decides to move first. He opens the door.

The first few trees are illuminated by the flood lights of the house. The thin trees that have grown up since the house was built. The woods beyond these are completely still. He doesn't see anybody. He pulls on his boots and steps outside.

He hears Cooper barking in the distance.

"Cooper!" he calls into the dark woods. He feels exposed. Reaches into the house and turns off the floods.

Cooper's barking at somebody.

He closes the backdoor to his home, and puts the empty six-pack beneath the tarp of his snowmobile. He goes into the garage and grabs the Louisville Slugger that leans in the corner. He waits for his eyes to adjust to the dark and then steps toward the woods.

There's a path that leads into the old woods behind the trees on their property. He walks on the path into the old woods, through the wet mud. He can hear Cooper barking like mad. The path goes up a hill. The moon is out now, and he can see.

It's chilly now that the sun's down. He should have brought a coat.

He doesn't hear or see anybody.

He follows the path toward the sound of Cooper's angry barking. Suddenly it cuts off with a rapid whine, and Paul knows that Cooper's hurt. Cooper never whines, never cries out, except once when he was a puppy and his cage collapsed on him.

He runs toward the sound of Cooper's whining. Someone's beating Cooper.

He rounds a bend in the forest. Then he's airborne— flying backwards—he feels the air leave him, smashes against the ground and spits up into the air.

Stars. The suffocating stars. He looks at the stars through the naked branches of a few trees. The wooden bat is gone. The dog is whining nearby, and he can't get his breath. In the darkness of the forest path, he feels for his bat with both palms, but he can't find it.

He rolls onto his side, looking around for his attacker, looking for the serial killer, the detective, somebody. His lungs are empty and scalding, and he's choking, on his hands and knees now, choking into the dirt, coughing it all up, and still he can't breathe, but he manages to get partially off the ground, and look around, fists clenched for the attacker.

He takes in air with one long gulp. He slowly stands. He sees the branch just beside him and realizes what's happened: he ran off the path in the darkness, and struck the low hanging limb of a tree. The dog is close now. He starts to move forward toward Cooper's whining. He steps on the bat, loses his footing as it rolls forward, twists his ankle, and falls to the mud of the forest path again.

He rolls to the side in the mud and pulls the bat from beneath him. He sees Cooper, whimpering as he hobbles down the moonlit path. His front right leg is broken or missing—his head hung down as he whimpers and limps toward Paul.

Paul stands and holds the bat, ready to strike Cooper's attacker.

Cooper reaches Paul and looks up at him. Paul touches his head—Cooper howls in pain. Paul kneels down. Cooper's whiskers are bloody. Paul touches Cooper's whiskers; Cooper whimpers and then gives a slight, almost ashamed growl. He can't find the cut. He looks at Cooper's front right leg in the darkness, picks it up, and the dog howls again.

He feels them then—porcupine quills cover Cooper's front right leg. He pulls at them and the dog fills the quiet night air with a humanlike howl that sounds like a child's cry, so human it unnerves Paul. He swears and apologizes to Cooper and pets him, and the dog howls again. Not bloody whiskers, but quills that cover his face. Then he panics and stands and looks at the dog's hind quarters and belly—they appear free from quills. He picks up the big dog and leaves the bat and walks back to the house.

He carries Cooper into the dark garage. He turns on the lights, still clasping Cooper tight to his chest. He puts Cooper on the work bench in the far corner of the garage, and pulls the chain of the fluorescent light fixture above it. In the bright light he examines Cooper's face: a few quills are dangerously close to his right eye, and many jut out of his nose, which is bleeding. Many more cover the sides of his snout, like thick black whiskers.

"Oh Cooper, poor Cooper," he's saying and: "Easy boy, it's okay Cooper, good boy, we'll fix you up, oh poor boy."

He tries to pull a couple out. Each time he pulls one out it tears out chucks of skin, and Cooper, who never complains, is howling. There are quills inside Cooper's nostrils. He gets a set of needle-nose pliers and pulls out a few—Cooper howls with each chunk of skin Paul yanks out. The dog's nose is bleeding freely now.

Suddenly Cooper chokes, and coughs. He's choking on the blood, so Paul wedges a thumb back behind Cooper's back molar on the left side and opens Cooper's mouth. Inside, quills are wedged in the tongue and gums and back where the larynx must be. He immediately puts down the bloody pliers and lifts Cooper up again by the hindquarters and stomach and pulls him to his chest. He puts the dog in the back of his truck, and then realizes that he's forgotten his keys. He goes back inside.

On his way to the living room, he walks past the painting called "First Hunt" that's of a black lab standing beside a group of ducks, and past a photograph of himself, Susie and Brien Grace kneeling in camouflage in a field with their shotguns, and Cooper sitting there alert, ears cocked, and a bevy of ducks laid out before them.

He finds the keys and heads back to the garage and to Cooper.

On the way, he opens the windows between the cab and bed. The wind howls in, but he can hear Cooper whining in the back. Paul is talking to him.

"It's okay, big guy. Just hang in there, Coop," Paul yells over his shoulder. "Hang in there. Good boy. Good dog. We're almost there."

He stops when he sees the emergency lights behind him. He looks for his driver's license. He realizes that he left it at home, and that he's covered in mud and probably smells like a distillery.

"Good evening, Paul," it's Jimmy's young deputy.

"Hey Mark," Paul says.

"Matt," the officer says.

"Right, listen—"

"You been drinking tonight?"

"It's an emergency."

"It better be—you were going twenty over."

"My dog, he's in the back. He got attacked by a porcupine. He's in pretty bad shape. It's an emergency, some of the quills—"

As if on cue, the dog gives a yelping whine again.

Matt goes to the back of the truck and shines his flash light through.

He comes back up to the pickup's cab.

"Okay, here's the deal—if you follow me to the animal hospital, I'll escort you, but I'm going to give you a ticket for speeding, and I'm going to escort you back home when this is over. You're only getting off easy because of Jimmy, got it?"

"Thanks Matt," Paul says, putting the pickup truck in gear.

The veterinarian has a salve for the quills. He gives Cooper a slight sedative and gets him up on the examining table.

"They're barbed at the ends," he explains. "And heat expands them. That's why you can't pull them out, why they go in easy, but stick there. They're like arrows at first, but they expand into fish hooks."

He puts the salve carefully on each one; the whole time he talks to Cooper and moves his hand in slow but firm strokes on his non-injured hindquarters.

Once that's done, he carefully pulls out each quill, even those in the nose and throat. Then he gives the dog a topical ointment, a shot to fight off infection and a bottle of pills to keep a fever down.

Matt is waiting for him outside, arms folded across his chest.

Paul carries Cooper, wrapped in a blanket and sedated, to the bed of the pickup. Matt lowers the bed. Paul slides Cooper in and puts the medicine on the dash of the truck.

Matt hands him a ticket for going 20 over in a 50 mile an hour zone.

"I had Jimmy call your wife," Matt says. "So don't drive, she'll be here soon."

"I won't, I appreciate it," Paul tells him.

"And don't drive if you're tanked. Call somebody next time, okay?"

"I'm sorry officer," Paul says.

Just then, Susie drives into the lot.

"Goodnight Paul," Matt says, getting in his squad car.

Susie takes one look at him and at the mud that covers his clothes and hair.

"Jesus Christ," she says.

"Yep," Paul answers.

"I got home and you weren't there. Then this call. What the fuck?"

"Yes," Paul agrees.

Susie gets in the driver's seat and slams the door.

While Susie glares at him, Paul goes to the bed of the truck and moves Cooper to the backseat of Susie's car. Her expression softens a bit at the sight of Cooper's drooping head. He goes back for the medicine and locks up his truck for the night.

Paul gets in the passenger side and straps himself in. Susie doesn't speak to him.

She pulls onto the county road that will take them back

home.

He can hear Cooper in the back seat, breathing deeply in his sedated sleep.

He watches the headlights illuminating the dark wet road before them.

He puts his temple against the window and feels himself drifting off. The mud is like it would feel if the guy in the woods had shot him, and the blood and bone were matted and coagulated in his hair.

A light snow fell, and fog partially obscured the ski hill.

She skied down the face of the hill and looked very pretty. He stood near the flat of the valley, watching her ski toward him. After two wide sweeping turns, she headed past him toward the chair lift. He followed her.

Almost no one was on Powderhorn, and they'd agreed to take the chair up to the top. She would ski a groomed trail, while he took a run through the woods; then they'd meet up at the bottom and take the chair up to the top and ski down for lunch.

The ropes were down, and no one was in line as they poled to the loading zone. Nearby, a ski bum with a nametag shoveled snow onto the chute, and a Bob Marley tune came over the stereo. The big wheel of the machine brought the chair around swiftly, and they sat into it. She sat on the right, and he on the left.

The hill was covered with new snow and fresh tracks. The chair took them up and away from the flat plain, toward the face of the slope that was covered by aspen and pine trees. They did not speak to each other, and that, he supposed, was a part of their arrangement.

She took off her gloves and motioned for him to hold her hands. Her hands were red from exercise, and her nail polish was chipped and fading.

He slid his gloves and poles under his left leg; the chair swung just a bit when he shifted his weight. He smiled at her and gently held her small hands in his own on the chairlift.

She had delicate wrists and pretty hands.

He thought she was delicate. And very beautiful.

Soon it would be three o'clock, and the runs would be nearly empty, and they would ski down to the restaurant, where the busboys would be vacuuming and cleaning up, and they would find a quiet corner and have lunch and eat apple strudel and drink hot wine. They'd take one last run or two, and then drive back through the dark woods to the cabin and have a jacuzzi.

She squeezed his right hand once as the chairlift neared the top, and she said something, but he didn't hear her. He was looking at her hands and remembering how she'd cried out the night before.

She slid her hands out of his hands. She clutched her poles and gloves in her right hand as they approached the top, her ski tips at the ready, and held the middle pole with her left hand. The diamond in her wedding ring was very large, and he knew he could never have afforded it.

Their skis touched the packed snow that covered the boards of the ramp at the top, and they stood and skied down the plank and away from each other toward their separate runs.

14

Tom watches as Kristen walks through the cabin. She is naked and beautiful.

She pours two glasses of a Napa cabernet sauvignon, and he watches her body, each imperfection somehow making her body more perfect, more beautiful than any woman he's ever been with before. She sets a glass of wine on the table beside him. She places a single beautiful knee on the couch a moment and bends slightly to kiss him. She smells of chlorine from the jacuzzi. Then she goes into the master bedroom suite. He hears the shower running.

Tom sits up on the couch and wraps a towel around his waist. He goes out on the balcony, where the two filets he placed on the grill earlier are beginning to sizzle and their aroma fills the night. The cool evening air feels good after the heat of the hot tub, sauna and shower. Snow lines the railing. Below, through the naked oak and birch trees, the bay of Lake Grace is frozen over and dark, and above and to his right, Tom can see the northern lights slowly sweeping up and down above the treetops of the forest.

And in the distance to the west, above the forested shoreline, he can also see the lights of the island town of Grace, which when his great grandfather arrived here over a hundred twenty years ago was still just an outpost on the edge of the wilderness, just a depot for mining and logging. Tom was conceived in that old town.

And when he dies, he wants his ashes to be scattered in this lake.

The steaks are nearly done, so he flips them and looks up at the wavering northern lights. Then he grips each of the filets with metal tongs, pulls them off the grill and places them on a plate. He goes back inside, sliding the balcony door behind him, and checks the potatoes in the oven. It's a casserole of sorts: potatoes finely sliced and covered with grated parmesan cheese. He also tosses a caesar salad.

Then he stands in the living room, sipping his wine. He feels good from so much exercise, five days' worth, and he stands there, breathing, filling his lungs with the fresh Northwoods air.

There's one of Drew's paintings hanging on the wall. A landscape portrait of northern Wisconsin. It's arguably decent. Maybe a little too realistic.

There's another of Adam's Martin guitar, which is actually quite good.

People wanted to know why Drew didn't turn out to be a painter. Tom knew, but he never said: it wasn't a lack of talent: it was a lack of vision. It was the subject matter he chose to depict and the style he used to depict it. That, and the need to please his father, which was why Drew was still trying to run the company, even though his father had already passed on him. That's why he'd gone to law school. Anyone else would have moved to Palm Beach or the Hamptons by now.

But Tom will not be able to afford the life that Drew can, or that Adam could.

He and Kristen are enjoying one of the few luxuries left to him; they are staying at his family's cabin up in Grace. The last thing from his great-grandfather's will that Brien and Tom still had any claim on, the big old log cabin sitting on a bay of Lake Grace.

And Tom knows that Kristen has been here, years ago, at the Fisher's nearly identical cabin across the bay, with his cousin Adam, back when they were engaged.

And that Brien thinks she's unstable.

And that Brien's interest in her is more than a professional one, or a collegial one, or a friendly one.

And that he too is deeply in love with her.

And that now she has decided to wear her engagement

ring. Maybe that would help with her depression. Tom doubts it; in fact, he thinks the opposite; still, he has decided that it wasn't his place to say.

She calls to him from the bedroom. She wants to make love with him. Wearing the ring that Adam gave her. Tom has a problem with that, but when he crawls into bed with her, all he can think is how damn gorgeous she is.

After they make love, Tom and Kristen have dinner. The steaks and potatoes are cold, and Tom heats them up in the oven.

They eat their salads while the oven warms their food.

Kristen finishes her salad first. Then she sets down her fork on the side of her plate and looks at Tom.

"You've stopped writing," she says.

He nods.

"Why?" she asks.

"I used to think it was important. That it mattered somehow."

"But now you don't?"

"No. Maybe. I don't know."

"Why did you start?"

"It was fun at first."

He stands and gets the steaks and the potato dish from the oven. The heat of the oven feels good on his shoulders as he pulls the metal plate out with an oven mitt.

He sets a plate in front of her and then sits opposite her with his own plate.

"It stopped being fun?" she asks.

"Sometimes it is. But sometimes I write about stuff defensively."

"Defensively?" she asks.

"Things hurt you, you know? Like when something bad happens. So I write about it, because it can't hurt me if I write about it."

He cuts into the steak and adds, "But that's not true."

The filet is medium rare. He takes a bite.

"Because you feel it," she concludes.

The food is very good. Tom chews for a moment before speaking.

Tom nods, "More so. More so than when it's just made up. Even more so than when it happened the first time."

She is looking at him, eating. She doesn't say anything, so he continues: "The pain becomes more intense on the retelling."

Kristen thinks about that and nods.

"Pain is relative," she tells him.

Those words make his stomach feel sick.

"But I want you to try, okay?" she tells him. "We'll both try."

"To do what?" he asks, lost in the conversation.

"To live with the pain," she says.

Tom nods.

Tom wakes in the night, and Kristen is crying.

The bed is shaking. She's trying to be quiet.

"Oh Kristen," he says. "What's up? What's the matter?"

She doesn't say anything.

"Is it Adam? Or Craig?"

She lets out a sob.

He turns on the light. Her face is wet with tears.

"I fucked up, Tom. Okay?" she says.

"Okay," he says.

"Just turn off the light and go back to sleep," she says.

"Tell me," he says.

"I can't," she says.

She leaves the room. He can't sleep.

He finds her in the living room, staring at the remnants of the fire. Tomorrow, they'll drive back to Chicago, and he will stay with her for a time before driving back to

Appleton.

"It's Adam, isn't it," he says gently. "It's too close."

"It's the same as with Adam," she says.

He looks at her, full of understanding and sympathy.

"And different too," she adds.

"That's the problem, I think," Tom says. "It's too close for you."

"You're right," she says quickly.

Tom has a dream that night. He is skiing with his cousin Adam on a huge mountain. The chain rose out of the fog of Lake Superior, and it reminded him of Colorado, but he was convinced it was Tibet.

He has to leave, and to leave Adam there, on that mountain, and a black helicopter takes him away, and he looks back at the long stretch of dark blue and white mountains as beautiful as a picture of the earth from space and as infinite as the night sky.

Back in Lincoln Park, they find a place to park near her apartment. They are barely inside the door when Tom tries to kiss her. But Kristen pushes him off, and tells him she wants to grab lunch—she's starving.

They go to a little café that has tables outside beneath heat lamps. She orders a bottle of cabernet franc and finishes most of it herself. The waitress approaches and Kristen orders a steak and then digs into the bread. Tom orders a salad Niçoise, not pronouncing the z sound at the end, pronouncing it "nee-swah."

"So that's how they're pronouncing Niçoise in Appleton these days?" Kristen asks between mouthfuls.

Then she orders a second bottle. And a third.

Tom pays the bill, and they walk back together. She walks a few steps in front of him the whole way.

Back at her apartment, she slops down onto her couch.

Tom stands there, uncertain.

"Kristen, what you said," he begins, "up north—"

She has a hand over her face and interrupts him.

"Look Tom, just stay the fuck away from me," Kristen says, annoyed.

"What? Why?"

"I tried," she says. "I really did. But I can't do this anymore."

"What do you mean?" His heart hurt.

"Everyone that gets close to me gets hurt," she says.

Tom nods: "I was afraid you'd think that."

He sits beside her and places a hand on her shoulder.

"Don't think that way, okay?" he says gently.

She turns away from him, arms across her stomach. She bends over slightly for a minute, as if she might be sick. She is moaning. She is not right.

He reaches out for her again and places a comforting hand on her back.

"They weren't your fault. They were accidents."

She stands, crying. She heads for the door and right out it.

"Tom, just stay away," she manages before the door slams shut.

Left alone in her apartment, Tom goes to the balcony. Outside is Chicago, where he was born. He spent little time here as a child, but somehow the city has always seemed like home. Lincoln Park is across the street, teeming with people enjoying the spring air.

He cannot conceptualize himself without her. It just doesn't make sense. But he can't stay here.

He has to let her go. It's too close for her. Adam, then Craig.

It's too close.

Craig handed her a shot and smiled.

She took it, touched it to his shot glass and then to her friends' glasses.

Then she slammed it back.

15

Paul calls her cellular phone again, but Kristen ignores his call.

She stands in the unfinished loft in Milwaukee that may become her office and apartment someday.

She is trying to make her mind up, but she can't.

The bar was beginning to spin. She could feel it. She was losing her grip.

She grabbed onto Craig's arm, and he steadied her.

"We have to leave," she told him.

"Just one more shot," Craig gestured to the bar, where he'd just paid for a round.

Craig passed out the shots to Tom and the others.

"We have to leave," she said again.

He handed her the shot. Kristen lifted her shot and held it up with the others.

She tilted her head back and gulped it down. She was looking at the ceiling when the light began to darken, and she felt herself falling backwards. She was on the ground suddenly, and there was a loud noise, and Craig was helping her up.

Her friends were making loud noises, cheering for her, patting her on the back.

She felt herself stumbling as they left, and she leaned on Craig, who led her to her car. She fastened her seatbelt and drifted off.

She wants to call Tom. She wants to have a normal life.

But it isn't possible anymore.

She calls the sheriff again, the one she knows is

investigating her brother.

She can't do it, and hangs up.

Kristen woke up in the morning, and her head was pounding.

It was already eleven o'clock.

She tried to think. She remembered the bar. Dancing with Craig. Then something happened.

She found her way into the bathroom and took a long, hot shower, standing with her head beneath the stream of hot water for many minutes. The shower began to run cold by the time she turned it off.

She made coffee and ate what breakfast she thought she could hold down: a piece of dry wheat toast. She skipped her vitamins, but managed to take an ibuprofen.

It wasn't until she went to the bathroom that she realized something was wrong.

She defecated, and it felt wrong.

When she looked into the bowl, she realized that a snot-like substance was surrounding and clinging to the fecal matter. She felt hot and sick all at once, realizing what it was. She reached and felt it. Semen.

She reared back, dizzy. Then she vomited.

Without thinking, she flushed the toilet.

She thinks about calling Tom.

She thought she was incapable of love. That it was impossible for her.

That they'd missed each other.

But she isn't sure anymore.

And she did love him. She did.

She thinks of calling. Thinks of the call. Envisions it.

It goes to his voicemail.

She imagines what she would say, "Tom. I'm sorry. I'm so sorry we missed each other."

.

The doorbell rang. It was Craig.

He held up two six-packs of craft beer with a smile.

How's the hangover? he asked.

She said nothing.

She walked right into the bedroom. He crawled in bed with her. She watched his eyes widen in surprise as she took off her clothes. As he stood and stripped off his clothes quickly, she found herself shaking, and she rolled over. He lay back down. He tried to roll her over and kiss her, but she grabbed him and moved him toward her backside.

This is how you like it isn't it?

What? he asked.

Come on, do me, just get it over with, she whispered.

He allowed her to move him.

Suddenly she stopped him, asking, Is this how you did it last night?

What are you talking about? he asked.

When I was passed out? she asked. She rolled over and pushed him hard.

What? he stood and looked at her.

She knelt on the bed and continued: I won't have sex with you, so you wait until I'm passed out and then do that?

What are you talking about? he demanded again.

She punched at him, trying to hit him in the face.

What the fuck? he asked, shielding himself, backing off.

He put on his clothes.

What the fuck, Kristen? he asked again.

She grabbed a nearby book and threw it at him. She stood, found a shoe and threw it at him. It smashed into a painting on the wall, which fell to the hardwood floor, and the glass shattered.

He was out the door and did not look back.

The deputy, Matt, is about her age and is definitely checking her out as he leads her back to Jimmy's office.

The sheriff is muttering something as they walk into his office—it sounds like Italian, but she only hears a snippet. Something about fire and belief.

"Hi Sheriff Baker," she says.

Before he disappears back into the labyrinth of the Department, Matt nods at her, giving his best cowboy impression, touching his hat and saying, "Ma'am."

Jimmy stands and shakes her hand.

"Kristen," he says. "Well now, aren't you a sight? What can I do for you?"

"I need to talk to you," she says.

"You come up all the way from Chicago to see me?" he asks.

"Actually I was in Milwaukee for work, so it's not as far," she says.

"Still an hour and a half," he says.

"It took me just over an hour," she says quickly, then adds, "But I wasn't speeding."

He smiles at her kindly.

He gestures to a plastic chair that sits before his antiqued desk. She sits and smiles back at him.

"What'd you like to chat about?" he asks her.

When Craig was gone, she sank down against a wall.

She stared at the broken picture on the floor, and she began to cry.

She punched herself in the leg. She punched herself again in the leg. It felt good, the pain felt so good, so she slapped her face, but that didn't feel right somehow, and then she hit her clenched fists against her arms and legs as hard as she could. She punched herself in the stomach and then picked up the picture on the floor and severed one of the limbs of the frame from the rest of it and smashed it against the floor so that there was no glass in the frame, and then smashed it repeatedly against her legs, arms and stomach.

She hesitates and then says, "I want to talk with you."

"What do you want to discuss?" the sheriff asks her.

She looks at him for a long time.

"It was me," she tells him, and once she begins talking, she can't stop.

After she meets with the sheriff, she heads back to Chicago, but makes a quick detour north through the downtown of Two Rivers to drive past the diner.

She passes by outside.

She can't bring herself to go inside or to see her mother. Or Paul.

She finds herself crying. She calls Brien.

She gets his voicemail.

Hi, you've reached Brien Grace. Please leave a message. Thanks.

But she can't bring herself to leave a message.

What message could she leave?

She thinks about that for a time as she drives through the old decaying town. She could text him, and she thinks of a text to lure him—he would laugh sympathetically, with understanding and sorrow and love, and would call her back if she sent this quotation: "I am alone, now, truly alone, and absolutely isolated from any known life. I am it. I feel this powerfully—not as fear or loneliness—but as awareness, anticipation, satisfaction, confidence, almost exultation."

Although she is worried she might actually feel just that, she does not text him. Brien is broken, nearly as broken as she is. His clinical outlook now has replaced his old funny, philosophical self. Wild, kind and easy-going.

Now guarded. Careful. Wounded. Religious. It's sad really what the war did to him. She doesn't want to add to the torment. A hero. They were all her heroes.

Leaving Two Rivers, she drives past the rusted tugboats in the river. Rusted factories. Old shops: some abandoned, some still clinging on.

She talks to herself, quoting some of her favorite passages from Brien's dissertation: To dwell is to garden.

She decides to drive south, along the lake.

Maybe it would cheer her up.

Lake Michigan has been whipped up into a frenzy, and she watches the waves smash the shore as she heads south, back toward Manitowoc, where she'll head west and catch the freeway south.

She whispers, Being and time determine each other reciprocally, but in such a manner that neither can the former - Being - be addressed as something temporal nor can the latter - time - be addressed as a being.

The road turns toward the west and then southwest, following the lake to her left.

Ahead of her, to the southwest and in the distance, the factories of Manitowoc loom as giant gray monstrosities as the cold dusty sun dies into a bank of winter clouds.

The possible ranks higher than the actual.

Craig and Tom were in the casino playing roulette and black jack. They were betting heavily.

Tom was due to ship out in a couple weeks. Craig was to start BCT in about a month.

Tom was getting crushed. Craig eventually took his winnings and just stood back, watching his good friend lose and laughing a bit.

Finally they gave up, and Tom and Craig went up to the bar.

I coulda had class, Tom was saying afterwards, joking around, quoting Brando, I coulda been a contenda, I coulda been sumbuddy, insteada a bum.

Craig knew he was joking, but also that he was actually pissed off he lost.

It didn't matter, Craig was thinking. It was all done now. What ifs beat what is out of the gates, out of the five-deck shoe, but after that the what is is all that matters, and the what ifs don't mean shit. All your hoping and praying and crying and thinking won't change what is. What's done is done, it is what it is, and there isn't anything that's going to change it ever. Never ever never. Forever and never, amen.

16

Craig hated this job. Only temporary. A way to make money. Get cash, before figuring out whether to go to college or join the army.

Twenty an hour. Cash.

He stood outside his father's house in Two Rivers in the cold as the big truck came up in the dark with its headlights on.

This isn't a permanent thing, Craig thought. He's just moonlighting.

Mark, who knows his dad from way back, has a hurt back. Needs someone to pick up the slack for him, so he doesn't lose his seniority with the company.

The weirdo who worked with Mark opened the door and stood on the running board, leaning out and giving him an odd salute. Craig held up a hand briefly, gathered his backpack and coffee mug, and climbed up into the truck.

The weirdo, Oscar, made Craig sit in the middle seat, between him and Mark, which wasn't a seat at all, but just a metal hump that rose between the driver's seat and the passenger seat. Must house some mechanism for the big truck.

Oscar slid in beside Craig, and Craig felt confined as Mark put the truck in gear.

Inside the truck was warm, and Mark greeted Craig with a nod before hauling the big steering wheel to the left and pulling the truck back into the street.

Oscar was bitching about the upcoming election. He hated both Gore and Bush. Thought we should have more choices. Thought it was going to be a close election. Who gives a fuck?

They pulled up to the first street, and the cans were lined up along the road.

He and Oscar got out and pulled the black plastic carts from the side of the road.

Craig worked the left side of the street, while Oscar worked the right.

The cans varied from house to house: old-style frozen metal cans, plastic black tall bins with rollers, brown or tan or green squat plastic cans. They dumped the garbage bags from the cans into their respective carts and when they were full, they took them to the back of the truck and dumped them into the hopper. Every so often, Mark used the crusher blade to compact the trash.

Most of the trash had been mercifully bagged and tied shut. A few cans, though, had been tipped over in the night by raccoons, the plastic bags torn through by little claws. They spent ten seconds or so with a shovel, scooping the scattered items into the cart, just dealing with the terrible smell.

It was better though than in the summer when he had subbed for Mark. The colonies of white maggots wriggling in the bottom of every tenth can made him nearly puke every time. There was no getting used to it. Writhing individually, but moving like some singular animal.

The morning was slow at first, and Oscar had finally shut up. They finished four streets and then worked their way back toward the first. They left the neighborhood, and as the sun was rising in the cold darkness, they began to work on a twisted street lined by trees. Some old ravine they've turned into a subdivision.

Now the morning was picking up, and Mark began to chatter between jobs. He'd been in the army. He wanted Craig to sign up. Good benes, he said, Little action and good benes. And you get to shoot guns all the time. Blow shit up.

Oscar and Craig left the warm confines of the garbage truck for the next route.

When it was done, they climbed back in, and Mark

continued to chat about how he should sign up.

Craig was still thinking about college, and as they drove to the next neighborhood, he said so.

You would have gone before now, Oscar told him. Trust me I know education, you would have gone before now.

If he wants to go, let him go, Mark said.

You won't learn shit in college that you don't already know, Oscar said. Seriously, I learned the hard way, after I'd spent two hundred thousand dollars.

Bullshit, Mark said.

What? I did, Oscar said.

Mark made a sort of groan in the back of his throat and looked out the driver's side window.

I know this, there's nothing in college or medical school or graduate school that you can't learn here, right fucking here in this truck, Oscar said, slamming his hands down on the dash board for emphasis.

They pulled down the long forest road to the dumping site.

Seriously, it's all about learning the spirit of a thing. The soul of a thing. Something people in school don't know anything about, Oscar was saying.

But Mark wasn't listening to him. Ahead of them were three squad cars and five officers dressed in cowboy hats and long coats.

They all had shotguns pointed at the truck.

Craig was raised up, and vulnerable, sitting in the middle on the hump that separated the two seats. Craig immediately raised his hands, something he'd never done before in his life. Oscar raised his hands too, and Mark reluctantly did too.

Ah, shit, Mark said.

Nobody do anything stupid, Oscar said, grinning, and Craig looked at him. If any of them did something stupid, it would certainly be Oscar. One of the officers stepped up to the truck as Mark opened the door. The officer pointed the shotgun in at them.

Marcus Agamovich? he asked.

Craig realized he was talking to Mark, who gave a reluctant, Yeah.

I'm Sheriff Baker, and I have a warrant for your arrest.

Mark breathed out a long sigh and looked up at the ceiling of the truck.

Craig was amazed. He couldn't believe it as the sheriff read Mark his rights: Mr. Agamovich, you have the right to remain silent, anything you say can and will be used against you in a court of law. You have the right to an attorney. If you cannot afford one, one will be provided for you.

Mark finally stepped down from the truck, and once he had been cuffed by a deputy, the other men raised their shotguns, pointing them into the air, so that they were not pointed inside the truck. Craig lowered his hands.

You boys are free to go, Sheriff Baker said, looking up at Craig and Oscar. The sheriff turned back to his squad car. Craig didn't move; Oscar clambered down from the passenger side and made his way around to the driver's side. He climbed up and slammed the heavy door shut. Craig slid over to the passenger seat, watching Mark's bowed head in the back of the squad car.

Gawd Da-yam, Oscar said, pretending as if he had a southern accent. Now how 'bout that sheeyt for a Wednesday morning?

They took the truck the rest of the way to the dump site and dumped it while they watched as the officers took Mark away in the back of the sheriff's squad car.

Well, Craig, Oscar said, It seems you've been promoted.

Is that so? Craig said.

That's right, Oscar said.

Nope, Craig said, shaking his head, Today's my last day.

Why's that?

Oh. No reason, just because.

Then the company's gonna need to find a new squad for this rig, Oscar said.

Why? Craig asked.

Because I got a new job as a trucker, and start next week, Oscar said, We was training you to take over for me, seein' as how you haven't made a—a—a—

Craig looked at Oscar, who continued, suddenly formal: A decision on your dilemma as to whether to attend college or defend the country as a serviceman.

Oscar pulled the leveler, and the truck shuddered and lowered the bed back into position.

The room was empty.
Concrete walls.
The only thing to fill it was his own thoughts.
His own memories.

17

The door is constructed of metal. It's heavy. There is no way to open it without a guard. Oscar looks at it. There's nothing else to do.

He stares at it for hours before the guard arrives.

He has been in solitary in the Winter Correctional Facility for three days.

The door opens with a loud banging sound as an electric current makes the heavy metallic bolts fire open.

The guard pulls it open toward him a bit.

"Stand up and face the wall," the guard says.

Oscar does as he's commanded.

"Place your hands behind your back."

He does so, and the guard enters and shackles his hands together.

"Put your feet together," the guard says. Oscar is wearing the white socks they give everyone, and the brown plastic strap of the thin sandals runs over the white sock between his big toe and his other toes. When Oscar complies, the guard shackles his feet and runs a line between his feet and his hands.

The metal shackles are cold on Oscar's hands and feet, and his feet are cold, and the orange jumpsuit he wears is so thin, he constantly feels like he's on the verge of coughing.

"Turn around," the guard commands. The guard has gloves on, and he takes Oscar's right arm and leads him out of the holding cell.

Once they are back in his unit, beyond the triple unit of electrically locked solid metal doors, the guard unshackles Oscar.

"Only good behavior now, Friedrich," the guard tells

Oscar as he swings the shackles in several long circles.

Oscar walks through the open door and into the lobby of the pod. The guards are all in the central unit that is shielded by dark glass and is dark inside, so he can only see shadows of them occasionally, when they stand and walk from one terminal to another.

He sits down at a table.

"You lookin' te die?" a black man sitting at the table whispers.

Oscar looks at him: "To what are you referring, kind sir?"

"This my table," the inmate says.

Oscar stands, bows with a flourish, and moves to another table.

His buddy Mark from the old days is there in the cafeteria. Oscar guesses he's been in and out over the last eight years—since their stint together in Two Rivers on the garbage run. And they did a bit of time together at the Red Granite last fall when Oscar was revoked for a time, but Oscar didn't get an opportunity to speak to him because they were in different housing units.

Oscar makes his way over and sits down beside him. Mark wears a look of confusion. Oscar shakes his hand.

"Haven't seen you in a while. What'd you do?" Oscar asks.

Mark says nothing.

"I went through Dodge, how about you?"

Mark nods: "Everyone goes through there."

"That's a real clusterfuck, hey?"

"Yep," Mark agrees.

Oscar gestures to the walls of the Winter facility.

"Did you know that there are one of these in every county?" Oscar asks.

Mark looks at him.

"Some of them have two or three. Milwaukee has like

five."

"So?" Mark says.

"Then there's the sheriff county lockups. The jails. They're near the courthouses. And the police all have jails too. All those facilities. That's what they call them. Facilities."

Oscar starts laughing, "We lose our faculties in their facilities."

Mark says nothing.

Oscar continues: "They say they're full, but that's bull. They ain't really full. That's just them talking, so they can build more."

"Who?"

"The intelligencia, friend. My class of people. And the politicians. And the rich. They just want to build more and more barracks and prisons."

"You got a point?"

"No point, friend," Oscar says calmly. "Just a premise. You know what a premise is?"

"I know what a fucking premise is, man," Mark whispers. "You got some sort of big thought, and I wish you'd just shut the fuck up."

"Hey, friend, there's no bad will here," Oscar says. "No bad, no bad, no bad intentions. Just a premise."

"And what's that?" Mark says evenly.

"You ever see the airports, the private airports?" Oscar says calmly. "They got one of those in every county too. They're surrounded by barbed wire, just like the jails. Just like these facilities. Just like the army barracks and the train stations and the factories. All surrounded by guards and barbed wire."

"I don't get what you're getting at," Mark says, annoyed.

"When the end comes, that's how they'll get us rounded up."

Mark grunts.

"They will be rounding us up—well, not you and me, they already got us. But the rest of the people—the good people—the rest of humanity. They'll round them up, and put them into the prisons, by the truck loads: hundreds, thousands, tens of thousands."

"How will they do that?"

"In cattle cars," Oscar says simply with a thin smile. "You ever seen cows in them, as you drive by, through the holes they have in the side? Now imagine them filled with people, with their hands sticking through the holes. They'll fly them into each county and then take them from the airports right to the courthouses in cattle cars and then straight to the prisons."

Oscar closes his eyes. He can see it: filthy fingernails sticking out through the circular holes in the metal of the cattle cars. Hear it: the low drone of the wheels of the heavy trucks interrupted occasionally by the ruts of the broken highway.

"Why? Why would they do that?" Mark demands. Oscar looks at him.

"To control them," he says. "And so that they have a food supply."

Mark looks around the room and then back at Oscar.

Oscar continues, "So that they can eat them."

Mark stands and moves to another table. His fists are clenched. He immediately begins to whisper to another inmate.

The trucks will whine on the roads as they carry their fodder to the courthouse.

Mark is still whispering to the other inmates.

Oscar knows what they are talking about, and he doesn't like it. He stands up on one of the metallic tables. He sees the shadows moving in the control room behind the tinted black glass. He knows he only has a few moments.

He raises his arms in the air and stomps on the table.

"I am the lone wolf!" he proclaims. "I am the Wolf King!"

"Here we go again," one of the white inmates mutters.

The guards are hurrying over. The inmates stare at him. A guard approaches and makes a snapping, pointing gesture at him, while nodding in an exaggerated manner and putting a hand on his duty belt.

Oscar ignores him.

"Do you hear me?" he demands. "Do you fear me?"

Prisoners begin catcalling.

"Man think he a wolf!" one yells.

"Fear you?" an inmate says in a mockingly high voice, making a smacking noise of disgust and adding, "Cracka, we own you."

"We're all owned!" Oscar shouts back. "We all owned from the day we got born! Every one of you owned from the day your mama shit you out! And now they feed us this crap?"

"Go fuck yourself," someone yells back.

The guard has pulled out his Taser and is eyeing the crowd. Oscar kicks a plate from the table, and it clatters against the floor.

"And I don't mean just the food! I mean every damn thing! The rules! All their fucking rules! One hour in the yard! Only light is one speck of space overhead in the rain! One yard of space for all us animals! The smoke from the factory poisoning us day and night! Lights out at eight! No books for all us animals! Not allowed to use the workout room or the library unless you blow the blue shirts! Divided by race! Three choices for us animals! Black mob! Mexican cartel! Or the fucking Nazis! Join one or get AIDS and die! How do you like eating this shit? Don't you love eating this shit!"

They are all standing and yelling back at him and at each other.

"How do you like the zoo?" He exclaims. "How do you like your zoo?"

"Buddy, get down!" the guard yells at him, but he's looking around at the other inmates. There are more guards around the table now, and Oscar stamps his feet and chants: "We love our zoo! We love our zoo! We love our zoo!"

Some of the inmates start chanting with him. Leaders of the white, black and Hispanic inmates are pointing at each other and arguing.

"We love our zoo! We love our zoo!" The inmates chant.

"Down! Now!" The guard shouts.

Oscar points at him and shouts, "This guy wants to eat your brain for breakfast!"

The whole place erupts.

Five guards rush him at once, and drag him down and away through the chaos.

Back to solitary at last.

Oscar is grinning as they carry him off.

A hypothesis is a proposed explanation for observable phenomenon.

A hypothesis that is tested becomes a working hypothesis.

A working hypothesis, upon being universally accepted, becomes a theory.

A theory differs from a law because scientific laws are considered universal and invariable facts of the physical universe, and as such they are analytic statements, usually having empirically determined constants.

18

Suddenly it's spring, and those persons still wearing winter coats, or even sweaters, seem outlandish and foreign. The change is undeniable, radical and enduring.

Winter hung on and hung on and hung on to the land and their souls, and then late winter arrived, more inhumane than the winter snows, more troubling than the winter sorrows: cold, wet, brown. Yet all along it is coming, something undeniable is happening, full of hope, if not light nor warmth, and then all at once it is here.

It is that the land has become green once more. The forests, the farms, the fields, even the suburbs and towns are suddenly filled with green. Even the interstates and highways are no longer frozen, filthy and salted-over corridors, but avenues populated by green deciduous trees, various grasses and even flowering plants.

Even the chilly nights, frosted-over mornings, or the rapid plunge of temperature in mid-day as the wind shifts and brings in an arctic blast from the north or from that chilly inland sea called Michigan does nothing to minimize the significance of spring in eastern Wisconsin. Seven months of brown and gray and white and black. And then the sudden resurgence of green land beneath blue sky.

As simplistic and basic as anything in the world, and yet almost nothing amazes Brien more than this change in the natural world itself. He will think about that change the night after he returns from Winter, while working on his dissertation, thoughts triggering others: thinking of the seasons; the migration and hibernation of the animals; the impact of seasons on our moods, the melancholy of fall, the joy of spring; seasonal affective disorder; the return of Persephone to her mother; the failed journey up of Orpheus with his lyre; the planetary change as our orbit causes the tilting of earth's northern pole toward our star; a blue ball, frozen on the top and bottom; a bright oblong, in reality only slightly colder at the poles, endlessly spinning through the darkness.

Time and Memory: What stands in the way of the ability to perceive the "present" for the being in time?

PAST	PRESENT	FUTURE
Rejection (Denial K)		Ideation (Denial I)
------------------------------	X	-----------------------------
Idealization (F, G or D)		Imagining (Fa, De or L)

Definitions:

Where X stands for the being situated in the present moment, unable to perceive the present actuality.

Where Rejection (Denial K) is the inability to perceive present actuality, prior to its becoming past actuality.

Where Idealization (F, G, or D) is the purposeful or unintentional inability to recall past actuality.

Where Ideation (Denial I) is the inability to perceive present actuality and understand its import on future actuality.

Where Imagining (Fa, De or L) is the purposeful or unintentional inability to envision future actuality.

Where Denial stands in the way of intelligence in terms of a being's capacity for data storage.

Where K and I stand for Knowledge and Insight.

Where F, G, and D stand for Forgetting, Glorification or Demonization.

Where Idealization and Imagining stand in the way of a being's capacity for data retrieval.

Where Fa, De, or L stand for Fantasy, Depression, or Lack of Foresight.

Where Actuality is defined as objective truth, or that truth beyond the perceiver's subjective perspective.

.

Brien arrived in the town of Winter at 10 in the morning.

He'd left Appleton at six, and made it to King before seven. He had a great breakfast at the King's Table, and drove the rest of the way up to the town.

On the drive, his thoughts were clear for the first time since Kristen's break down.

He was going to do his job at $80/hour and go home to his wife. He wasn't going to speak with Kristen again. She had Paul and Tom to care for her.

Brien stopped at a gas station, filled up his truck and bought a soda. He drove past the old shops in town, all sorts of mom-and-pop shops that Brien wanted to check out, but he was in a hurry, and so he continued on toward the farms. He'd listened to sports talk shows and alternative stations on the way up until the radio stations had all turned to static or religion. His thoughts had wandered during the drive. If superstring theory dictates nine dimensions, then there must really be nine times four if time is truly the fourth dimension and interacts with each. Or maybe it's just three to second power before time is factored in, and three to the third power after, and possibly add one odd one for time's dimension again.

The prison loomed before him on a plot of barren land atop a hill. The Winter Correctional Facility.

He'd never been to the town of Winter before, and it had taken some navigating.

He got out and locked his truck. Snow was coming down, and the wind was picking up. He walked toward the first building, which was the entrance, separated from the rest of the prison by a big yard.

Inside, a guard sat at a large open desk beside a metal

detector and a scanner.

"Brien Grace," he told him, and the guard looked at a clipboard and nodded.

"Put your bag on the belt, it has to go through the scanner, plus any keys, belts, or anything else that's metal."

Brien complied.

"You can lock up your keys and the bag in a locker. Here's a token," the guard said, handing him a worn yellow token with slots running the length of either side, and pointing to a bank of lockers that lined the back wall.

Brien did what he was told, then the guard pointed a thumb at the wall and went back to reading his book. Brien realized that he was supposed to walk through an ugly, pale green metallic door that had a thick window installed. As he approached, the latch inside gave off a buzzing sound, followed by a loud click. Brien opened the heavy door and stepped inside an alcove, where there was a second metallic door, precisely like the first.

Once the first door had slammed shut, the second door too gave off a loud click, and he opened that door too. Outside, there was a small paved area: a triangle that was about forty feet in diameter at its base, lined by fences topped with narrowly spaced coils of razor wire. It was like half of a baseball diamond, and opposite him there was a heavy fence door. He walked to that door and waited. A security camera pointed down at him.

Beyond this new gate, three guard towers overlooked an open field on either side of a concrete walkway lined on either side by high fences topped by razor wire.

The fenced door clicked open, and Brien walked through. He was now in a narrow run of fencing topped with more coiled razor wire that stretched up a small hill from the fenced door to another building—part of the main complex of the prison, Brien assumed as he walked in the cold, as opposed to the portcullis where he'd stored his personal effects.

He reached the far door; it was a door with black-tinted glass this time, and he heard the latch click open. He opened that door, just as heavy as the other ones. Inside, there was a reception desk opposite him beyond a plate glass window, but the guard inside just pointed to his right.

Brien turned left and walked where the guard had pointed. There he saw yet more doors, a series of three panels of glass, transparent, set in the sickly green metal. Again, he heard a click and opened the first door.

He entered a library of sorts. There were a few tables here and there. And a few rows of short book shelves, about four feet high, against two of the far walls. There were several inmates meeting with people in plain clothes. There were four guards sitting at a huge desk that was cordoned off from the rest of the room. One had his feet up on his portion of the desk. Another had a pen and gestured with it at Brien.

"Mr. Grace, right?"

Brien nodded.

"You here to shrink some heads?"

"You betcha," Brien said.

The guard gave him a curious look, part mischievous, part suspicious, and then nodded.

"Your freak of a client sure needs it," he said.

"Cut it out, Daniel," the guard with his feet up said, gesturing and adding, "He's in Room 8, right down over there."

He was the Captain. He had on a white shirt.

Brien walked toward the little room, opened the door, which was unlocked, and walked inside.

His client had a shaved head.

"What do you think of my fortress?" he asked.

"Your fortress?" Brien responded with a look.

"Do you know how difficult it is for people to get at me in here?"

"Who wants to get at you?"

"People. Enemies," he said nonchalantly.

"Okay," Brien said. "Mister—"

"Call me Wolfgang, okay?" the prisoner interrupted.

"It says here your real name's—"

"Just call me Wolfgang, or Wolf for short. Got it?"

"Yeah, you bet." Brien decided that Wolfgang was going to try to claim a lack of competency to proceed.

"Okay, Wolfgang," Brien said. "Your lawyer is a friend of mine."

Wolfgang appeared unimpressed.

"So I know you'll have good representation."

Wolfgang said nothing, then swallowed and said, "So do I have to comply with this court order?"

"No, but if you don't, I'll have to note that for the judge."

Wolfgang sat back, looking cold and angry.

"Let's start with an AODA assessment," Brien said.

Wolfgang denied having any problems with alcohol or drugs.

"I noticed you went to medical school," Brien said.

"Yeah, that was a brilliant idea."

"You left?"

"Flunked out. Bastards kicked me out."

"And you were charged with forging prescriptions around the same time?" Brien asked.

"Look," he said, formal. "I did get charged, I did get convicted, and after my initial confinement, I was released from that crime."

"Onto extended supervision," Brien said.

"Yeah, onto E S."

"But now you've been revoked."

"It's a short time," Wolfgang smirked. "I got five months on a two year E S run."

"Okay," Brien said. He paged through the report:

"And you were kicked out of medical school because you were forging prescriptions for whom?"

"Friends," Wolfgang said nonchalantly. "Colleagues. Acquaintances."

"Yourself?" Brien asked.

Wolfgang shrugged.

"So why the name change?" Brien asked.

"What do you mean?"

"You changed your name from Oscar DeMareni to Friedrich Corvus Wolfgang Aristotle Drakos."

"I used to study metaphysics in college."

"Really?"

"That's why I went into anesthesia. I figured it was the closest I could come to God."

"Knocking people out?

"Exactly—inducing a trance-like state. What's the difference between a spiritual meditative trance and an induced medicated one?"

"The drugs?" Brien suggested.

"Yes, but what if they are the same states? All these thousands of years, the yogis in Asia and Christian mystics of Europe have been trying to get at a state of consciousness, and modern Western science leaps over all of them in a few short years and produces something so amazing, so dramatic, because it relaxes a person to the state of peacefulness only written about in Christian and Buddhist legends."

"Nirvana," Brien stated.

"Something like that. Non-consciousness."

"So, is that why you had the fentanyl? The midazolam?"

"I'm not a mystic. Actually I have terrible insomnia."

"And you took these that night. The night of the accident with your rig?"

"Yes."

"Why?"

"I can't tell you that."

"I thought you wanted to get better."

"I do."

"Look, all I'm going to tell the judge is whether or not I think you're competent to stand trial."

"I was trying to kill myself."

"Really?"

"I think so."

Brien makes a note and says, "Tell me more about that night."

"I took them, and then I got in my fully loaded rig and started driving, the wrong way, toward Michigan, and then I took more. That's all I know, and all I remember, but you do the math."

"Where were you driving?"

"I don't know, but I know it was a fully loaded rig with petrol."

"Were you going to crash it?"

"Like I said, I was loaded with petrol, and loaded with pills, and driving east. I don't know—there's a pretty big Lake there with a couple big piers, and the nuclear power plant, and a couple other chemical plants and factories."

"Why would you do that?"

"Because I'm depressed?" Wolfgang suggested.

"Have you been depressed your whole life, or did this start when you were kicked out of medical school?" Brien asked.

"When I was a kid, I was happy, until something happened."

"Something bad?"

"Buddy, you don't know the half of it," Wolfgang said.

When he was a child, in first grade, Wolfgang and another kid were brought by a nun to the office for disciplinary measures, but the secretary had to leave for a family emergency, so the principal took him back to his little house next to the school. The principal was an old man.

He told the other child and Wolfgang, whose name was Oscar at that time, that he was the "prince-i-pal, the primary pal, for all the kids." But that he had to discipline them now. The man who disciplined them said he would be right back, and he did come back, wearing a long white robe.

The man who disciplined them took down their pants and spanked them both briefly, but then he was nice, and he dried their tears, and he hugged them close and wrestled with them and tickled them and kissed them and made them touch each other. The other child was a girl, and the prince-i-pal made him do things to her, all the while the prince-i-pal's hands were busy, moving beneath his long white robe.

Brien knows all about this person, this priest, because he was Brien's priest too, and did similar things to kids that Brien Grace knew.

To kids like Brien Grace.

And to Brien Grace too.

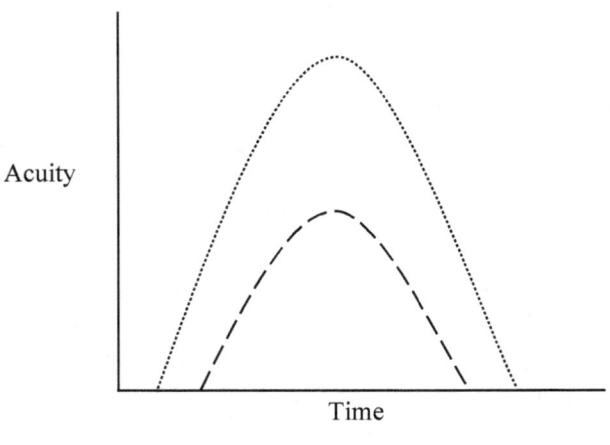

Acuity

Time

Passive Acuity: ....
    (Passive Data Capture, Storing and Retrieval)

Active Acuity: — — — — — — — — —
    (Active Data Capture, Storing and Retrieval)

Brien immediately began to collect his things.

"That's it?" Wolfgang said.

"Yes," Brien said. "Thank you for your time."

"Am I cured, doc?" Wolfgang said jokingly.

"Undoubtedly," Brien said.

"Indubitably," Wolfgang said formally.

Brien said softly, "Seriously, you should set up a meeting with the prison psychologist and maybe he'll refer you to the psychiatrist if that's necessary and required. I wasn't here to perform any form of counseling, just to evaluate your ability to stand trial and the likelihood of success of certain defenses."

"Like insanity," Wolfgang said.

Brien shook his head, "You know that's not one of the defenses Mr. Fisher is exploring."

Brien looked at Wolfgang, who was shaking his head with his eyes closed. Wolfgang said sadly and with affect: "I don't know what I know anymore."

Brien ignored this. The walls of the place felt more barren to him, and his stomach felt sick. He had begun to sweat and felt a bit dizzy. He pushed the button on the wall for the guard to release him, but nothing happened.

"Anyway, sorry it took me a while to get up here to Winter," Brien managed to say apologetically. "But it's been a tough few months."

"Why's that?"

"A friend of mine was shot. Hunting accident."

"I was wondering when you'd come round to that, Columbo," Wolfgang said sardonically.

"What are you talking about?"

"Look, I'll tell you what I know, okay, just leave me alone after that."

Brien stared at him as he continued: "I was locked up with Mark—Marcus Agamovich—and anyway, he must've had a falling out with somebody, because he started getting these letters, while he was in prison, letters threatening him."

Brien was listening carefully to Wolfgang. All of his behaviors had the mark of psychosis. But this—this false confession is the sort that psychopaths or schizophrenics are known for. He'd even adopted a casual, almost country attitude when he spoke: "Anyway, he gets one letter, a letter that really really scared him. And that was when Mark said, 'There's somebody messing with me, and when I figure out who it is, I'm going to kill him.'"

"And what did you say to that?"

"Nothing, I didn't say nothing."

"Why not?"

"What was there to say?"

"Well, was he serious?"

"Yeah he's always serious."

"But you didn't do anything."

"No. I didn't."

"And then what happened?"

"That day? Nothing."

"But something did happen, right?"

"Yeah."

"What happened?"

"There was a shooting up north."

"When?"

"It was while I was still locked up. But after Mark got released."

As soon as he made it through security and collected his things, Brien called Drew.

"What's the verdict?" Drew asked.

"He's definitely exhibiting signs of a disorder."

"Yeah, tell me something I don't know."

"He thinks he killed Craig."

"What?" Drew nearly shouted.

"Well, he essentially confessed to being Craig's murderer. Pretty sad, really."

"I don't get it," Drew stated.

Brien explained: "He took the hunting accident that I mentioned in passing and he tied it into his own mental train of thought. Then tried to pin what he perceived as a murder on someone else. Classic false confession, simple transference. It's sad."

"Thanks Brien," Drew said. "Keep track of your mileage and hours, and send me a bill."

"You got it," Brien said.

"And Brien," Drew said, "One more thing."

"Yeah, Drew," Brien said.

"If Tom goes up to Grace, or is in Two Rivers, just have him keep it on the down low with Kristen," Drew said.

Brien said nothing. He didn't know where it stood

between Kristen and Tom.

"I mean it's cool that they're both helping each other and all, but she was Adam's fiancée," Drew said. "You think it doesn't tear my mother up to see your kid brother with her? When she sees them up north in Grace, or down in Two Rivers."

"I'll talk to him," Brien lied.

Brien left Winter and tried to take a short cut down to Stevens Point. Winter is far west of Grace, which is north of Stevens Point and Wausau, and he thought he could figure it out.

But he quickly became lost in a series of icy, barren farm roads. He backtracked and became more confused and lost. He took a turn too quickly, and the truck suddenly skidded to the side on the ice—he had to reverse steer as it fishtailed back and forth, several times, until at last he brought it under control. He pulled over and brought out a map. He looked at it, and felt cramped in the truck, his shoulders aching as he studied the map. His cellular phone rang; it was Megan.

"How's the shrink?" she asked.

"I'm lost," Brien said to her. "I'm so lost."

"Really?" she asked.

In the distance, a farmer was moving an old rusted thresher on a parallel road up on a hill, but there was no road connecting this gravel road with that one, so he couldn't ask directions even if he chose to do so.

"Yeah, I pulled over on the side of the road," he said. "I don't think these old farm roads are even on this map."

"Brien," Megan said, concerned, almost strict. "Get home."

"I'm trying,' he said, laughing, "But these farm roads, and woods, I don't know this area like I know Grace. And the roads are covered with ice."

She continued, more sternly than before: "You come

home, right now."

Brien turned on the overhead light and studied the map. He could hear Megan breathing on the other end of the line, hear his children in the background talking to each other, playing. The map was topographical, the sort Brien loved: hills, rivers, lakes. The whole area looked like a big sponge; there were so many lakes and swamps. Then he saw it, running like a vein through the woods. It was not a short cut. It was the way home.

"I'll be right there, Megan," he told her.

He is home. The evening in the west is a panoply of pink and purple as an echelon of clouds embrace the spring sun.

He is in the front yard, playing a form of baseball combined with tag with his kids in the cool spring air. Megan has warmed croissants with brie in the oven and has opened a bottle of Merlot.

His cellular phone rings in his jeans pocket. He pulls it out. It is Kristen.

He lets it go to voicemail.

He examines his client's file, paging through each of the documents and studying them carefully. Then he comes to the warrant. To search his client's house.

He frowns as he studies it. Looking at the judge's signature line.

It isn't signed.

19

March was back and forth; ice one day, rain the next. Yet all of the snow has finally melted, revealing the crap in the yard that had been buried: kids toys, dog shit, stuff Drew or Sharon forgot to bring in before the winter snows, and now they're paying for it. He spent yesterday morning picking it all up, and then he had to pack.

He is glad that this is the time, his time. His father is going to put him in charge of the company; he's certain of it. Sharon and the kids are waiting for him in the foyer of the house, beside their bags. The cab will take them to the airport, and then they will go to Florida.

But Drew has one more chore: for that stupid pro bono case he's working on. He calls up the detective, the one who calls his company Razorsharp.

The detective is right to the point: he's raised his hourly rates.

"I have something I need you to do," Drew tells him. "I need you to interview somebody, ask him about a shooting."

Drew watches the dull cold houses roll by as the cab takes them to the airport.

He argued a motion before Judge Crandon three days ago.

And he won. The judge had stared at him almost sadly as he made his arguments, and as he deposed the deputy.

The judge even questioned the deputy: "You mean you didn't have a warrant? After all that?"

"No," the deputy admitted. "Well I did, but it wasn't signed—I thought it had been, but there was a mix up in the office."

"A mix up," the judge grunted.

And Drew had said, "It's the fruit of the poisonous tree, your honor. The warrant wasn't properly executed. Therefore, the search, all of it, it has to be stricken, and the charges dropped. Even the premise of the warrant is under suspicion because the sheriff was acting as a caretaker when he took the evidence."

The district attorney was furious and had lost his composure; he was paging through his file, trying to come up with a counter argument. There were none. He half-heartedly argued for exigent circumstances, but Judge Crandon just gave him a sneer.

"Mr. Fisher," the judge said reluctantly and softly. "I'm afraid that you're right, and that it is my determination that the evidence regarding the majority of the charges against your client must be suppressed. Therefore, the charges shall be dismissed, and it is the Court's determination that counts four through twenty have no legal basis or merit, and that no further argument or evidence shall be heard, short of a timely appeal by the State. Furthermore, the Court shall accept a responsive brief from the state filed within five business days regarding Counts One and Two, and explaining why the evidence there should not be suppressed and why these two charges should also not be dismissed."

Then the judge looked down at the ADA and added, "However, I strongly encourage the state to reconsider its offer for settlement of this case."

And yet Drew has felt nothing but bad ever since. Now, as they approach the airport, he is watching the road, wishing he'd never taken the case.

The pool at his parents is a long rectangle. Four sculptures of impish children pour water from buckets or cups into it, and the water flowing against its surface makes a pleasant sound. At the head of the pool, where the diving board used to be before his parents removed it, is a great flower pot, and Drew has often wondered if his parents knew of the symbolism: the four children representing himself and his three living siblings, who all have children, and the flower pot being a sort of urn to his brother Adam, who never will.

Drew is sitting on the side of the pool with his feet in it. Sharon is glaring at him from a raft. They are having another fight. A fight in whispers, below whispers.

Then his cellular phone rings on a nearby glass table.

Drew gets up to answer it.

"Don't," Sharon says, tears in her eyes, but Drew walks to the table and picks it up. It's the detective. He walks away from the pool as he says, "You conduct the interview?"

"Yep," comes the voice. "The great wolf king allowed me an audience."

"And?" Drew asks.

"It was him that did it."

"How do you know?"

"He just tried to frame his friend Mark Agamovich for Craig Bunder's murder," the detective says.

"So?"

"So, I wasn't asking him that. He made a leap and started framing somebody else."

"A psychologist I know thinks he's making it up."

"If he's making it up, he's a damn good liar," the detective tells him. "If he's making it up, there's got to be some other connection there."

Drew considers this.

"Oscar DeMareni ain't even his real name," the detective adds.

"No?"

"He changed it twice before."

"What was it?"

"The last name was Seahulls. I remember that."

"You don't have the first name?"

"I can't remember. Something random though. But even that wasn't the first time he'd changed it. His real name's Allen Huccashes."

"No wonder he changed it."

"Yeah, no kiddin'. But the guy's nuts, that's why."

Drew laughs.

"Oh, yeah, and there's one more thing you should know."

"What's that?" Drew asks.

"He said he was incarcerated on the day of the murder. I looked it up. He wasn't."

Drew thanks him, eyes closed.

"Send me your bill," Drew says.

"You want a report?"

"No," Drew says immediately. "Don't send a report. No need."

He hangs up. He turns and looks at the pool. It is empty.

He looks inside and sees Sharon through the broad glass doors of his parents' winter home; she has thrown on an outfit and is leaving with the kids.

Drew rolls his eyes.

That night Drew's mother has a priest over—her priest, who is the priest that married Drew and Sharon. Sharon is not there. She was supposed to be. She is not there.

Drew puts in a cd; it's a band that Adam loved, and an album they released a few years after he drowned.

When his mother is in the other room, the priest leans forward, and they have a quiet conversation about what to do.

"You've got to try, Drew," the priest says. He is talking about saving his marriage with Sharon. The band is singing: *they thin my heart with little things, and my life will change.*

"I know Father," Drew says. "I will."

Drew flies home alone.
He wants to meet with the detective again, get the full story.
Then he will meet with his father.

He sits outside the restaurant, watching Paul clean up the place, listening to the chatter of the dispatch.

He has a warrant. He doesn't plan on using it yet though.

20

Jimmy is sitting at his desk, doing some paperwork.

Rick calls up, and Jimmy answers.

"Investigator O'Reilly, to what do I owe the pleasure?" Jimmy asks.

"Sheriff, I'm just calling to tell you what I'm sure you already know," Rick says sourly.

"What's that, Rick?" Jimmy asks.

"The rifling pattern for Paul Krukowski's rifle doesn't match the one from the bullet."

"Yes, I did hear that," Jimmy says. "And I am awfully sorry about that."

Rick is silent for a time.

"Any leads?" Rick asks quietly.

"No, but you're welcome to come down here and buy me breakfast anytime you want to bet on a case again."

"Thanks anyway, sheriff," Rick says.

He hangs up loudly, which doesn't sit well with Jimmy.

Jimmy is interviewing the last of the hunters in Craig's group. Bert Vance is tall and has a full beard.

"You work with Brien Grace?" Jimmy asks.

"Yes, we're both in the same graduate program, and probably going to open up a practice together."

"You were in the woods on Monday morning?"

"Yes," Bert says, shifting slightly in his chair. "Yes, I was."

"You got a deer?"

"A little spike buck," he says. "I was hunting the southern side of the woods, not far from the ravine, a little clearing. I was behind a log, and there it was."

"And you carried it to the road?"

Bert nods, "I tied its hooves to a stick, carried it to the road on my shoulder."

"Near the ravine? The road above the ravine and Tributary Seven?"

"Yes."

"Okay," Jimmy says. "So, you see anything on the road above Tributary Seven?"

"Not really," he says.

"Sounds like you saw something," Jimmy states.

"Maybe, I don't know if it'll help," Bert says.

"So what'd you see?"

Bert is cautious.

"I saw a truck coming down the logging road," he said.

"That's it?"

"Yep," he said. "Told you I didn't have anything for you."

"What kind of truck?"

"It was a Ram. A silver Ram."

Jimmy pulls out a photograph of a truck.

"Could this have been the truck?" Jimmy asks.

Bert studies it a moment.

"Yes," he says slowly. "It could have been that truck."

"You see the driver?"

"No," Bert says. "No I didn't."

After some general questions, and other pleasantries, Jimmy thanks Bert, shakes his hand and escorts him out. He finds himself in his office, sitting, staring out at the bleak day.

Three months ago, Jimmy was in his squad car, looking at the dilapidated house of the trucker whose life he had saved. The storm had finally subsided, leaving snow piled several feet high.

Jimmy looked at the house, saying, "A yellow fog presses against the window."

Matt walked up from his squad car, giving him the

thumbs-up sign. He had gotten the necessary paperwork, gotten the key from the landlord.

"A yellow smoke," Jimmy muttered, and he opened the door of his squad car.

Matt keyed the door, and Jimmy and Matt entered. It was hot inside and filled with the heavy scent of winter dust, and the sound of a heater that was going full blast. Jimmy felt himself beginning to sweat beneath his heavy winter jacket.

While Matt looked around the small entrance that served as a living room, Jimmy went into the kitchen. There were pills on the counter. Jimmy pulled on his gloves, pushing them with his index finger, looking at them. They were imperfect: brown and square and not smooth. There was no imprint of a word to designate their origin.

Jimmy bagged them. He held them up for Matt to observe. Matt whistled, impressed.

They opened up the cabinets and found, among the cereal boxes and cans of food, more unmarked jars of pills and bottles of an odorless liquid.

"I'll check out the upstairs," Matt volunteered, disappearing into a narrow corridor.

He opened door beside the kitchen that led into darkness. Jimmy flipped a light switch on, and the dingy basement stairs greeted him. Cobwebs and filth lined the walls. He walked down, whispering, "Licking its tongue in the lingering rain, forgetting the black ash falling on its back."

The basement was unremarkable: a washing machine, a dryer, a laundry chute. A rusted old bike leaning against a concrete wall. A tool bench with a few disorganized tools. The far wall was made of wood. There was a door in the wall with a padlock on it.

"Slipping past the terrace, a sudden leap in the dark October night."

Jimmy approached the door. He studied the lock, then went back over to the work bench and looked at it for a time. He carefully picked up a crowbar and walked back over to the padlock. He slipped the crowbar beneath the metal of the latch, whispering, "And there may be time to ask, do I—"

The wood splintered as he made a sudden thrust, and the metal fell away. He reached in and pulled a string for the light bulb.

Inside there was equipment. He was amazed.

He'd seen a crack house and a pot farm before, but this was a sophisticated labyrinth of Bunsen burners and tubes and refrigeration units. Everything required for making homemade drugs.

There was a map on the far wall. Jimmy got out his video camera and documented the evidence. He heard Matt come down the creaking stairs and then walk to the doorway, where he stood in amazement.

Jimmy turned off the camera and looked at Matt.

"Wow," was all Matt could manage. Jimmy nodded. They spent a few minutes looking over the equipment.

Before he left, Jimmy looked at the map.

"Matt," he said. "Look at this."

There were markers in the map of the United States. Pins with dates written beside them.

"What is it?" Matt asked.

"I don't know," Jimmy said, musing, "Maybe the dates and places that he delivered these drugs. Maybe the deliveries coincide with his runs as a trucker."

Matt nodded, adding, "I'll check with his petrol company to see if he was in those towns."

Jimmy's truck is parked on a country bridge of County Road J, idling above a creek. It's beautiful here.

Why not? he says.

He looks at the pretty stream running over the black

rocks beneath the old bridge.

You've done it before, he says aloud.

Then he is angry and whispers, You don't know up from down anymore. Hell, it could have even been you. But you know it couldn't be you.

Four years ago, he and Matt had entered a crack house.

The police had already scoured the place, and the detectives had all been through too. Matt got bored eventually, and he went out.

Jimmy had put this guy away, so he took a special satisfaction of walking around his old house. This guy had called himself the Buffalo Soldier. And one day he killed a cop. The Soldier had also been responsible for selling several tons of crack cocaine.

Jimmy had sat down in his arm chair. It was very uncomfortable.

Jimmy thought about how the Soldier had stolen a car and made a run north.

He rolls down the window, and the cool spring air enters his squad car. He closes his eyes and listens to the pleasant sound of the river as it runs beneath the little bridge.

You think it was. Then you know it wasn't. But you don't know. Because we don't know anything really. We just guess or think we know. But we don't know. Not really.

The water runs beneath the bridge.

When Jimmy caught up with the Soldier, his car had broken down. About a half a mile from this creek.

Later, a local policeman from this township found it. When they went through the car, they found several bags of crack, paraphernalia, and a blow torch. They did not find a Magnum, a nearly empty bag of crack cocaine, and a metal glass pipe.

They never found his body either, Jimmy thinks, as he sits idling on a bridge above the creek.

Someday they will though.

A corpse shot seven times, lying deep in the woods. The shooter had a chance to reload twice. Perhaps they'll even be able to reconstruct how the cop-killer fled up the creek for a mile after being shot through the knee cap and in the shoulder.

How the Soldier slipped in the creek, dropped the Magnum after squeezing off a single round, and then fled, unarmed, begging for his life, up into the forest.

How his pursuer got his feet soaked, patiently walking up the creek, retrieving the Magnum from where it lay in the water amid the rocks, before heading into the woods, following the crimson trail the Soldier left on the trees and grass.

How the Soldier was shot three times more before he began to crawl.

"It had known them, it knew all," Jimmy says aloud.

He's in his squad car, on County Road J, thinking about what he should do, planning it all out, and thinking about his recent meeting in his office most of all.

Jimmy had been in his office, trying to answer a question, prior to the unexpected meeting. It was a simple question: how are Mark and Craig related?

Mark served with Craig's dad in Vietnam. They're both good old boys.

If it wasn't Paul, then maybe it was Mark. But why?

Or Drew. Or Brien.

This would do to drive him mad. That was when Matt walked in the room with Kristen, who looked more determined than anyone he had ever seen.

And then she proceeded to tell him a story that he didn't believe.

That's the truth? he asked.

That's the truth, she said, unflinching.

You did it, he said.

Yes.
You?
Yes.
Because of what Craig did?
Yes.
He didn't believe her. So he didn't arrest her.

The question is one of belief. One of trust.
Can you trust her?
Can you trust yourself?
You have always chosen to fail beautifully.

It's time to become serious, like your father. Pick up your guitar for the last time, and then say goodbye.

The chromatic scale. Christians made it, a modification of the ancient Greeks', and they built a message into it. Twelve possible notes, one for each of the apostles or perhaps the months, but only eight may typically be played, thus giving the various major or minor scales and keys. Why is eight superior to twelve? The eight directional points on a compass? Who knows? They created it a long time ago. Post Romans. All you remember from music theory is that they wanted to avoid the diminished sixth. Eight main keys each with eight notes, beginning and ending at that same beginning, so seven notes really, but twelve keys, and many more are possible, depending on how strange a sound one is willing to accept.

Today is simple, a simple trust, and so a simple scale.

Pentatonic. C and A minor. Move up the fret board: the notes come to you, uninvited.

The song is lovely.
But it is time to stop playing now.
It is time to put away the things of childhood.

21

Adam was stretched out on the bed with his shirt off and his guitar resting beside him. His hair was still wet from the jacuzzi and shower.

Kristen walked in with a towel wrapped around her and sat down beside him. She nodded at his Martin guitar.

You haul that all the way up here from Appleton, she said softly, But it's just sitting there. You gonna to play it?

Sure, Adam said quietly. He sat up, picked it up gently by the neck with his forefinger and thumb, and positioned it lightly on his lap. He played a song he was writing for her. The cadence was steady, and he picked the song softly from the strings as if they were fragile and might shatter if touched too roughly. There were no words, just a sad, pretty progression: C Am C Am Am7/G G C/F Am C Am C C. C Am C Am Am7/G G C/F C/F C Am Am Am. C/F C Am G C/F C Am G Am Am C/F C. C/F C C/F C C/F C/F Am Am C/F C/F Am Am C/F C C C. C. He strummed the last note once and fully, letting the chord ring out, bringing in the low E string by placing his ring finger on the third fret and his pinky on the A string's third fret, a positioning Brien Grace's father had taught him as a boy.

Then he tuned it down to a dropped D, an alt-tuning he loved, and he played a song he loved, singing: All the leaves will burn, in autumn fires and then return; all the fires we burn, all will return.

Kristen left the room for a time.

She returned, and Adam could tell she'd been crying.

She was wearing the diamond ring that he'd given her. The diamond ring purchased with his father's money. The company's money.

What's the matter Kristen? You're so distant, Adam

said.

No I'm not, Kristen replied. I'm right here. Right here.

She lay back covered in sweat beside Adam. He'd held her tightly as she came. And then again as they came together.

They were both trying to get the thin air into their lungs.

Adam held her still, feeling her breathing next to him. He began to chuckle.

She looked at him, confused for a moment, and then she too began to laugh. They held each other tenderly, laughing at their good fortune.

Adam was mulling it over. There has to be a way to make money.

His own money.

All the money he had was his father's. Company money.

Maybe his music, or maybe a different business. He can't take over his father's business, even though his father wants him to run it. His father wants him to run it because he scored well on the GMAT, enough to get a scholarship for his MBA, and because he did well at Kellogg. But Adam wanted something more, something that was his own.

She rolled over against him, naked in the darkness, interrupting his thoughts.

I made a mistake, Adam, she whispered. A big mistake.

I know, he told her.

You know? she leans up on an elbow, peering at his face.

About you and Craig? he asked, Sure.

Why didn't you say anything?

That was a long time ago.

She turned away from him.

He can make out the outline of her hip in the darkness.

Why did you do it? she asked, her voice breaking.

You're right, Adam told her. I messed up too. So who am I to judge?

She said nothing.

Anyway I forgive you, Adam told Kristen.

She turned to him. Adam could see in the darkness that she'd been crying once more. He didn't want her to be sad.

Can you forgive me? he asked.

She smiled and crawled into his arms.

Sure, she said, Why not?

Adam played one more song for her on guitar before they left the Upper Peninsula. It was a good song, and she knew it was about her on at least one level of its metaphor, but he never told her the name.

Summer

Supposing truth were a woman—what then?

22

Paul is weaving on the road, from his lane to the gravel shoulder and back, and from his lane into the oncoming lane. But there's little traffic, just the occasional trucker or pickup. He keeps bringing up her number from the contacts of his cellular phone, looking at the number, and then hitting the end button.

The road takes him through the farm country, up to his new home. His home that is not his home at all really. His new temporary house.

It is high summer, a couple days before the Fourth, and hot. He rolls down the windows, turns off the air, and lets the humidity seep into his truck and his skin.

He focuses on the road as the last amber glow fades into the west and as abandoned farmhouses and rotted out old barns flash by on either side. These old 40 acre farms are all dead. They were all purchased starting in the seventies and united into a series of huge complexes. Every so often, there would be a conglomerate manager's gigantic barn complex beside his brand new ranch house, complete with flood lights and modern equipment, surrounded by mile after mile of carefully cultivated corn, wheat or spinach. And in between, there's a couple dozen decaying barns; rusted tractors lined in a row and cars without windshields sitting on blocks; empty boarded up houses and fallow fields; ruined windmills and collapsing sheds.

Fuck it, he thinks. He's making the call. He puts his cellular phone to his ear.

He listens to the phone ringing, and he knows with each ring that he shouldn't be calling. She might pick up any moment, and at each ring, he tells himself to stop, hang up. But he listens to the rings, feeling ashamed and excited and sad.

He hangs up immediately on hearing her new voicemail. His heart feels like a new hole has just opened. And they were right—all that shit he'd heard in the songs and poems in high school about your heart aching, actually physically aching. It's true. His heart really hurt.

She's ignoring his call, or maybe she's gone out tonight, or maybe she has someone over. Maybe he should spend more time at better places than Griffins, find some friends, find someone who will come over. To his new place. Or to their house. Their old house. The bed is still there—nothing else really. He could use that bed, and maybe he'd feel better. His mind races. It shouldn't be this way, but it is. It is what it is, and it's awful. Truly awful. He is surprised by how much it hurts his heart.

On his left hand on the top of the steering wheel, he has an imprint on his finger where he's worn his wedding ring for twelve years. He took it off two weeks ago. But every day for twelve years, it makes an impression in the skin, in the muscle beneath the skin. More than an impression. Like a memory in the physical makeup of his hand. He wonders how long it will take for the skin and muscle to grow out and the mark to disappear.

It's okay to cry about it, Brien told him. You know you can go ahead and cry about it.

And coming from anybody else, he would have thought it was cheesy as hell, some line from a get-well card or a pop song. But he was so sincere. The way he said it, softly and without affect: It's okay to cry about it.

Of course he did not cry about it then, there in his father's restaurant. But he thought about it.

He thought about that as he drove home, and he kept thinking about it once he'd pulled his car up and into the attached garage. He went into that house that seemed so empty, and he found himself staring at the time, the digital, green numbers on the microwave.

She hadn't taken the microwave. He assumed she'd probably considered it, and maybe even rummaged around for a tool, and then given up, leaving it there and him here, looking at the time.

The morning before Susie dropped by with the papers, Brien's wife was waiting for him outside the restaurant in her Tahoe as he was heading in to work.

She rolled down her window. Paul walked up.

"Hey," he said quietly.

She had tears in her eyes.

"It's okay Megan," he told her.

She couldn't say it. He nodded to her gently.

Her Tahoe smelled of spoiled milk, dirty diapers, and old McDonalds fries.

He said patiently, almost whispering, "Just give me the message."

"She's coming over today. She wants to talk," she said. "I'm sorry."

Paul nodded. He knew.

That first night he did not cry. The next night, however, he walked into the dark kitchen of their empty home, and that's when it happened. He broke down—shaking and sobbing. He knelt on the floor and wept until Cooper came over and found him and licked the tears from his hands.

The next morning after crying in the kitchen, he called in and told his mother he wouldn't be in for work, and he called around until he found a new place to stay.

And he moved as much as he was able to his new home, the temporary new home, an old farmhouse he was renting. Across the street there was an abandoned farmhouse.

Get your shit moved in, he told himself. He moved it in in a haphazard way, and then poured some food and water for Cooper, and went out to Griffin's Pub.

Tonight, as he rounds the last bend, his headlights illuminate the old place across the way, its windows boarded up, its door painted black, its roof slack and burnt through in two places.

Then he pulls his truck up to the old barn in back of the farmhouse. He throws the truck into park and kills the engine, his keys sounding loud and obnoxious in the summer stillness. The farmhouse is a four bedroom place, although Paul thinks only one of them is big enough to be considered anything more than a glorified closet, and it's almost as dilapidated as the place across the way, and it rents for $300 a month.

Paul opens his flask of Jack Daniels, but it's empty. He opens the truck door and is annoyed by the blinding light from the truck. He pulls himself out of the truck and walks up to the house. Cooper greets him with a bark and comes trotting up with his head lowered—embarrassed at having been caught off-guard, sleeping, Paul thinks.

Paul finds the bottle of vodka he put in the freezer, and pours himself a little nightcap.

He pulls out his wallet and puts it on the wood counter. He has her new address written on a piece of paper in his wallet. That's the toughest thing. Knowing he could drive over there. But that would just add to the problems, and he's decided he has to stop hurting her and hurting himself, and he can't do anything to make things worse. He won't sin anymore.

He walks outside and lets Cooper out. Cooper won't step out from behind him.

"What's wrong boy?" Paul asks.

Then he hears it—coyotes howling in the distance. It sounds like immature kids calling and yelling to each other simultaneously.

Cooper gets his courage up, and steps out onto the porch, and lets out a long growl, followed by a quick, loud bark.

That's right, Paul thinks.

Then Cooper sits down and listens, his ears cocked.

Goddamn coyotes, Paul whispers at their jabbering howls.

Things were amicable between them.

They spoke to each other through their lawyers now.

They hadn't even said goodbye to each other. Not really.

When Susie showed up at the restaurant, she had the papers in a manila envelope with her. She was hugging them to her chest, like a school girl with an algebra book or a poetry notebook. She didn't say anything, she just looked at him, with this look on her face. He couldn't place it— she looked sad and curious and excited at the same time. That look really bothered him, and he thought about saying something about it, but decided against it.

She leaned over and peered past his arm. His mother was behind him, working in the kitchen. Then Susie straightened and returned her eyes to his face.

"Hi Paul," she said, and actually let a tear roll down her face. He stared at her, feeling his expression remain static, hard, unchanged.

"I'm so sorry," she said. "I—"

Susie held out the papers, and he took them, looking at her. He didn't need to open the envelope, didn't have to read them; he knew what they were. And he didn't care— he didn't care, didn't care, didn't care, in the least. That's what he told himself. And he opened up the envelope by wedging his thumb in the top of it and drawing it across the opening. And that, he knew, would cut him, and it did cut him, but he didn't care. And he walked up to the register and fished out a pen from behind it and he didn't read them and he signed the back page with a flourish and dated his signature, and initialed each and every page, each and every fucking page, he whispered to himself. And he shoved them back in the envelope, and he walked back slowly and carefully, delicately handed them over, and then he smiled at her, and watched as she, mouth slack, took a step back, wavered a moment, like an unhooked fish that has been returned to a lake and is regaining its faculties, and then, hugging the papers to her, turned and ran out of the place.

As the sleep leaves him, Paul hears the sound of a lake swallowing a rock. It is pitch black in the old farm house and still, but he can no longer hear the coyotes.

There were two possibilities. Two possible scenarios. Maybe three. He knew he'd spend a lot of time exploring them now, but it was too late.

The next day is his day off, so he drives up 10 toward Steven's Point. On the radio, they're playing an old song about a gun fighter in West Texas and his love for a Mexican girl. He listens to the lyrics of the old song. It's a good song, about love.

But that's not how it is when you're in love. It's not longing—it's loneliness. Loneliness because you have to do things the world demands of you, but you can never explain it to her fully, and what you have to do changes you in a bad way, and then she's gone, and then the loneliness is over, replaced by aching and pain.

He crosses under Skeleton Bridge, and then over a small bridge above the tiny Rat River, and continues driving for what seems a long time. It's hot today and he has the windows down, because the air conditioning just annoys him. He takes a bypass they've set up on Highway X, then gets back on 10.

He crosses over the winding stream called Tomorrow River twice and pulls off on a side road. There's a stretch of woods between the farms, and he pulls over onto the gravel shoulder and lets Cooper out. The dog immediately begins running through the weeds, tall grass and wild flowers between the woods and the road. As Paul steps to the weeds to piss, the dog bounds into the woods.

While he pisses, Paul watches Cooper bounce through the woods like a deer flushing and treeing squirrels, marking the territory like Paul is doing, until Cooper disappears from view.

He zips up his pants and walks along the forest line. The day is hot and humid, and the cicadas are giving off their annoying buzz, each one lasting for at least ten seconds and sounding louder than the last. He'd heard that these locust only emit the sound when it's above 85 degrees, like some insect temperature gauge. Fucking locust.

"Cooper!" he calls once.

Maybe he should just let him go, just let him slip back into nature. Somebody would pick Cooper up, take care of him. He immediately dismisses the thought as stupid melancholic bullshit. And maybe there are coyotes up here.

This feeling sorry for myself—it's so stupid.

He watches the woods for Cooper as he walks the length of them. He keeps thinking how odd it would be if somebody were in those woods, staring at him. How out of place they would look against the backdrop of forest, they wouldn't even have to be wearing blaze orange, they could just be wearing normal clothes, and they'd look completely out of place. And then if that person were to take a step toward him.

Suddenly Cooper pounces out of the woods before him and lands on something in the field beside the road. He nudges and paws at it. Then Cooper comes trotting back, head high, with a mouse dangling from his jaw.

"Give it," Paul says, adding as if it were a duck, "Release."

And Cooper drops the mouse onto the gravel shoulder. Its neck is bent. Paul takes a stick and moves it, but it's limp. Its tiny mouth has a speckling of bright blood above it, from its almost humanlike nose. Paul leaves it for the crows.

They continue up north. Paul makes it to Waupaca and keeps going, and ten miles later he's on a two lane road with his window down, and as he passes an oncoming pickup truck hauling sheet metal on a trailer, his pickup takes a bump at the same time the trailer next to him takes the bump in the road, and Paul blinks as he's bounced upwards, and through the open window, hears the sound of the sheet metal bouncing next to him, and in an instant, he realizes that a piece of sheet metal, improperly harnessed, might come flying into the cab of his truck, and it would be like a movie that just stopped running, it would be that sound and then nothing.

But the sheet metal is properly harnessed down, or the bump in the road is not enough to jostle it loose, and Paul drives on for a few more miles. At the next road, though, he turns around and heads back toward Two Rivers via Appleton.

When she left, he knew. He knew it was over. But he didn't do anything rash until after he'd signed the papers.

That night after she came in to the restaurant, he took the pictures out of the albums and the shoe boxes. Fifteen years of pictures. Of memories. And he went through and tore them all in half. It took him over an hour. He kept the ones of the dog or that had other people, and the ones of him. He shredded the ones of just her into little pieces.

The next morning, though, when he woke and called to get his new place, he felt different, and he put the torn and shredded pictures in a shoe box and drove to Appleton. He parked in front of the restoration photography store, and took the box inside. The man behind the counter raised his eyebrows briefly when he saw all the ruined pictures.

"I need you to mend and copy these," Paul told him. "And make a duplicate set."

The owner nodded briefly, understanding. He'd seen this before.

On his way back from Skeleton Bridge, he stops in Appleton and picks them up, paying two-hundred, sixty-three dollars and eighty-seven cents for the pictures.

Without thinking, he drives to the post office. He pulls out his wallet in line and gets out the piece of paper on which he had written her new address. The address was weighing him down, and it's time to be free of it, he tells himself. He sends the duplicates of the restored photos to Susie's new address.

A note enclosed says, "You may need these one day. Paul."

He throws away the address on his way out of the post office.

That night is warm, and Paul has on a Brewers game. He used to be a fan. He supposes that he still is, but they are a tough team to love after the All Star Break. He watches the game, following the stats, realizing that these guys are just kids, that he is watching a sport of kids. Even the oldest one on the team, Counsel, he's just a kid really. And the others, even the big men like Fielder, they're just big kids really. And we send these big kids off to fight our wars, or look up to them for their ability to hit or throw a ball.

He turns off the television and pours himself a whiskey and coke.

He sits outside with Cooper.

That's when he hears it. It's low, and at first he thinks

he's imagining it:

Babbling. An old man babbling.

It's coming from the abandoned house across the way.

Even Cooper hears it: he cocks his ears and looks at the house.

It sounds like an old man saying, Oh why, sick, oh why, that's the sick, oh may, oh my, oh mind, oh why, oh why, oh that's, oh that's the sick.

An old man is in that abandoned house. A crazy farmer or an old hobo, or maybe a homeless veteran.

He goes back inside and pulls out his Maglite from one of the boxes, and then goes back out and shines it over the darkened abandoned farmhouse across the road. There's nothing. The person's inside, or behind it, or lying in the long prairie grass that surrounds it.

An old man lying in the grass or camping in the abandoned house and babbling.

Oh why, oh why.

Or somebody died in that old house.

Oh may, oh my, oh why.

Or maybe somebody will die in it someday.

Oh why, that's the sick. Oh may, oh my, oh why.

Ghosts should be able to haunt the past, Paul thinks. Susie believed in ghosts. He doesn't believe in that shit, but if they can haunt the future, they should be able to haunt the past too.

The next morning, he walks across the hot paved road with Cooper to the abandoned house. It's all boarded up. There's no way in.

He spends a few minutes looking for footprints in the mud in back or impressions in the long tall grass, but there's nothing.

Cooper is bounding through the brush, hunting.

In the middle of his shift at the restaurant, Paul walks

out front to check on his mother. See if she's keeping up with the orders. But it's pretty sparse.

Jimmy, the sheriff, is sitting there at a four-top table beside the booths with two guys who are both dressed like mechanics.

Jimmy waves him over and introduces him. They are farmers, hired hands, guys that have worked a bunch of the conglomerate farms, including the one he is staying on. Frank and Al, who are focused on the cheeseburgers he just cooked them and their beers. Jimmy hasn't touched his egg salad sandwich or his soda. Jimmy shakes Paul's hand and pulls out a seat for Paul, and Paul joins them.

"So I hear you moved out there to Frank and Al's neck of the woods for a while," Jimmy says after the introductions and some small talk.

Paul nods.

"Sorry to hear about you and Susie," Jimmy says softly.

To Paul's left, Al is silent and eating his burger. He's been working with machines recently, a thresher or a tractor, and the smell of oil hasn't completely come off of him.

"It's only temporary," Paul says, and he thinks about time. "I mean I'll get a new place once we sell the house."

Jimmy says something to Frank, but Paul isn't listening; he's thinking about ghosts and that it makes sense if they're able to haunt the present after they die that they should be able to haunt the past before they die.

"I used to stay there when I was working that conglam," the one named Frank says to Jimmy. "The old Burton place."

"Yeah," Paul says. Paul feels like having a beer, but decides to wait until he's back in the kitchen, prepping for the dinner rush.

"Nice place," Frank says between mouthfuls.

"It's alright I guess," Paul says. "Nice enough

anyway."

Frank nods.

"Was the place across the way boarded up when you were there?" Paul asks him.

"The McKellen farm? It's been abandoned for years," Frank says, chewing the burger. Frank has nose hairs protruding from his nostrils just above the whiskers of his mustache that move slightly back and forth as he chews.

"Is it haunted?" Paul asks jokingly.

"How do you mean?" Frank asks, shrugging. "Like a real ghost?"

Paul smiles. Jimmy's looking at him.

Frank puts his burger onto the pile of fries on his plate and takes a sip of his beer. He says, "There was something about old McKellen who died out there just before he got foreclosed, he went crazy, got cabin fever I guess, I remember that story, but I don't remember anybody ever saying it was haunted."

Paul remembers a ghost story his father used to tell him when he was a kid about an old farmer, who lived next to a cemetery, losing his sanity one winter, going mad, refusing to sell the land, refusing to pay his taxes, getting foreclosed on, screaming that it was his land and they'd never take it from him, and trying to shoot (and getting shot by) a sheriff that had come to foreclose on the place; they buried him in the cemetery, but whenever there was a big rain storm, his corpse was found out of the grave and back on his old property.

"What's up, you seeing ghosts Paul?" Jimmy asks.

Paul manages to force out a laugh.

"Last night, I sat out on the porch and I swear I heard an old man babbling. My dog heard it too. An old guy whispering total nonsense. I went over there this morning, and it's all boarded up, and there weren't any tracks or anything."

"Now that's a downright mystery," Jimmy says, and

there's something in his eye, as he finally takes a bite of his sandwich, that Paul doesn't like.

Al gestures at Paul with his burger and says, "That's not a ghost."

Paul looks at the stranger who has finally spoken.

"That's the coyots," Al tells him. "You got coyots?"

"Yeah," Paul answers. "I heard the coyotes howling the other night. Sounded pretty weird. Scared the shit out of my dog."

Al nods; Paul has confirmed his theory. Al swallows another bite and wipes his mouth with his napkin. Paul sees that his fingernails are filthy.

"The babbling isn't really even them though. The babbling is the rabbits," Al tells the table. "That's the sound that rabbits make when they're being eaten by coyots."

23

They fastened their packs and started up the path.

The path was an old logging trail, an old logging railroad line called the Milwaukee Road, but the railroad had long abandoned this branch. They'd pulled all the rails out years ago. Only the rotting wooden planks were left, buried in the ground, almost absorbed back into the earth. And the occasional twisted, rusted spike.

They walked side by side through the tall yellowing grass between the pines, firs and deciduous trees until the wooden planks became more and more sparse and seemed to disappear entirely, and the forest narrowed and narrowed, and they were forced to walk single file. He took point, and she followed him through the forest.

There were mosquitoes and dragonflies everywhere.

The woods were filled with different types of trees. In his boredom, he began naming the types of trees, cataloging them: red pines, white pines, balsam firs, Hill's oaks, hemlocks, red oaks, birches, bur oaks, American elms, fireberry hawthorns, mountain maples, red maples, silver maples, sugar maples, beeches, black ash, green ash, Bebb's willows, jack pines, white spruces, black spruces, speckled alders, tamaracks, white cedars, butternuts, American bladdernuts, mountain alders, black cherries, pin cherries, chokecherries, American basswoods, quaking aspens, big-toothed aspens, heart-leaved birches, paper birches, yellow birches, alternate-leaved dogwoods, balsam poplars, American mountain ashes, northern mountain ashes, downy juneberries, smooth serviceberries, ironwoods and Canadian plums.

Every mile or so, they had to stop to brush off wood ticks. They talked about the ticks as a way of reassuring each other—wood ticks, unlike smaller deer ticks, do not carry Lyme disease.

He pulled the wood ticks out of the woman's braided hair, and she checked his neck. They hadn't dug into the flesh yet, but they brushed off a half-dozen or so every time they stopped. They looked each time for the smaller dangerous ticks, but didn't find any.

He liked hiking, liked camping, liked the process of it all—the thoroughness of planning, the organization of packing, the physical exertion of hiking in ten miles and setting up camp—but the time was passing too slowly. He wanted to be at the lake.

For a time, he tried the mantra she had recommended to him: Ahnunggokwan. She'd said it meant Star World in Chippewa, which she said should be called Anishinaabe, or at least Ojibwa. He could not envision a world of stars, but it was a beautiful idea and the time did seem to go more quickly.

Midway in, five miles in, they stopped at a wooden bridge spanning a river and propped their packs against the wooden side rails and had lunch. Below the green and gray lichen-covered rails, the fast clear water was running over black, gray and blue rocks, and everything around them was so green.

They fought for a moment about the map. He'd lost the map. Left it in the car back in the parking lot beside the trailhead. They fought, but he said he knew the way to the lake, and she said something unkind as she always did. She was polite and kind to friends, acquaintances, even strangers. She was the cruelest to those she loved most.

He bit his tongue. This was going to save them.

He clambered down to the river and filtered water into their canteens with the pump. The water was clear and cold, and the filter removed any natural microbes or manmade contaminants. There was always talk of the heavy metals in the water of this region from the old mines, but he didn't know if there was any truth to it.

He climbed up the hill to the bridge and gently tossed her canteen to her.

They sturdied their gear and hefted up their packs. She took point and walked in front of him. He stared at the back of her hair and her pretty braided lock swinging back and forth as she walked.

They needed saving. That became his mantra for a few thousand yards of hiking through forest, interrupted only by the occasional sunny meadow.

Then they came to a stretch that had been destroyed. Huge tire treads cut through the mud. Not a single tree remained, just mud and a few weeds here and there. They didn't know who'd done it—just that they'd clearcut a whole section.

The two of them surveyed the wreckage: this was national forestland; some of it was old growth forest. She propped her pack against her knee and brought out a camera. She took a picture of the broad expanse of dirt.

They each took a long pull from their canteens. They were sweating now and would be drenched soon.

They marched for a half mile in the mud in the intense sunlight, waiting to reach the other side of the wasted section.

They welcomed the forest, although it meant more difficult hiking, but the shadows were cooler. The air beneath the canopy felt lighter too somehow.

Every so often, he'd tell her to turn right or left, north or west, deeper into the forest. They were weighed down by their packs and by their lives. She'd lost the baby, after he'd told her he'd left graduate school, failed to finish his doctorate in philosophy, sent their world spinning. It was his fault. That was his mantra for a few miles as he navigated the twisting paths from memory: it's my fault, my fault, it is, it is, mine, my fault, my fault, my fault.

During a tick check, she pulled him close and kissed him and smiled, and then turned with her heavy pack and continued through the forest.

When they reached the hill surrounded on three sides by the large beautiful lake, it was nearly sunset. They stopped and set up camp, scarcely noticing where they were, the beauty of the place. Setting up the tent took ten minutes.

The sun was red and hot by the time they finished, and nearing the horizon created by the treetops of the forest that rung the lake. They walked down the path to the sandy, deserted beach of Bear Lake on the eastern side of the peninsula. It was a plane of glass that mirrored the forest that rung it and the darkening blue sky above it.

His wife was staring at the lake intently.

She unbuttoned her flannel shirt. He made sure he didn't ruin it by saying something stupid. She took off her t-shirt and pulled off her black sports bra. She had a lovely body and pretty breasts. He sat and pulled off his boots and socks, and let his tired feet sink into the cool brown sand. He pulled off his wet shirt. She wasn't looking at him as she unzipped her jeans, focused on the water.

Brien is sitting on a wooden bench of the wooden dock of their bay on Lake Grace surrounded by forest: mostly red pines, white pines, oak trees and birch trees. He has a line in the water that he cast out into the middle of the bay, his bare left foot on the plush handle. It's just a simple pole he's jerry-rigged together with twelve pound test, a bobber and a hook with a worm on it. He's got a foot on it because he is also playing with his fly rod, making lazy casts into the center of the bay, near the bobber of the other pole. He should really cast into the shadows of the trees on the eastern shore, take out the canoe or row boat and hug the shore and see what's there. But the lake is in a drought now—it's been for the last five years or so—and now it's down a full four feet, which is the worst it's been in over one hundred years.

So he's content right now to just be playing with the lines while his children nap up at the cabin. His three beautiful kids.

It has been a busy week, and he and Megan have hardly had a moment to themselves.

Brien is thinking about when he and his wife went camping. It was nearly a decade ago. It solidified things between them, and they conceived Sean.

She had been studying for her master's degree in English at the time and taking a Native American literature class. She taught him some words. Anishinaabe words. He'd thought about that language, and Etruscan, Tibetan, Latin. All over the planet. Languages that had died out or were dying. Like great rivers and lakes, just drying up.

He hears Megan on the dock; she has walked the long stairway of white and gray river stones that formed steps in the forested bank of the lake, from the old rustic cabin on the hill above to join him on the wooden dock. She walks to the far edge of the dock and stretches, looking out at the beautiful forest that surrounds them in this simple bay of this pretty lake that is named for his ancestors.

He puts down the fly fishing rod and hooks the hook of the fly onto the rod. Their dog, Fynn, stirred on the other end of the dock suddenly, where the boats were: she looked up from where she lay in the shade of the boat cover, drying herself off, and seeing it was Megan, put her head back down. Brien realized that Fynn hadn't heard Megan; the retriever's ears must be filled with water from fetching the sticks he and his sons had thrown off the dock.

He looks at Megan. She is beautiful.

Suddenly he realizes that he has a fish on the line. It nearly drags the pole out from beneath his foot. He reels it in. It feels big, but when it comes out of the water, it's just a little rock bass. Too small to keep.

He looks in its mouth and sees that the hook is in deep. The worm is half-way down, deep among the ringed interior of its throat, the vessels of which look like strands of clear cellophane noodles or rice vermicelli.

Dangling the fish from the line, he smoothes back its fins with his left hand and gets a hold of the wet rubbery skin. The fish tries to twist out of his hand. He holds on and wiggles the line to loosen the hook out. It's far down in there. He reaches a finger in, and tries to get it, and the fish's teeth, like tiny pebbles, clamp down on his fingers—shocking but not painful. He needs a needle-nose pliers and turns to his fishing box, but Megan has already opened it and pulls out a set and hands them to him without a word. He wiggles the hook, but he can't get it.

He looks at Megan.

"Sean is going to kill me after all that catch and release talk," Brien says. He nods at the fish. "He thinks they're puppies or something now."

Megan says to him, "One pull. If it comes out, we release. If not, we eat him."

"Are you going to clean him?"

"Sure," she says.

He yanks on the line and hears an almost instant click from inside the fish's throat and head, and the fish suddenly becomes stiff, and he knows he has killed it. He breaks the line with the pliers and hands her the fish almost immediately, knowing there is a sheepish look on his face.

"Glad you said you'd clean him," he says.

"Jesus," she says. "You're serious?"

Brien laughs and says, "Seriously, I have to make dinner."

Megan takes the fish up to the cabin, and he follows her. Fynn charges up to Megan and trots beside her, looking at the fish for a few steps with his ears cocked, before peeling off the stone path into the woods to tree a squirrel.

Brien starts the grill and waits for the coals to get hot. He makes vodka tonics for each of them, and then, amused, watches as Megan gets a wooden cutting board, a towel and a carving knife.

The grill is hot now, and he puts brats that have been boiled in beer and onions onto it. With a heavy, dramatic sigh, Megan sets the cutting board loudly on a red picnic table beside the grill, eyeing Brien and then rolling her eyes.

She cuts the fish open; Brien is always amazed how much blood they have, and how red it is. She uses the towel to wipe up the thick line of blood that has shot from the rock bass across the cutting board.

Brien flips the brats as Megan proceeds to gut and fillet the fish. She walks into the kitchen of the cabin. He hears a fork rapidly scraping against the bottom of a bowl. She's beating an egg and milk. She comes out a few minutes later with two small fillets, no more than two fingers or so, that have been dipped in breadcrumbs.

"You amaze me," he says.

"Wish the feeling was mutual," she says.

He laughs and places the tiny fillets on the grill. He cooks them with the brats, places the brats back in the brine, and serves the fillets as an appetizer. The kids love them. Brien takes a bite. It is delicious; she added some garlic to the crumbs.

"Wow," he tells her. She smiles.

He is thinking about Bear Lake again.

They didn't make a fire that night. They swam naked in the lake until dark, and the stars arrived, filling the sky and the waters around them.

They dried themselves and dressed in silence.

They walked up the hill and to the southern end of the peninsula, then down the hill to the old oak tree that jutted out at an angle, pointing southwest, over the calm lake. The stars were intense and the Milky Way was out, and all of it was reflected in the waters of Bear Lake. They talked about the vastness of the universe, the billions of galaxies, billions of galaxy clusters they've found, and the possibility of life. She talked about the Anishinaabe culture and their reverence for the stars. He talked about the infiniteness of the multiverse, the dimensions of time, the idea that we live again in another universe. Perhaps a few details get switched around.

They kissed, and later she moved down his body and unzipped his jeans. As she moved her mouth over him, he watched the heavens and the lake.

Later in the tent, he went down on her, and she moaned, and then she got on top of him and moved over him, her hair falling into her face, and again he could see the stars through the open sky window above her beautiful face and body as she whispered and moaned and cried out. He never remembered being so happy, never imagined he could be as happy.

Afterwards, he stayed awake and watched her in her sleep. Her eyes were moving rapidly. He looked through the window at the top of the tent. The stars were still out and incredibly bright, and he could still see the Milky Way.

He thought about the baby and wondered if it would have been a boy or a girl. If it had been born to them and was happy in another world, in another universe.

She stirred in her sleep and muttered something.

He imagined that she'd said, "Star world."

They are waiting in his father's old boat in Main Bay. An evening hush has fallen over the whole of Lake Grace. There are other boats that dot the water of the great bay here and there, green and red dots of light, and the smell of the water dominates the night.

Brien is sitting at the wheel of the Mastercraft, watching his wife, who is cuddling beneath a checkered blanket with his children.

It could fall apart, he thinks. Like Paul's marriage.

And he couldn't stop it from failing, from falling apart. Like chaos theory. Fragments and fractals. Disintegration. Break down, disorder. Entropy, falling. All is vanity.

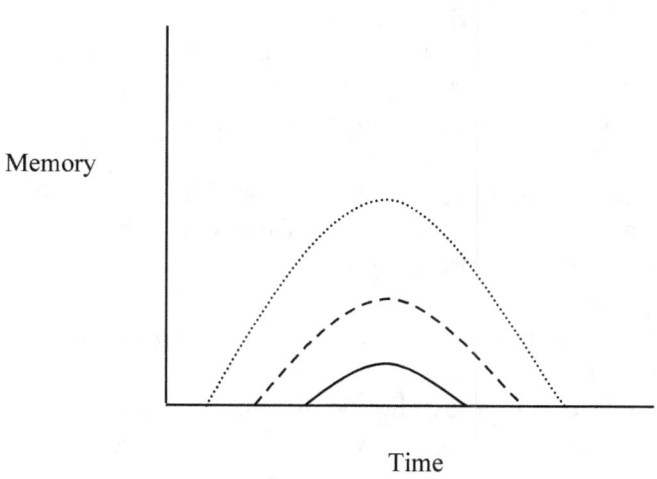

Memory

Time

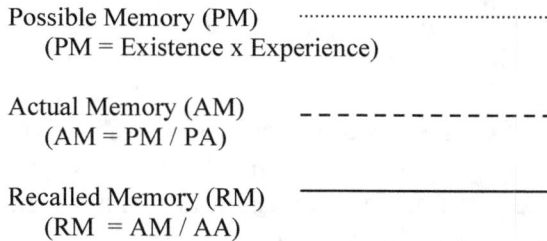

Possible Memory (PM)
   (PM = Existence x Experience)

Actual Memory (AM)
   (AM = PM / PA)

Recalled Memory (RM)
   (RM = AM / AA)

.

"It's all rigged," Paul said. They were in his restaurant, and Brien was trying to console Paul, telling him it was okay, and that he could let it out, even cry about it, if he needed to.

"Rigged?" Brien asked.

"Well, not rigged," Paul recanted. "A stacked deck."

Brien waited. Paul was trying to tell him the truth.

"What do you mean?" he asked patiently.

"I mean it's all a game to make us play in their world, in the world of home and kids and all that, and the funny thing is I never wanted any of that crap, and now suddenly, now that I will probably never have that, now I want it."

Brien nodded.

A squad car drove by the restaurant, and Paul was suddenly distracted.

"I can't believe how many cops there are," Paul said.

Brien sat back, saying, "I had to speak with Jimmy about the accident. The last time I saw Craig that morning. When Drew picked him up to head out. All that."

"It's bad enough to be losing Susie, but to have to answer questions all the time," Paul said.

Brien said, "He asked me what I saw. I didn't see anything, that's what I told him. I didn't see anything."

Paul nodded. They were silent for a time. Paul was looking out the window of the diner at the street outside. Everything had become fully leaved and beautiful and the green leaves were waving in the warm wind.

"But I did see something," Brien added softly.

Paul looked up at Brien.

"I saw a truck. It had the same dent in the fender on the front driver's side bumper that yours has."

Paul said nothing.

"Saw it near the dump. Of course, somebody else was

driving it. Big crazy beard and glasses. Looked like Jerry Garcia."

Brien laughed and watched as Paul managed to force out a smile.

"Anyway, it wasn't, couldn't have been you, right? Right, Paul?"

"Yeah, I wasn't anywhere near there."

He leans back in the Mastercraft in the big dark bay beneath the stars and takes a sip of his beer. He's thinking about his conversation in the restaurant with Paul, when Paul said he wasn't near the Noname River on the day Craig had died.

It was in that moment there in the diner that Brien realized that Paul was trying to tell him the truth, but it had eluded him. Just like Kristen. The truth of it was deeper than we were willing to admit. The insignificance of us. The lack of significance of everything. The randomness.

But there was something more, Brien was convinced of it. But Paul wasn't convinced, and perhaps he never would be. Brien had felt himself shift into his profession and resume his role as psychologist, the role that he abandoned so recently. He shifted and moved into a different place, with a different role, and he began to tell Paul the contradictory truth that Paul probably already knew: that he has the ability to save his marriage for himself but not for Susie because she is an independent being and must want to save it for herself, but in order to save it for himself, he first has to be honest with her.

He looks at Megan, who is sitting in the back of the boat, whispering with their children. I have pushed her away, and perhaps she's with someone, like Susie is. You don't know that though: I might be wrong, might be right.

A loud sudden blast: the boom echoes throughout the bay, and a single flare trails up into the night. It bursts into a shower of green lights, and everyone in the boats in the bay lets out a collective cheer.

Need to lighten up. Just worried because of how bad a shape Paul is in, how bad things are for him. Transference. Shifting everything from Paul onto himself. This is not a matter of intellectual rigor—this is how we live.

"Daddy, look!" Sean exclaims, running up to sit by him. Brien points to the fireworks and talks about each one with his son. From the stern, over the heads of their younger two children, Megan smiles at him. He's going to hold on to this, for now and for as long as he can. Hold on, even if it makes him a fool. He smiles back at her.

They watch as each shot fills the night, each one like a galaxy, like the universe, flowering out like God's own fire into the void of the cosmos, unique and perfect, before collapsing into darkness once more.

24

"That's not what we're talking about here," Susie says. She lies back on the pillow and covers her nakedness with a sheet. Drew looks at her and puts an arm behind his head.

"What are we talking about?" he asks quietly. Usually they don't talk at all.

"Whether I'm just your hotel girl," Susie says. "Is that all I am to you? A hotel screw?"

"That's not what I was saying," Drew says. "I just want to keep it simple, that's all. For the time being."

"I'm not the one who's making this difficult," Susie says. "I'm divorced."

"I know," he says. "I just want to be honest with you."

"Like before?" Susie asks.

"Before I couldn't, and now, I'm not sure."

"Before you were sure you couldn't."

"Look, I'm sorry, I don't know, I mean I didn't know whether my marriage would end, or whether yours would," he says. "I just think—"

He stops himself and frowns.

"What?" she asks, looking up at the ceiling.

"I think you need time, that's all," he says softly.

"For what?"

"Time until the marriage is completely over."

"It is," she says.

"And for me to figure out how to end mine," he tells her, standing to get dressed.

25

Adam knocked on the door of Craig's duplex.

After a moment, Craig opened the big heavy door. The thin, dark veil of the screen door stood between them.

"Look, Craig," Adam said quickly, "I'm not here to start anything."

"Okay," Craig said.

"I just want to know if it's over between you and Kristen," he said.

Craig was serious: "That ended a year ago."

Adam was relieved. He could propose to her now.

"Thanks," he said before leaving.

26

At the bar, the band was playing a low folk song with a sweeping violin. They'd been drinking too much, Craig knew that, but the cadence of the music filled the room, and Craig took her into him arms. She laughed a bit, and then they swayed like that, happy for a time.

Later, though, the band quit, and the sound blared from the speakers. There were shots, and she suddenly needed to go home. He walked her out and back to her place. He kept her upright.

At her place, she was nearly passed out. Craig carried her up to the house. The door was open. That's just the way the town is. Still, Craig always locked his doors.

He set her down easily on her bed. She was asleep.

"Kristen," he whispered. "Kristen?"

No response. He pulled back her covers and slid her into the bed. He thought about staying, but he had to be at the recruitment center in the morning.

Outside, Craig fired up his bat. He took a hit and then looked at the night. Nothing, just nothing. He stepped down the porch stairs and out into the darkness.

There's a war on, he told himself as he walked to his car. He's going to be a soldier.

He wished he could have had the foresight to have become a marine.

Pray for war. Semper fi.

27

Kristen breaks down and calls Brien one night in late August.

Miraculously he picks up.

"Look out at the moon," Brien tells her almost as soon as he picks up.

She walks to the window of her balcony.

"It'll be in the southeast, it's just rising," he says. "It's the closest to the earth that it will be in our lifetime."

She looks out, and there it is, rising majestically over Lincoln Park and the Lake.

It is huge; the face of the moon is amazingly visible.

"This only happens once every hundred years," he whispers. "Can you see it?"

"Yes," she says. "Yes I can."

It seems intimate to her, the two of them in different parts of the Midwest, looking up at the same moon. She doesn't understand. Why's he doing this? Is it true that the moon is that close to earth, the closest it will be? Or is it just that famous optical illusion, the moon illusion, which makes people see the moon as larger than normal as it rises and sets? Surely he knows of the illusion. It's a classic example of perception. She holds up a thumb, closes an eye, and the moon appears smaller.

Still, it feels like a real moment to her, it might be a real moment between them, and she tries to surrender to it. Then Brien ruins it.

"Kristen," he says, "I want you to be careful."

"Why, why are you saying that?" she says.

"Because I do. I just do, okay?"

"Okay."

"I want you to call Paul. Or Tom. Or someone. Okay?"

"Sure, Brien," she says softly.

"And you know that I am always here for you, right?"
"Right," she says, hanging up.

28

Tom's cellular phone is getting a bad signal.

"Look," Tom says to Kristen, "You know I love you."

"Yes," he hears her whisper over the static.

"But I just don't know if we should be together."

Kristen says nothing.

"Last time wasn't so good," he adds.

"I know," she says. "I'm sorry. I was in a bad place."

"Honestly," he says, "we were pretty messed up together."

"I just," she begins, her voice cracking, "I just want another chance."

"I'll have to think about that," Tom says. He hears her hang up on him.

29

It is August 31st. The National Weather Service has issued a frost advisory up in Grace. The sheriff has returned from a vacation up there with his family.

He is only in his office for a few minutes when Matt announces that Paul Krukowski has arrived. Paul closes the door to the office and turns around slowly, like an old man. Jimmy stands and shakes his hand.

"I'm here to talk with you," Paul begins, sitting his big frame down into the plastic chair against the wall opposite Jimmy's desk. He looks at his worn leather shoes and the linoleum floor beneath them. Concerned, Jimmy sits down as Paul folds his hands together and begins.

"I want to confess," Paul says. "I'm here to report my actions."

"Shut up Paul," Jimmy says. Paul snaps his head up.

"Before you go and say something stupid," Jimmy says. "I want you to listen."

Paul watches him, listening.

Jimmy sits back in his chair, musing, "I think about jurisdiction a lot. See, mine is confined, basically, to crimes committed in this county. So, I don't have jurisdiction over, say, something that happens way up north. But if I hear of something, something criminal, I have a duty to report it. A duty to tell other law enforcement what I learn or observe."

Paul is silent.

"Look, Paul," Jimmy says. "I know that your sister had an encounter with Craig. And I know it was, in a word, bad. And I know you were hunting on the weekend that he died."

Paul doesn't take his eyes off Jimmy, who is leaning back, and looking up while he talks, looking at the ceiling.

"I think that sometimes a person goes overboard with power and thinks they can do whatever they want. You and I were both in the Gulf, so I know you know what I'm talking about. Don't get me wrong, most are heroes. But some just get messed up. They go overseas, and then they go overboard. When it was our dad's generation it was Vietnam or Cambodia, and when it was our granddad's it was Normandy or Okinawa. Now they go to Baghdad, or Afghanistan, and come back and think they can take and take and take, think it's owed to them for what they gave up, or nearly gave up."

Jimmy's phone rings, and Paul jumps in spite of himself; Jimmy glances at the old phone and lets it ring.

Jimmy speaks just a little louder now: "Now you correct me if I'm wrong, but that's what I think happened to Craig, but I don't think that's what happened to you."

Jimmy leans forward and opens up a drawer of his desk. He pulls out a plastic bag and flops it down on the desk. There are pictures in the bag. And next to it, he sets a report.

Paul looks at the pictures. It's a gun stock of a Winchester rifle, it's beat up. When Jimmy's sure that Paul has realized what the pictures in the bag are, Jimmy pulls them out and thumbs through them a moment. The phone is still ringing, more like an alarm clock than a phone.

"This stock was found in Lake Michigan. A tax accountant found it, washed up on his private beach. In Sheboygan," Jimmy says with a slight smile. "There's no finger prints. The surf washed it clean, even sanded it down a bit."

Jimmy looks Paul in the eye.

"And, of course, there's no rifling pattern because there's no gun barrel."

Paul keeps his face expressionless. Jimmy is pretty sure Paul needs to sober up, though. Jimmy pulls out pictures he took of the shooter's blind and the line of sight to the victim's blind. Paul is staring at the pictures. Jimmy drops them onto the desk.

"Here, look at this," Jimmy says, pulling out an individual photo. "Here's something, see this? This is a picture of a footprint. I got a couple pictures. Rothco jungle boots. Size twelves. The person only left two prints. Pretty damn good actually."

Paul is now silently staring at the single photo of the footprint frozen into the mud just outside the shooter's blind.

Jimmy adds, "I could get a subpoena. But of course, the boots that made these footprints aren't at your house. Those boots are in the bottom of a garbage heap somewhere. Probably way Up North, right? Along with the rest of the clothes."

The phone stops ringing and silence fills the office for a time. Then the phone starts up again.

"Look," Jimmy says, leaning back, still ignoring the phone. "I know that every man like you, who's a good man deep down, has a conscience that eats away at them. I've got a conscience too, and it eats away at me for the things I've done. And the law is the law."

Then he sits back up.

"But there's more to it than that," he says. "A person has a right, even a duty to defend themselves. Judge Crandon and I talk about that all the time. We have rights in this country, and one of them is the right to protect and defend what's yours and those you love. Hell, it even says so on the side of my squad car, 'To protect and defend.'"

Jimmy thumbs through the report and the pictures again. He sets them down and continues slowly: "I could tell you that I could build a case with this picture here, with these pieces of evidence, but I couldn't, not really. And not without a confession. And again, it's not my jurisdiction, so it's not my problem. What happened to your sister, though, that was my jurisdiction."

He stops for a moment and then looks at Paul.

"And I don't know what I'd have done, if the situation were reversed. I could sit here and tell you that I would've turned the other cheek if I were in your shoes, but I can't say I would've for sure, so how's that protecting and defending? And maybe there's a need for the truth, maybe there's more to justice than just justice, maybe we need to have things in print in order for a true truth to emerge from the mess that's this life, but I honestly don't think so. I don't know for sure—that much I can tell you—but I just don't think so.

"And I also know there's almost no evidence. And so, if you want to confess, you go ahead and do that. But honestly, you've suffered pretty bad already."

He's enumerating on his fingers now: "Lost your house. Your wife. Your sister's losing her mind."

The phone abruptly stops ringing in mid-ring. Paul manages to rouse himself.

Paul stands and sways a moment—a boxer after a right hook. He pulls out Jimmy's silver pen from his coat pocket. His hand is shaking as he places it on Jimmy's desk. He slowly makes his way to the door of Jimmy's office.

"Thanks Jimmy," he manages quietly as he leaves.

Jimmy raises his eyebrows and nods, "Anytime, Paul."

When Paul leaves, Judge Crandon calls, needing Jimmy to arrange a favor.

Jimmy spends the next part of the day making calls, and the rest of the week in face-to-face meetings with the person who can deliver for the Judge.

30

Darkness. Oscar is strapped to something metal. He doesn't know where he is or how he got here.

A shape made of light and the voice of a man comes out of the darkness.

Oscar cannot see his face.

"Hello, Oscar," he says. "Good morning."

"What have you done to me?" he asks.

"What do you mean?"

"You've done something to me," he says, then with a realization, exclaims happily, "Why—why you've drugged me haven't you?"

"No," the man says. "You're just having a nightmare. And you won't remember it tomorrow. Just relax."

Oscar looks at him. Everything is fuzzy.

"You see," the voice says. "I'm you. We're the same. You and I. I'm you, and you're me."

"We're the same," Oscar repeats. "You're me?"

"Yes, you're Oscar, and I'm Friedrich."

"No, wait," Oscar says. "I don't want to be Oscar. I want to be Friedrich."

"You're still Friedrich, the wolf king. You can be Wolfgang too. But you need to tell me what I want if you're going to stay that way."

"I want—I want to be Friedrich," Oscar cries, pleading, "Let me be Friedrich."

"You can be Friedrich."

"How?" Oscar asks suspiciously.

"You have to play nice. If you want to remain in control," the man says.

"What do you want?" Oscar moans.

"Were you dealing drugs?"

Oscar smiles, but doesn't say anything.

"Strike one. How about Craig—you know a guy named Craig?"

"Who?" he asks.

"Strike two," the voice says. He clears his throat and asks a third question.

"The map," he says. "Tell me about the map. What does it mean?"

Oscar doesn't say anything.

"Have it your way," the man says.

Oscar feels the world slide suddenly, as whatever he is strapped to is tilted backward into the shadows.

Then there is something over his face, a towel, and then water pours over him in the darkness. He is drowning in the darkness.

The wet towel is gone.

"Were you selling drugs?" the voice asks him. "To who?"

"I don't—I don't know," he says, gasping for air.

Again the towel is over his face. He is drowning again.

His heart pounds, and he can't breathe.

The towel is gone. He knows he nearly died that time.

The same questions. Then the towel again.

Again and again. Drowning in darkness, awaking to coughing and demands from the figure of splintered light.

After the seventh round, he answers them.

The map is a map of completed projects. Projects with women. The dates and locations that he met with them.

What would he do when he met with them?

Give them the liquid.

What would the liquid do?

Let him do what he wanted.

How many have there been?

He doesn't know. Dozens.

Where?

Everywhere. Wherever he was trucking. But never in Manitowoc, his home.

How did he pick them?

He doesn't know.

Where was the closest?

In Appleton, the woman in Appleton.

The woman was in an Appleton bar. She was with a man.

And there was a wolf in the bar with them. He watched her from across the bar, his hunger for her consuming him.

The wolf knew the man she was with. They used to work together, pick up garbage together sometimes.

But the man she was with didn't recognize him, or was pretending not to know him. Pompous little bastard.

She had a drink on the bar, next to him, as he smoked a cigarette.

It was noisy, and the man and the woman were partying, weren't paying attention.

The wolf took the drink off the bar. He allowed a bit of liquid to fall into her drink. Then placed the drink back on the black surface of the bar.

That wolf, he moves off and watches the two of them. Watches as the drug takes hold of the woman, watches as she stumbles and as she falls.

But the man is always with her. So there's no opportunity.

A waste of the liquid. He hates when he wastes the liquid.

The man doesn't leave her side.

He has wasted the liquid again.

When they left the bar, he followed them to the parking lot. They were parked near his rig. He started his rig, and followed them at a distance of a few blocks. It was five miles before the man stopped in the driveway of a little house.

He pulled to a stop on a side street, shut off the engine and killed his lights. He watched as the man struggled with the woman, and he watched as they went up the steps to their house.

He waits for the young man to leave. Maybe the young man won't leave, and he'll have wasted the liquid, have to go back to the bar tomorrow night or to a different one the following night when he's back on the road.

But the man walks out the front door, sooner than he thought. He sees him smoking a cigarette on the porch. The man leaves, and the Wolf's heart begins to pound.

Questions from the figure of splintered light. Oscar recognizes him before he continues his confession. Friedrich is an angel of light.

The door was locked. He walked around to the back of the house. One of the windows was open. He took either side of the screen in his gloved hands and twisted it back and forth until it gave. He crawled inside, got on the floor on his hands and knees, and felt his way through the house to the bedroom.

His thoughts are precise. He feels his heart beating tightly within him. He rolls her over on the bed.

She's out cold. His thoughts are clear. The madness will come later, but now his desire and the fear of being caught almost overwhelm him as he unbuttons and unzips her jeans and pulls them down.

He carefully puts a pillow beside her stomach and rolls her on top of it.

Even in the dim light from the streetlamp outside, he can tell that she has a lovely ass. He worms his way out of his jeans and climbs on top of her. He puts his hands on either of her shoulder blades and hears the wind leave her lungs as he pushes down.

Afterwards, he tries to be cautious.

Be careful, he tells himself. Put her back the way you found her.

Who was she? What was her name?

He doesn't know; he never knew.

What was the man's name?

The man he worked with, the guy from the truck, sitting in the middle when Mark got arrested.

What was the man's name?

He tells them.

Fall

31

Brien Grace knows he is going to die, but he is not afraid.

The knife is pointed toward his throat.

It all started over something stupid. He got off the Red Line at Addison, not watching where he was going, and bumped into this kid, knocked him down. Now the kid has a knife. Brien's smiling, thinking how stupid all of this is, and then he realizes that it's pretty stupid to be smiling at this kid, who's probably fifteen or sixteen, and who has what appears to be a switch blade pointed at him.

Not scared—he's concerned, and he stops smiling, and he starts to say, "Now just wait a minute" or "this is stupid." But the kid makes a subtle gesture with the knife. This makes Brien more concerned.

But Brien isn't scared. He's been scared before and faced danger before too, but he's never faced death, not in the immediate sense, and even though he knows this is dangerous, and even though he realizes that with each passing second it's getting more dangerous, he's not scared.

He looks the kid in the eye. Everyone else on the platform has gone silent. There are only five people behind him, all unarmed. And the kid has three friends with him. Odds are one of them has a gun, a pistol, a piece. They won't show the piece unless they need to.

"Look man," he manages to say, "I'm old enough to be your dad."

The kid doesn't say anything, just points the knife.

"Get his bills, holmes," one of the others whispers.

The kids are white, and that's the part that makes Brien want to burst out laughing. He knows he shouldn't, but he just can't take this gangster attitude from a bunch of skinny white kids.

Back home, they're all shaken up by a family friend from Two Rivers, who was robbed at gun point while delivering pizza in Milwaukee, and got shot to death, because he fought the guy.

So he knows that he should take this seriously.

Still, instinctually, he's not at all afraid.

And he finds that odd.

Two weeks ago, Brien was bow hunting.

Paul was shooting, but Brien wasn't shooting, just helping. He didn't even own a bow, nor an archery license. They'd often hunt like this in the woods that border a farmer's field, not far from Two Rivers, hours south of the hunting camp of Manitou.

The buck approached the stream, his tail flicking. In the wooden blind overlooking the stream, Paul pulled back the string of his composite bow.

The buck leaned his head down to drink, and Paul let the arrow fly.

The buck immediately sprinted up the hill, away from the stream, and Brien realized that the arrow had bounced off the buck's front right leg. No need to track the blood trail in vain through the field or woods beyond it—there won't be any blood.

"Ah shit," Paul muttered. The buck turned back at the top of the hill briefly, snorting, raising his head, and then ran away, over the hill.

"He'll be back," Brien said. Paul nodded, and silently nocked a second arrow.

"What you know about my dad?" the kid wants to know. Brien is about to beg off the question, then realizes that the kid has brought out his free hand, and is shaking his palm at him, demanding his wallet.

Brien brings out his wallet. That's when he realizes

it's empty.

"What?" the kid says, his face scrunched up in mock disgust and disbelief.

He makes a move as if to cut Brien, and the kid's sudden movement is enough for Brien to move, to try to sprint past the kid to the exit, and he feels the knife rip through his bomber jacket, and he knows the blade has passed through the cloth right above the right pocket, and through and into his rib cage.

Brien spins, just like back in football in high school, spinning away from the defensive back, and sprints for the exit: down the stairs, down the corridor and the deserted fluorescent station, toward the sound of the Chicago traffic. He hears them following him.

They will chase him to the hospital, but he knows he won't make it there.

He is relatively calm as he considers this and as the street flashes by. He has to find a cab.

His lungs will fill with blood. He'll die before he gets there.

Brien and Paul were silent. The buck approached the stream again, following almost precisely the same hoof-marks in the mud.

Paul drew back the black composite bow and waited.

The buck seemed to be filled with bravado as he stepped down to the stream, stomped a hoof and snorted once, then put his big head down and drank.

Then he pulled his head up and turned, exposing his rib cage.

The arrow flew right at him and hit him behind the shoulder. It was a perfect kill shot. The deer spun around and began to run, north, parallel with the stream.

His head was drooping as he ran. He sprinted upstream with his head lowered, then cantering, but it was as if he was trying to run with his forehooves above his head.

Must be losing its muscle control. Or its vision. Or both.

The buck ran like that, erratic and jerking, its front hooves shooting up above its bowed head, then it leaned to the side, and ran to its left, and fell into the field grass.

Brien thinks he might vomit and feels a strange, nauseating sweat break out across his entire body. He clutches his side as he runs. He isn't going to make it.

He hears their footsteps echoing through the city streets.

No one will believe that he died running from a gang in Wrigleyville. That's when he runs into the cab, which is going slow and slams on its brakes. He rolls across the hood, still holding his side.

He opens the backdoor and is in the cab, yelling, "Go-go-go!"

Paul came over with some jerky from the bow hunt. Megan got him with a sad hug, and Brien watched Paul struggle to maintain his composure. Megan had lunch with Susie not three days before.

Later, they were watching the Packers game, eating chips. Brien couldn't help talking about Rodgers and Favre and Thompson. Half of the state hated Favre; the other half hated Thompson.

What a complete debacle, Paul kept saying when Megan was in the room, but when she was out of earshot he'd say, What a clusterfuck.

I mean you don't remove the arguably the greatest player to ever play for your team, for an unknown commodity, Brien said, adding, Arguably one of the greatest to ever play the position. They were one play away from going back.

Total clusterfuck, Paul said and finished his beer.

Brien said, And the odds of a second Favre, a Montana to Young transition, is slim to none. Don't get me wrong, Rodgers is playing well, but the whole team is so out of synch and screwed up right now. But we'll see how it plays out I guess.

Paul grunted strangely and was silent for a long time, staring at the television set.

Finally Paul broke the silence.

I already got my buck, but I'm going to come up anyway, he told Brien.

Brien nodded. Paul was talking about the deer hunt up north, about coming up to Manitou.

Then Paul asked, Do you think Megan can watch Cooper during the hunt?

Sure, Brien said, That way Fynn has someone to play with.

The intern is young and very nice as he examines him.

"You're lucky," he says. "The wound's mostly superficial. No veins or arteries. The cleaning and bandaging went well. We'll give you a tetanus shot."

The intern nods to the nurse, who leaves the room to prep the needle.

"What were you doing again?" the intern says cautiously. "I need to ask because the police will want a report."

It's none of his business, but Brien tells him that he wanted to see Wrigley at night. He does not tell him that he changed his mind halfway to Lincoln Park, decided to head back up to Rogers Park, where his hotel was for the Psychology and Veterans conference he was attending.

Later, Megan calls. She's worried about him.

"When will you be home?" Megan asks.

"I'll be home as soon as I can," Brien says.

.

Being

Time

Existence: — · — · — · — · — · — · — · — · — · —

Experience: — · · — · · — · · — · — · ·

Passive Acuity (PA) ··
    (PA = Passive Data Capture, Storing and Retrieval)

Active Acuity (AA) — — — — — — — — —
    (AA = Active Data Capture, Storing and Retrieval)

Possible Memory(PM) ··
    (PM = Existence x Experience)

Actual Memory (AM) — — — — — — — — — ·
    (AM = PM / PA)

Recalled Memory (RM) ——————————
    (RM = AM / AA)

Note: Chart also applies to future events by changing PM, AM and RM to Possible Foresight (PF = Existence x Experience), Actual Foresight (AF = PF / PA), and Accurate Foresight (AcF = AF / AA).

.

There was no question in his mind as he watched the game with Paul that something was wrong with his friend. Then he received the email from Kristen just as Megan came into the room and sat down next to him. He turned off his cellular phone and put it in his shirt pocket. The Packers were going to lose the game.

On the way home, Brien approaches Holy Hill Road, and pulls off the freeway for gas. He steps out and walks to the pump beneath a sky filled with layers of clouds, dark blue and gray.

After he fills up, he decides to head west to the Basilica. He drives through the winding hills and forest up to the old church.

The beauty of the turning leaves against the dark, swirling sky.

God did not create death. Nor does He rejoice.

A sparrow, a single leaf.

He parks his truck and walks up to the entrance. He takes the stairs up. There's an old monk sitting on a stool outside with a black leather book. A prayer book or a Bible.

Is it open? Brien whispers.

The monk looks at him; Brien believes he hasn't heard him.

Cold one today, hey? The monk asks him.

Yes, Brien says.

Must be global warming, the monk chides, That's what they'd have us believe. But we know the world is much older than that, don't we?

Brien recognizes a moment to bond with the priest, but his convictions get the better of him.

May I go in? he asks.

Yes, yes, The monk says.

Inside the chamber is silent. His footsteps echo until he chooses a pew near the front. There are crutches lining the southern wall, near the Shrine to Mary.

He kneels. The old wooden kneeler creaks, and the echo fills the empty hall.

He prays in the stillness.

It is a prayer of thanks.

32

It is well past sunset when Paul walks into the hunting camp, and he shudders at the sudden explosion. Everyone bursts out laughing, but Tom is howling, and that's how Paul knows that Tom Grace is fucking around again.

But this time it sounds like he's genuinely hurt himself.

He is howling and running through the dark camp.

He runs up to Paul, his eyes closed.

Paul grabs him. Tom is covered with blood, brains, something. He smells of gun powder.

"Are you alright?" Paul demands.

"Here, take this Kruk," Tom shouts. He gives him the shotgun and runs, waving his hands like a kid who has touched something gross, to the mess tent. Paul examines the gun. The shotgun is a black Browning Silver Stalker and is covered with a slick and sticky substance.

Everybody is laughing hysterically at Tom's antics. That's when Paul figures out what Tom has done. He's blown up a melon with a slug from his shotgun at nearly point blank range. The melon is all over him.

Paul owns a similar shotgun, but he's never used slugs in it before. He's only used birdshot in it, but it is loaded with buckshot tonight.

Drew Fisher and Brien Grace are in genuine hysterics, doubled over in pain.

They stand up, and Drew gasps, "That little fucker," and they both go right back into it again. Brien snorts, and then Drew starts laughing so hard at that that he has to spit into the ground. Paul is laughing too now, but not like Drew and Brien, his laugh is more of a defensive one, standing up to rather than joining in their hysteria.

.

"What's the matter, Kruk?" Brien asks later.

Paul looks at him.

"Nothing. Really, nothing," Paul says.

"Busy day tomorrow," Brien says.

"You know it," Paul says.

Then Paul backs into one of the deer hanging on the line and somebody shouts, "Hey! Watch it, you'll knock them down."

Paul bows slightly, and then takes a heavy slug of his fifth of Jack.

Tom Grace has a toast.

"To our brothers," he says between the campfire and the hanging deer.

Everyone raises their drinks simultaneously and solemnly. Paul finds himself raising his mug of whiskey and ice too.

"To our brothers we've lost," Tom says. "To our brother Adam, and our brother Craig. Neither of you were perfect, but you were both blessed, and you were all taken by God before your time."

They all raise their glasses and drink, and Paul drinks too and then suddenly he begins to cough.

There were two scenarios, and Paul did spend a lot of time thinking about it as he'd known he would. The first scenario was bad, and it was the only one he'd considered that fall. The second scenario was worse, and it meant worse things.

It's an eye for an eye.

But they saved him, he reminds himself. Spared him from the shame. But they also committed the greatest sin.

And he could have been innocent of it all. That's true

too.

And if he was innocent it is much worse. But even if he did it, Paul knows Craig shouldn't have been killed.

Paul can't sleep. He needs to sober up. He lies in his cot for a long time, then gets up, and brings out the pack of cigarettes he bought on the way up. He isn't a smoker. Still he lights one after the other anyway, looking at the Graces' tents and the Fishers' tents and the stretch of pine trees between them moving hauntingly in the wind and the cold stars above, and shivering in the dark.

Paul sits in the blind and waits for the dawn.

He's gotten away with it all.

It's like what they said in the old days. He's made it out alive, and that was all that matters. He's made it. He's made it, and he can live with it.

A deer is moving in the valley below. He can hear it, but he can't see it yet. He has the wrong gun anyway, but he wishes the earth would hurry up and turn so he could get a look at the thing. The earth needs to turn and bring the dawn.

33

When Brien and Megan drove Tom to the Base, their oldest child, Sean, wanted to come along. Brien would be shipping out in a month. It was Tom's turn now.

Tom was dressed in his uniform. Sean thought that was cool. He sat in a booster seat in the backseat of the truck beside Tom and asked him questions about the army the whole way to the base. He wanted to know about officer training and guns and tactics.

Their mother was watching Brien's second child, who was just a baby.

A satellite or meteor was falling through the western sky, slowly burning through the evening sky. It was green, and slowly falling like a bright emerald, high above the light of the dim orange of dusk. None of them had ever seen anything like it, and they said so.

"A shooting star!" Megan exclaimed, pointing.

"Too slow," Tom said, shaking his head. "It's a satellite on a weird trajectory, or a satellite falling."

"Gatsby's green light," Brien said emphatically from the driver's seat.

"It's the end of the world," Sean said beside Tom.

"I can't stand being in this town anymore," Kristen said. They were in Two Rivers, but she meant more than Two Rivers. She meant in the Midwest, and she meant in the United States, and she meant in her own head.

"So let's leave," Tom said.

"I'm gone already. It's the town in me. It's the town in my soul, I don't want any of it, ever again. I don't want to see or talk with another person from this town ever again for as long as I live."

"What about me?" Tom asked. This was before their trip to Michigan, before their breakup. She sighed and allowed him to put his arms around her.

"We could be happy," Tom told her.

She was trying to be kind, "I know you want us to drive off into the sunset together. And that's sweet. But it doesn't work like that Tom—people don't really get what they want."

Brien and Tom set up Manitou as their father had taught them and waited for him to join them at the campfire. It was their third hunt with all three of them together.

On the way up, Brien had driven their father's truck from Two Rivers, having earned his license a few weeks prior. Brien should have been happy, but he wasn't.

It wasn't fair, Tom had decided. Tom would have to wait years to drive. And here Brien was acting spoiled.

Tom had decided he was old enough for some things, and without Brien or their father knowing, he'd listened to Brien's tape of The Unforgettable Fire the whole way up on his walkman and read the sixth book in the Elric series that he'd taken from Brien's room. When he finished the book, he had watched as the land changed from farms to forest and had felt a sense of something magical happening.

Still, the next day in the woods, he'd felt an unexplainable sadness come over him. Eventually, sitting in his tree stand, he'd decided his own mood had been caused by Brien's sourness.

After the first day of uneventful hunting in the woods, they were building their fire in the pit when their father walked up with Paul and Paul's father.

"Now here's what we've been missing," his father said, and he held out his hands to warm them, adding, "No pale fire here. This here's the real McCoy."

Brien muttered something. Tom thought it was

something about vanity.

Paul and his father went to change their boots. Tom watched as their father warmed his hands and the light of the fire danced on his face.

Brien smirked and threw a stick into the hot center.

Tom took a log and threw it on the fire, saying nothing, thinking about the space shuttle: the sudden burst over Cape Canaveral; then twin smoke columns peeling off from the great white cloud on an otherwise perfect day, and the voice of a man, calm, narrating the range and speed over the wreckage.

Their father looked at Brien, and then at Tom, smiling softly, almost sadly. Their father raised his eyebrows, glanced at Brien and then looked back at Tom for an answer, but Tom just shrugged his shoulders.

Their father nodded once. He went to the old cooler, opened the lid with a loud creak that interrupted the stillness of the hunting camp, and brought out a beer. He opened it, poured the beer into a plastic cup and took a sip. Then he rejoined his boys at the fire.

"What's wrong Brien?" their father said softly and looked into the bright fire they'd built.

Silence filled Manitou for a time. Their father was eyeing Brien carefully, looking worried.

"Nothing," Brien said, eventually adding, "Life."

"In what way?" their father asked, and then he took a sip of his beer.

Then as serious as anything he had ever said, Brien asked their father, "Do you think there's a God?"

Their father released a quick breath from his nose into the cup, and the sound echoed throughout Manitou. Then he sat on his haunches, set the cup on the pine-needled ground beside him, and carefully placed a stick onto the fire. He looked up at Brien and nodded with a serious expression that covered a smile.

Then he asked, "What makes you bring that up,

Brien?"

Brien looked around the campsite as he spoke as if trying to find evidence for his words: "The way it just spins. We think of it as an arrow, going from the past to some great future, but it just spins and spins, getting worse all the time."

Their father thought a moment and said quietly, almost whispering, "You don't think there's a purpose to this?"

"No," Brien said.

Tom listened to the wind and looked into the darkness beyond the ring of firelight that lit the hunting camp, and he hoped that they could start talking about Lynn again, why last year was his last season, and what an arm he had, and how good Lofton was, and whether Wright would ever as good as Lynn, and when the team would stop looking like a train wreck.

Tom noticed that their father was staring at the tops of the pine trees. Tom looked up, squinting to see if there was a squirrel's nest or a raccoon up there, but he didn't see anything. Beyond the canopy of the pines, he could see that the stars were out and bright.

"You know," their father said, "I honestly think God has a sense of humor. He creates an amazing kid named Brien. Who's filled with ideas and spirit and talents, not to mention blood and bone and cells and molecules and atoms and subatomic particles. And he creates his equally amazing brother, and his *somewhat* amazing father. And sets up all of this amazing world, sets it all spinning with all of its beauty and complexity. And the sun and all of this amazing solar system too, spinning through the cosmos. Through all of this amazing galaxy with its billions of stars. In all of this amazing universe with its billions of galaxies. And all of this universe is just a fraction of an infinite number of other universes, all stacked on top of each other like beautiful planes of glass."

Their father was now staring at Brien as he said, "And

then in one of those universes, in one of those galaxies, in one of those solar systems, on one of those planets, that amazing kid named Brien Grace, who's made of flesh and blood and bone, matter and spirit, all of it complex and wonderful, down the tiniest infinitesimal particle or the simplest thought or resolution, that kid, that amazing kid, asks his amazing brother and his somewhat amazing father, 'Do you think God exists?'"

Tom laughed, but Brien said nothing.

"You know, Brien, faith isn't about certainty. It's about a philosophy and choice and a way of living. Living for others."

"I don't want to talk about that," Brien said.

"Why not?"

"Well, what if we're wrong?" Brien said to his father. "We live life a certain way, but nobody else does. We have a code, but no one else follows it. You know?"

"Then we're the biggest fools on the planet," their father said.

"No," Tom objected.

"Yes," their father insisted, "If we're wrong, we're the biggest fools on the planet."

Brien kicked at the dirt. His jaw was clenched.

"I don't want," Brien began, then stopped and frowned, then continued, looking at the flames, "I don't want to be a fool."

"Look," their father said. "Brien."

Brien would not look up at him.

His father whispered something, which Tom heard as, "Sanctify them in your truth."

Brien looked up and asked, "What?"

Their father smiled at him and said, "Hey, I didn't really mean that we're fools, I was just playing around."

Then their father added, "Look, it's like a coin flip. You live a good life, and there's a God, and you get an eternal reward. If there's no God, you still have lived a good life, which has its own rewards."

Brien shrugged, "Like how."

Their father said, "It's not about outcome, it's about process. A life for others is a life of meaning, regardless of the outcome. And life is difficult. Your lives will have difficulties, things you can't even imagine now will hurt you and those you love. But it's how you deal with those problems, how you act in the face of those obstacles that matters."

They were all quiet for a time.

Finally their father spoke, "Do you want to hear my favorite quote, the one I think about all the time when I look at the two of you?"

Brien asked facetiously, "Is this the part where we get some of the hunters' high spirits?"

And at that, their father laughed, back to his cheerful self again, and he opened the cooler with its noisy lid. Tom and Brien looked at each other with smiles as he poured beer into two cups.

Tom looked into the cup his father handed him. There was foam and a bit of beer in the bottom, but only a couple sips. Still, the strangeness of its smell alone seemed magical to Tom.

Their father held up his own cup until they touched for a toast. Then he said, "No one after lighting lamps puts them in the cellar, or under baskets. Instead, we put them up on tables in the top rooms, so that they provide light for the whole house, and so that all who enter may see their light."

The leaves are beginning to turn in Appleton.

Tom decides to get some writing done. He is working on a tough scene. He writes a sentence: All these physical moments in time adding up to precisely nothing.

But he's thinking about her. She's in the next room, the bedroom of his apartment. He hears her packing her things. She has to be back in Chicago for work.

She has told him that she is certain she loved Adam. And Tom knew that. Tom isn't sure about the others: Craig and Brien. She won't talk about either one. And she won't talk about their relationship, and its future.

But he hopes she loves him now.

He continues working on the play.

She kisses him before she leaves, lingering there a moment.

Then she is out the door without a word.

34

Jimmy is reading the newspaper. It's a shame.

And it's his fault.

Two people have died over this. And he could have stopped it.

Jimmy has incontrovertible evidence.

He has had a plan for some time. It's his fault, and now he has to set it right.

As he stands and gets his keys, he mutters, "Ridiculous fool."

No one is in the evidence locker. He goes to the back of the chicken wire fence they've jerry-rigged together that serves to keep out the janitors and non-authorized staff to the wooden pallets sitting atop two-by-fours, which he and Matt hammered together a few years back. As he puts on his leather gloves, he looks down for a moment and can see his reflection in the linoleum floor. But it is only a moment, and then he is searching the pallets.

He finds what he is looking for. It is something hidden. Three items. There's no need to sign them out as they have never been signed in. He places them in a backpack and zips it shut. He heads to the garage.

On the way out, Matt is on his way in.

"How's it going there Matt?" Jimmy asks.

"Feeling sleepy, you?" Matt says, holding a cup of coffee.

"Just feeling like it's time to retire."

"You're too young yet, Jimmy. Don't you pull a Favre on me."

Jimmy laughs and responds, "I'm old, I'm old."

.

He pulls his squad car to a stop a block away from the little house. It's fairly pathetic looking.

He watches the cold house for a time and whispers, "Are they singing?"

A woman is walking with a child down the cold street.

She continues on, oblivious to his presence. He pulls out the Magnum, and screws the black oblong object onto the barrel carefully, muttering, "They won't sing for me."

The sky is threatening: it could be rain or snow.

Jimmy steps onto the porch and rings the doorbell. It doesn't work, and the screen door is latched, so he knocks on a worn wooden board that props up the ceiling of the old screen porch. He waits for a bit and then knocks again.

Oscar opens the front door, and immediately his eyes widen.

"What's wrong, Sheriff?" he asks suspiciously.

"I just need to ask you a question or two," he says. "Mind if I come in?"

Oscar steps out of the house onto the porch, shutting the door behind him.

"Yeah, I do mind," he says, folding his arms and glaring back at Jimmy.

Jimmy doesn't remove his gaze from Oscar.

"I just need to talk with Friedrich, the mighty Wolf king," he says.

Oscar laughs and shrugs, "I'm terribly afraid that there's no one here by that name."

Jimmy keeps his steady gaze on him. He can feel the Magnum against his rib cage, wedged there beneath his jacket by his left elbow.

Oscar drops the pretense and says simply, "You see, I'm clean, officer."

He holds his arms out to the side, as if asking Jimmy

to inspect him.

Jimmy smiles, "Then this'll be a brief visit."

Dropping his arms to his side, Oscar asks, "Don't you have to have a warrant or something?"

Jimmy tells him, "That's fine. I'll call your P O too, okay? We can chat about all this later. Once you're charged with and revoked for obstructing an officer."

Oscar rolls his eyes, "Fine just come on in."

Oscar steps up, flicks up the latch on the screen door and turns back inside. Jimmy opens the door and follows him onto the porch. When Oscar turns the handle of the door, Jimmy feels his heart start racing, and he tells it to knock it off.

"Shitty weather, hey?" Oscar says as he opens the door and walks into his living room.

"It sure ain't warm," Jimmy answers, following him inside and pulling the Magnum 44 with the long thin silencer from his jacket. He points it at the back of Oscar's head and flicks off the safety. Oscar suddenly stops in mid-step at the noise—his shoulders shrugged up and tense.

Oscar begins to say, "What do you—"

All at once, the back of Oscar's hair bursts with bright blood as his skull splinters, and the body falls forward as if the head were the weight of a bowling ball. His feet are in the air a moment, and then they too flop against the floor. A circle of bright crimson quickly spreads across the fibers of the carpet, radiating out from the body.

Jimmy unscrews the silencer and puts it in his jacket pocket. He holsters the weapon. He pulls a plastic bag from his pocket. There a few crystals and a pipe inside.

He opens it slowly and removes the crack pipe.

He rubs Oscar's inert fingers on the glass pipe, and then places it in Oscar's hand. He puts the nearly empty baggie on the table in the living room. Then he steps away from the corpse, toward the door, which he shuts behind him.

35

Tomorrow is the first day of winter. Drew is buried in paperwork. He has traveled up to Grace with two bankers boxes full of files.

He got up this morning in the pitch black of his bedroom of the dark cabin. He pulled the curtain away from his bedroom window, and the old wood pile that he and his brothers had stacked back when Adam was still alive sat just outside in the darkness of the morning.

He made coffee, scrambled eggs and toast, and lit a fire. Then he got to work at the dining room table of the kitchen of the cabin with the fire crackling on the other side of the room. The sun rose behind the clouds and a gray half-light filled the cabin.

Three cups of coffee later, he managed to bill out three files, dictate four letters, and make a significant start on an answer to interrogatories.

The phone rang once while he was working. He ignored it.

Then his cellular phone began to ring.

He looked at the caller id. It was Sharon.

He ignored the call and continued working.

Now, he stands and goes out onto the porch and looks out at the little forest-lined, iced-over bay that leads to a bigger bay of Lake Grace.

I don't know what to do, Drew told his father on the phone. He had just returned from his disastrous Florida trip, and his client was weighing heavily on his mind.

Yes, you do, his father said simply.

I do, he stated.

Yes.

Do you know?

Of course I know Drew, his father said simply. I always know.

What should I do?

Come in, Drew. We'll talk.

Drew sat back in the black leather chair at the conference table. It was a Saturday, and the office was all but empty. The corridors were dark, and but for this room, most of the lights were out.

"I just think this guy needs help. Needs to be monitored. Or something. Because something isn't sitting right, especially his story about Craig."

His father sighed and placed a fist on the glass conference table. He smiled and said, "Drew, I'm sorry I got you into the middle of this. This is a bad case, and this guy is a sick man."

He leaned forward and said evenly, "But you won. And that's your job. You're a lawyer. And as a lawyer, you have an ethical obligation to keep your client's secrets, right?"

"Yes. That's my point."

"Good," his father said, nodding. But there was something more to it, and his father asked him a question: "What is a lawyer?"

"What do you mean?"

"Exactly that."

"An officer of the court."

"That's right. An officer of the court," his father said, seizing onto that thought happily. "And as such, you have certain obligations, right?"

"Yes," Drew said.

"Like what?"

Drew rolled his eyes and said, "Zealous representation of your client. Candor to the tribunal. To report crimes."

"Exactly," his father said emphatically, pointing at him

and nodding. His father suddenly closed his mouth, leaned back in his chair, folded his arms and looked at his son.

Drew knew that it was only if you were certain of a crime occurring, to prevent injury. But Drew thought a moment and smiled grimly, "Who do I tell?"

"You tell Crandon."

"I thought Crandon was the devil."

"He may be the devil, Drew, but he's our devil."

"What then?"

"You stay out of it. You go up north get some R&R. Crandon will help your client, get him whatever he needs."

They were silent for a time. The idea of getting away for a bit did seem inviting.

"I could do this for you," his father said. "But it's time you grew up. You tell him yourself."

Drew was silent for a long time, and then asked, "And Sharon?"

"That's over Drew. I'm sorry, but you just got to let her go."

The judge's chambers consisted of a long room with a huge conference table and a large desk at the end. It always felt strange to be in the informal setting of a judge.

Look, Judge, he said, I'm not telling you anything you don't already know, okay?

Okay.

But the guy, this guy, my client. I think he needs help.

Don't we all, Judge Crandon said.

There was a long pause. Drew didn't know what to say. Then he added, A lawyer has a duty to report if his client is going to commit more crimes.

And you think he is?

I don't have any evidence.

But you wouldn't be here if there wasn't something. Something significant.

Drew made the briefest of nods.

The judge leaned back in his chair, considering this.

Drew enters a store in Grace.

He stamps the cold out of his feet and jumps around just a bit.

He picks out a newspaper and a box of ammunition. He sets them on the counter.

"You got a permit to hunt polar bears?" the cashier asks him.

"Nope," he says. "Just heading over to the range. Gonna practice a bit."

He grabs a *Journal-Sentinel* and asks for a Powerball ticket.

"Can you believe the Jets? They're falling apart," the cashier says as he rings him up for the paper, the rounds, and the lottery ticket. "Serves him right for retiring in the first place. Can you believe he wanted to play for the Vikings?"

Drew nods and laughs, "Yeah, what a weird sight that would be."

36

Kristen was standing in her empty apartment, watching the first snow of the year falling into the dark predawn of Lincoln Park. She held a ticket in her hand.

Her cellular phone began ringing. It lay on the wooden floor beside her ipod. Beside them, her folded white rain coat lay atop her black suitcase.

She walked over to the phone and looked at it.

Paul was calling. She had to answer it. She owed it to him. She picked it up.

"Hi Paul," she said softly.

"Hey Kristen," he said.

There was silence on the line.

She knew she should fill it. She walked to the kitchen, thinking of what to say. What could she say to him?

When they were young, they hunted together. Paul had taught her in the years following their father's death. He explained that they'd be poaching if they used guns, so they used cameras instead of rifles. They found animals in those days in the wild: they took pictures of whitetail, ducks, song birds, eagles, falcons, crows, wild turkeys, seagulls, bats, squirrels, chipmunks, field mice, rabbits, badgers, even an occasional fox.

He taught her where to sit for the best shot. Shooters X and Y form Z, the kill zone. Taught her how to be patient. Told her not to worry, taught her to control her mind. Hunting is about readiness, about patience. It's a matter of skill and a matter of luck, but mostly a matter of patience. Of letting them come to you. The prey won't even see the hunter, until maybe just before the end, when it's already too late.

If you miss, I'll make the shot, he always told her with

a smile. And his pictures of the deer, birds or other animals were always more centered. Better somehow. More perfect.

When she was old enough, Paul taught her to shoot.

When she was in high school, he took her to the range so she could practice her marksmanship, and she often went bird hunting with Paul, Sharon and Cooper.

She shot bottles too up north with Adam on their property in Grace. She was better than Adam. Nearly as good a shot as Paul.

It was a part of who she was.

Aim carefully. Inhale deeply. Exhale completely. Re-aim. Squeeze gently and slowly. It explodes instantly—an array of colors briefly catch the sun.

There were bottles now, empty bottles, in the recycling bags lining the white counter in her kitchen. She'd poured them down the sink two weeks ago. She was starting over.

Paul was on the line. Not a part of the process of starting over. This call—going to set you back. Feel the sadness welling already.

"I just wanted to say goodbye," he said softly.

"You know?" she asked. She hadn't told Tom. Hadn't told her mother even.

"You're leaving," he stated, sounding genuinely happy for the first time in a year.

"Yes," she said.

"That's good," he said kindly.

Silence. All those years he had always tried to protect her, but she'd always believed she never needed it.

"How are you?" she asked him.

"I'm at peace with it all," he told her.

"Yeah?"

"Yes."

"What does that mean?" she asked, beginning to cry.

"It means goodbye, Kristen. And good luck," Paul said.

He will read over his dissertation. None of it will seem to matter now.

Psychoanalysis is a terribly efficient instrument, and because it is more and more a prestigious instrument, we run the risk of using it with a purpose for which it was not made, and in this way we may degrade it.

He will weep—for all his good intentions, he has failed. All our thoughts are merely guesses.

He'll know that she will be his only solace.

In the blind, he watches the day return to the land. Below him, he can see the Noname River. He pulls a gun out of its sheath.

The gun is not his rifle. It is his shotgun.

He checks to make sure the safety is off. He turns the gun around and places the barrel in his mouth.

He puts his right hand beside the trigger guard, supporting the stock in his left hand, and looks up at the clouded sky through the bare branches of the trees. He puts his thumb against the cold steel trigger and thinks to move his thumb and suddenly the light of the sky and the leafless branches stretch out in long individual streams of light and color and shade and then fade to darkness and then he is no more and that is all.

He wrote for a long time. His new play was about the process, about the struggle when life becomes difficult, and about finding meaning in that struggle.

It began to snow while he was writing.

When he stopped writing, he realized she'd gone.

He realized he did not know if she would ever return.

He looked over his notes and was struck by a phrase he'd written:

All these physical moments in time adding up to precisely nothing.

His first thought was: It's a split infinitive.

On his way back to the Department, he will be narrating the longer of the two poems he memorized when he was a young man, as the snow begins to cover the town once more: I have seen them in the waves.

He will turn on his left turn signal and make a slow, gradual turn so as not to skid out on the newly formed ice.

Their long hair white and wicked.

There will be a child and his mother waving to him. It will be Megan Grace and one of her sons. He hasn't seen them since the funeral. He'll wave back as he passes them. Then he will return his attention back to the road.

While the wind whips the white water.

He will have to wait at a long traffic light.

A motorist crossing the intersection will slam on his brakes upon seeing his squad car, then continue down the avenue.

He will wait at the light and then head to the storage locker.

We have slept in a cold cave below the frozen sea, he will whisper above the chatter of the dispatch. He will approach the lot enclosed by a barbed wire gate. When he rolls down his window, the intense cold will invade the warm squad car.

He will enter a code into the metallic panel, and the gate will slowly slide to the side. He will wave to the guard as he continues to the back of the lot.

Wringed in seaweed, black and brown.

The lock on the storage unit will be frozen to the ground. He'll kick it once to free it from a thin layer of ice and snow, and then bend down and spin the combination into it.   He'll heave the metal garage-like door up and open.

He'll go to the very back of the locker.

He'll kneel before a large safe and unlock it.   He'll place the evidence in a lockbox in the metal safe in the very back of the storage locker and lock everything up.

Then he will get back in his squad car, shut the door against the cold, and head for his office down the wintry, deserted street.

Noises wake us, and we drown.

He lays cash on the counter for the lottery ticket and the other items.

While the cashier rings him up, he pages through the newspaper.

All these people in the paper. Dead, sick, poor, hurt. The machine is ringing out the lottery ticket. It's all just a crapshoot, he is thinking as he pages through the paper, while the cashier is counting out his change.

He stops on the page that makes his heart jump. His client is dead. There's a picture of the house where he was shot. He pulls out that section, and an article predicting an arctic storm in the Midwest falls out and open onto the counter.

"Well, one thing's for sure," the cashier says, gesturing to the page, "it's getting colder."

He looks up at the cashier, gathering up the paper; the news that shocked him has already sunk in and registered.

"Yeah," he agrees, heading for the door. "Winter starts tomorrow."

She'd paid too high a price. She was certain of that.

She looked one last time around her empty apartment. Everything had been put into storage, or had been sold, or given away. Everything was in its proper place.

In her hand, she clutched the overseas ticket. One way.

She would vanish now. It had to be now. Tomorrow would be too late. It probably was already.

She left her apartment and rolled her suitcase down the hall to the elevator. As she passed the square black trashcan in the hallway, she tossed her cellular phone in it.

She waited at the elevator, thinking about it all. Thinking about her dream.

She'd had a dream last night: she and Adam standing on the crown of a mountain, an ancient mountain.

Adam had told her one word before the dream had ended.

Chance.

Acknowledgements

Several years ago, I wrote a short story called *The Stone*, and it won a prize. That short story became (essentially) the first chapter of this novel. However, the novel took many years to write.

After I wrote the short story, I worked on a book of short stories, of which several chapters of this book were a part. Later, I submitted the story *The Stone* to the Aspen Writers Foundation in hopes of being accepted to the juried workshop. I received a scholarship and attended the Aspen writers' conference. There, I worked with Pam Houston, who encouraged me and invited me to attend the Tomales Bay writers' workshops in California. Pam continued to work with me after the conference, read the collection, and realized that there was a novel running through it. She then helped me shape and edit this book. I cannot say enough about the help that Pam gave me by encouraging me and helping me to create and hone this novel.

I would like to thank all of the people with whom I have worked in an artistic capacity or collaborated on various writing projects, who have encouraged my writing, and who taught me how to write. This group of wonderful, interesting people includes Ginny Schauble, Jim Kearney, Jim Arndorfer, George Doty, Leonard Casper, Elizabeth Kirschner, Robert Chibka, Francis Sweeney, Cecil Tate, Dean Kaplan, John Bergstrom, Ellen Hunnicutt, Tom Bontly, Sheila Roberts, John Goulet, Cam Tatham, Robert Siegel, Gordon Weaver, Dave Pincus, Chris Grimes, Drew Maxwell, Pam Houston, T.C. Boyle, Nick Flynn, Ron Carlson, and especially my father.

Thank you to the English department of Boston College; the graduate creative writing program of University of Wisconsin, Milwaukee; the Aspen Writers' Foundation, the Aspen Summer Words program and the Aspen Writers Retreat; the Writer's Institute at the University of Wisconsin, Madison; Milwaukee's Spring Writers Conference; the University of California, Davis creative writing program; and the Tomales Bay Workshops.

Thank you to my good friends and my loving family, and thank you most of all to Kerry for allowing me to pursue this dream.

I would also like to thank Wisconsin. The people, the lakes and woods, and the towns of Wisconsin, especially northern Wisconsin, have given me enough inspiration for several books.

About the Writer

 JOHN BOLGER has a doctorate in creative writing. He also has a law degree. John lives in Milwaukee, Wisconsin, where he works as a lawyer and a writer, and where he is raising three sons and a patient dog. He is currently working on two books of related short stories and several novels. *The Hunters* is his debut novel.

If you enjoyed *The Hunters*, please send John an email at his Resolute House author email: John@ResoluteHouse.com.

Story

Story Press